Advan

Napole

Napoleon's Gold is set in the Thousand Islands, where Thomas Pullyblank spent his summers as a youth, and which he brings to life in a novel that will draw readers into the stories, tales, fables, and history of the region and his beloved Saint Lawrence River. The author's narrative gifts, erudition, brilliant dialogue, and rich imagination make this a must read. This novel is at once a page-turner and a work within which the author's musings and reflections on life, death and religion will leave the reader deeply moved.

> —*Warren Roberts, Ph.D., Distinguished Teaching Professor, History Department, University at Albany*

Napoleon's Gold is a lively and well-written book, based on subjects that interest all islanders—finding treasures and meeting characters that come alive on the page. Pullyblank handles the detective work wonderfully and at the same time helps to "raise the bar" of Thousand Islands culture. We at *Thousand Islands Life* e-zine were lucky to have shared three chapters of the book over the winter of 2011, now we get all the pages, from front to back. Thanks Thomas for a splendid read.

> —*Susan Smith, Editor,* www.ThousandIslandsLife.com

Napoleon's Gold is a good yarn with a touch of coincidence and magic. Pullyblank's affinity for the Thousand Islands and Saint Lawrence River regions and his obvious knowledge of the life and history of its people enriches the account and will delight North Country dwellers and readers in general.

> —*Carolyn Schuler, Ph.D., author, professor, professional storyteller, former North Country librarian*

Napoleon's Gold

Napoleon's Gold

A Legend of the Saint Lawrence River

Thomas Pullyblank

Square Circle Press
Voorheesville, New York

Napoleon's Gold:
A Legend of the Saint Lawrence River

Published by
Square Circle Press LLC
137 Ketcham Road
Voorheesville, NY 12186
www.squarecirclepress.com

First paperback edition 2011.
Printed and bound in the United States of America on acid-free, durable paper.
ISBN 13: 978-0-9833897-0-5
ISBN 10: 0-9833897-0-5
Library of Congress Control Number: 2011929789

Publisher's Acknowledgments
Cover: © 2011 by Square Circle Press. Cover design by Richard Vang, based on *Napoléon à Sainte-Hélène* by François Joseph Sandmann (1820).

Epigraphs: Part 1, Steven Englund, *Napoleon: A Political Life*, Harvard University Press, 2004 (both quotes); Part 2, John Keats, *Of Time and an Island*, Syracuse University Press, 1987; Part 3, T. S. Eliot, "The Dry Salvages" in *T. S. Eliot: The Complete Poems and Plays, 1909-1950*, Harcourt, Brace & World, Inc., 1971; Fin, Steven Englund, *Napoleon: A Political Life*, Harvard University Press, 2004.

The author's personal and professional acknowledgments appear in the Afterword.

This story is dedicated to my parents, who took me to the Thousand Islands when I was a child and allowed me to fall in love with the place, and to our neighbor Carol Brown, who gave us a home to stay in when we went there.

Contents

Napoleon's Gold

Part One

For how to describe or explain this man, though it has been tried and tried ... ? As what do you characterize Napoleon? As Hitler? As Prometheus? Both analogies, and even Jesus Christ himself, have been invoked, but the man ... was very far from any of them. One might rather say that Napoleon is a character unfinished, like Hamlet; and like Hamlet a puzzle, full of contradictions, sublime and vulgar ... equally menacing and thrilling, with Sphinx-like qualities of good and evil and mystery.

Steven Englund
Napoleon: A Political Life

From America you can continue to make your enemies tremble.

Lazare Carnot to Napoleon Bonaparte
June 1815

Chapter One

"AN EXTRAORDINARY SITUATION of bewilderment and pain demands an extraordinary response," said the bishop from the office chair at Saint Cyril's in Alexandria Bay. "The community, family, and especially you, my son, need the extended opportunity to grieve and, when God has willed it, to begin the process of forgiveness."

I sat across from the bishop at the desk he occasionally borrowed from the parish priest. A breeze blew through a window behind him from the Saint Lawrence River, just a few blocks to the north. I was the reason there had been no funeral yet, a week after my parents' and brother's deaths on that same river.

"Burial will be held at the family's convenience," the obituary had read. But my own need to bury my grief under as much denial as possible was in direct conflict with my parents' desire to spread the grieving process out across the traditional three stages of vigil, funeral mass and committal. It was a week after their deaths, and I had been putting the church and funeral home off long enough.

"As you know, no planning need be done by you," the bishop continued. "Your mother and father both made detailed arrangements years ago, for themselves, for Patrick, and, as the case may be, for you. All you must do now is surrender yourself to the care of your Divine Father and your Mother Church."

I traced my finger over the back of my hand. The skin there was sunburned and dry from spending most of my

waking hours piloting my uncle's Chris-Craft up and down
the river in the vain hope of finding the man who, I was
told, had been drunk and who had caused my father to lose
control of his antique Lyman and crash it into an island
dock. The man I was looking for was tanned and tall, I was
told, and was piloting a small Bayliner that day. I spent a
week searching. I found no sign of him.

The bishop, in what I took to be the "extraordinary response" to which he had just referred, got me into his borrowed office by chasing me down in his own boat and convincing me to come ashore and give him fifteen minutes of
my time. I followed him to the village dock and up the hill
to Saint Cyril's, and there we sat, he talking of grief and forgiveness, and me listening, not yet grieving, nor anywhere
close to forgiving.

"Think too of others in need. Your aunts. Your uncles.
Your brother's classmates. The many people your family
called friends. They need closure, just like you. I assure you,
as impossible as it may seem, you cannot force it to happen.
Nor, for that matter, can you prevent it from happening.
Let go of your anger. Allow this grief to move through you
and into the hands of God. Allow forgiveness to happen in
time. Closure will come, it will come, but only if you let go
and trust us to do our work."

There was a long hesitation, during which I could feel
my defenses slipping. Now that I was off the river I was
tired, and being tired I found it impossible to maintain my
guard. I closed my eyes and prepared myself to speak. The
bishop stayed silent.

"All right," I finally said, doing an emotional one-eighty
and wanting to get the entire process over with as quickly as
possible. "Can we hold the vigil tomorrow night and the
mass and committal on Wednesday?"

"Of course, of course. My deacons will make the necessary phone calls."

The bishop stood, walked around the desk and took

hold of my hands. I too stood, and received his words of blessing and kiss of peace with genuine appreciation.

"May I preside?" the bishop asked after he had walked me back to the village dock.

"Of course," I said, feeling as if I had no real choice in the matter.

"I knew your parents well, Thomas, and I will find it an honor to commend their souls and your brother's soul to God. Be confident that your church will serve you well." He cleared his throat. "I assume you'll want closed caskets?"

"This wasn't in my parents' arrangements?" I asked.

"It was not," the bishop said with some gravity. "But I'm sure, having known your parents so well, that they would've wanted closed caskets."

"Fine, then," I said. "Closed caskets are fine."

The bishop blessed me with a sign of the cross.

"Thank you," I said.

THE CHURCH DID SERVE ME and my extended family well in the three-part ritual. The vigil, held at the Knights of Columbus Hall in Alexandria Bay, was as cathartic as a wake is supposed to be, filled with food and drink and conversation and crying on shoulders. The funeral mass at Saint Cyril's was attended by almost two hundred mourners from all over the United States and Canada who came despite the short notice. The mass itself contained several fine scriptural and musical expressions of Christian hope amidst despair. The bishop's eulogy was touching, theologically rich and brief.

The committal, a somber affair on a cool and drizzly day, was, to me, the most meaningful segment of the ritual. My parents had rejected the death-denying character of so many modern burials, with their tents, Astroturf grave coverings and an overabundance of flowers, and had instead instructed us to literally bury them by tossing clods of dirt into their graves, first with our bare hands and then with shovels.

When I tossed in the first clod my uncle, Jack Hibbard, a lapsed Methodist living in Florida, looked at me, shook his head, and said, "Dead is dead, Tommy. Dead is dead." I was glad to know that closure had come more quickly for others.

My journey through the grieving process had at least begun for me that day. I know in retrospect that the first step came as we sang *Jesus, Savior, Pilot Me*, my mother's favorite hymn, to conclude the mass.

I had questioned the veracity of religious thinking before and would do so again, but at that moment, with even agnostic Uncle Jack singing at the top of his lungs, I believed that I knew this bit of God's truth: that the particulars of death don't matter as much as the faith we hold at the moment death inevitably comes. Or, for that matter, the faith we hold when we begin to process something that seems worse than death.

Having taken the first step of letting go, the second step came naturally when, during the committal and after throwing in my share of dirt, I made up my mind to take a leave of absence from graduate school at the State University at Clinton Falls and build houses with Uncle Jack in Florida.

"God or not," he had told me at the wake when he invited me to join him for a few months, "it's hard, honest work that heals our wounds."

It sounded good to me, despite the agnosticism and especially since I knew that staying in upstate New York would most likely lead me back to the compulsive ways of living that had left me with nothing more than an empty gas tank and sunburned skin. I resolved to work hard under the southern skies, to silently pray as I hammered and sawed, and, when free, to read the dozen or so Psalms of lament the bishop had recommended.

Chapter Two

THAT WAS FIVE YEARS AGO. I share that brief account of the funeral proceedings as a sort of prologue, because what happened then defines the emotional and spiritual context of the story as it truly opens now. Just as a tapestry's wooden frame is not part of the tapestry itself but is essential to the picture within, so too is my understanding of the events of September 1996, the essential frame for the story I now relate.

Grief, you see, has a way of cutting across time. Sometimes it resurfaces on its own terms like a rhizome touched by warm soil. When appearing thus, its recurrence is usually predictable, as the memory of my family tragedy was every year to the day of both the accident and the funeral. In this story the return of grief was something else, more aptly described by another terrestrial metaphor. What was for five years a barely active volcano, always alive, always simmering in my memory, erupted with a vengeance when a tectonic shift broke upon our nation with no clear warning.

I take full responsibility for this. It was my own obsessive behavior in the week after my parents' and brother's deaths that made my personal day of suffering a day that would become a national day of tragedy.

The telling facts of the calendar are these: the boating accident happened on Labor Day, September 2, 1996. My futile search for the killer delayed my conversation with the bishop until September 9th, the wake until Tuesday the 10th and the funeral mass and committal until Wednesday, September 11th.

When I woke up early in the morning five years later, on Tuesday, September 11, 2001, the volcano of grief was simmering just as it had for the four previous September 11ths. But I closed the night in much worse shape, under a full blast of confusion and anger and pain that burned with the return of old wounds as much as with the new trauma brought on by the terrorist attacks at the World Trade Center and Pentagon.

When the attacks happened, I was living and working in Brooklyn, finishing up a two-year fellowship with a nonprofit research institute affiliated with Columbia University. I shared the visceral panic of most city residents when news of the attack reached me. I gathered with my colleagues around the television to watch the second plane hit and the towers fall. I joined my neighbors on the roof of our apartment building to see and smell the smoke from across the East River. I went to a candlelight mass and prayed for the dead and the missing. Through all of this I lived as if in a dream, reaching out but not touching, looking but not seeing, living but not feeling anything besides a deep and intractable numbness.

I read again the eulogy preached by the bishop for my parents and brother five years before, a copy of which the bishop had sent me on the first anniversary of the funeral. In it he spoke about what makes a life complete. He asked, by whose measure do we evaluate such things? By the biblical standard of three score and ten years? By the shape of our life story's arc? If we evaluate such things from the human perspective we're bound to see a life taken by sudden death as incomplete and unfinished, lost to the dead just as they are lost to us.

But if we try to see God through the lenses provided by almost two millennia of Church tradition, as uncorrected as our limited human vision may yet remain, we might catch a glimpse of how the dead person's life fulfilled part of God's plan, however large or small that part may be.

"Jesus Christ died at thirty-three," the bishop reminded us, "not from a long illness but rather in a sudden rush of circumstances and through violence. By dying thus, Jesus Christ fulfilled the major part of God's plan, the healing of a broken world.

"Those who died similar deaths, unable to see the end approaching, blessed by the fullness of life until the moment of death, are closer to Jesus Christ than we might realize. With God in each of us, with God incarnate in them, they also helped bring God's plan closer to its climactic achievement of peace and love. As we feel our grief for what we and they have lost," the bishop concluded, "let us also pray for what all of God's creation might gain."

Try as I might, I could see nothing of God through any lens, and could see nothing gained by my personal loss from five years before or by our collective loss on that terrible day. This time, even praying the Psalms of lament did nothing to help.

That night, as drunk as I've ever been, I called my old family friend Louie Fratello in Clinton Falls and admitted in some kind of perverse relief that at least now my personal tragedy had been overshadowed by something much, much worse. Louie told me to worry about a feeling like that only if it survived the inevitable hangover. It did.

The next morning I called my dear friend Mindy Mc-Donnell, and we were on the phone for about an hour, sobbing more than talking, until exhaustion overcame me and I hung up as Mindy began repeating one "Hail Mary" after another. She told me later she repeated the prayer once for each of the estimated number of victims killed, and then three more for my parents and brother.

Other people gave solace, too. I received several messages from former professors at the State University, wondering if I was okay. Professor Roger Whittaker called and offered me a job. Julianne Radisson, whose family mystery I had helped solve in my first semester back from Florida after the funeral, sent me a postcard from Williamsburg, Virginia, where she lived with her mother Martha, a former history professor at Clinton Falls and now an interpreter at the colonial village. Uncle Jack invited me to come build houses again.

One bit of empathy provided an unexpected first thread to be woven into the tapestry that was framed five years before. It came from Jens Erlenmeyer, a graduate school buddy who had returned to his native Germany after finishing his dissertation on inter-war American Socialism. He sent me an email on the night of the attack, which gave me, as a professional academic might say, the theoretical grounding for many of the important life decisions that were to follow.

Dearest Tom,
My heart bleeds for you and for the many other Americans I grew to love during my stay in your generous country. I shout out in echo of John Kennedy's words to Germany in our distress: "We are all New Yorkers!" We will remain by your side throughout your time of grief and recovery.

For you my heart bleeds most, because I remember what you go through every year on Labor Day and September 11th. So much death! So much grief!

Remember the words of Goethe: "Who never ate his bread in sorrow / Who never spent the darksome hours / Weeping and watching for the morrow / He knows ye not, ye heavenly powers."

Sorrow is not something owned only by you, my friend, and you are never alone in your sorrow.

Remember this always: the circle of life continues to spin. Do not forget your history. Do not neglect the sufferings and triumphs of the past, for they, too, will be your sufferings, your triumphs. The sufferings will give you commiseration, the triumphs hope. Keep them close by you, and you may for always touch the generations that have passed before you and reach forward to offer a gift to generations yet to come.

The past will heal you, Tom. As much as it may pain you to confront your past, you must travel through that valley in order to emerge into the bright light on the other side.

The past will heal you. In the face of the future uncertainties that we all confront, do not forget your past.

Yours truly,
Jens

I pondered the message for hours, especially the last two paragraphs, suspecting that Jens was just as drunk and twice as wise as I was. I read it to Mindy when I called her the day after the attacks.

"What do you think he meant by all that?" I asked when I finished reading.

"For one, it's more important now than ever for us to do our work well."

I was doing an historian's work, although not in the classroom. Jens, I knew, was doing research and some teaching in Berlin. Mindy was teaching American history in Buffalo on a post-doctoral fellowship. We were all dedicated professionals who yearned for our craft to have meaning.

Mindy continued, "For example, I've scheduled an extra seminar to help kids figure out what it all means. It isn't easy, but has our work ever been needed more?"

"My work is useless, Mindy," I said. "Worse than useless. Cataloging the papers of colonial Dutch landlords means nothing to me now. Nothing to the world. I can't even think about it."

"The past is more than your job, Tom. It's how God shaped us. Shaped you. It's who you are. Jens was right about that, although he'd never use the religious language."

"That past is gone, too. Dead. Gone. Remember?"

"That past is never gone! You can always recapture it!"

"Not in this case."

"Well," she suggested with her usual pragmatism and a hint of frustration, "you're almost done with your appointment, right? So finish up your work for the sake of finishing. Then move on. Find yourself. Heal finally."

From anyone else, the final directive would have sounded like a criticism. Coming from her it sounded more like a prescription born of kindness.

"Jens again," I said. "Do you really believe the past can heal?"

"Your experience with the Radisson family past proves that," she said. "Arriving at the truth, putting lies to rest once and for all. That restlessness born of deceit and falsehood destroyed. Yes the past *can* heal. And the past can be brought back to life."

"All right. How?"

"Again, think about how little we knew then and how much we know now about Josephine Strong and Antoine Radisson. Or Theodorick Crane and Mary Strong, for that matter. Most of their history, too, was dead for all but a few people. Now anyone can read about it and see it alive and free. You wrote your dissertation on it, for goodness sake. Freddy Teed started it with his exposés, but you put it all together."

I knew she was right, despite my comments to the contrary, and I had turned the same example over in my mind several times since reading Jens' email.

Moreover, and more personally relevant, the uncovering of the Radisson family story had revealed two or three historical caves from my own past that needed further exploring. Not least of these caves belonged to Benjamin Fries, a.k.a. Albert Hartman, a fugitive from the law who was wanted for vehicular homicide. He had known the Radissons and my graduate school mentor, Peter Langley, and had shed much light on what had been hidden in the Radisson family past. He was part of my past, too, as he had known my family when we summered on the Saint Lawrence River, and had spoken of his relationship with my parents in language that left me more than a little curious.

Was there perhaps a bud or two of history from my own family tree, dormant yet still alive, in Ben Fries' cave? I knew the difficulties of answering this question. I hadn't heard from him in four and a half years, since just after Julianne Radisson and I visited him to inquire about her family. The letter I wrote in reply to his was returned undeliverable. I now had no idea where he was or how to get in touch with him. But I knew that if I were to discover anything about my family past I would have to encounter Ben Fries again, either in the here and now or in the there and then.

"I've been thinking of going back north," I said.

"To Clinton Falls?"

"Further north. Back to the river."

"Oh," Mindy said, recognizing the implications of my answer.

Truth be told, I had started the journey north several times since moving to Brooklyn. On at least a dozen Fridays I had rented a car and driven out of the city with the intention of spending a long weekend in the Thousand Islands. I owned a cottage there that had once belonged to my parents. It was just down the road from where Ben Fries had lived. It was in sight of the island dock into which my father, cut off by the drunk speedboater whom I had not found and had not yet forgiven, had crashed his antique Lyman, killing my family. I had gotten as far as Utica once on my journeys north, but had never made it all the way there.

"Is Ben Fries still there?" Mindy asked, spelunking down into that conversation topic of old.

"He moved on," I said.

"Do you know where?"

"Back in 1996 he moved to New Brunswick. But the letter I sent him came back with that pointing finger telling me he no longer lived at that address. I don't know where he is now."

"So the last time you saw him was when you and Julianne visited him."

"Yes," I said. "I never told you this at the time, Mindy, but I also received a letter from him soon after that, just before he moved away. He knew my parents, and my father knew his true identity as Albert Hartman."

"That doesn't surprise me. I'm sure life can get a bit insular up there."

"Mindy, Ben said he was more valuable to my father free rather than in jail. He said he paid a high price for that freedom. What did he mean by that? Why didn't my dad turn him in? Their relationship was more complicated than I realized as a kid, that's for sure."

"Another historical puzzle," Mindy said. "This one's closer to home, though. You should make it top priority."

I smiled for the first time in days. "Thanks for the affirmation," I said.

"As soon as I can manage it I'll drive up and visit you. See what you've found. See if you're healing. Maybe towards the end of October. Maybe Thanksgiving. Whenever I can. I promise you, though, I'll do it."

"Really?"

"Yes really."

"Thanks for that, too."

"And, oh yeah, it's good to hear you perking up a bit, Tom. Even something as bad as what happened yesterday doesn't mean it's the end of the world. We still have to live our lives. It's good to hear you talking about living yours."

A final "thank you" was all the response I could manage.

"Message received loud and clear," Mindy said. "Now go take a nap. Stop drinking. Stop watching TV. Get some rest."

AND SO I PREPARED TO LEAVE. My final two weeks of work were easy enough to endure with the help of my colleagues, the return of Major League Baseball after a time off for national mourning, and the assurance that I would be leaving as soon as my time at the institute ran out.

I had never considered myself a New Yorker, had not liked living there, in fact, but in those two weeks, as I prayed with others and as we allowed the wounds of 9/11 to be salved by priests, politicians, columnists, counselors and each other, I felt closer to the city and its people than I ever had.

Finally, on September 27, 2001, I packed up a rented Ford Taurus with everything I owned besides what was in the Thousand Island cottage that I had not visited in five years. I drove through the Bronx on the Major Deegan and onto the Thruway. I honked when I passed Newburgh and was finally, to my mind, upstate. I saw the lights of the American span of the Thousand Island Bridge just after eight o'clock that night.

It was not quite as extraordinary as the bishop's response five years before, but at least decisive action provided some hope for relief from this new and aggravated condition of bewilderment and pain.

Chapter Three

MY PAST. I KNEW I WOULD FIND SOMETHING OF IT when I arrived at the Thousand Islands—the sufferings and triumphs
hinted at by Jens, clues to my family's connection with Albert Hartman/Ben Fries, perhaps even some degree of healing from my grief. But I never expected to begin finding
anything so quickly. Even less did I expect my personal
quest for answers to be immediately and inextricably linked
to one of the river's most famous legends.

I had heard the tale of Napoleon's gold, of course, as we
all had while aboard the tour boats out of Alexandria Bay,
Clayton or one of the Canadian river towns. And I suppose
that as my favorite tour boat tale the story was already part
of my past. But that was a frivolous preoccupation of my
childhood, or so it seemed. The story as I knew it was usually told in the following way.

When Napoleon lost his final battle at Waterloo in June
1815 and abdicated the French throne, a group of family
and friends hatched a plan to escort him out of Europe,
preferably to the United States. Napoleon consented to the
plan, but the water off France's Atlantic coast was con-
trolled by the British navy, and the former emperor was unable to flee. In July he was taken captive by the British, and
by October he was a prisoner on the isolated South Atlantic
island of Saint Helena.

Napoleon was a prisoner, but his older brother, Joseph,
and several friends of the family did succeed in getting away.
Joseph purchased several properties in America. One prop-

erty was in Cape Vincent, New York, at the foot of the Thousand Islands, where the waters of Lake Ontario become the Saint Lawrence River. It was here that they hoped Napoleon would settle, once past the British blockade or, after Napoleon was finally exiled on Saint Helena, escaping from the remote island prison.

Napoleon never made it across the ocean. He died on Saint Helena in 1821, still a prisoner of the British. And although Joseph Bonaparte did make it to the United States, he eventually settled near Philadelphia, and only set foot in northern New York on a few occasions.

Nevertheless, Cape Vincent still celebrates its bit of notoriety with an annual French Festival in early July. The festival climaxes in the wish-fulfillment of French émigré hopes, the entry into town of the "Emperor Napoleon Bonaparte" saddled on a white horse, at the head of one of the best small town parades you will ever see. The festival has more meaning than this fiction, however, as many families from Cape Vincent to Clayton, my mother's maternal family included, boast French or anglicized surnames, and can trace their lineage back to the post-Waterloo expatriation and, in many cases, beyond.

The core of the Napoleon's gold legend is this. In July 1815 a lone French vessel, bound for Cape Vincent, slipped by the British blockade. It crossed the Atlantic. It got past the British defenses at Louisburg and onto the Saint Lawrence. It got through several of the rapids upriver from Montreal. The ship almost made it, but as often happened in those days before the dredging of canals and the eventual opening of the Seaway, it hit a shoal or capsized in a rapids and sunk somewhere upriver from Prescott. Neither the ship nor a ship's manifest was found, nor was anyone quite sure of the vessel's name. The tour guides insist, though, and many local historians concur, that on board the ship was a large supply of gold, meant to maintain Napoleon's high standard of living in the relative wilderness of the New World hinterlands.

So much for what I knew—or, more accurately, half-remembered—of the story when I drove the long journey north from Brooklyn in late September 2001. Within an hour of my arrival, I discovered that there was much more to know, and that the knowledge, or at least the search for it, was very close to home indeed.

I WAS IN THE LOUNGE of Il Castello Ristorante in Alexandria Bay, needing dinner after the long drive. I was sipping a beer, and had just ordered the surf and turf when a series of pictures behind the bar caught my eye. When the bartender saw me looking closely at one of them he asked if I was a hockey fan. I should have guessed that something was up because he had been treating me with an air of friendly familiarity from the moment I had walked in the door.

"My father was a huge hockey fan," I said, "which is why, I suppose, he and my uncle are up there arm in arm with the Esposito brothers."

The bartender was a tall man with thick, black-rimmed glasses and two tufts of charcoal-grey hair on either side of his otherwise bald head. He smiled and offered me his hand. "I'm Martin Comstock, Tom, and I've been wondering when you'd come back."

I shook his hand, then paused for a moment to see if I remembered him from my time in the Islands, from the funeral, from anywhere. Nothing. So to avoid the obvious question I asked instead, "When I'd come back? Not if?"

"No, not if, although after five years of waiting some of the others have put big money on if. I, however, always knew that when would be the winning bet."

"The others?"

"More of your father's friends. I'm sure you'll meet them sooner or later. As a matter of fact, they'll be at

Jimmy's Tavern tomorrow evening if you're not too busy. There's always a place for you at Jimmy's."

I nodded. "You've been expecting me."

"Well, you haven't put the cottage up for sale. Your cousin Andrew's been mowing the lawn and shoveling snow for you. We knew you'd come back someday, at least to check it out."

I slid my empty glass his way. "I drove up from Brooklyn today and, frankly, could use another one of these."

"Mi cervesa es su cervesa," he said, laughing quietly.

"Gracias," I replied.

Comstock got me a fresh glass from the cooler. "You missed the season," he said. "The river's practically empty by now. People are fools to leave this early, you know. The beauty's just begun. We need it more than ever this year. Well, after what happened on 9/11."

"I didn't come as a tourist, Martin. I'm not here only for a weekend."

He stopped the tap, my glass half full of Genny, then resumed the pour. "You're moving in? Now?"

"Right after I finish dinner." I gestured out towards the parking lot as he placed the beer on the coaster. "Everything I own is in the rental car outside. Everything I own except for what's been sitting in the cottage, that is."

"Well, I'm sorry," he said, with a wave of his hand. "It's just that most people are doing the opposite, putting up their shutters and driving away this time of year."

I tipped my glass and drank a long swig. "Not me. I just drove six hours here, and tomorrow morning I'll be taking the shutters down. I expect there's a hammer and screwdriver around the cottage somewhere."

Martin Comstock smiled and poured himself a half glass of Sprite. "You're an historian?"

"Sort of. I did research work in Brooklyn. I haven't taught in several years."

"But you know your history, don't you? You know how

to sort through stuff and figure out what happened and what didn't?"

"If only it were that easy," I said.

"You did it with the Radissons, right?"

"I had lots of help. But yes, in the end I did."

"Well, without being presumptuous, I'd like to say that once you get settled in and get to know your father's friends, you're in for quite a treat. Historically speaking, that is."

"I look forward to it," I said, although I was not quite sure what he was talking about.

"Your father's work is waiting for you. Your cousin Andrew says he didn't touch it, left it exactly like it was on the day ... well, like it was five years ago."

"The day my family died," I said. "Don't worry. I can handle it." I took a swig of beer and tried to change the subject anyway. "Were you really betting on if and when I'd come back?"

He smiled and waved his hand. "Well, not betting so much as considering the odds. We were trying to figure out whether you'd continue your father's work. We read about what happened in Clinton Falls, with Congressman Radisson, and thought it might be right after that."

"I went to Brooklyn instead to do that research work."

"And the years went by," he said, and then sighed. "And the world has changed. Well, have you visited their graves yet?"

"First thing I did when I got here," I said. "I was lucky I had a good flashlight. The plots need some sprucing up. I'll head over there tomorrow with some mums."

"Good man." He nodded. "You won't have to do anything back home. As I was saying, Andrew has been diligent with the upkeep and left things exactly as they were." I assumed he meant the cottage. But then he said, "Your father's work was important to Andrew, too, you know. As important to him as it was to the rest of us."

My father's work. Martin Comstock had referred to it three times already. What did he mean? Not the newspaper, I knew, which my father had lost about a decade before he died. Not Preserve the Islands, either, the international environmental group that Ben Fries had started and my mother had supported most among my family. That had been in the hands of committed, capable professionals and volunteers for years.

I asked him directly, "What work?"

"Again, I don't want to be presumptuous." He looked at me curiously as he wiped and hung wine glasses. "You didn't know what your father was doing when you were growing up? Besides the newspaper?"

"All I cared about when we were up here was swimming and fishing. When I was in my teens I didn't know much at all about what he did. I remember him spending the morning hours in his study, listening to his Beethoven records, and then going out on the river for half a day. Sometimes I'd join him and he'd pull me on the water skis. Sometimes we'd dive together and look at the easier shipwrecks. I never joined him on anything other than the easy dives, though. Overall, I didn't ask questions, and he kept his study locked."

"Andrew hasn't told you anything?"

"We've spoken maybe twice in five years," I said, "when he needed some money for roof repairs and again for plumbing fixtures. Andrew and I haven't been close since we were little kids, Martin. He's like Uncle Jack. They both like to conserve their words."

"Well, maybe he was just being discrete," Comstock said after a pause while the waitress brought my dinner. "Or maybe he was waiting for you to bring it up. We never did come to any consensus on how to involve you in it."

"Bring what up?" I asked as I buttoned my bib. "Involve me in what?"

Martin Comstock wiped down the bar to my left and

my right, then fidgeted with the salt and pepper shakers that the waitress had placed on the other side of my dinner plate. I half expected him to ignore my questions and go fill them up. Then he said, "Well, what Andrew was keeping to himself, what we know for sure, is that right before your father died he thought he was once again close, I mean really, really close, to finding Napoleon's gold."

The punctuated crack of the lobster shell as I squeezed it between the pliers was as good of a reply as any I could have spoken.

Chapter Four

Martin Comstock returned to finishing his other closing time chores. He did not press me for further conversation.

"Okay," I finally said, after eating all the lobster and half the filet. "Let me get this straight. First, my father was moonlighting as a treasure hunter." I shook my head and laughed. "I thought he dove for recreational purposes only."

"Nope. His purpose was a higher one, you might say."

"Apparently. Second, my father thought he was very close to finding the most famous, half-legendary sunken treasure on the Saint Lawrence."

"Half-legendary, huh? I guess you could call it that."

"Third, this wasn't the first time he thought he was close to finding it. So far so good?"

"So far so good," Martin Comstock affirmed.

"Did his search for Napoleon's gold involve Ben Fries?"

Comstock nodded thoughtfully. "You could just as well ask if Ben Fries' search for Napoleon's gold involved your father. The answer to both questions would be a resounding affirmative."

I felt a strange sense of calm, as if reassured that my trip north had not been in vain. I sent Jens Erlenmeyer a telepathic thank you.

"What do you expect from me?" I asked. "It sounded like you want me to take over my father's research and continue his quest."

Martin Comstock smiled. "Quest? Well damn. Charlie Flanagan's quest. I haven't heard it called that in a long,

long time." He turned off the track lights above the wine glass rack. "Of course, whether you continue his work or not is your decision."

"How long has it been?" I asked.

"Well, it all started twenty-five years ago. In 1976. That was quite a year up here on the river, the year that changed everything."

"But he didn't find it then, right? And twenty years later he thought he was close to finding it a second time?" I finished the last bite of the beef. "Martin, did he and my mom and Patrick die because of Napoleon's gold?"

"I can't say," he answered immediately.

"Can't or won't?"

"Can't, for several reasons." He turned off the neon lights in the window. "Five o'clock tomorrow at Jimmy's. We'll be there. We'll be waiting for you."

I MET MY FATHER'S FRIENDS, as invited, the next day at Jimmy's Tavern, where one or another iteration of their group had gathered each and every Friday for almost twenty-five years. They called themselves the "River Rat Reporters." They met to discuss Thousand Island happenings and, while doing so, to drink beer as heavily as possible while still remaining able to talk. The composition of the group had not changed much since it was formed in the autumn of 1976. My father was dead, Ben Fries was gone, and my cousin Andrew had taken over Uncle Jack's place at the table when Jack moved to Florida. The group sat at a round table in what Martin Comstock called the "space of honor," just to the left of the entrance door and under an oval stained-glass window.

I walked in shortly after five and Comstock motioned me over. The men were drinking glasses of beer poured from pitchers. My cousin Andrew had one ready for me before I sat down next to him.

"Damn, Tommy," he said, "I haven't seen you since the funeral. And we've talked, what, twice since then?"

"About the color of roof shingles and about copper versus PVC plumbing fixtures," I said, shaking his hand. "Thanks for all your work, Andrew. Heron's Nest looks great."

"You made a good move choosing plastic. A dozen cottages have been broken into and stripped of their copper pipes the last few years. Easy pickin's for burglars."

"How are your mom and dad?"

"They're great. I'm headed down there after I finish up a few jobs here on the river. You should come down again sometime."

"I just might do that," I said.

Andrew smiled and shook his head. "Damn, it's good to see you again, cuz."

Martin Comstock stood and gestured around the table with an arm. "And this is the rest of our vaunted company." He pointed around the table at three of the men. "These figured on when," he said, "the others, only if you'd return."

"I'm Tom Flanagan," I said, offering my hand to each of them one at a time. "I guess you already knew that."

There were laughs as we shook hands, which quieted when Comstock sat down and hit the bottom of his empty beer glass against the table. "Gentlemen," he said. "I had the pleasure of meeting Tom less than twenty-four hours ago over the surf and turf special at Castello's. He informed me he's moving into Heron's Nest, and not just to visit." He looked at me. "Since you and I have already met, Tom, let me introduce you to the others." Several of the men exchanged glances, smiles, and nods.

He motioned to the man at his right, who was thin and bony with stringy blonde hair sticking out from underneath a Husqvarna baseball cap. He wore cut-off denim shorts and had a pack of Marlboro's rolled up in his t-shirt sleeve. The thin man's face reminded me of my own five years before when I was searching for my family's killer—unshaven for a few days, sunburned, and more than a little uncomfortable with being on land.

"This is Billy Masterson," Martin Comstock said, "fishing guide extraordinaire. He'll find you the last Muskie on the river before the poor fish itself even knows where it is."

Billy Masterson nodded my way. "I'll catch the effer, too," he said.

Comstock shook his head and smiled. "Next is James Pembroke, our token Canadian. He's a former river pilot and now the captain of the *Thousand Islands Queen* out of Rockport. In my opinion, it's the finest tour boat from either shore. Back when he was piloting the big boys he had more near misses with salties and freighters than any captain on the river. Each one, he likes to say, was a near miss with a purpose."

"For that comment you can drink the dregs," said Pembroke, who then emptied the pitcher into Martin Comstock's glass. As he was getting up to refill it he said to me, "Call me Jim."

Jim Pembroke was a tall man, almost as thin as Billy Masterson but with a more prominent belly. He was well-dressed in a yellow button-down shirt and sport coat. His hairline was receding, like Martin Comstock's, but he kept his remaining hair cut short.

"You know Andrew Hibbard, of course, son of Jonathan 'Jack' Hibbard, master builder and Florida defector. Andrew followed in his father's footsteps as owner and operator of George Hibbard Construction, and is now considered the man to call when your island home needs help."

Anyone looking at Andrew and me could tell the family resemblance, handed down through my mother, Mary, and his father, Jack Hibbard, especially identifiable by the dark hair and in the incongruent combination of aquiline nose and double chin. But Andrew did not wear glasses, had a goatee, and over the years had bulked up through hard physical work and, ignoring his Methodist heritage, by heavy eating and drinking.

Martin Comstock continued his introductions. "On your right is this evening's guest of honor, Mike Slattery. Today he celebrates his fortieth birthday for the twentieth year in a row." A mock cheer went up among the men. Jim Pembroke set the full pitcher of beer down in front of Slattery. "And, oh yes," Comstock added, "the Honorable Mr. Slattery also happens to be the Bay's current mayor."

"For five friggin' terms," Jim Pembroke said. "For just as long as he's been forty. Try as they might they can't vote the bastard out of office. No wonder you Americans are so enthusiastic about mandatory term limits."

Mike Slattery was short and squat, his shoulder length grey hair tied back in a pony tail. His thick grey beard gave the impression of wisdom. His hands were strong, I found as he offered me a shake, which told me that any wisdom he had acquired was obtained through more than just book learning.

"Happy birthday," I said while refilling Slattery's glass. He tapped my glass with his full one and nodded.

"And last, but certainly not least, at least when accumulated fortune is the measure, is Raphael Ostend, son and heir of Gabriel Ostend, who is no doubt son and heir of another angelically named Ostend ..." Martin Comstock gestured with an upraised palm.

"Michael," affirmed Raphael Ostend with a polite smile.

Comstock smiled in return and continued. "Michael, then, made the family fortune as a luxury haberdasher, plying his trade in your old haunt of Clinton Falls. Gabriel moved the business to Puerto Rico where labor is cheap. Raphael here shifted the business plan to designer baseball caps, which are to the American man in the twenty-first century what felt bowlers were to him in the twentieth and silk top hats were in the nineteenth."

Mike Slattery put an arm on Ostend's shoulder. "Our

dear Ostends are also the token remnant of the glory days of the Islands as an upper-crust resort paradise. The Pullmans, the Bournes, the Strausses, the Emerys, the Boldts. They're all gone, but the Ostends are still here. His family has owned the Ostend Group for over a hundred fifty years, their castle Valhalla for almost as long."

"Group?" I asked, not knowing that the Ostends owned more islands than the two upon which Valhalla was built.

"My great grandfather bought all seven of them for just under five thousand Canadian dollars," Raphael Ostend said.

"What's their price tag today?" Andrew asked. "Thirty mil? Forty?"

Ostend smiled, and assured us that they were not for sale, and therefore had no price.

He wore designer blue jeans and a cuff-linked white shirt. Under the right cuff was a watch that I guessed was worth as much as my entire wardrobe. His face was spotless and smooth, with only a hint of a wrinkle on his brow. His white hair was perfectly combed with a left part.

I knew of the Ostends, of course, as did everyone who lived in Clinton Falls or summered in the Thousand Islands, but I could not imagine my father drinking with one of them—drinking beer no less—and had an even harder time reconciling Raphael Ostend with his other bar buddies, especially Billy Masterson.

"The Ostend Group's sure as hell in the way," Jim Pembroke said. "Three of my closest near misses came over there. Worst section of the channel if you ask me, especially for a pilot who doesn't know what he's doing. Rookies coming upriver don't realize you can get a few yards away from the cliffs and still not be in any danger of hitting them. They crowd the damned channel and leave the downriver boats nowhere to go." Pembroke finished his glass of beer and poured another, as if to cap off his argument.

"Why didn't you just stop and let one ship at a time pass?" I asked.

At the word "stop" Jim Pembroke contorted his face into an exasperated scowl, then burst out with a "Ha!" and a handclap as I finished my question.

"You can't just stop a freighter," Mike Slattery said quietly, leaning towards my ear. Then, to bail me out, and speaking of boats, he asked Raphael Ostend about the condition of the family yacht.

"I'm in the process of turning it over to the Antique Boat Museum," Ostend said. "I think they'll begin offering tours on it next season."

"The *Archangel* is the only photo op on the river that rivals Boldt Castle and Captain Pembroke's passing freighters in popularity," Martin Comstock explained. "I, for one, hope they make postcards."

"Whew, bet they'll be raising the price of admission to pay for that acquisition," Andrew Hibbard said.

"It's a donation," Raphael Ostend corrected.

"Why the hell are you givin' it away?" asked Billy Masterson. "Too expensive to maintain?"

"Actually, no," said Ostend without a hint of smugness. "I've reprioritized these past few weeks. I'm downsizing my personal life, trying to help as many people as I can with what I have." Ostend took a ring with two keys out of his pocket and handed it to the captain. "Which reminds me, Jim, the museum people know you're coming."

"Commendable charity," said Mike Slattery. He and Raphael Ostend both drank their remaining beer and re-filled.

Andrew looked to his left and asked Billy Masterson, "How's fishing these days around the Ostend Group?"

"Useta be good before the zebra mussels. Now you can see eighty, ninety, shit, a hundred feet down in some spots." Masterson shook his head and swallowed a glass of beer in one gulp. "Zebras ate the plankton and left nothin' for the fish. Ruined the whole effin' food web. Nothin' in there now to waste your time on."

Martin Comstock looked around the table. "Unless you're hunting for sunken treasure," he said.

Billy Masterson pointed a finger at him. "Now findin' that is something the zebras can help you with."

There was a pause as Comstock looked at me. He and the other Reporters waited for my reply.

It was not the first time in the past twenty four hours I had considered the potentially selfish motives of these men in being interested in my return and in my possible resumption of my father's work. Martin Comstock's comment, however, did not trigger the usual awkward response of avaricious men, as I had expected it would. No one looked away from me as I scanned their eyes. No one twitched or took a sip from their beers. No one even gazed in anticipation for my answer. Either these men were excellent poker players or they had more complicated motives than mere greed. All of them were drunk by now, too, their inhibitions lowered by what I counted to be seven pitchers of beer consumed among us, with another two full ones on the table.

Concluding that the pause was not an uncomfortable one, I decided to test my hand, trusting from the slip of paper I found in my father's office and now had in my pocket, that he had probably left a few more good cards, perhaps even an ace, in the hole.

"Sunken treasure," I said. "Martin told me last night that my father believed he was very close to finding Napoleon's gold." I motioned around the table. "You all expect me to carry on his work. You expect me to keep hunting." I leaned forward towards Billy Masterson. "And you hope I do indeed find it."

"Actually," Mike Slattery said, "we're just as divided in our opinion of the treasure's existence as we were in our predictions of your return. I, for one, like most other sensible people here on the river, think there's nothing to hunt."

This surprised me, and I swallowed more beer to try to hide it.

Billy Masterson responded next, his speech slurred now and his syntax impaired by the beer. "We're sure as shit not foolish enough to think that a heap of gold wouldn't lead to more effin' trouble than they're worth. Shit," he continued, his math skills faltering as well, "Captain Pembroke already has two kids with at least three different women from both sides of the border. Imagine what a stash of gold like that would do for his child support payments. The bitches would have him in family court for years on end."

As the rest of us laughed, Jim Pembroke reached over and cuffed Billy Masterson in the head, causing Masterson's hat to fall on the table. Pembroke picked up the cap and tossed it across the room.

"We're not manipulators, Tom, if that's what you're thinking," said Andrew when the laughter died down and Billy Masterson had retrieved his hat. "None of us is here to stab you in the back and take the gold for ourselves."

"If—I repeat—there is any," said Mike Slattery.

"We're not manipulators," Raphael Ostend repeated. Then he opened his hands in a gesture of reminder and continued. "And yet, at the same time, all of us have, in one way or another and to varying degrees, allowed Charlie Flanagan's quest for Napoleon's gold to shape our lives, whether we believe in its existence or not."

"Allowed?" said Jim Pembroke with a hint of anger. "For over twenty years now I've tried to keep as clear as possible from this nonsense. I didn't allow a goddamn thing."

"It's still part of your story," insisted Martin Comstock, "just as it is for each one of us."

Pembroke grumbled, but nodded slightly all the same.

I looked at Raphael Ostend. "Are you saying my father manipulated you?"

Ostend shook his head. "Not at all. What I'm saying is

that we were drawn to him by the immediacy of his quest. Each of us has been shaped by our responses to what Charlie Flanagan sought. There's no way we could've avoided it, just as there's no way Charlie could've resumed his quest without the guidance each of us had to offer. It was a symbiotic relationship, not crass manipulation."

"What do you expect from me?" I asked.

"Clarification for our stories," Raphael Ostend said. "As I just explained, each of us is connected to Napoleon's gold and your father's quest for it. Charlie knew that." Ostend sighed, finished his beer and placed his glass upside down on the table. "Tom, right before your father was killed he asked us to tell him our stories. Not just in snippets and fragments like we'd told them before, to him and to others, but completely. He wanted to hear them, perhaps needed to hear them, but he never got the chance."

I produced the half sheet of paper from my pocket— the one good card of my father's I had already found. I placed it on the table facing Raphael Ostend. He and the other Reporters glanced at it and exchanged looks that, again, revealed nothing.

Typed on the half sheet of paper were these words:

```
BILLY M. -- GLOW
CAPTAIN JIM -- OIL
MAYOR -- PICNIC
OSTEND -- PORTRAIT/PHOTOGRAPH
HIBBARD -- D'BLANCS
COMSTOCK -- ????
```

"Your stories," I said. "I assume this is the order in which my father wanted to hear them. If you don't mind, I'd like to honor his memory by hearing them myself in the same order."

"Well, we definitely need to tell them," Martin Comstock said quickly. "We need to tell our stories. We would have done it five years ago with Charlie had the accident not happened. That's exactly what we should do now, with Tom, in the order he suggests. If we're going to figure out anything, it's going to be through our stories."

"You're assuming that, once everything's put together, we'll know what Uncle Charlie knew," Andrew said. "I, for one, highly doubt it will all add up."

I could see a few of the others ready to respond, perhaps in agreement with Martin Comstock, perhaps with my cousin. Taking no chances, I spoke quickly. "I'm the historian," I said, "and I'm also Charlie Flanagan's son. If my first impressions of my father's work at Heron's Nest is any guide, I think I can fit together a few things, maybe a piece or two of information that you didn't know. So yes, tell me your stories. We all need to hear them."

I took a final swig of beer and added with a self-conscious rhetorical flourish, "and maybe together we'll discover the true source behind the gleam of Napoleon's gold."

The men nodded their assent, and Billy Masterson spoke for them all when, looking right at me, he poured himself another beer and said, "Eff yeah!"

Chapter Five

IT'S TIME, I suppose, to describe the two most important settings of this tale, the Saint Lawrence River itself and my cottage, which my great-grandmother Hibbard had named Heron's Nest. I've hesitated to discuss the settings not because of any difficulty in my describing them, nor because of any dictates of story structure, but rather because of my fear that the one would bring to the surface the lava-like grief of my parents' and brother's deaths, and the other would carry with it a deep feeling of regret that my family wasn't here with me to enjoy this place that had been so beloved to all of us for so many years.

But it only took me a few days to understand that my experience of the present and hope for the future were only partly tied to the sorrows of the past. After moving around furniture, replacing some old wall hangings with new ones, and kayaking on the river, I knew there was something to be said about what I heard at the funeral about how new growth often springs from destruction.

The first few days I was there, I worked on the cottage, much as my mother had done every May when opening it up for the season. I removed the shutters from the windows, swept the wood floors, and then cleaned them and the flower-patterned wallpaper with Murphy's oil soap. I vacuumed the rugs and upholstery with the old Kirby and washed the windows with Windex and newspapers. I turned right side up a cabinet's worth of coffee mugs, mismatched drinking glasses, plates and bowls. I cleaned the cast iron skillets and Dutch oven with dry salt and a water rinse. I planted some mums of the same colors I'd planted at the cemetery along the walkway to the front porch. Andrew had kept the chimney clean and in good repair, so I chopped some wood and kindling and kept warm by firing up the old cast iron stove rather than using the electric baseboard heaters.

In the mornings, after stoking the coals and re-igniting the fire, I would walk around the place with a cup of coffee, surveying the collages of family pictures that my mother loved to make on rainy days. I would go to the room where Patrick and I had slept on the nights we didn't camp out in the boathouse in our sleeping bags. I would eat lunch and drink a couple of afternoon beers on the screen porch overlooking the river, rocking slowly on the metal gliding coach that I used to vigorously ride as a kid.

I spent some time in the boathouse, too, which still contained Jack Hibbard's Chris-Craft, the boat I had been in when the bishop found me and convinced me to finally lay my parents and brother to rest. All in all, as I reacquainted myself with Heron's Nest I felt glad that it was mine. The living presence of so many good family memories served to comfort rather than depress me.

But anxiety threatened to overwhelm all that whenever I entered my father's study to search for clues about his quest for Napoleon's gold. The study, housed in a large third floor crow's nest overlooking the river, was built for privacy, secrecy even. A pilot's bridge is perhaps what Jim Pembroke would have called it. Certainly in my youth my father had guided all of us Flanagans and Hibbards as we picnicked and played and read our novels and newspapers in the lawn below and on the fishing dock beyond. He piloted the *North Country Daily News* from there, too, discussing story ideas with his reporters over the telephone and writing his own thrice-weekly columns on an orange Olivetti typewriter.

His Beethoven records were still stacked vertically on a

shelf between a set of speakers. I found the turntable on top of an amplifier in a corner across from his desk, and opened the dust cover. The Seventh Symphony. Had Andrew not touched it? Was this the last music my father had listened to before he died? I turned the amplifier on and moved the arm to the second movement, the Allegretto, and was surprised to find the sound relatively scratch and static free. With the music playing, with the swell of violins and tympani filling the room, I continued to look around.

Maps of the river hung on a wall and were marked up with different colored inks, for what purpose I did not know. Below the maps, correspondingly-colored note cards were tacked to the wall. My father had written something on each of them that looked to me like dates, initials and some numbers whose significance eluded me. I wondered if the maps and note cards were related to the list of River Rat Reporter names I had found the morning of my first visit to Jimmy's.

I sat at my father's desk and read his diving journals. He had made a record of all his dives over the years, beginning with his initial dive in 1972 to see the *Islander* steamboat wreck off Alexandria Bay. After that my father saw most of the known shipwrecks in the Thousand Islands: the *Keystorm* near Frederick Bourne's Dark Island; the *Major Henry*, with its dual front and back propellers, resting partially exposed at Mandolin Island; the *A.E. Vickery* near the Rock Island Lighthouse; the *Oconto*, just across the channel in the same section of the river; the *Iroquoise/HMS Anson*, the oldest known wreck dating from the time of the French and Indian War; the *Sir Robert Peel*, blown up by Bill Johnston and his band of pirates near the Wellesley Island base of the American bridge; and, finally, the *Kingshorn*, an oddity for the many large stones that somehow ended up on its wooden deck, presumably after it had sunk.

An interesting theme as my father returned to these sites over the years was the variation in visibility, from poor in the summer due to algae and weeds to clear in the spring before the plants started to grow, to magnificent year round once zebra mussels invaded the river in the early 1990's. The last few years of his life were clearly his best years of diving.

But what work had my father done on Napoleon's gold other than the cryptic map markings, the note cards, and his list of Reporters' names? There was no mention of his search for the gold in any of his diving journals. Might he have devoted a separate, secret journal to that quest? The lack of evidence made the historian in me uncomfortable, and I wondered as I sat in his chair, with the Seventh Symphony drawing to its magnificent conclusion, whether the gold, like several other river legends, had no basis in reality.

I RECEIVED SEVERAL VISITORS at Heron's Nest in those first days. Mike Slattery and Raphael Ostend stopped by to see how I was getting on. Several neighbors came by, too, including Stella Donaldson, who had bought Ben Fries' old cottage a few doors down when she had divorced her husband of twenty-three years and Ben had moved to New Brunswick. I was tempted to ask her if Ben had left anything in the cottage, in the attic, perhaps, or in a spare closet, but my politer instincts prevailed. She did make me an open offer to visit for afternoon tea anytime I needed company. I promised to take her up on it.

Father Napier from Saint Cyril's made a pastoral visit on a warm sunny afternoon, and we spent over an hour sipping cans of beer and watching the river from folding chairs on the shore. We talked about parishoners' comings and goings. We talked about baseball. He never asked me if I would be returning to church on a regular basis. I never admitted to him that I was still having a hard time seeing anything of God through the Church's lens. I did appreciate the visit, though.

My most interesting visitor was Walter Maitland, a

friend of my father's and former board member of Preserve the Islands, though not a River Ray Reporter. I found out later, online, that he was actually former Ambassador Walter Maitland, and had become a full-time resident of the river when he retired from the United States Foreign Service in 1993. Like Stella Donaldson and Father Napier, like the River Rat Reporters, Maitland was kind to me in those early days of my living at Heron's Nest. He even offered to take me out on his antique wooden boat next season when it was fully repaired and again seaworthy.

A FEW DAYS OF CLEANING THE HOUSE and conversation with neighbors left me in need of exercise and fresh air. On Sunday I lowered a kayak from the boathouse rafters. I loaded the kayak onto a 1993 Ford pickup I'd bought on Saturday when I returned the rented Taurus. I launched in Westminster Park on the other end of Wellesley Island.

The sky was blue and cloudless, the water clear and cold —a perfect day to be out. The river was deserted, as Martin Comstock had intimated, and I got to see and hear and feel the Saint Lawrence with an honesty that few shared in this age of motor boats and guided tours.

What struck me most about the river, especially given the premise of the Napoleon's gold story, was the power of the water, even though dredging had given it wider and deeper channels via the Saint Lawrence Seaway. I could feel the tug of the current as I paddled into open water beyond the small canal between Wellesley and Mary Islands, around Mary Island and across from Zavikon, into the Lake of the Isles between Wellesley and Hill Islands and finally into Canadian water. When I turned back into the American channel of the Seaway, I could feel the volume of five Great Lakes worth of water coursing under my small, and at that moment very fragile, kayak. It was a calm day in late September, but I knew that in high summer when a storm tracked up from Kingston or in springtime when the west winds blew from Superior to the Atlantic, that even the dredged channel could not contain the fierce violence of this water. I understood how ships were wrecked here.

I also understood how earlier people, not estranged from nature by technology like we are, were awed by the river. I thought of how the first French and English explorers processed their initial encounters with these waters. Several of these explorers had come from the Radisson family, whose history I had learned in Clinton Falls when I returned there from Florida. In contemplating these things, I could feel my connections with the past starting to fuse together again, just as Jens Erlenmeyer had suggested and Mindy McDonnell had affirmed.

I also made new connections with the past, the most intriguing of which was with the First Nations who had lived on this river for centuries before the Europeans came. As I plied the water in my plastic kayak, not so differently than they had in their wooden bark ones, I wondered what their experience was like; what they thought of this river and its islands.

I got some indication of this near the Canadian span of the international bridge, having put in at Ivy Lea, Ontario. The current was more challenging there than anywhere else on the river, with rushing and swirling water that flowed up and over underwater hills, down into underwater valleys, and between islands of pink granite whose cliff faces rose vertically from many feet below the surface to twenty, thirty and forty feet above it. Dog tired at one point, my arms flimsy, I coasted to the Canadian shore and was surprised to see a series of carvings in the rocks, six to ten feet above my head.

Some of the pictures were of human figures, others were clearly animals, still others were combinations of the two. There were geometrical shapes—circles, trapezoids, parallel lines both straight and curved. There was what looked to me like the river and its islands, the water I had just paddled through indicated by spirals and curved lines that went away from the islands. Fortunately I had my digital camera, and I took several dozen pictures of these magnificent First Nation petroglyphs.

There were calmer places too, just as awe-inspiring as the swift channels, nooks in the shoreline and hideaways between islands that might have deluded a less cautious man into thinking the river was benign. Some people appreciate beauty more when paired with sublimity, and to them the quiet lagoons and marshes and hidden coves of the Thousand Islands are made more special by the deep water dangers that lie around the corner.

I found these spots as well over the next few days. I floated silently in Eel Bay, where the sunshine-infused, greenish-blue water looked like the Caribbean. I thought the resemblance might have been a product of the unstoppable reproductive power and insatiable appetites of the zebra mussels. Around Grindstone Island I encountered bays where sea smoke hung like fire when the river was warm and the morning air cool. On the Canadian side I paddled through passages between island cliffs thirty and forty feet high, the reflected pink granite walls turning the water a subtly shifting shade of purple. In the Canadian Admiralty group I spent several hours recharging my spiritual batteries in Half Moon Bay at Bostwick Island. This was a sacred place, where boaters have gathered to enjoy summer Sunday vespers services since 1887. Called the "tallest cathedral" by Islanders, it was, to me, even more awe-inspiring when empty. On the mainland near Clayton, I paddled around the marshes and bogs that narrowed into French Creek and provided shelter and food for herons and muskrats, frogs and speckled trout.

Having seen the Thousand Islands again from a kayak rather than from the deck of a tour boat, I thought I understood my father's love for the place and what fed his obsession for resurfacing the river's most celebrated secret. At least now I had the emotional grounding for this work of his that I was expected to continue.

Chapter Six

THE FOLLOWING SATURDAY, a week and a day after my first evening at Jimmy's, I kayaked downriver from the Boldt Yacht house on Wellesley Island and into the collection of Islands known as the Summerland Group. My plan that afternoon was to paddle around there for a while, then head back west towards Boldt Castle and around the Sunken Rock Lighthouse, which sat atop one of the most dangerous shoals on the river. Then I would cross back over to Wellesley Island, go home, and grill a steak.

As I was about to leave the Summerland Group I was hailed by a thin man with wet hair wearing a diving suit and holding a blow torch, standing on the shore of a small forested island with one secluded cottage and a three-bay boathouse. Only when I got close and he took off the mask did I realize it was Billy Masterson.

"Almost finished," he said after catching my attention. "Come ashore and I'll pop open a couple beers."

"Finished with what?" I asked after he had helped me out of my kayak and we had pulled the boat out of the water.

"Dismantlin' the Snell's dock," he said.

"The Snells?"

"Desmond and Georgia Snell. They own this effin' rock. They took their cabin cruiser back to To-ron-to last week, and it's my job to bring their dock in and shut the place up for the winter. Hey, where were you last night?"

"I was housecleaning," I said. "Take no offense. I'll be there this week."

We moved to the kitchen, and when Billy Masterson opened the refrigerator I saw canned beer, cold cuts, an unopened gallon of milk, a large hunk of cheddar cheese and a squeeze bottle of mustard.

He snapped open a can of Genny Cream Ale and handed it to me. "I have a cabin over on the north side of Grindstone," he said. "I cut back on my heat bills by caretakin' places like this. I have four of them from here to Chippewa Bay. Check on one every month or so from now 'til the end of April."

"Do the Snells know you've moved in?" I asked.

"Not sure," he said thoughtfully. He winked, and I nodded in return to assure him I would keep his squatting a secret.

"What about you?" he asked. "You all moved in?"

"I am," I said. "It's good to be back in the place. I barely remembered it until I got to spend some time there alone. I cleaned the whole place up. Planted some mums. It's been a good week."

"Alone time's what I love most about the river," Billy Masterson said. "When it's just me and the water, me and the fish—that's when I'm in heaven."

"I'll be in heaven when I'm dead," I said. "This world is nothing but pain and sorrow."

"I'll drink to that," he said, and downed the whole can of beer. He scratched his head and added, "You gotta admit, though, even if you believe what you just said, that this place is as damn close to heaven as you're gonna get."

"Not for me," I said. "My parents and brother died here."

He retrieved another beer from the fridge and cracked it open. "Sorry to rain on your pity parade, but so have thousands of other people, many of 'em on the water. Death is sure as shit, Tom. I for one'd rather go here than anywhere else. Especially than in one of those effin' towers." He shook his head quickly, as if shivering, then pointed to a chair. "Here, sit down. Stay awhile. You and I got some talkin' to do."

I sat and sipped my beer, taking in the ceramic tile and pink granite luxury of Desmond and Georgia Snell's kitchen. I wondered from our conversation so far if Billy Masterson was religious. I asked him as much when he returned in a pair of denim shorts and a black long-sleeve t-shirt that read "Molly Hatchet" in peeling vinyl letters across the chest.

"Born and raised Catholic," he said. "Still go to confession." He moved towards the door. "Get yourself another beer. Come on out. I need a smoke."

We sat on a log at the island's shore near a small fire pit. The river was calm, the water just barely rippling in the breeze, the seagulls flying in circles overhead in their endless search for food.

"Do you go to Saint Cyril's?" I asked, referring to my family's summer church in Alexandria Bay where the funeral was held on September 11th five years before.

"Saint Mary's," he said as he lit a cigarette. "You know my motto?"

"What?"

"Sin in the Bay, confess in Clayton."

I laughed. "I appreciate your distinction between the profane and the sacred."

"I'm good at the profanity part," he said.

"We all are. It's the sacred we need help with."

Billy held his cigarette in the air and nodded. "You know what's most sacred to me?" he asked. "Even more than a church?"

"That's easy," I said. I pointed with my beer can towards the river.

"Damn straight," he said, "even though they try their best to ruin it with their shippin' channels and oil spills and their regulated water levels and Sea-Doos." He almost spat out the last words, and his mouth was twisted in disdain as he spoke. He took a swig of beer and smiled. "But try as they might they can't do it. Whatever they put in the river eventually washes away, you see. That's why this place is as close to heaven as we're ever gonna get." Billy Masterson cleared his throat, then said in a baritone voice, "Then the angel showed me the river of the water of life, as clear as crystal, flowin' from the throne of God ... down the middle of the great street of the city."

I added, mimicking Billy's baritone, "And there will be no more death or mourning or crying or pain, for the old order of things has passed away."

A-effin'-men to that," he said.

"You know what I've always wondered?" I asked. "How the Book of Revelation can be so reassuring and at the same time so bizarre."

"You mean the seals and scrolls and the four horsemen and the whore of Babylon and the plagues and the beasts and all that shit?"

"Don't forget the white rider with his blazing eyes of fire and a sword coming out of his mouth."

He nodded. "Try this on for bizarre. Last spring I saw a dead cow floatin' down the river. It was belly up, and on top of it was a calf. The calf was lyin' down, and its mouth was clamped to its mother's teat like a pair of vice grips. I slapped myself to make sure I wasn't dreamin'."

"How exactly is that as close to heaven as we can get?"

"The cow was dead. Everything living dies. Shit, how the hell else do you expect to get to heaven? Anyway, as I said before, at least it died here, on this river.

"Think about that calf," Billy continued. "That calf was still alive. Who knows, maybe its mom got hung up on an island and the calf made it to safety. Maybe it's still alive today, munchin' on some of that nice Wellesley Island grass of yours. Stranger things have happened."

"For example?"

"For example, stuff back before the Corps started regulatin' the water level all the way out in Niagara Falls. Houses washed away. Carriages with the dead horses still attached. A guy in his tub, drunk and passed out. They said when he woke up he stepped out to get his towel and got the surprise of his life! Is that any more bizarre than what's in Revelation?"

"That was real."

"That was when the river was real. Today it's just a glorified canal."

I nodded, thinking through his argument. I had spent a lot of time on the Saint Lawrence since my arrival, and had been impressed by the power of the river's current. How much stronger had it been before being dredged and regulated by the Army Corps of Engineers, harnessed by modern civilization? I recalled that even Charles Dickens commented on the ferocity of the rapids during his 1842 journey downriver from Kingston to Montreal. I began to appreciate that the river's power might have a mystical affect on those so inclined.

"Tell me if I'm getting your point," I said. "Let's try to imagine what a writer with an apocalyptic bent living two thousand years ago would've done with that image of the cow and calf. A sign of things to come? A glimpse of God's plan revealed? A metaphor for fallen and redeemed humanity?"

"You're gettin' my point," Billy Masterson said.

Billy's love of the river opened the door to a topic that I hadn't yet broached with any of my father's friends save Martin Comstock, diverted as I was by reacquainting myself with Heron's Nest and the river. I took the opportunity to step right through. "Are you a member of Preserve the Islands?" I asked.

He shook his head. "Naw. I'm not much of a joiner. I

certainly do respect 'em. How could I not with the work they've done for the river?"

"My dad used to say that," I said. "My mom was enthusiastic, but my dad kind of just stayed off to the side. You know what I think it was?"

Billy Masterson puffed his cigarette and raised an eyebrow. I had a hunch that he did indeed know what it was.

"I think he had it in for Ben Fries."

"Sure as shit," Billy Masterson said, nodding. He snuffed out the cigarette and put the used filter into his shorts pocket. "Your father sure did have it in for good ol' Mr. Fries." He pronounced the name with an exaggerated syllable, like "Freeeeeze."

"I was only a kid back then," I said. "I never knew why he felt that way. I always thought it had something to do with pesticide use on a golf course."

Billy Masterson laughed, then glanced at me as he lit another cigarette. "You mean Ben didn't tell you the real story? Not when you came to see him five years ago with that brunette?"

"How did you ..." My words trailed off in surprise that Billy Masterson was aware of my visit with Julianne Radisson to learn what Ben knew about my mentor's death and about her family's past.

"One of my caretakin' gigs back then was two doors down from Heron's Nest," he explained, "in the other direction from Ben's. Shit, when I saw you comin' that day I thought you might be movin' in. And with a chick like that ..." He licked his finger and touched the lit end of the cigarette, causing a distinct and surprisingly loud hissing sound.

"You knew Ben?"

"Did I ever. More than once Ben Fries gave me reasons for a visit to the confessional." He stood up and stretched. "Remember that we're all supposed to tell you our stories? To explain about your father and the gold? My story is about the gold, and it's also about why your father had it in for Ben Fries."

Chapter Seven

BILLY MASTERSON WENT INSIDE and made us ham and cheese sandwiches. He built a fire with driftwood kindling more quickly than I had ever seen done before. He sat back down and told me his story.

"I've always loved fish," he said. "Ever since I can remember—and I have memories from back when I was four or five—I have always loved fish. My earliest memory is bein' neck deep in water out in Eel Bay. I was standin' there, my dad was in a skiff anchored just a few yards away, and just like that he jumps in the water and starts splashin' towards me like my leg's about to get bit off by a barracuda. It wasn't a barracuda, of course, but it was close. There were three big ass carp swimmin' around me, and I stood there with my legs spread wide, like the bridge to Canada, as they swam under me like salties.

" 'No wonder the fuckers didn't bite your fuckin' balls off!' my dad yelled, which, incidentally, also provides my first memory of hearing an f-bomb. The carp didn't bite me, didn't bother me a bit, in fact. My father's language did, though. And I resolved soon after that to never use f-bombs myself."

"Ah," I said, smiling. "That's why you say 'eff this' and 'eff that' all the time."

"Hey, it's a step in the right direction, isn't it? Maybe a future Masterson'll be an effin' poet."

We both laughed.

"You're a fish magnet," I said.

"I am. I don't know why, but the fish always seem to come when I ask 'em. Only in this river, though. It never works anywhere else. If I go down past Cape Vincent or over to the Black River or Lake Champlain they ignore me. Here, they listen to me. They like me. There's somethin' about them, or somethin' about this river, that draws 'em right to me."

"They come when you ask them?" I said. "When you ask them verbally?"

"No, not verbally, although I did yell a lot in those days. This is gonna sound weird, but how I understand it is that it works like Aquaman on those old TV cartoons."

"Telepathy?" I asked.

Billy Masterson tipped his head, as if to say I could use that word if I chose to.

"Anyway," he said, "I took my first fishin' party out when I was twelve. My dad was supposed to do it, but he was so hungover he couldn't even get out of bed. My mom was cryin' her eyes out 'cuz we wouldn't have food for her and my sisters that week if we didn't catch these Canadians a muskie. And so I volunteered with my feet, walkin' out the door and down to the dock while my dad barfed and my mom bitched.

"Well, to make a short story shorter, we caught fifteen bass, eight pike, five walleye and two muskies that day. We did it just by lowerin' the bait where I felt it was the right place to lower it, and by trollin' for the muskies where I knew they'd be. Where they, or the river, *told* me they'd be. When we got one on the hook I'd whack it with a baseball bat and that would be the end of that.

"The tourists were from Quebec. They spoke just a few words of English and I spoke no French, but when the fish started pilin' up they had no complaints in any language. They couldn't've cared less that a piss-ant kid was leadin' 'em to anglin' glory."

"When was this?" I asked, having no clue how old Billy was.

"Summer of '75," he said. "I was twelve, as I mentioned, just about to turn thirteen. My next client after the Canadians? The next man I took out fishin'? None other than Benjamin Fries, who had just moved up from Pittsburgh, or so he said, and was itchin' for some fresh seafood. By then my father figured out he was better off at home watchin' TV and drinkin', and I was better off in a boat earnin' the family's money. So when this guy knocked on our door askin' for help on the river, my old man didn't complain about me takin' him out. Didn't complain either when I came home with twenty dollars from a poor man who just wanted company and some conversation. The lazy bastard was fast drunk asleep. At least my mom and sisters could get some food."

As Billy Masterson took a break to stoke the fire, I considered what he'd said about Ben Fries being "a poor man who just wanted company and some conversation." My cynical side suspected that Ben had been using the naive twelve-year-old to gain knowledge of the river and make his alias and alibi more credible, having just eluded the law on charges of vehicular manslaughter. My compassionate side guessed that Ben was hungry for friendship during those early years of his new identity, and with his historian's eye would have relished time with a common man of the river just as I was relishing the same now. But such self-interested slumming seemed just as cynical as my first thought, and now I, sitting here on the Snell's island shore, could be implicated in the same. Before I could work out the further implications of these assessments, Billy Masterson resumed his story.

"I fished for three years, just about every day, even when the river was frozen. I honed my skills to a pretty sharp level in those years, catchin' whatever I wanted to catch wherever I wanted to catch it. I brought home money from the tourists and brought home fish for my mother to fillet and cook. Ben joined me a lot, sometimes payin' me as his guide, other times pitchin' in by cuttin' tackle or relinin' my poles. I guess you could you say we became friends."

But before I could ask the most important question, Billy Masterson answered it. "We all knew who he was. I don't see how he could've thought we didn't. Even I knew and, shit, I was just a kid."

"Why didn't anyone turn him in?"

"He was more valuable to us free," Billy Masterson said, shocking me with words that not only echoed but outright plagiarized what Ben Fries had said about why my father hadn't turned him in.

"Think about what he did," Billy continued. "In July 1976, right after the oil spill, he organized a community meetin' to discuss the Powers-That-Be's plan to open the Seaway to year round shippin'. He convinced all of us— your mother, Mike Slattery, Raphael Ostend, shit, even my old man—convinced us all he was right. Year round shippin' would have changed this river beyond recognition. Destroyed it more than the Army Corps could ever do with their dredgin' and their regulatin' river levels. Ben Fries was right, and he fought against everything that threatened our islands and our water.

"Besides, I can't think of a single person up here, American or Canadian, who gives a rat's ass about the government agents who were lookin' for him. Many of us here hate 'em. We decided as a group that we'd keep our mouths shut and protect Ben from 'em. Not all of us joined Preserve the Islands, but we joined together to protect the man who started it."

"Was he ever close to getting found out?"

"Naw, not really. He looked different enough than he did in that last picture, the one in the papers. If anyone came snoopin' around we all just played dumb. 'Nope, never seen him,' we'd say."

"And Napoleon's gold?" I asked, totally unsure of what the connections might be.

"The gold's what introduced me to your father," Billy Masterson said, "and the gold's what came between your dad and Ben Fries."

"How?"

"To tell you that I'll have to make a long story longer."

"Go ahead."

"I fished for three years, okay? Then I got tired of it. I got tired of doin' my father's work for him. I got tired of givin' him the money I earned. This might sound strange, but most of all I got tired of gettin' to know the fish on my terms and not on theirs. Do you know what I mean?"

"I have no clue what you mean," I admitted.

"When you catch a fish you pull it out of the water," he said. "I wanted to know the fish *in* the water. I wanted to familiarize myself with their element."

"What did you do? Go back to Eel Bay and start spearing them?"

"No, never done that, although it's a good idea." He laughed. "What I did was take up divin'. I got myself some second-hand equipment and took up divin'. It turned out to be the stupidest, most dangerous thing I ever did."

"You still do it, right? You were just down there before I came by. Dismantling the Snell's dock."

"Divin' itself wasn't the stupidest thing. Teachin' myself was the stupidest thing."

"I see the distinction."

"It was easy at first on the other side of Grindstone where the water's calm and clear. I'd go ten, twenty-five, fifty feet down. I'd look for the fish and follow a pike or muskie 'til it hit the afterburners and I couldn't keep up with it any more.

"Then I tried it over here, on this side of Wellesley. It's completely different on this side. The currents are crazy. The shoals sneak up on you. I found that out the hard way in July 1978. I was fifteen and fearless. I thought with my skills of marine life attraction I might swim with a sturgeon. Now I did swim with a sturgeon eventually, and it was a big effer, too, about six feet I guess. That was a few years later, in 1981. In 1978, when I was fifteen, I was stupid."

Billy paused and played with the fire again. "I motored over here in my putt, just to this side of Sunken Rock, dropped anchor and dove in. I had no clue." He shook his head. "I had no effin' clue."

"What happened?"

"At first I fared well in thirty or thirty-five feet of water. Then things got dicey when I tried to turn upriver and couldn't, then tried to turn back to my boat and couldn't, then tried to surface and couldn't. I was caught in this nasty underwater current, and could only follow it downriver. Let it take me where it was goin', not where I wanted to go. Fifty, seventy, eighty-five, ninety—I felt like I was being pulled both away and down. The map I looked at later said I ended up in water a hundred thirty feet deep, and I was only about fifty or sixty feet from my boat.

"I knew the river was like this, underwater hills and valleys of granite. Shit, did you know there's an underwater waterfall over by the Lost Channel, right near the Canadian bridge? Depth goes from fifteen to two hundred fifty feet, just like that," he said, snapping his fingers. "I useta putt around all day back then watchin' the depths change, learnin' the curves of the river bed. I never knew it from under the water, though. I never knew what those curves could do to a current."

"What did you do?" I asked, instinctively shrinking back a bit from the water for fear that I'd fall in and have to do the same thing.

"I floated," Billy Masterson said. "After about ten seconds I stopped panickin' and floated. If this was my end, then so be it. I was prepared to live or die as the river decided. Just like that guy in the bathtub. Just like that cow.

But I was pretty confident, given my affinity for the fish and their affinity for me, that their river would either let me live or kill me gently."

"You obviously didn't die," I said. "And you obviously didn't float all the way to Massena."

"No shit, Sherlock. And I'll tell you why I didn't float all the way to Massena. Because I was plucked out of the river like a perch plucked up by a tern."

"By whom?" I asked.

"By your father! With Ben Fries and Jack Hibbard next to him in that big ol' Lyman of his! The bastard reached down with one hand and stopped me, then pulled me back towards the boat, then tied a line around me, and Jack and Ben hoisted me out of the water. I must have gotten out of the current by then, because apparently I was only two feet or so from the surface at the time." He shook his head. "I was just startin' to feel my freedom, too. Had I gone on I might've become part of the river, I might have become ... oh, shit, never mind. Let's just say your dad and Ben Fries and your uncle Jack plucked me out of the river and ended all that."

"Let me guess," I said. "My father, Ben and Jack were searching for Napoleon's gold."

"Bing-effin'-o!" Billy Masterson said with a slap on his knee. "I didn't know that at the time, of course. But a few weeks later I was learnin' scuba from a friend of your father's in Clayton. I was getting' along fine, applyin' my previous knowledge to the instruction of Mr. Marcus Holliday. I was about to hop in the water, preparin' my last exercise, about to receive my certificate when your father came to see me."

" 'You aren't much afraid of the channel, are you kid?' he said.

" 'Not a bit.' I answered.

" 'Even after your incident?'

" 'Why should that scare me away? I had plenty of air

left. Shit, I could have kept on floatin' 'til I hit land.' I wanted to piss him off because I was fifteen and thought he was actin' like a prick. 'In fact,' I said, 'my intentions were to keep on floatin'. See what happened. But then you intervened. Ruined my intentions.'

"Your dad laughed his ass off at that one. He repeated, 'As I said, kid, since you're not much afraid of the channel, I might just have some work for you …' "

"Searching for Napoleon's gold," I interrupted, becoming annoyed that Billy Masterson had once considered my father a prick. But then I recalled that, when I was fifteen, and except for when we were waterskiing or diving ourselves, and sometimes even then, I had considered him a prick too.

"That's right. We spent the next year and then some searchin' far and wide for Napoleon's gold." Billy Masterson shook his head. "Napoleon's effin' gold."

I waited in vain for him to continue. "Did you find it?"

"Well, that's the interesting part," he said, his expression turned serious, his voice more reflective. "We went downriver near the shoals of Brockville, down near Chippewa Bay and Singer Castle, over near the Sister Island lighthouse. Up this way we searched off Dingman's Point and in the Manhattan Group. I dove under the American bridge and into the Upper Narrows. We spent a lot of time around the Sunken Rock Lighthouse and Cherry Island. We looked around over near Heron's Nest. Summer dives, winter dives. We spent years doing it. He sometimes went down with me, sometimes I was on my own. Did I ever have fun, too! I dove and floated and followed the contours of the riverbed like I never imagined I could. I saw timber from shipwrecks that was in perfect condition. I saw logs, entire logs, that must have been two hundred years old! And I saw fish. Did I ever see fish! I swam with that sturgeon during one of our expeditions." Billy Masterson shook his head, and I took the opportunity to interrupt him and ask my question again.

"Did you find it? The gold?"

He shook his head and gave an open-mouthed smile that looked fake from the first crack of his lips. "I live in an unheated shack over on Grindstone. I eat what I catch and grow. In the winter I caretake for several fine citizens who may or may not know I'm here. Do you think I found it?" His expression mellowed and he laughed genuinely and then waved an unlit cigarette my way. "I'm bullshittin' ya' Flanagan. I never got it out of the water, never called Geraldo Rivera to come up and open the chest, but I do believe I found it. And get this …" He leaned closer and placed the cigarette in his mouth, then took it out again. "I found it on the one and only dive I took with Ben Fries and without your father."

"How did that happen?"

"Because somehow Ben Fries knew exactly where to look." He paused and lit the cigarette, his voice becoming serious again. "It happened like this. I went down myself that day and I could see everything. I mean *everything*. The day was perfect. Late afternoon. Mid August, 1982. The sun was shining deep into the water. I could see the weeds and the different colored layers of rock and the fish—my God, there were a lot of fish out that day. Big effers too!

"I was feelin' good, I don't know how to explain it. Keen, I guess, like after a good shave. I'd been in the water for ten, fifteen minutes when I saw this glow in the distance. At first I though it was sunshine on some pink granite. I rolled over on my back and realized it couldn't be the sun because the glow was coming from the other side of a pretty steep drop off that was in shadow. Besides, it wasn't like a reflection. It was a glow. Like a bulb.

"I got closer and the glow got brighter. I could make out what looked to me like some banged up wood and metal around the glow, definitely an old ship. The glow got even brighter. I swam towards it, and got to about ten feet away." Billy Masterson paused and exhaled a large cloud of smoke. "When I got to about ten feet away a current hit me like a truck and turned me around, back towards the boat. It seemed like a current, but then again it didn't." He shook his head. "I don't know, the more I think about it the stranger it becomes. The current, or whatever it was, hit me and I couldn't go on. I tried again and again, with the glow gettin' brighter and brighter. Shit, it was like it was cheerin' me on to reach it.

"I couldn't do it anymore, Tom. My tank got empty. I ran out of gas. You know what's weird? When I stopped, the current stopped too. The water became calm, but I could not go on. I returned to the boat. I looked back once before I broke the surface and saw the glow dimmin' now behind me. It wasn't because I was swimmin' away from it or because my vision was blocked by the cliff or anything like that. It was like one of those fancy light dimmers the Snell's have. It shone bright, then dimmed. It was like it knew I was going away and faded. Like a curtain pulled over a sunny window. Or a smile fading from your face. That's the only way I can describe it. Like losing a smile. Then Ben helped me out of the water and back into the boat. I told him to take me home right away and tried to hide my eyes from him."

"Where was this?" I asked. "Over near the Rock Island light?" I was thinking about where my parents and brother had died in the boating accident.

Billy Masterson was obviously uneasy about the question. He took a long drag from his cigarette and, without looking at me, quietly answered it. Puffs of smoke came from his mouth and nose as he talked. "I have no effin' clue where it was. Ben Fries picked me up at my Grindstone cabin and offered me two hundred dollars to go with him and dive. The one condition was that I keep a hood over my eyes until we got there and I went under, and put the hood back on immediately when I came up. He didn't tell me what we were lookin' for or where we were goin'. From where I was in the water before I went down and from where I was when I surfaced I could see a few islands but it could've been anywhere. Or at least ten or twenty other places.

"I was nineteen then. I wanted the two hundred bucks. Since that day I've gone down into the river a hundred times tryin' to find it again. I never did. I saw some marvelous things, but I never saw the gold again."

"Did my father ever see it? Uncle Jack? Did Ben go back and look again?"

"They couldn't have. I never told any of 'em what I saw," Billy Masterson said. "Well, I never told Ben Fries. I never told Jack. I did tell your father, eventually, but that was only a month or two before he died. But he must have known that Ben knew somethin'. They got into a whopper of a fight a couple months after I saw the glow." He took another drag off the cigarette and looked right at me. "Shit, Tom, would your dad still be alive if I hadn't told him?"

We were silent for about ten minutes. I was staring into the fire, thinking about how angry my father must have been with Ben Fries in 1983 and with Billy Masterson in 1996. How would my father's life had changed if either one of them, especially Ben, had been more up front concerning the gold's whereabouts?

While considering these things I was nudged in the shoulder by Billy Masterson. I looked at him and he directed my attention to the sky in front of us.

My jaw dropped when I saw it. There, from about thirty degrees above the horizon to almost directly overhead, hung a curtain of light that waved and swelled in the sky as if blown by a steady wind. The light changed from blue to green to orange to yellow, and shifted again to red, magenta and then back to blue. In all my time spent on the river it was the first time I'd ever seen the *aurora borealis*.

"They say it's the river of Heaven," Billy Masterson said quietly, just above a whisper. "The one from Revelation. They also say the river up there sometimes overflows its banks and falls into our river down here."

As the northern lights cycled back through the spectrum again, Billy Masterson pointed up and said, "See that right there? That orangish yellowish color? That's exactly what Napoleon's gold looked like the day I saw it. I don't think it was real metal gold on that ship, Tom. I don't think it's real metal gold down there. I think it's some of that, some of Heaven's river up there. I bet Napoleon himself stole it and, who the hell knows, poured it into a bottle and sealed it shut. The French effer tried to become God, Tom. He tried to conquer heaven along with everything else he took." Billy Masterson paused. "You know what else?"

"What?" I squeaked, totally absorbed by what I was seeing and hearing.

"That color? That gold? Every time I see it in the sky I want so effin' bad to see it again in the water."

I could hear the regret in Billy Masterson's voice and even heard him choke up a bit, as if he were fighting to hold back a river's worth of tears. I turned to face him then, but he was already walking back to the Snell's cottage.

Chapter Eight

WHEN THE LIGHT SHOW ENDED Billy Masterson directed me to a spare bedroom in the Snell's summer home and left me in silence. He was already gone when I awoke before sunrise, out fishing for lunch, I guessed. Refreshed after a good night's sleep, I paddled back to the Boldt yacht house through some beautiful patchy fog, loaded up my kayak and headed back over to Heron's Nest. I ate French toast and syrup for breakfast, and thought about the night before.

What was I to make of Billy Masterson's story? I never would have pegged him such a mystic. And the sense of guilt and loss he exuded at the end of his tale had pricked a raw nerve from my own past and had shaken me a little. While sipping a second cup of coffee I read the Book of Revelation and some poetry of William Blake to put the spiritual nature of Billy's tale in perspective.

I went to my father's study and quickly found the initials "W. M."—my father had a sense of propriety—on several orange note cards that corresponded to orange markings on the map. There were four of them, mostly in the Alex Bay area, which suggested to me two possibilities: either these were places they'd searched before Billy accepted Ben Fries' offer to dive in exchange for money in 1983, or they were places where my father had searched in 1996 after Billy told him about what he'd seen. The problem was that the cards contained what seemed to be a month and day notation, all of them in August or September, but no year. The more important question seemed, how much did Billy Masterson's tale bring the hearer (whether myself or my father) closer to knowing the actual whereabouts of Napoleon's gold? I hoped that the second story I heard would provide some answers, or at least no new questions.

FIRST, THOUGH, I NEEDED TO SPEND some time catching up with my cousin. On Wednesday afternoon I paddled over to Hibbard Island, just upriver from the American span of the Thousand Islands Bridge, and found him unloading groceries from his boat.

"You should call first, cuz," Andrew said as he threw me a rope to pull me in.

"If you weren't home I would've kept on paddling and stopped by tomorrow."

"Getting good use out of that thing, aren't you?" he asked, referring to the kayak.

"Closest thing to heaven," I said, mindfully repeating what Billy Masterson had said to me a few days before.

"I prefer power," he said.

I helped Andrew take the groceries into the house and unpack them into a huge stainless steel refrigerator that sat between an oven and a dishwasher, both of them also stainless steel and very expensive looking. We returned outside to enjoy the warm air, and as I sat down on the deck Andrew broke open a bag of chips and handed me a can of Genny.

"This place is incredible," I said, admiring the cottage Andrew had built and property he'd developed, both with his father's help. The house had rosewood paneling and Adirondack pine floors salvaged from earlier jobs, tall plate glass windows behind us and on two other sides of the house, a whirlpool hot tub with an incredible view of the bridge, and a perfectly manicured lawn with a pink granite seawall; all of it bespoke of worldly success and the determination to enjoy the fruits of that success.

"If you think you like it now, wait ten minutes," he responded. When I asked for more he simply said, "In ten minutes you'll see what I mean."

"Do you get a chance to enjoy all this?" I asked. "It seems you're always working."

Andrew took a sip of beer. "How'd you know that?"

"Word of mouth. The other Reporters."

He nodded. "I put in about sixty hours a week. I sleep for six hours, eight on the weekends, so that leaves me six to eight hours a day to enjoy Hibbard Island and all its amenities. That's my high summer schedule. Now and again, in May and early June, this time of year, I get even more time for R and R."

"Do you still go to Florida?"

"From right after Thanksgiving to late April. Just as I've always done."

"You said your mom and dad are well?"

"They're getting old, like the rest of us. My dad wants me to move down there full time. I love this place too much, though. My heart is here."

"I can see why."

"Although I could make a hell of a lot more money down there. Something you learned five years ago."

After a couple more minutes of idle chat I glanced at my watch and saw that the ten minutes were up. Just as I was about to ask Andrew again what the big surprise was, I turned and saw the big surprise itself emerging from behind a row of fir trees that sheltered the yard from the southern sun.

It was an ocean-going freighter headed downriver, heavily loaded with massive bins of grain. It was painted green below the ballast line and white and red above, and flew the Greek national flag. It was also no more than twenty yards from where we sat.

"Holy crap," I said.

"Plug your ears," Andrew recommended, then pulled a rope to his right that rang a bell attached to the flagpole.

The bell wasn't that loud, I thought, and uncovered my ears only to have them assaulted by three long blasts from the ship's horn. I instinctively looked behind me to see if the plate glass windows would hold up.

"Don't worry about the windows," Andrew said laughing. "They're industrial strength." He pointed. "This here's the *Bellerophon*. We see it every year. It's one of my favorites."

The aft deck was now drawing into view. I could hear the ship's engines as loud as, but much lower in pitch than, a riding lawnmower. I spoke loudly. "You enjoy this?"

Andrew was smiling, clearly relishing it. "Do I enjoy the ships? I love the ships! I still keep track of which ones come by, just like you and I used to do as kids. One of these days I'll take you out on my boat and teach you how to ride their wake. Can't do that in a kayak!"

When the vessel passed we were able to talk at a reasonable volume again. My cousin continued, "I love the ships, and I love the Seaway. My favorite activity off Hibbard Island is go up to Massena and watch them go through the locks. You ever been there?" I shook my head. "You should see the games those pilots play. It's the equivalent of doing doughnuts in the school parking lot." He looked at me suspiciously. "You *have* done that?"

"Yes, I've done doughnuts," I said. "It was my mistake. I just assumed that you, being a river lover, would have misgivings about the Seaway."

Andrew waved me off. "I've never been one of those island huggers like your mother or Masterson or Ben Fries. I'll fish as much as any other guy, don't get me wrong, but I do believe there's room for both ships and fish on this river. I'm a multi-use guy, you might say."

"You're not a member of PTI?"

"No, but I do enjoy their fundraisers. Especially the concerts."

I went to finish my beer but the can was already empty. "Billy told me his story the other night," I said.

Andrew laughed and finished his beer. "Want another?"

"Sure."

"Come on in."

I got up and followed him into the kitchen, and after getting two more cans he joined me on a bar stool at the counter, which was made from butcher block.

"Masterson's mysterious glow," Andrew finally said, having crunched down a few handfuls of chips. "Any thoughts?"

"It's an interesting story," I said.

"That's euphemism, right?"

I nodded.

"Good. I didn't pay much attention in English class, to the perpetual chagrin of your mother. But I know it's euphemism because the accurate way to say it, cuz, is that Masterson's story is goddamn unbelievable."

"What parts of it don't you believe?"

"I believe Napoleon's gold exists. I believe it's somewhere here in our river. Does it glow? Did it draw Masterson in like a magnet pulls metal shavings?" Andrew shrugged his shoulders. "By the way, that's another reason I stay here and haven't moved to Florida."

"You want to find it," I said. Andrew nodded. "You want to keep it." Andrew nodded again. "Are you willing to share it?"

"Sure I'd share it. My proposal to the River Rat Reporters is that we share it among ourselves after giving a certain percentage of it away to charity."

"What percentage?"

"Depends on the gross value."

"What charity?"

"Depends on who finds it."

"Did you share this idea with the others?"

"Yes ... well, no, I never really got the chance."

"You've been a River Rat Reporter for how long?"

"Five years. Ever since the accident."

"Five years, and you haven't had a chance to share your idea with the others?" Andrew smiled enigmatically and sipped more beer. "Tell me, why did some of the others say they weren't interested in finding the gold? What was it that Billy said? That it would bring more problems into their lives than it was worth?"

"Billy said that because there are other groups looking for the gold, not all of them favorable to the River Rat Reporters."

"Other groups?"

"Yes, other groups. Rival groups. When word of the gold started getting out in the late seventies and early eighties, other people started forming diving teams to find it. Not all of them were friendly with your father and Ben Fries."

"Are these other groups still looking for it?"

"With ever higher expectations now that the zebra mussels have cleared out the water. Believe you me, cuz. These other groups wouldn't be giving an ounce of the gold to charity. I call them The Undesirables. 'Undies' for short."

I laughed, then paused for a moment and sipped my beer. "Have you ever considered joining forces with these Undies?" I asked.

"I have," Andrew admitted. "I'm loyal though, Tom. More than anything else, in fact, I'm loyal to my family and to my friends. All I've been trying to do, with little opportunity so far, is convince the others I need the gold." Andrew chugged his beer. "I work my ass off, Tom, and the only reason I have something to enjoy for it is that my father and I built this place on an island he bought many years ago for back taxes. With the government sticking its hand deeper and deeper into my pocket, I for one need the gold. George Hibbard Construction, Inc. might not be around too much longer otherwise. That would be a very sad ending for everyone involved."

I took a long sip of beer and tossed the can into a recycling bin. None of Billy Masterson's mysticism in Andrew's point of view, I thought, although I did sympathize with his financial plight.

He offered me another beer, but I had a tough upstream paddle ahead of me and wanted to get home before dark so I declined, said goodbye, and slipped on my PFD.

"See you Friday?" Andrew asked.

"See you Friday," I said.

As I got into my kayak, Andrew went inside and turned on his stereo. He returned to the lawn with another beer, and I could see him playing air guitar and hear him singing John Cougar Mellencamp's *Authority Song* as I paddled away, his voice loud but fading as the distance between us increased.

So I was there at Jimmy's, sipping a beer, keeping an eye on the baseball playoff game and playing the puck bowling machine as I waited eagerly for the others to show. The crowd seemed less friendly that night than it had on my first night at the bar. Several men in flannel shirts sitting around a table near the back of the room looked at me with scorn and then turned away as I waved to them. I wondered if they belonged to Andrew's Undesirables.

I considered for a moment going back to them and asking outright if they could tell me anything important about Napoleon's gold. But then Billy Masterson arrived, looking refreshed and well rested, and pulled me by the arm to the Reporters' table of honor.

"Hey, Flanagan," he said. "Glad to see I didn't scare you off with the tale of my amazing journey."

"God appears, and God is light / To those poor souls who dwell in night / But does a human form display / To those who dwell in realms of day," I said.

"Been time travelin'?" he asked. "A Masterson gonna write that a hundred years from now?"

I laughed. "Actually, it's William Blake," I said. "Lived in England in the late eighteenth and early nineteenth centuries. You should check him out sometime. He was an artist as well as a poet. I bet if you look closely enough at his paintings you'd see that golden glow again."

Billy Masterson gave a noncommittal grunt and ordered a pitcher of beer. I wondered if he even had a library card.

Just then Jim Pembroke came through the door and greeted us, Laurie the bartender and several other people at the bar with a series of loud hellos. "The other shitbirds'll be late or not here at all," he said after he bought a second pitcher of beer. "Comstock is with his mother in Watertown, Hibbard is dealing with an emergency foundation collapse out in the Manhattan Group, Slattery has a budget meeting and Ostend is off in Puerto Rico. Let's play a few games and converse until I lose my inhibitions."

"Then what?" I asked.

Jim Pembroke slid the puck in my seventh frame and hit a strike. "Then you'll hear my story," he said.

He retrieved the puck and asked if he could use the rest of the game as a warm up. I said okay and took the time to use the men's room and ask Billy Masterson if he knew about my father's maps and note cards.

"Never been in his study," he answered in what seemed to me an elusive tone, "although I knew he was keepin' track. Four of 'em with my initials on 'em, huh? Around Alex Bay? Seems to me that would be some of the places we went to before Ben took me out that day."

"What about the places after?" I asked. He reminded me that he did not tell my father about what he had seen until many years later, and that they never looked for the place together thereafter. I knew I would have to look more closely at my father's maps, and so dropped the subject for now.

I heard the bowling machine's bells and whistles register for a new game. "Ready?" Jim Pembroke said, handing me the puck.

"For your story?"

"For some Flash."

I noticed there were indicator lights for only two bowlers. "You're not playing?" I asked Billy Masterson.

"No effin' way," he said. "I learned long ago that playin' against Captain Pembroke means an automatic loss."

I had played the game too as a kid and teenager, and knew from the six frames I had already bowled that my timing and coordination were still pretty good. I took the puck and slid it down the alley, and the pins made their familiar crunching sound as they folded up together for a strike. But my timing was a bit off—I let go a split second too early—and the flashing lights above the alley stopped at only six hundred.

"Step aside, son," Jim Pembroke said. "Let the master practice his craft." With a backward stretch of his leg that reminded me of a sprinter in the starting block and with his elbow acting as a fulcrum, he made a perfect left handed shot, perfectly timed to the red lights at the center, for a perfect eight-hundred-point strike.

"A lefty," I said as I took my place at the machine. "That was considered diabolic back in the old days. Bodes ill for you." I thought I would make the boast count, too, as I shot the puck with the straight-on flat-handed delivery I had grown comfortable with in my youth.

"Nice technique," Jim Pembroke said after I got the eight hundred point strike. "Technique alone won't catch me, though. Your mistake in the first might be your only one, but it'll be enough for me."

He was almost right about the first part of the statement, that my mistimed strike might be my only mistake. We battled point-for-point through seven, with Pembroke clinging to his lead. He was perfect in both form and execu-

tion, firing the puck on the same trajectory, at the same
speed and with the same results shot after shot. Billy Masterson, who had settled into a chair a couple tables away, exclaimed that he once saw the captain fire twenty-three perfect strikes in a row. The feat certainly impressed me, and I
hoped the comment would break Jim Pembroke's luck. But
it did not, and he cruised through the eighth and ninth like a
machine. I made only one more mistake, a one-pin spare in
the ninth for five hundred points, and we went into the bottom of the tenth with me up ninety-one hundred to seventy-two hundred. At least I had put some pressure on him.
He would have to strike out to win.

He did strike out, with three perfect eight-hundreds to
make it twelve in a row. When the machine stopped its
ringing and dinging I gave him a mock bow of obeisance
and then shook his hand.

"Twelve more frames like that breaks your record," Billy
Masterson said, clapping his hands slowly.

"Unfortunately, not *the* record," said Jim Pembroke.
"Spuds Perry has that with six perfect games in a row.
That's over fifty-seven thousand points for all you math
whizzes out there."

Pembroke turned and pointed to a Kodachrome photo
of a gray-haired, smiling fat man with a can of Genesee
Cream Ale in one hand and the can of shuffleboard alley
wax in the other. He was standing in front of the same machine we were playing, and the scoreboard indeed showed
perfect scores for players one through three.

Pembroke continued, "We used to take turns back then
seeing who could rack up the most points in accumulating
games. You could only progress to playing two quarters if
you got ninety-six hundred in one game, and then after two
onto three, et cetera, et cetera. Spuds got as far as six games
in a row. No one else came close."

"When was this?" I asked. I noticed in the picture the
captured image of a baseball game on the television above

the machine that had now been replaced by a larger set at the far corner of the bar. The batter looked to me like a Cincinnati Red.

"October 1976," Jim Pembroke said.

I was right. "The Big Red Machine," I said. "The year they rolled over the Yankees. I remember crying when I read the results of game four in my dad's paper."

"Good year for Spuds Perry. Bad year for the Yanks. Bad year for the river. Worse year for me." Jim Pembroke took two quarters out of his pocket. "More on that later. First I've got something to prove to Mister Masterson."

We played a second game, and Pembroke cruised along frame after frame with his consistent delivery and his perfect results. But I was perfect this time, too, and we entered the tenth tied at seventy-two hundred.

And then, after two more strikes, having tied his record, Jim Pembroke faltered. Looking back, I cannot decide if his mechanics were wrong, if some background noise had distracted him, or even if he had missed the shot on purpose to offer me a chance at victory. Regardless of why it had happened, the fact was that Pembroke's final shot went a shade too far inside and left him with a seven-ten split. I struck out in the tenth for my first perfect game ever.

Pembroke smiled. He complimented me, shook my hand, and then looked over at the picture of his old friend. "I guess ol' Spuds is my guardian angel," he said, "looking over my shoulder and protecting me from hubris." He smiled again and shook his head, keeping the rest of his thoughts to himself.

Chapter Nine

IT TOOK ANOTHER HALF HOUR for Jim Pembroke to lose his inhibitions, as he had put it earlier, and begin his story. He did so rather abruptly, in the middle of a conversation about our picks for the baseball playoffs. I thought the Yankees would roll through everyone, despite the game one defeat. Billy Masterson liked the Astros' chances. Jim Pembroke was indifferent since neither the Blue Jays nor the Expos were in it.

As I was commenting on how long in tooth Atlanta's pitching was, Pembroke ordered a six pack of Moosehead from Laurie, put on his captain's coat, and said, "Come on. Let's get out of here for a while. There are ears around that I don't want to hear what I'm about to say." He gave a slight nod towards the "Undies" in the back of the room.

Billy Masterson and I followed him out the door, around the corner and down to the village dock. As we approached the water Billy stopped and pointed, a broad smile on his face. "Is that what I think it is?" he asked.

"The *Archangel*," Jim Pembroke said. "Ostend asked me to run it up and down the river a few times to check its performance before I deliver it to the Antique Boat Museum. We're going to check its performance while I tell you my story."

"Hot damn!" Billy Masterson said with glee.

I shared his sentiments as we boarded the boat. It was a magnificent yacht, a "woodie" from the river's classic age, at least eighty feet long, over four times as big as my father's

Lyman. It was paneled in cedar, polished to a bright sheen in the early evening sun, and its gunwales were edged with chrome. It was fitted out with fine, soft leather everywhere else, on the bucket seats, wainscoting, steering wheel, the hidden cooler into which Billy Masterson put three of the Mooseheads, and, even, I found out later, the toilet seat. There was a stateroom and a library, three bedrooms and a playroom. A small galley in an enclosed aft cabin was also covered in expensive leather and the fixtures were made of polished chrome.

And the *Archangel* was fast. The river was mostly empty, allowing Captain Pembroke to run it full throttle after he steered around the Sunken Rock shoal, turned upriver and straightened out into the wide stretch of deep water off Alex Bay. We must have hit fifty knots. Pembroke later explained that the boat had been refitted with high performance diesel engines, which surprised me because I couldn't smell a whiff of fuel. Pembroke slowed down as we approached Cherry Island and the nearby shoals, came to a stop, and put the boat in neutral. He began to tell his story.

"You remember the CANCO-2000 oil spill?" he asked me.

"I was just a kid, but yeah," I said. "It was 1976, wasn't it? I couldn't swim anywhere that year and my father was gone for an exceptionally long time. It sucked."

"Your dad was workin' cleanup," Billy Masterson said. "My father was too, and Ben Fries. Shit, we all were, tryin' to save the river."

Jim Pembroke looked right at me. "I was piloting the boat that hit Pullman Shoal and almost ruined the river," he said. He held my gaze. "June 23, 1976. That's why now, twenty-five years later, despite the fact that I'm actually not to blame, I'm schlepping tourists around in a boat with a fake aft paddle wheel rather than earning glory on the big freighters and salties."

I took a swig of beer to help myself work through my

surprise at Pembroke's admission and his subsequent denial of responsibility. Trusting his sense of fairness, I asked him about the issue since he was, after all, piloting the ship that leaked three hundred thousand gallons of oil into the river in the first place, two weeks before the nation's bicentennial no less.

"Some people did argue that I was responsible," Jim Pembroke said. "I just do what I do, and I do it the best I can. I know I can only control so much. I'm always willing to accept responsibility for what I do. I also recognize that others have to accept responsibility for what they do. In this case, I made the proper orders to get the boat upriver safely. The captain and his wheelman countermanded those orders. The result was a collision with Pullman Shoal that breached the aft starboard hull."

"And you kept goin'," Billy Masterson said, pointing the mouth of the beer bottle at him. "You kept goin' all the way to Clayton before you hit *another* shoal and finally dropped anchor."

"I'll assume your 'you' is generic," Jim Pembroke replied. "I hope it is anyway, because my denial of responsibility is perfectly legitimate. I couldn't do a damned thing about it personally." He had his beer bottle almost to his lips, then returned it to the cup holder when I asked him why. "I was detained," he said. "That's why."

"Detained?" I asked. "By whom?"

"By the captain and his crew," he said.

I shook my head and laughed softly, comprehending nothing. "If you want me to understand what you're saying, you'd better go back to the beginning," I said.

Jim Pembroke nodded and took his drink, then started his tale in earnest.

"THE BEGINNING GOES BACK to my initiation to the Saint Lawrence, which I received courtesy of my father, one of the best river pilots in the Seaway's first generation. I often joined him on the bridge when he boarded a ship going downriver from Cape Vincent. Or I'd join him and my mom in the car and we'd board in Massena or Ogdensburg going up. I learned everything from him at a very early age. I learned where the shoals were, what the currents or the wind could do to a ship and how they could change due to shifting conditions. I learned how to read the weather more accurately than a machine could. I learned to figuratively extend my legs and arms into the ship itself, becoming one with the vessel, so I could feel the water beneath me as if I were swimming. This was all in the first years of the Seaway.

"I memorized charts," he said, pointing to his head. "I had them all up here by the time I finished high school. I climbed the hawsepipe, serving as mate with my father and several other top captains on the river and across the Great Lakes. When I was finally ready to take the licensing exam, it was a snap."

"What's a hawsepipe?" I asked.

"The window the anchor chain comes through at the bow of a ship."

"You climbed the corporate ladder. Or rose through the ranks."

"Exactly. In other words, I had no formal schooling, something that would bite me in the ass later on after the oil spill. My father was damn proud of it though, right up to the day he died. I still am."

"I'm curious," I said. "Did your father know about Napoleon's gold?"

"Probably not. Few people did in those days, up until the late seventies when the story became more popular. Besides, my father was a man with a deep and abiding faith in Canadian enterprise. He believed in progress. He believed in the Seaway. He was part of that generation that built dams and highways and dredged rivers for the good of Canadian industry. Had he known about it in the same way that I know and Billy here knows and your father knew, he might have changed his mind. But back then he was committed to doing the things that could help build Canada. No, my father was a doer. I was, too, until the oil spill changed my life."

Jim Pembroke paused and took a sip of beer. "On that day I came aboard ship in Massena," he said. "The boat was Canadian, on their way to Cleveland with eight hundred thousand gallons of oil. The crew was Middle Eastern with a few Americans, which was odd. A mixed crew usually didn't serve on lakers, only salties, but because the Middle Easterners were scheduled to sail from Cleveland to Morocco a few days later on a Liberian freighter filled with grain, the Arabs got a last-minute contract with to deliver the oil to Cleveland, then transfer to the Liberian ship for their trip home. The Americans were there to bring the vessel back to Montreal. Captains usually don't serve on Canadian lakers either, but they needed one that day. I got the call late at night on the twenty-second.

"I got on board in Massena, and I knew there was trouble before we were even through the lock. When I met the captain he was arguing with the first mate, the wheelman and another man, a well-dressed Arab who obviously was not a member of the crew. The well-dressed Arab was short and stout, like a bulldog, and he wore a large ring engraved with some sort of twisted snake symbol on his left hand. His eyes were like ice. He bothered me." Pembroke paused and took a sip of beer. "Still does."

"The men were discussing which channel to take. I figured there wasn't much to argue over, given the shipping regulations and all, so I intruded into their circle and moved my finger along the American channel, tapping my fingertip west of Cedar Point for emphasis. The wheelman shook his head vigorously and said something in what I guessed was Arabic. He pointed to the map around Alex Bay and got more agitated by the second. The well-dressed Arab was trying to hush the wheelman, speaking softly but with authority and moving his hands up and down in the air like he was lifting weights.

"I excused myself and went out on deck." Pembroke paused to hit the engine and turn the boat to face west, up-river. "The fog was thick that morning. I could see the running lights maybe ten yards down the length of the ship, but nothing at all out in the river. I didn't like being out there in the fog, but I needed some down time before we got to the Brockville Narrows and the fun started. After about five minutes of peace and quiet the well-dressed Arab joined me.

" 'My apologies for Hassan's over-reactive behavior,' he said. 'He's a good sailor, but he has been away from home for a long, long time.'

" 'What's he so worked up about?' I asked.

"He looked at me for a few seconds as if translating in his head. 'He does not want to go by the place you call Cherry Island,' he said.

"Now I knew a fact or two about the area's history before I started captaining the *Thousand Islands Queen*. One of them was that Nathan Strauss, who had made millions of dollars from Macy's department stores in New York City and had donated much of it to various Zionist groups, had built his mansion, Olympia, on Cherry Island. I also knew enough about geopolitics to understand that Egyptians and Israelis were not exactly on the best of terms. I mentioned as much to the well-dressed Arab.

" 'Hassan does not know this Nathan Strauss. Hassan is a Copt, an Egyptian Christian. He does not subscribe to what was revealed to the Prophet, and is therefore no enemy of Israel. I come from Lebanon, and have spent much time in Egypt. I have knowledge of Strauss and his money. I have no quarrel with long dead Americans, however, only with the Israelis who take land from Arabs in their wars.'

" 'Why doesn't your Hassan want to go past Cherry Island?' I asked.

"The well-dressed Arab tapped his ringed finger on the

railing. 'Ah, that would be difficult for me to explain,' he said, 'for Hassan is a Copt. Nevertheless, I trust you will lead us safely through these thousands of islands with no difficulty.' He looked around us, trying to change the subject. 'Is this fog a danger?'

" 'Damn straight it's a danger,' I said, getting annoyed.

" 'Do things unseen give you fear?'

"I assumed he was talking about the river, of course, so I shook my head. 'Look there,' I said. 'Did you see that channel marker?' He shook his head. 'I didn't either. What I can do in this fog and what your captain and wheelman cannot do will get us through safely. I know this river more than I know myself. I know there's a channel marker there because I've been counting the seconds since the last one I did see. I know every channel marker on this river, my friend, where the last one was and where the next one's coming. My job is to get cargo and human beings through these islands. That's my job, and I take pride in doing it well. Now go get Hassan, and translate for me so I can figure out why the hell's he's on pins and needles. If we want to get through to open water we need to be on the same page. Hassan needs to follow orders.'

" 'It is difficult for you and Hassan to be … to share the same perspective, as it is for most Westerners and Egyptians, and has been for a very long time.'

" 'I don't give a damn if he's Egyptian, Polish, Chilean or Swahili,' I said. 'All I care about is that we hear one another and work together.'

"The well-dressed Arab nodded, then asked if he could tell me a story. I said go ahead.

" 'When Napoleon and his French armies invaded Egypt almost two hundred years ago, they were met with much resistance. There was the ruling Mameluke elite, of course, but common Egyptians in large numbers also refused to submit to French occupancy.'

" 'The French tried many efforts to endear themselves

to the Egyptian population. One such effort was to share with them music. To this end, a French orchestra played military marches, fanfares, Mozart, Haydn, all of this music in an attempt to connect with the Egyptians. The music made no impression whatever on the Egyptian listeners. Exasperated, the orchestra played an old sentimental song called "Marlborough," and the crowd responded with cheers and dancing. It was quite extraordinary. The French were confused. The orchestra played the song again and again, to the continued delight of the people.'

" 'What's your point?' I said.

" 'My point is that even when they are closely connected, Westerners and Arabs often fail to realize that the connection even exists. You see, Captain Pembroke, "Marlborough" was originally an Arabic tune, brought to Europe over four hundred years before Napoleon and his expedition sailed. It was brought to Europe by King Louis IX and his Crusaders, another French army that attempted, and failed, to conquer Egypt.'

" 'I said it once and I'll say it again, what's your point?'

"The well-dressed Arab hesitated for a moment, then said, 'you and Hassan may be searching for the same thing. If you listen to him, you both might find what you're looking for. Someday, you might understand this.'

"I pointed a finger right at him, fed up with his stories and his defending Hassan. 'You tell the wheelman to start listening to me,' I said.

" 'You are a brave man, Captain Pembroke,' he said with a cold smile, and left.

"He returned a few moments later with Hassan, who was sweating. The Egyptian was, in fact, scared as hell.

" 'Hassan has been on this Saint Lawrence River before,' the well-dressed Arab said. 'He says there is an old and unseen evil in the water of this river. Hassan is a very insightful man, Captain Pembroke, despite his idolatry.'

" 'Unseen evil?' I said. 'What evil?' I waited for him to

translate and for Hassan to answer. Hassan just shook his
head and repeated what I'd quickly learned was 'no' in Arabic.

" 'Hassan will not say.' I guessed that the well-dressed
Arab already knew and wouldn't say either. 'Hassan would
only say before this time that the ancient and unseen evil
was awakened by the French.'

" 'What the hell's this evil have to do with him following my orders to get us safely into open water? And what
the hell's he mean by the French? Why should I care about
the damn French?'

" 'The French evil will pull this boat down,' the well-
dressed Arab translated between Hassan's shouts, 'and take
all our lives with it. Stay out of the American water. The evil
awakened by the French will pull this boat down.'

"I was beyond angry now. 'Tell Hassan I've been piloting lakers and salties up and down the American channel for
eight years and have never allowed one goddamn boat to be
taken down. Tell him to pull his act together now for what
he's been hired to do. He'll follow my orders or he'll be relieved of duty.'

"As the well-dressed Arab relayed my instructions, Hassan again grew agitated. He lunged towards me, and, according to the well-dressed Arab's translation was shouting 'The
French evil will deluge us all!' I punched Hassan in the gut
to slow him down. I ordered a couple of the Americans to
restrain him and take him below deck until we reached Lake
Ontario and I gave the all clear. He'd see we wouldn't get
deluged, I thought, and hopefully get his marbles back. If he
didn't, he'd be hearing it from the authorities."

Jim Pembroke paused to swig his beer. I glanced over at
Billy Masterson, who was listening to the story with a slight
frown on his face. "What?" I asked him.

"I don't want to interrupt Captain Pembroke's story,"
Billy Masterson said with a politeness that failed to mask the
urgency of his thoughts.

"Go ahead," Jim Pembroke said.

"Well, it's just that Hassan was wrong, Jim, as I've told you several times before. What's there in the river, what's still there in the river, isn't evil. I saw the gold with my own eyes. It filled me with good. Now that oil you and your crew spilled? That was a different story. That was evil."

"I'm sorry to have upset you, Billy," Jim Pembroke said with a genuine tenderness that surprised me. "You know as well as anyone that all these years I've withheld judgment on whether your glow was good or evil, or if the damn gold even exists, or if it does exist, exactly what it is and what it means. Right now I'm just repeating what Hassan told me. It's his opinion. Not mine."

Billy Masterson nodded.

Then I said, wanting to hear the rest of Jim Pembroke's story, "You were detained when the CANCO-2000 hit Pullman Shoal?"

"Detained just as we hit it," Jim Pembroke said. He put the *Archangel* in gear, and we slowly moved upriver as he continued. He spoke loudly over the sound of the engine. "I got us through the Brockville Narrows and past the Sunken Rock without much trouble. It was right about dawn then, and if you looked carefully enough through the fog you could see just the bare hint of the silhouettes of the downriver islands. But we were heading upriver, so I had to pull out a trick from my father's bag. By going out onto the deck and looking back and seeing where we were, I knew exactly where we were going. In a couple places the buoy lights were just visible enough for me to discern. I was able to identify from memory which one was which.

"As we passed the glow of Alex Bay, I could hear something happening below deck. We were moving at seven knots, exactly what we're doing now. I told the substitute wheelman, one of the Americans, to keep it steady for fifteen more seconds, and then to turn slowly to the starboard, a degree every five seconds, for a total of thirty seconds or six degrees. We were on twenty-seven. There was little room for error. I was about to order a turn back amidships when I heard Hassan running up the metal stairs to the wheelhouse. I knew it was him because I could hear him yelling that same damn bullshit about the boat being pulled down by the French evil that he'd been yelling before."

Jim Pembroke cut the engine again and quieted his voice. "It was right here. Right in this spot. Before I could get the order to the American wheelman, Hassan body-blocked me to the side, grabbed the wheel from the wheelman, and turned it hard starboard. I got up and lunged towards Hassan, but was pulled back again by the captain and the first mate, who were helped by the inertia of the turn. One of them hit me in the head with something hard. I fell to the floor, and before I passed out completely I could hear the scraping and ripping of the hull against the underwater granite of Pullman Shoal." Jim Pembroke shook his head. "I'll be damned if the last person I saw was the well-dressed Arab smiling and wagging his ringed finger in my direction."

Chapter Ten

JIM PEMBROKE finished his beer, rested his palms on the wheel, and looked at me, and then at Billy Masterson. I was at the starboard rail, looking down at the granite shoal below us that steeply sloped into deeper water.

"That's my story," Jim Pembroke said. "The rest of it belongs to others."

"Who?" I asked.

Pembroke sighed. "The Arab captain might tell you that he finally realized the severity of the situation several miles upriver and dropped anchor. The Coast Guard would tell you, as they told every commission that heard them testify, that they responded immediately upon being notified of the incident and placed booms around the vessel to contain the oil. People like you, Billy, and your father, Tom, and Jack Hibbard and Ben Fries and hundreds of others like you would say how the Coast Guard and the Seaway and the river pilot had all failed in their obligations and had put the burden of cleanup on you, the good citizens of the river. Boards of inquiry in the United States and Canada would tell you, as they told news outlets from all over the country, that they fully investigated the incident and arrived at the proper conclusion, which was that the river pilot, Captain James Davis Pembroke, was the sole responsible party."

Jim Pembroke put the *Archangel* back in gear, and we moved fast upriver, past the Gilded Age cottage-mansions of Millionaire's Row, underneath the American span of the Thousand Island bridge, past Andrew's island, through the spectacular stretch of water along the west end of Wellesley Island that's called the Upper Narrows, past Thousand Island Park and Heron's Nest, and into the open water between Clayton on the mainland and Grindstone Island on the river. Jim Pembroke once again stopped the boat, presumably where the CANCO-2000 had run aground the second time.

"What would the well-dressed Arab have said?" I asked him.

"That's the interesting part. That's also where Napoleon's gold enters the story again." Pembroke paused. "That's not my tale to tell, Tom. It's your father's. I can only tell it second hand and, I believe, with your permission."

"Please tell it," I said, eager to hear more.

"Your father called me a few days after the spill, the day before he started working cleanup, and assured me that as angry as the spill had made him, he didn't blame me for it happening. He knew … shit, we all knew, that it was bound to happen someday. All the dredging in the world couldn't completely tame the Saint Lawrence, and if the Seaway people insisted on sending poisons like oil and mercury and PCBs and pesticides up and down it on ships, then we knew the poison would end up in the river sooner or later. He asked if we could discuss this more for a few minutes the next day.

"Well, the upshot of the meeting was that your father promised to do all he could to find the well-dressed Arab and get his story. He called some newspaper friends of his in Kingston, who called some newspaper friends of theirs in Montreal, who were able to identify the well-dressed Arab as one Naguib Malqari. He was indeed from Lebanon, and also a citizen of Canada, and his family had made a fortune in the Mediterranean tourist trade. Malqari was also neck deep in the violence of the Lebanese civil war. Having found him, your father went to Montreal to meet him in the middle of November 1976."

"He did?" I asked.

"He did. He went to Montreal and met Malqari. He told him my situation, and Malqari replied that although he sympathized with me he could not help me directly as he was returning back to Lebanon shortly to tend to some important business. He did offer me an apology through your father. He told Charlie Flanagan to reassure me that I had played an important role in an unfolding drama on the world stage. Malqari gave your father a check for a thousand dollars, made out to me. When I got it I tore it up. I wasn't about to enslave myself to that man's money. It was probably rubber anyway."

"What was the unfolding drama Malqari referred to?" I asked, already guessing the answer.

"It turns out that the reason Malqari had been on my boat in the first place was to find the location of Napoleon's gold. He'd heard about it from a Canadian tourist some years before, he claimed, and had committed himself to searching for it as soon as he got the opportunity. Malqari explained to your father that he believed Napoleon's gold would help his side win the Lebanese civil war. Malqari wouldn't answer the question of exactly how it would help, but your father guessed, correctly I think, that the gold would finance weapons purchases."

"That wouldn't have made my father too happy."

"No, it didn't. Nor was your father happy when Malqari first asked, then demanded, that Charlie help him find the gold. As I've explained, his first attempt at finding it himself did not turn out well.

"Malqari had come to Montreal to interview sailors who had traveled the river. He met the wheelman named Hassan, who told him about a strange sense of foreboding he'd experienced on several trips up the American channel. A few more interviews with Hassan convinced Malqari that Napoleon's gold had triggered the sense of foreboding the way an underground well sets off a dowsing rod. Hassan's common sense had been so affected by the feeling of malice that he couldn't remember exactly where he'd experienced the sensation, only that it was somewhere in the American channel, somewhere near Alex Bay.

"Naguib Malqari arranged for passage aboard the CANCO-2000 to Cleveland, Ohio. It would be inconspicuous, he thought, obviously not factoring in the dangers inherent in moving oil up the Seaway. Hassan was his canary in the coal mine, as it were. The rest of the story is the story I already told you, the one I can claim as mine."

"My father obviously didn't help him," I said.

"No, he didn't. He was pretty shaken by the encounter, though. I could tell that much because he wouldn't talk about it for days after he got home. Finally, one night at Jimmy's and with the help of several pitchers of Genny, I was able to get him to loosen his tongue."

"What did he say?"

"Basically, that Malqari scared the shit out of him." Jim Pembroke took a sip of beer. "Oh, it's true that your father stood up to him when they were discussing things in Montreal. He stood his ground and refused to help Malqari with any of his schemes. Afterwards, when he looked back on it and recalled Malqari's ... well, Malqari's will power, he was very afraid indeed."

"Was that the last you ever heard of this Naguib Malqari?" I asked.

Jim Pembroke hesitated, measuring his words. "Yes. Well, no. I never saw him again in person, although I'd always thought I would. Your father received news a couple years later that Malqari had been seriously wounded in the fighting for Beirut, and apparently had died sometime in the winter of 1977. According to your father's source he was quite the hero, too, throwing himself on a grenade to save some civilians under attack from the Christians. Believe me, that news was some relief to your father. Still, for a few years after the spill I'd always expected to see Malqari again on the river, perhaps even on the *Thousand Island Queen*." Jim Pembroke laughed softly.

My mind wandered back to Jim's story. "When Malqari was on the CANCO-2000, how did he avoid questioning by the Coast Guard?"

"He wasn't on the ship when I came to. The Arabs would say nothing. The Americans didn't know anything, not even his name. Your father asked him in Montreal where he'd gone after we hit the second shoal. Malqari answered that he made it to shore and thence back to Montreal. Charlie asked if he swam, walked, or drove. Malqari merely smiled and restated that he made it to shore and thence back to Montreal."

"And Hassan?"

Jim Pembroke shook his head. "Your father and I kept our eyes on crew manifests for years, but saw nothing to trigger our suspicions. Of course, he could have been going by another name."

"The Coast Guard didn't question him?"

"The problem was that none of the Arabs besides Malqari spoke English. The Coast Guard had no Arabic in-terpreters."

"Didn't the Americans stick up for you?"

"Shit no. They sat back and allowed the blame to fall on the ugly, self-educated Canadian. Tom, did you see those guys in the back table at Jimmy's, the guys whose ears I didn't want to hear what I had to say?"

"Are they the ones my cousin calls 'Undesirables?' "

"Yes, the 'Undies,' " Jim Pembroke said.

"I saw them. They gave me dirty looks."

"Several of them were on the CANCO-2000. They've been giving me dirty looks for twenty five years."

"Nice," Billy Masterson said.

"Should I try talking with them?" I asked.

Billy and Jim looked at each other for a moment, then Billy changed the subject. "Not long after that Charlie got you that tourist boat gig, right Jim?"

Pembroke laughed. "It was indeed Tom's father who got me the job, with Raphael Ostend's added recommendation. I puttered around for almost two years, and then just before the 1979 tourist season I got the call from the Rockport Boat Lines. Despite what I said earlier about preferring to pilot the lakers and salties, Tom, I'll be thankful 'til the end of my days that I can at least pilot something on the river. Along with his moral support, I have your father to thank for that too. Piloting the tour boat gave me and Charlie the perfect means of keeping an eye out for Hassan."

"You were also the first to tell the gold story on a tour boat," Billy Masterson said.

"Damn straight," Jim Pembroke said with a smile. "I heard it from your father, Tom, and then shared it with the masses. Charlie wasn't happy about it at first, but after a while, when he saw how well I told it and that I didn't give away his secrets, he agreed it was the right thing to do. Besides, if Hassan did come back, hearing the story of the gold might have exposed him. I told it first, then the others in Gananoque, Brockville, Alex Bay and Clayton picked up on it. These days, it's one of the most popular stories on the river."

At that Jim Pembroke turned the *Archangel* back downriver and took us back to Alex Bay. The sun was setting at our backs, causing a salmon sky to appear above us, bordered by a deepening purple glow to the east.

"Look there," Jim Pembroke said. "See that dark blue arc on the horizon? It's actually the shadow of the earth on the upper atmosphere. Perfect conditions tonight. Damn, that's beautiful. My favorite sight on the river."

I finished my beer and watched the blue arc deepen, then fade, and finally disappear.

WE DOCKED THE BOAT, spread and secured the canvas cover, then walked silently back to Jimmy's. I was glad to see Mike Slattery greet us from the table of honor when we entered.

"How's the budget look?" Jim Pembroke asked as we sat down.

"Worse each day. Sometimes I think we should go back to riding horses and buggies on dirt roads." Mike Slattery paused and smiled. "I saw you bringing Ostend's boat back in. You guys have a good ride?"

"Jim told us how my father first heard of Napoleon's gold," I said.

"When was that, Jim?" Mike Slattery asked, clearly annoyed.

"1976. From Naguib Malqari. When Charlie went to Montreal to confront Malqari in November 1976."

Slattery disagreed. "The hell it was," he said. "He heard it first about a week before the oil spill. I was there. Besides, why do you think he'd go all the way to Montreal to confront Malqari in person? If he wasn't already drawn in by Ben Fries he would've called Malqari on the phone."

Pembroke considered this for a moment and nodded. "That may be so," he finally said. "Malqari simply might have confirmed what Charlie already suspected, that the gold was in the river, probably somewhere in the American channel. But Charlie certainly didn't commit to looking for it until after his trip to Montreal."

"I'll agree with that much," Mike Slattery said. "It was after Malqari that Charlie started looking for it. But it was before the oil spill that he first heard of it."

"That's your story?" I asked Slattery, referring back to his comment. "How my father first heard of Napoleon's gold? Before he met Malqari?" I also silently wondered why the two men were arguing about such things now, many years after the events had taken place. Hadn't they discussed all this before?

"Partly," he said. "It's also about how the oil spill and

the gold and everything else that happened that summer bound your dad and Ben Fries together. And, for that matter, bound me and Ben Fries together. But my story is really about your mother, Tom, and her life."

That surprised me, but Mike Slattery smiled and shook his head, and quickly continued speaking.

"Damn, those were good days. Even with the fear and exhaustion and the cleanup and all the other crap going on, those were damn good days. Momentous days. Don't listen to what Pembroke tells you about how bad they were. That's just his Canadian pessimism talking. Those were good days, and the river wouldn't be what it is today without 'em."

Chapter Eleven

THE SETTING OF THE FIRST ACT of Mike Slattery's tale was a perfect late spring evening at Heron's Nest, just after the end of school and a week before the oil spill. A steady southwest breeze warmed the air and kept the bugs at bay. Mike Slattery, my parents, Ben Fries, Uncle Jack and Aunt Nancy Hibbard were outside enjoying cocktails and grilling barbeque chicken and burgers on the Weber. Andrew and I were playing with our Hot Wheels cars in the sandbox. Patrick was crawling around the yard, alternatively charming the adults and throwing sand at his older brother and cousin. Here is my reconstruction of the story Mike Slattery told.

It had been Mary Flanagan's idea to invite Ben Fries over for the cookout. She had met him several months before at an ecumenical Lenten potluck at Saint Cyril's. She had insisted he come over to meet some of the river's "good citizens" before the summer season began in earnest. He had enthusiastically accepted the invitation.

The conversation had started light, with discussions of the weather, the return to glory of the New York Yankees, the upcoming Montreal Olympics, the American Bicentennial, and whether Queen's *Bohemian Rhapsody* was quality music or, as Jack Hibbard had put it, "garbage."

"It's about the angst of an entire generation," Ben Fries said.

"Angst schmangst," Jack Hibbard said.

"Say that ten times fast," his sister Mary Flanagan challenged.

"It's about how an entire generation has been manipulated by the previous one," Mike Slattery said.

He sang the opening verse, just a little off key. Mary Flanagan and Nancy Hibbard chimed in for the next verse. The result, once Mike Slattery adjusted his pitch, was a harmony that was not half bad. The ladies emphasized a decrescendo by lowering their heads, then they lifted up their empty cans of Schlitz as if saluting with Zippo lighters.

Charlie Flanagan put down the spatula and tongs and applauded, a smile on his face. Patrick crawled into the circle of adults and joined suit.

Jack Hibbard booed and hissed. He rose to get another round of beers from the cooler and a Bloody Mary for my father, and took the empty cans from his sister and wife. "Bad music and bad beer go together, I guess," he said. "I'll take the good stuff, Barry Manilow and Genny Creamers any day of the week."

"I love it when you get romantic!" Nancy Hibbard said. She sang, with Mary Flanagan joining her in unison, one of her husband's favorite tunes, *I Write the Songs.*

"No wonder this generation has angst," Mike Slattery said, pouring out the dregs from his can of Genny Cream Ale and tossing the can into a growing pile of empties. "I can agree with you ladies on Queen, but not on Barry Manilow and certainly not on that piss water you drink. Half the country's in angst, the other half's clueless. And Schlitz used to be the ambrosia of the gods. How the hell'd all this happen?"

Charlie Flanagan pointed the spatula to Make Slattery. "You could be onto something there. Father D'Agostino tells us that Jesus turned water into wine. Ergo, the people who turned Schlitz into urine must be the Antichrists. Whaddaya think Mary?"

My mother stuck out her tongue.

"That's actually a pretty accurate commentary on American big business," Ben Fries said. "They brew piss water,

ruin sports teams, destroy the environment with their oil refining, and perpetuate the military-industrial complex. Definitely the collective Antichrist."

"Watch what you say about the military with Jack
around," Nancy Hibbard whispered.

"What?" Ben Fries said. "The military-industrial complex was Eisenhower's phrase."

"Yeah, but he was President, a good American, and a
good Christian." Nancy Hibbard frowned. "Jack's just a
good American."

"Pussy-footing around the military issue is bullshit,"
Charlie Flanagan said. "If Kent State taught us anything it's
that you can't even send a kid to college these days without
worrying about him getting killed. If you avoid the hit and
run, the gunshots'll get ya. Isn't that right Ben?"

"The age of complacency is over," Ben Fries said, nodding, either unfazed by or oblivious to the fact that Charlie's
comment was directed towards him and implied knowledge
of his secret identity. "There's a new edge to life these days
that might be with us for a long, long time. The angst'll get
worse before it gets better."

"Angst or no angst, we're still lucky as hell to live in the
best country on earth," Jack Hibbard said while returning
with the drinks, obviously ignorant of the intervening conversation. "Would any of you argue with that?" He looked
around and saw shaking heads. "Good," he said. He smiled
and handed out the beers and gave my dad his Bloody
Mary.

"The real question is why it's so great," Ben Fries said.
"What exactly is it that makes these United States of America the best country on earth? We Americans often argue
the case for exceptionalism, but we just as often fail to offer
sufficient evidence for it."

"It's easy," Jack Hibbard said. "Freedom and the second
amendment make America great."

"The great outdoors," Mike Slattery answered.

"The pursuit of happiness," said Mary Flanagan.

"Fireworks!" I apparently yelled from the sandbox.

Ben Fries nodded. "All good things, true. But America's best quality is that we Americans can make ourselves into whatever we want to be." He turned to my dad. "What do you think, Charlie?"

"Good point about self-invention," Charlie Flanagan said, causing the grill to flare up and sizzle as he flipped the chicken.

"I meant what do you think about what makes America great? What's your answer? Do you even believe in American exceptionalism?"

"You want my answer?" My dad asked. Ben Fries nodded. "I'll tell you what. You can read about it in my next three columns. They address that very question."

"Give us a hint, Charlie!" Mary Flanagan said. "Tell us, or I'll sneak up into your crow's nest and read it myself."

"Yeah," seconded her brother Jack. "Tell us. If it's bullshit we'll let you know right away. Save you the public embarrassment."

"It's never bullshit with Charlie," Mike Slattery said. "Still, that's no reason not to tell us."

"All right," Charlie Flanagan relented. He took a sip of his Bloody Mary and smiled. "For my money, the best thing about this country is the way it began in 1776. The revolution itself is the best thing about America."

All the adults looked at him in anticipation of more. My cousin and I started singing *Yankee Doodle*.

"We began it all," Charlie Flanagan continued, "right here, with our revolution. We started the end of kings. Just imagine what the world would be like if we still had kings."

"I remember that warning from Father D'Agostino," Mary Flanagan said. She cleared her throat, then continued in a voice as close as she could get to a male preacher's:

He will take your sons, and appoint them his horsemen. And he will appoint captains over thousands, and captains over fifties; and will set them to reap his harvest and to make his instruments of war, and instruments of his chariots. And he will take your daughters to be cooks, and to be bakers ...

". . . et cetera, et cetera, et cetera. I forgot the next few verses. I do remember the last part, though:

He will take the tenth of your sheep: and ye shall be his servants. And ye shall cry out in that day because of your king which ye shall have chosen; and the LORD will not hear you in that day."

"Second Samuel," said Mike Slattery. "Timeless words of wisdom, those."

"As true now as they were then," Ben Fries said. "And as true now as they were after our so-called revolution."

"So-called?" Charlie Flanagan said from the grill. "What the hell do you mean so-called?"

"Haven't you read Williams or Schlesinger?" Ben Fries asked. "The trend towards the imperial presidency didn't begin with Nixon, you know. The revolutionaries themselves—Adams, Washington, Hamilton, Madison—wanted to curtail the revolution soon after they started it because they feared the dangers of popular sovereignty."

"I remember that from reading the *Federalist Papers* back in college," Mike Slattery said. "Didn't a group of men write an Anti-Federalist Papers too?"

"Tom Paine helped write them," Ben said.

Charlie Flanagan said, "Ah, but he wasn't an American. He was British."

"The anti-Federalists even got angry at Jefferson," Ben Fries added. "And later, even Jefferson overstepped the bounds of presidential authority. He's usually been made out to be a radical republican, but he wasn't radical at all compared to Tom Paine, or to Theodorick Crane here in New York, or to other revolutionaries from Haiti, say, or, especially, France."

At this Mary Flanagan sang, swinging her fist in front of her, "Allons enfants de la Patrie / le jour de glorie est arrive!" She smiled triumphantly. "The French sure didn't allow *their* daughters to be turned into cooks and bakers!"

"Excuse my wife," said Charlie Flanagan. "Her paterfamilias may make her a good English Hibbard, and she may be Irish by marriage, but her true loyalties are obviously with her mother's side of the family, with the French."

"Je t'aime, trop," Mary Flanagan said.

"No trace of Frog in me," Jack Hibbard claimed. "How the hell'd that happen?"

"Adoption," his sister offered.

Jack reached over and lightly punched her on the leg. My mother slapped him away as if she were swatting a mosquito.

"Can we please get back to what Ben just said?" Charlie Flanagan asked. "He just claimed that some Haitian and, especially, French revolutionaries were more radical than Jefferson. I can see that. Are you also implying that the Haitian and French revolutions were more important than the American one?"

"Well ..." Ben Fries drew out the word as he considered his answer. "Yes," he said definitively, "I will say that. I'll say more, too. The French Revolution was the first true revolution, the one that gave the word revolution its current meaning. The Haitian revolution, which scared the pants off slave-owning Mr. Jefferson by the way, was the first to follow the model of the French revolution, which every revolution since then has also followed."

"You mean the Russians, Chinese and Vietcong?" asked Jack Hibbard.

"Yes," said Ben Fries. "The Russians, Chinese and Vietnamese all followed the same pattern; the overthrow of a

powerful ruling minority by a previously powerless op-
pressed majority."

"I don't mind 'em killing kings, but you can keep your
Communism to yourself," Jack Hibbard said angrily.

"What do you mean by saying the French gave new
meaning to the word revolution?" Nancy Hibbard asked,
placing a calming hand on her husband's arm. "I'm Canadian, by the way. A neutral observer in all this because we
don't have revolutions."

"Remind me later to correct you on that," Ben Fries
said. "As far as meaning is concerned, how is the word revolution defined in reference to celestial objects?"

"Well," Nancy said, "the earth for example, revolves
around the sun. One year around is one revolution."

"Where does the earth end up after three hundred sixty
five and one quarter days?"

"Back where it started," said Jack Hibbard. "What the
hell's this got to do with peasants hacking the heads off aristocrats?"

"Nothing," said Ben Fries, "which is exactly my point.
The original meaning of the word revolution, the meaning
up to 1789, anyway, was the astronomical meaning, to return back to where you were. That was what the Americans
were hoping to accomplish, a return to the generally leave
us alone …"

"Laissez faire!" interrupted Mary Flanagan.

". . . yes, a return to the generally lenient economic conditions that the British kings and Parliament allowed before
the mid 1760's, before the Stamp Tax. The American rebels
didn't want to create something new. They wanted to return
to the old way of doing things that had made so many of
them rich. John Hancock in shipping, George Washington
in land speculation, Thomas Jefferson in slaves. They were
all made rich thanks to the lack of British regulation."

"Getting rich sounds good to me," said Jack Hibbard.
"Let's add that to the list of reasons why America's great."

"Let's," Charlie Flanagan said. "Let's also remind ourselves that we were able to get rich because there was no king to take our money. That's what makes our revolution the best. What did the French do to expand the world economy? Besides adding a word or two?"

"My point is that there *was* a king while Americans were getting rich before 1776," Ben Fries insisted. "And Americans prospered just as much before the revolution as they did afterwards. In that sense, the American Revolution didn't change a thing. But the French," he continued, his hands moving now to emphasize his points, "the French intended from the beginning to start something completely new, something so new and so different that it would be unrecognizable by and unacceptable to the old regimes of Europe."

"They wouldn't have made one step forward without the American example to follow," said Charlie Flanagan, tongs in hand. "We were first. That makes us best."

"The French did kill more aristocrats," Jack Hibbard said. "Doesn't that count for something?"

"Wasn't it Thomas Jefferson who said that to make an omelet you have to break some eggs?" Mike Slattery asked.

"Pauvres oeufs," said Mary Flanagan, frowning.

"I thought you loved your revolution," Jack Hibbard said to his sister.

"I love Napoleon," Mary Flanagan answered. "And without the revolution there would've been no Napoleon."

"Ah ha!" said Charlie Flanagan, snapping the tongs with excitement. "There's the fault in your argument, Benjamin Fries. Thank you, Mary dear, for pointing it out. Leave it to a teacher to bring us to truth."

My father moved away from the grill and started walking around the others. "If the French Revolution was so monumental, so world-changing, then how do you explain Napoleon? Wasn't he just another king? Didn't he succeed in putting the pre-revolution Humpty Dumpty back together again?"

"Meet the new boss, same as the old boss," Mike Slattery said. "More timeless words of wisdom, this time courtesy of Peter Townsend."

"The kings of Europe hated Napoleon!" Mary Flanagan said.

"Yes they did," said Ben Fries, "because his style of rule was revolutionary, in the new, French sense of the word. Think about what he did. He brought constitutions to conquered places where kings and emperors had previously forbidden them. He opened all positions to talent rather than to family name. He channeled the energies of the French people into the greatest slayer of kingdoms that the world had yet seen. He ..."

"He almost ended up in Cape Vincent," interrupted Jack Hibbard.

"It's true!" Mary Flanagan said, picking up Patrick as he scooted by. "Some family friends bought him a house, shaped like an upside down cup and saucer of all things, and prepared for his arrival. But the British got him first. We should know. Our family was waiting for him. Oh, Ben, you must join us for the Cape Vincent French Festival this year. French bread, croissants, Napoleon on horseback. It's almost like the British hadn't even gotten him."

"Thank God they did," Charlie Flanagan said. "Just imagine the trouble he would've caused over here if they hadn't. He would've tried conquering the whole river, island by island."

"Are you kidding me?" said Mike Slattery. "He was fat and weak by then. Completely ineffective and barely able to stay awake half the time. Didn't you see Rod Steiger in *Waterloo*?"

"Now that's *really* good music!" Mary Flanagan said. With Patrick in her arms, she stood up and started dancing in circles as she sang, in a faux-Scandinavian accent, Abba's *Waterloo.*

Patrick smiled and laughed, triggering the same response from his mother, then his father, and then from the other adults.

"There she goes with her damn Abba again," Jack Hibbard said, his face sliding into an exaggerated grimace. "Dictator inspired disco."

"You shouldn't pick on Abba," Mike Slattery said. "They've got more historical content in their music than any band since The Who. Have you heard *Fernando* yet?"

Jack Hibbard shook his head. "I'm not picking on Abba. I'm picking on Napoleon. I've never shared my sister's adoration for the little fart. I'm glad the British got him."

Nancy Hibbard shook her head. "Sorry, Jack, I'm with Mary on this one. Wouldn't the signs have been great? 'Bonaparte slept here!' And the business? 'Napoleon short stack for one ninety nine! Free coffee!' Imagine the tourist dollars!"

"There's more to the story than Napoleon not making it here after Waterloo, you know," Ben Fries said once the laughter quieted a bit.

"What more to the story?" Charlie Flanagan asked.

"His friends did buy him the house. You've probably seen pictures of it, the old cup and saucer house in Cape Vincent, as Mary mentioned. They also prepared for his arrival in other ways." Ben sat forward in his chair. "What most people don't know is this. There was a French corvette, name unknown, that was commissioned by Joseph Bonaparte and was on its way to Cape Vincent when it sunk somewhere in the river. A British sloop, the *Goodspeed*, was right on its tail for much of the journey, hoping to steer the French corvette to Fort Haldimand on Carleton Island. But when it got to Kingston there was no sign of the French ship. Captain Terry of the *Goodspeed* interviewed people up and down the river, asking them if they'd seen it. The last report of it was in Brockville. Captain Terry communicated his findings to the Admiralty, which concluded, reasonably, that the French corvette went down."

"When exactly did this happen?" asked Mike Slattery.

"The summer of 1815, just after Waterloo."

"Don't sing," Jack Hibbard said to his sister.

"Why's this important?" asked Charlie Flanagan. "Was Napoleon's hat on board?"

Ben Fries smiled. "Possibly. What's important is that also on board the nameless French corvette was a large supply of gold and other treasures, some of them quite exotic, bound for Cape Vincent, sent ahead to await the arrival of the Emperor, former Emperor, himself."

"Gold?" said Nancy Hibbard. "Really?"

"Where'd it go down?" asked Mike Slattery.

"Holy shit," said Jack Hibbard. "How much gold?"

Mary Flanagan gave Ben a strange look, then turned away before he could meet her eyes.

"Yes, really," Ben Fries said, answering Nancy Hibbard first. "No one knows where it sunk, though. Somewhere upriver from Brockville, but that's as much as we know. It could be anywhere." He pointed out to the river, towards the Rock Island lighthouse. "It could be right there, Charlie, just a stone's throw away."

"How much gold?" Jack Hibbard asked again.

"No one knows. But he was Emperor, after all, so you can imagine it was quite a bit of gold."

Charlie Flanagan was turned towards the grill, putting the cooked food on a serving platter. "How'd you learn all this, Ben?" he asked.

"I'm an avid reader," Ben Fries said. "And I've dabbled a bit in research. You know how it goes, Charlie, hit upon the right sources and you can learn a lot about what was once unknown. Especially now, in the microfilm era."

"I see," Charlie Flanagan said abruptly, turning from the

grill and walking back to the cottage with his head down, not looking at anyone. When he got to the front door he yelled, "Okay! Burgers and barbeque are ready, people, so come and get it while it's hot. Let's go kids! Wash that sand off your hands! Mary, can you please get that bowl of potato salad? Nancy, can you get the ketchup for the kids?"

Chapter Twelve

"My mother liked Abba?" was the first question that came to mind. I asked it unable to hide my surprise at the fact.

"She loved Abba," Mike Slattery said. "She was singing all the time. Queen, Barry Manilow, Carole King, Dan Fogelberg. But Abba was her favorite. She and Nancy even went to see them in Ottawa once. It was sometime in '78, I think. Your mom said she had the time of her life."

"I remember my mom singing a lot, but I only recall the church songs. *Jesus, Savior, Pilot Me. Were You There. Blessed Be Thou Heavenly Queen.*" I took a sip of beer and laughed. "Damn. My father and his Beethoven? My mother and her Abba? I guess opposites do attract."

Mike Slattery tipped his glass at me at smiled. "There you go," he said.

"The night of the cookout was the first time my dad heard about Napoleon's gold," I said, returning to the important subject at hand. "A good five months before he met Naguib Malqari."

"Yes," Mike Slattery said. "It was also the first time I'd heard of it. Please recall, though, that I don't believe it exists, while your father obviously did. He found something more there to chew on."

"But when and why did he start looking for it?" I asked. "Was it Malqari?"

"That's my theory," Jim Pembroke said.

I looked to Billy Masterson for further answers.

"I only found out about it a couple years later," he

answered. "Remember? Your dad first told me after he pulled me up out of the water in 1978. He and Ben had been looking for it for a while by then, but I don't know for exactly how long."

"Two years," Mike Slattery said.

"But Ben knew where it was and presumably my father didn't, because Ben took you out that day when you saw it."

"I did see it," Billy Masterson affirmed, looking right at Mike Slattery.

Slattery shook his head and smiled. "You saw something, Billy," he said. "You can't prove to me or anyone else it was Napoleon's gold."

Billy Masterson glared at him.

I saw the conversation leading to a dead end, so I shifted topics and asked Mike Slattery exactly how my dad and Ben Fries were bound together.

"The initial cord was tied on the day I just described to you," Mike Slattery said. "And the cord was made of your father's knowledge of who Ben was. Looking back, it's obvious that your father knew Ben Fries wasn't exactly the man he claimed to be. Charlie's comment on getting killed at college—a harsh one don't you think?—was no doubt a reference to Ben's running over that Hollister kid back in '73. Then there was your dad's response to Ben's point about reinvention. Why Ben made that comment in the first place is beyond me.

"The most curious comment was Ben's explanation for knowing about Napoleon's gold. An avid reader? Dabbling in research? Come on! It wasn't just any professor who'd disappeared from Rochester a year before amidst scandal. It was an award-winning professor of American naval history. If anyone knew about Captain Terry's chase of this French corvette and the rumors that Napoleon's gold was on it, it would've been him."

"Sounds to me like hubris," Jim Pembroke said.

"Indeed," Mike Slattery agreed.

"Knowing about Captain Terry's chase is one thing," I said. "How'd Ben know about the gold?"

"We're not sure," Mike answered with a glance towards Billy and Jim.

"And my father never turned him in," I said. "Ben Fries said he was more valuable to my father free rather than in jail. Ben must have been referring to his knowledge of where Napoleon's gold was located."

"Makes sense to me," Billy Masterson said. "Ben tells your dad where the gold is and there's no reason to keep his identity a secret."

"Well ..." said Mike Slattery.

"The gold's real, Mayor," Billy Masterson interrupted. "I saw it with my own eyes."

"That wasn't what I was challenging this time," Mike Slattery said.

"What then?" I asked.

"I know for a fact that there was more than one reason for Charlie Flanagan to keep Ben Fries around."

"Did *you* know who he really was?" I asked.

"Your father's comments at the cookout had given me an inkling that Mr. Fries wasn't being altogether transparent. I found out for sure from your mother, Tom, a few weeks after the cookout, on the same day Ben Fries rose to greatness. I also found out from her that a stronger cord bound your father and Ben Fries together." Mike Slattery glanced at Jim Pembroke, then at Billy Masterson. "Neither of you know this part of my story," he said. "I've shared this part with no one, not even Charlie. Especially not Charlie."

THE SECOND SCENE in Mike Slattery's story took place in Alexandria Bay, on the night of the bicentennial fireworks over Boldt Castle. The CANCO-2000 had spilled its oil two weeks before. The people of the river, both American and Canadian, were doing the hard work of cleaning up the mess. Men, women and children of the river were physically exhausted by that point, working fourteen to sixteen hours a day in the heat, suctioning and shoveling the oil from the water, cutting by hand the oil coated vegetation on the shore, collecting and disposing of the hundreds of birds and fish killed by the poison, and carefully swabbing the filth from whatever creatures were unfortunate enough to get coated by it and were still alive.

The river people were emotionally exhausted, too, because they didn't know if their hard work would be enough to undo the damage that three hundred thousand gallons of toxins had done to the place where it wasn't meant to be. Could the wetlands recover? Could the fragile breeding grounds of osprey, cormorant, tern and heron be saved? What about the frogs? What about the fish? There had already been several moderate-sized fish kills. Would they increase in number and in frequency? All these questions were unanswerable on the day of the bicentennial celebration, unanswerable at least until the following spring when the birds and frogs and fish returned to their breeding grounds to lay and hatch their eggs. The unknown future brought a combination of fear and anxiety into the collective mood of the river people.

Mixed in with the fear and anxiety was anger. As Jim Pembroke had told me earlier that evening, everyone knew that a disaster like the CANCO-2000 spill would happen, given the existence of large scale shipping on a tamed, yet still dangerous, waterway. Now that it had happened, the anger of generations rose to the surface. Many people were angry, and not only about the oil spill. The Canadians whose lost villages had been submerged to widen the river and slow the most dangerous rapids. The cottage owners whose docks had been damaged and shorelines eroded by the swell and wakes that the ocean-going salties produced. The swimmers whose river was contaminated with gasoline and oil and urine and garbage that leaked unintentionally or was dumped intentionally by uncaring freighter crews. These people had been insulted, and the insults, latent for almost twenty years since the Saint Lawrence Seaway had opened, were, on the night of the fireworks, triggers for the angry reactions of the drunk holiday crowd.

Mike Slattery recalled seeing proud men from families who for generations had made a living fishing dump buckets of chum on the cars of Coast Guard and US Corps of Engineers Seaway officials. He saw women throw dead, oil caked cormorants onto the decks of ships as the vessels passed by the women's motorboats. Before the fireworks he heard shouts of "Fuck the Seaway!" and "Break down the dams!" from men and teenage boys, exhausted in every way after a long day's cleanup, who drank cans of beer by the case and waited for the release they hoped the fireworks would provide. And right before the show he saw Billy Masterson, all of thirteen years old in that bicentennial year, steering his father's boat up and down the river, eliciting the cheers of the crowd with his waving of a Jolly Roger flag and his firing of a makeshift potato cannon he'd made from an old piece of cast iron boiler pipe.

Into the midst of this fearful, anxious and angry crowd came Benjamin Fries, a.k.a. Albert Hartman, former professor of American naval history, fugitive from the law, wanted for vehicular homicide, who saw the chance to reinvent and redeem himself in a particularly appropriate American way on this particular American holiday. He had already spoken to a large crowd in Gananoque on Canada Day and had received much acclaim. Now, about a half hour before the fireworks were set to begin above the most iconic building on the river, Ben Fries once again brought the megaphone to his lips and spoke to a crowd yearning for leadership.

"My friends," he shouted, then louder, in an ever-growing crescendo, "My friends! We have gathered here today to remember and celebrate the birth of a great nation, a nation founded on the principles of government of the people, by the people, for the people! I ask you, neighbors, what has the government done for you lately? What has it done?

"Some of you might answer, 'The government is paying me good money for the cleanup work I did today. This money will help me send my child to college.' Could there be better work? Would this hard and dirty labor be here today to sadden and anger us had the government not betrayed us all by using our river as a highway for its toxins?

"Now, my friends, my neighbors, women and men of the river, the government wants to tell us that year-round shipping on our precious river is safe! Just days after we received proof that summer shipping on our river isn't safe, just days after the United States Army Corps of Engineers, the Seaway and the river pilots ruined our shores with their oil, just days after the worst inland oil spill this nation has ever seen, the government officials try to tell us that year-round shipping is safe!

"Safe, with the river bound by ice? Safe, with fog ten times thicker than it was on the day the CANCO-2000 ran aground? Safe, with frost making useless even the most sophisticated navigation and steering technology? Safe, we ask, with the Coast Guard's already flawed disaster response plans made useless by inaccessibility to the water? No, no, no and no!

"Can we trust our government to tell us what's right for us? Can we trust our government to tell us what's right for our river? No! NO!! AND AGAIN, NOOO!!!"

The crowd cheered loudly now, whereas before it had been listening with mostly silent attention punctuated by a few loud cries of assent. Ben Fries stood silent for a moment and let the cheering subside before concluding his speech.

"My friends, on this great day, the two hundredth birthday of our great nation, our nation founded on the principles of government of the people, by the people, and for the people, I call on you to join me and save our river! Preserve our islands! Together may the men and women of this great and mighty river, men and women on both sides of the border, work to maintain the beauty and grandeur that they tried to take from us and that we, knee deep in their muck, each day are trying to reclaim!"

The crowd cheered wildly. Women screamed. Children whooped. Men whistled with their fingers between their tightened lips. As people broke into small groups to discuss Ben's words, several comrades of his, including Mike Slattery, moved through the crowd with sign up lists for people wanting to receive more information about the environmental group that Ben Fries had just created.

The group was Preserve the Islands, one of the most successful international environmental organizations in the western hemisphere. Ben Fries and others visited door to door on both mainlands and on the water. They spoke at Veterans and Rotary and Kiwanis clubs. They wrote letters to newspapers and lobbied politicians in Albany and Ottawa and Washington.

Within a month two hundred people had joined. Within a year the organization could boast a thousand members. The Seaway never expanded. Winter navigation never happened. None of these victories would have come to pass without the CANCO-2000 oil spill. They might have happened, but not in the same way, not with the same intensity, without Ben Fries' leadership.

MIKE SLATTERY WAS MAKING HIS WAY through the crowd, collecting names and addresses for the Preserve the Islands mailing list, when he felt a tug on his pants. He looked down and saw Patrick Flanagan. He tussled the boy's hair, reached down and took his hand, looked up, and saw Mary Flanagan walking towards him, tears in her eyes.

"Are you okay?" Mike Slattery asked. He let go of Patrick's hand, but Patrick stood on a boulder and demanded that Mike take it back.

"I'm fine," my mom said, wiping a tear away. "How could I not be fine after that?"

"That was one hell of a speech."

Mary nodded. "I'm scared, too, Mike. Terrified, in fact."

"We all are, Mary. Who knows when this'll end? Sometimes it seems like our river's on borrowed time. It could be even worse next time it happens." Mike Slattery frowned and lowered his head towards Patrick.

Mary Flanagan looked up at the American flag flying over Boldt Castle, said, "Yeah, next time." She started singing the first verse of the Neil Young song, *After the Gold Rush*. Her voice grew quieter as she approached the end of the verse, her rhythm slower, and the words became mixed with sobs.

"Canada's own," Mike Slattery said when she had finished. "Mr. Young knew what he was talking about." After a moment's pause he shook his head, looked up and asked, "Where's Charlie?"

"He's on one of the fire department boats with Jack. Tommy and Andrew are with them, to watch the fireworks. I came down here with Nancy, but she met up with some old high school friends somewhere over there." My mother waved a hand to the northeast and then sat down on the ground. "Actually, Mike," she said softly, "I was looking for you."

"You found me," Mike said. "Did you sign the mailing list?"

My mother must have looked awful at that moment. Tired? Scared? Exhilarated? Probably all three, because Mike Slattery reached down and offered her the hand Patrick wasn't holding.

He said, "Talk to me, Mary. Please."

"I don't know where to start, Mike …"

"Try at the beginning. What's got you so upset?"

My mother's voice was quiet, almost imperceptible as

the percussion of the first fireworks filled the air. "I love him, Mike."

Mike Slattery laughed softly. "I know you do, Mary. You and Charlie are the envy of everyone on the river. You two ..."

"No," she said. "Well, yes. I love Charlie, too, of course, but I also love *him*, Mike." She made a gesture towards the river. "I love Benjamin Fries."

Mike Slattery sat down and placed Patrick on his lap and let the child gum his finger. "Jesus, Mary, I mean, wow. Have you two ... done anything?"

"No, nothing. Nothing physical." My mom shook her head vigorously, her jaw set. "All we've done is talk about it, about a lot of things, actually. And we kissed once, before we talked about it."

The two friends paused to watch a rapid-fire burst of fireworks that lit the sky in flying white, red and then blue streaks, which then whistled upwards to another explosion of all three colors at once.

"Are you going to do anything about it?"

"That depends on Charlie."

"What?" Mike Slattery had heard her, but did not understand.

"That depends on what Charlie does," she repeated. "You remember at the cookout? When we started talking about Napoleon's gold and Charlie grew so hostile?"

Mike Slattery nodded.

"I've heard that story before," she said.

"Really?"

"Yes, from my mother. She was French, you know. She lived in Cape Vincent for a time. She knew all about the French corvette and the *Goodspeed*. She also knew where the boat went down."

Mike Slattery looked at his friend suspiciously.

Mary Flanagan smiled. "Don't worry, I won't burden you with that knowledge. At least not yet. But that's not the most important topic that I wanted to talk about concerning that night."

"Go on."

"Well, it turns out that Ben has a history." My mother paused and brought her knuckle to her lips. "Mike, can you promise me you won't tell anyone what I'm about to tell you? Can you promise me you'll keep it a secret?"

"Of course, Mary. We've known each other since you were in second grade. I babysat you for seven years. We've shared secrets beyond counting."

My mom moved closer to Mike's ear and spoke just under the sound of the fireworks. Anyone paying close attention might have concluded that they were the ones in love. But no one was watching them. All eyes were directed towards the sky.

"Ben's real name is Albert Hartman, Mike. The same Albert Hartman from Rochester who was accused of that horrible hit and run in Albany a few years ago. He changed his name and came here to hide, but Charlie found him out."

"How?"

"As usual, Charlie put two and two together, then went one step farther than everybody else and got five."

"Will Charlie turn him in?" Slattery asked the question knowing full well that my dad hadn't yet turned him in, and also guessing, correctly, that to do so now, after the fireworks speech, might not be such a good idea.

"No he won't." My mom took a long look at the ground, a look that Mike Slattery might have interpreted as one of shame mixed with pride.

"Mary …"

My mother set her jaw and turned to look him in the eye. "I told Charlie that if he ever mentions Ben's secret to anyone, or if he ever turns him in, I'd leave him for good. I'll go away with Ben if we can get away fast enough.

Without Ben if we can't. I mean it, Mike. Charlie knows that. Charlie won't turn him in."

"Jesus, Mary. What about the kids?"

"I told him I'd take them, too. He'd have to sue me to ever see them again."

"I don't think you need to tell me how Charlie responded."

She did anyway. "It was just yesterday, Mike. It was after he got home from a very hard day of cleaning up. Tommy was grumpy and wanted to play baseball. Patrick, as you can tell, was teething. I told Charlie what I just told you and he shut down. He didn't say a word. He made himself a tall vodka and tonic, went up to his study, and listened to music all night. He was gone when I woke up this morning. Jack called a few hours ago to say he'd pick up Tommy on his way down and meet Charlie here. I haven't seen him all day."

"I'm sorry, Mary. I'm so sorry." Mike Slattery handed her Patrick, who was complaining about being hungry, and then took my mom's free hand.

They sat like this for the remainder of the show, a spectacular pyrotechnic display that has gone down in river history as one of the best ever. When it was over, with her ears filled with wild cheering even louder than that which had followed Ben Fries' speech, my mom noiselessly mouthed "thank you," and Mike Slattery answered by squeezing her hand and nodding his head.

"MY MOM HAD AN AFFAIR?" was my first question this time, and I asked it with double the astonishment I'd felt when asking if she'd really liked Abba.

"I wouldn't call it an affair," Jim Pembroke said. "I've had plenty of them, and it sounds to me like this was more like infatuation."

"Infatuations come and go," Mike Slattery said, "and they're usually foolish. Your mother's love for Ben Fries lasted for over twenty years, for the rest of her life in fact. She was quite serious about it. They both were. I can assure you of that."

"It was something more than infatuation but something less than an affair," I said.

"Your mother is what finally bound Ben Fries and your father together," Slattery said. "True, they looked for the gold together. Possibly true, that Ben Fries knew where the gold was said to be and didn't tell your father to keep him holding on. Definitely true that your father's life as he knew it would've ended had your mother left him because he spilled the beans about Ben."

"She obviously didn't leave my dad and run away with Ben. That would've ended my life as I knew it."

"She didn't leave Charlie, and that's to her great credit," Mike Slattery replied. "She put them into a competition."

"Competition for what?" asked Jim Pembroke. "To show the most attention to her? To find Napoleon's gold and make her rich?"

"They looked for it together, right Billy?"

"They were lookin' for it together when your father, Jack Hibbard and Ben Fries pulled me out of the river," Billy Masterson said, "and that was in '78, two years after this."

"Maybe it's more accurate to say that she put them into cooperation," I suggested.

"*That* would be a first for a woman," Jim Pembroke said with a grunt.

"Ever hear the one about keepin' your friends close but keepin' your enemies closer?" Billy Masterson said.

"Sun-tzu said that," I said. "The Art of War."

"That fits Charlie's personality," Mike Slattery affirmed. "Not a lion, but a fox."

I sat back in my chair. "Boy, now I know what Ben Fries meant about being more valuable to my father free rather than in jail," I said. "Free, my mother doesn't run. In jail, she's gone and neither man has her." I expected at least one comment, but the other three men were silent, none of them even looking at me as I waited for a response. "So Mike," I finally said, "when did you find out that my mother had drawn my dad and Ben together, whatever the nature of their relationship?"

"October 1978, when the two men once again tried to recruit me. Your father had just gotten word that Naguib Malqari was dead, and was just starting to publicly speak about his search for Napoleon's gold. For two years I'd refused to join the quest, but ended up doing so anyway, right here, at the very table around which we drink, and around which your father Charlie Flanagan, our great and good king, used to hold court."

THUS THE THIRD AND FINAL ACT of Mike Slattery's tale, a coda really, was set at Jimmy's, two years after the bicentennial and two months after my father and Ben Fries had pulled Billy Masterson from the river. My father's spirits were high because the Yankees were back in the World Series, because his newspaper was doing well, and because he believed that his search for Napoleon's gold, conducted quietly for two years with his fear of Naguib Malqari lurking in the background, was finally about to bear fruit. With, that is, a little help from his friends.

It was a "Jesus session," as the River Rat Reporters would come to call them, when their agreement was to speak honestly and completely, hiding nothing and dishing out only the necessary bullshit. My father had proposed a topic for the evening, which, not surprisingly, was the willingness of the others to help him in pursuit of Napoleon's gold.

"Still in, Billy?" my father asked.

"As long as you let me swim where the effin' hell I want, when the effin' hell I want," said the young Billy Masterson.

"Agreed, as long as you watch your effin' language. Benjamin?"

"What do you think, Charlie?"

"I'll take that as a yes. How about my brother-in-law?" Charlie Flanagan asked Jack Hibbard.

"I'm with you, Charlie," he said. "Might as well keep it in the family."

"That's three. Marty?"

"I'm a land lubber," Martin Comstock said. "But I'll gladly take my cut when and if you find it."

"Screw you. Slattery?"

Mike Slattery shook his head. "I'll give you three guesses, Charlie, and the first two don't count."

"Come on, Mike. Why not?" Ben Fries said.

"Because A—I don't believe it exists, B—I don't believe it exists, and C—I don't believe it exists."

"You're a doubtin' Thomas," Billy Masterson said.

"I'm a clear thinker," Mike Slattery responded. "Martin, if you weren't a land lubber, would you join in on this charade?"

"Well," Martin Comstock said, weighing the degree of honesty he'd reveal in his answer, "stranger things have been searched for in this river, and stranger things have been found, so I wouldn't necessarily rule out the possibility. I would, however …"

"For cripes sake, Comstock," Jim Pembroke said. "Would you help him or not?"

"Yes," Martin Comstock said. "I would."

"What about you, Captain?" my father asked.

"I don't want a damned thing to do with your gold," Jim Pembroke said. "I do want to clear my name, though, so if I can prove that something in the river caused Hassan the wheelman to screw up my life, then I'll do whatever I can to see it found."

"You're the odd one out," my father said to Mike Slattery.

Slattery, who had just been hired as executive director of Preserve the Islands, shook his head. "I've got more important things to worry about. And you do too, Ben, if you take some time to think about it."

"We've got plenty of people working on the winter shipping issue," Ben Fries said. "Besides, imagine how much the gold would help PTI's finances."

"Fool's gold," Slattery said, "or worse."

My father looked hard at him. "I've got a proposition for you, Mike. You do this for me and I'll do something for you. I'll reciprocate."

"What?"

"You know I've got friends in politics. Soon-to-be-Congressman Radisson, Governor Carey, Pat Moynihan, Walter Maitland. Help me find Napoleon's gold and I'll guarantee their support for Preserve the Islands."

Mike Slattery looked around the barroom. "What is this, Charlie? Tammany Hall North?"

"Mike, I need you. You know the river better than anyone here. Even better than Billy and even better than Captain Pembroke. I can honestly say I can't do this without you."

"*And neither could Mary*," Slattery thought. He had received the letter from her just a few days before, thanking him for his friendship and explaining why he should help her husband and Ben in their quest. He knew that Mary Flanagan's appeal had made a chink in his armor of refusal, which was why, he thought, he protested too much now that Charlie was asking him straight up. His armor was chinked, the offer of political support for Preserve the Islands had pierced it, so Slattery did what all proud but defeated knights do. He held his head high and surrendered.

"All right, Charlie. I'll help you," he said. "But I do so unwillingly, and I will always remain unconvinced that what you're looking for is real."

My father slapped the table cheerfully. "Good. That's it. Consensus. We're all in."

As became the custom at the close of Jesus sessions, the men sealed their conversation with a toast. My father offered it, with his beer glass raised high and with a smile on his face. "To Napoleon's gold," he said, "may it ever shine brightly in our lives."

MIKE SLATTERY SAT BACK and finished his beer. "There you go. There's my story. I did help your father, Tom. I helped by looking over maps with him—they're the ones hanging on his study walls with his strange shorthand. I helped by taking him out a few times on my boat when he couldn't find anyone else to accompany him. I promised to let him know if any Preserve the Island scouts saw or heard anything of note on the river, which they never did. And on Friday evenings, right here, I shook my head and told him his quest was a chimera. To that he never listened."

"Tell him about you, Mayor," Jim Pembroke said, tipping his glass towards Mike Slattery. "Tell him what Charlie did for you in return."

"Well, I served as executive director of Preserve the Islands for nine years. Charlie came through. We got the political support your father promised from Albany and Washington, especially from Radisson, Moynihan and Maitland. Thanks to the confidence generated by that I won the mayoral race with overwhelming numbers. I served two terms, took a break to sail around the world, and when I came back I was talked into running again. Here I am, Alex Bay's Grover Cleveland, back in office. And here's Preserve the Islands, as strong as ever protecting our fine river. Yes, Tom, Charlie Flanagan did indeed deliver."

I was still unclear about a few things. "Mike, you said Ben and my dad were still on the same page at this 1978 Jesus session. But that was two years after my mom informed my dad about her relationship with Ben. I always thought while growing up that my dad and Ben had quarreled over pesticide use on a golf course. What came between them? And when? Do you know?"

"There were certainly tensions between them from '76 on," Slattery explained. "But they lived with them, for Mary's sake, perhaps, or for the gold, or even for Preserve the Islands, although your mother was much more involved in that than your father ever was." Mike paused and sipped his beer. "Do you remember when your father got into financial trouble?"

"1985," I said. "After his reporter Freddy Teed dug up the dirt on H. Paul Gass and his banking irregularities. Gass and Harold Radisson brought the hammer down, and my father was forced to sell, then leave, the paper."

"They almost lost Heron's Nest for back taxes," Slattery said. "They simply couldn't pay them."

"But they didn't lose Heron's Nest," I said.

"No, they didn't. They didn't lose Heron's Nest because Ben Fries paid the back taxes, and continued to pay the taxes until ... well, until your parents died."

"That's why they quarreled?" I asked.

"To be honest, Tom, it seemed to me that your father let his pride get in the way. He hated Ben for what he did, although the rest of us interpreted it as quite the magnanimous gesture. But yes, they quarreled over that, and quarreled bitterly. Ben even stopped coming to Jimmy's on Fridays after that."

"That leads to my second question," I said.

"What?"

"How long did my father's first quest last? You've all told me that he resumed his search in the early 1990s, right before the accident, but when did the first one end?"

"Also 1985," Slattery answered. "The back taxes, Radisson's machinations, Ben's 'interference,' as Charlie called it. All of it was too much for him to bear. Your father just gave up. He kept diving, became even more active in the early '90's, in fact, but as far as looking for the gold, that much was over. He cut all ties with Ben Fries. Cut several important emotional ties with your mother, in fact. It wasn't pretty after that."

I didn't want to go into any more details of that ugliness, so I moved on to my final question. "You say my mother bound my father and Ben Fries together in their search for Napoleon's gold. You say she also broke down your resistance to helping them find it. Why, Mike? Why would my mother care? What interest did she have in their search for Napoleon's gold? Is there any way I could read this letter she sent to you?"

He was already producing the envelope from his windbreaker pocket. "Here you go," he said as he handed it to me and smiled. "I've held on to it for all these years. Never told your father about it, either. Take it home. Read it in private. It's yours now. I can say nothing more about it. Your cousin Andrew is in charge of that story."

Chapter Thirteen

I CONSIDERED FOR A MOMENT whether to take the letter and go home right away or to stay at Jimmy's, watch the Yankees and A's in game two, and wait for the next tale. My anxiety to read the letter sooner rather than later guided me to the first option and, besides, I didn't think I could concentrate on another River Rat story, if there was to be one, with the game in the background and with my mother's letter in my pocket. The Undies in the back of the room were also starting to grate on my nerves, cheering too loudly for the A's rather than for the Yankees, pointing my way and then laughing, or so it seemed, and even bumping hard into me when I went to use the men's room one final time before leaving. All in all, I had had enough of Jimmy's for that night.

I wished my friends well, and went outside into a cool, dry night with a waxing crescent moon. As I drove away in my new-to-me old Ford pickup, I found the ballgame on the AM radio and thought about that letter.

The historian's party game question came to mind. If I could, would I want to encounter a person from the past and ask her questions about something she had written? Or the Hollywood version, more appropriate in my case; would I want to be like Jodie Foster in *Contact*, whisked away by a technologically superior extraterrestrial civilization and placed on a beach with a simulacrum of a parent who would answer all my questions?

I decided that no, I would not want to do either. I

would have too many questions, too many things I would want to say, too much love to heap upon a plate that simply could not contain it all. I would be too much like Jodie Foster's character Ellie Arroway; in other words, unable to frame the right questions or correctly understand the answers. Now, five years after my mother's death, I was content to be served one morsel at a time of her life—and my father's—and to have time in between to savor each bite. It felt sacramental to me, beyond mere questions and answers.

I crossed the bridge onto Wellesley Island, sandwiched between two Canada-bound semis. I kept one eye on the rearview mirror half-expecting that one of the Undesirables was following me home. I turned off the ramp onto Jefferson County Route 100 and continued west on what was also known as Thousand Islands Park Road. I was approaching the hairpin curve into Thousand Islands Park, where one resident had hung a convex mirror and a "Honk Now!" sign, when I heard the A's take a 1-0 lead in the fourth. As I approached the curve I could see a pair of headlights behind me that, again, I thought might belong to a vehicle driven by one of the Undies. I could also see the bright reflection of my truck's headlights in the eyes of several deer foraging in the woods.

Driving and listening to the game, and paying too much attention to the car behind me, I saw the deer into whose haunches I was about to crash for only a second before it continued its run across the road to my right. I saw it for so short a time because I turned hard away from it, to the left, which caused my right wheels to come up off the ground for an instant and then my back wheels to kick out from under the truck. I tried to maneuver back onto the road but it was too late. The tail of the hairpin curve was straight ahead. I couldn't correct the turn fast enough to miss the tree. I did sound the horn, as the sign instructed, but only unintentionally when my chest fell upon it after my head hit the windshield and my legs hit the steering wheel and my body fell back and then forward from the impact of steel against wood.

THE FIRST PERSON TO VISIT ME in my Alexandria Bay hospital room was Martin Comstock. His first question, a predictable one, was, "Tom, be honest with me now. Were you drunk?"

"Not this time," I said. "Believe it or not, I only had about three beers over the four hours I was at Jimmy's and then out on the river. Ask Jim Pembroke. Ask Billy Masterson. They were with me the whole time. Hell, ask the doctor. I'm sure they've tested my blood."

He waved a hand. "Well, I don't have to ask anybody. I just wanted to hear it directly from you."

"A test, huh?" I smiled.

Martin Comstock looked at my ribs and my left collarbone, both of which were badly bruised and bandaged, and then down at my left foot, which was broken, in a cast. He moved closer and inspected my stitched-up face. "Deer, huh?"

"Big one. Eight pointer at least. I was just dreaming about it. The thing was looking me right in the eye. Wished I'd had a gun."

"In your dream or in real life?"

"In both, I suppose. How'd I get here, Martin?" I asked. I was thinking about the car behind me, the one I feared was being driven by one of the Undies when I hit the deer.

"Oh, Stella Donaldson brought you in. She was driving right behind you, on her way home from her monthly book club meeting in Clayton."

I laughed hard, which caused a shot of pain to travel across my ribs.

"What?" Comstock asked.

"Nothing. Just thinking about that deer again."

"Well, you've got plenty of time to think about it. You're not going anywhere anytime soon."

"Just back to Heron's Nest," I said. "I'll be fine once I'm there."

"Need anything? I can make a trip to Watertown for you anytime."

"Besides food and drink, nothing really. Actually, I could use an internet hookup. I have a laptop but I've been going over to the Clayton library to get online."

"You have cable?"

I nodded.

"Consider it done," he said.

"Thank you." I looked up at the television. "Too bad about the Yanks."

"Damn shame," he said. "I don't know how they'll get out of this jam. Clemens and Pettite already losers? Back to Oakland tomorrow?"

"Moose'll come through," I said, referring to the next starting pitcher, Mike Mussina.

"He'd better come through. Bats better, too." Comstock shook his head and looked out the window for a moment at the river. "What did you think of Mayor Mike's tale?"

"Intriguing," I said. "I never knew those things about my mother."

"She was a precious woman."

"I'm appreciating that more and more," I said. "And you were right about one thing, Martin, 1976 was quite a year up here. In general and in the lives of the River Rat Reporters."

"The Captain told his story, too?"

"I'm still not sure what to think of that. Hassan the wheelman. This Malqari character. The oil itself."

"Well, Jim's lived a long time with the guilt from that. Sometimes I wish Hassan the wheelman or Naguib Malqari would just show up at Jimmy's and tell him it wasn't his fault. Not that it would make any difference with the damn bureaucrats and review boards."

"Fat chance of Hassan showing up now," I said.

"Malqari either. He's long dead." I paused and took a sip of ice water. "Martin, how come there are question marks next to your name on my father's list of River Rat Reporter stories?"

"Because I don't have one," he said quickly and, it seemed to me, with some anxiety.

"Why not? You were there after all. It seems like you know everything that goes on around here."

Martin Comstock laughed loudly. "Me! Me? Well, at most, I'm just the master of ceremonies, introducing the real entertainers as they make their way to the stage."

"Or the bartender, mixing the drinks that others enjoy. And perhaps slipping in a little something extra." We laughed together, although I was becoming impatient. "You had to have told my father something. Apparently, even Andrew had something to say, even though Uncle Jack knew my mom ... which reminds me. I need to find out where my pickup is. I left the letter in the front seat."

"Your truck's at Caprara's," Comstock explained. "Insurance'll fix it right up. But your mother's letter to Mayor Mike is right here." He took it from his jacket pocket and held it up in the air. "I didn't lay eyes on it." He turned it around. "See, it's still sealed."

"Thanks, Martin."

"No problem. I'm also the deliveryman, you see, bringing the machine into someone else's home so that someone else's dirty laundry can be washed."

I WAS BACK AT HERON'S NEST the next morning. As promised, Martin Comstock had scheduled a service call from a cable technician. By the time Barry Zito offered his first pitch in game three, I was ensconced in a recliner-rocker with the television in front of me and a laptop with high speed internet on a side table that I could swivel back and forth as needed. I was on codeine for the bruises, cuts and broken foot, but I still had to be careful watching the game. Twice, when Jorge Posada hit a home run to give the Yankees the lead and when Derek Jeter made his amazing flip play to prevent the tying run from scoring, I cheered with too much gusto and tried to lift my right arm too quickly. I fell back into the chair with pain and exhaustion. That night after the Yankee victory, I slept well, right there in the chair.

Watching the games and reading about them online was about all the conscious activity I could handle for a few days. All the River Rat Reporters came to see me at least once, but we did not discuss Napoleon's gold during these first visits and there were no stories. They were being patient with me, I could tell. Or, more accurately, they were giving me the opportunity to be patient with them; patience being something I had never been good at.

I did not read my mother's letter in those first few days of codeine-haze convalescence. I kept it, unopened, by my side on the swivel table until I could approach it with a clear mind.

I lived thus for a week, watching baseball, sleeping and, once I stopped taking the drugs, waiting for my head to clear. By the time the Yankees had beaten the A's and were in the process of dispatching the Seattle Mariners, I was ready.

September 16, 1978
My Dear Mike,

I need to write you, after all these years of friendship, to ask you a most important favor.

I'm already in your debt for you being there when I needed you on the night of the bicentennial fireworks. I was becoming lost that night. I was on the edge of doing something that would have changed my life, Charlie's life, and, most of all, Tommy and Pat's lives forever. I needed someone to talk to, someone who'd listen. And only listen, mind you, not tell me what to do like Nancy would've or what not to do like my brother would've. I needed you, Mike, and you were there for me and gave me the strength to persevere.

I have persevered and will continue to persevere. Charlie and I have the boys. We have Heron's Nest. We have some money. We dance occasionally. We have a marriage and the kept promise of fidelity that was our vow. Beyond that we have little.

Time? He's either working on the paper, diving, or poring over his maps. I'm with the boys or volunteering at the school.

Conversation? It's all superficial. What's for dinner? How's the water? What time are you coming back from Jack and Nancy's?

A few days ago he came home before I expected him and he caught me weeding through the mums singing "You Don't Bring Me Flowers." He looked at me for a minute and went up to his study without saying a word. For a moment I thought he might've become as deaf as his beloved Ludwig.

I know he still loves me, Mike, and I love him. Things are just different now than they used to be and, well, you know what the song says about that.

Ben and I have our friendship and love, too, different from the love Charlie and I share, different from the friendship you and I share. We *talk* together, Mike, really *talk*. I feel alive when I'm with him. I feel like I'm a real person, not just a mother and wife, although I praise God for those roles, too.

I know that you and I once talked, back in the early days, about how my attraction to him might be because of his outlaw status. I certainly understand the romanticism of that! But our attraction is deeper. It's like the water in our seaway, deep and clear and a joint product of God and man.

Still, though, we have not been physically intim-
ate together, nothing beyond holding hands and giving shoulder rubs anyway. We agree that our love is
on a different level, another plane. We are not in a
torrid, desperate love affair like you might see on
television. Yet I am still, to quote another song,
"torn between two lovers, feeling like a fool."

This fool needs you again, Mike. As you already
know or will soon find out, Charlie and Ben, my Ar-
thur and Lancelot, are finally asking the River Rat
Reporters to help them in their efforts to find Napoleon's gold. Only the gold is not an elusive holy
grail, or a mere figment of their imagination. It's out
there, Mike, it's real. I know that. I need you to
promise me that you will stand by them, be stead-
fast, be their Bors, as it were, and make sure they remain safe and true to their task.

This means a lot to me, Mike, more than I'm
able to explain right now. This means a lot to my
family, to Tommy and Pat, in ways that they may
never know.

I cannot tell you anything else right now. I need
to find more certain knowledge myself, and I'm at
work on a project to do just that. But when I've
completed enough of my work and I can tell you, I
promise I will. It may be next year, it may be in ten
years. I don't know. I promise you, though, when
I've completed enough I will tell you exactly why I
need you to stand by Charlie and Ben's side.

I ask you this with the full understanding that
you're a Napoleon's gold agnostic. I'm not asking
you to believe, or even to actively help Charlie and
Ben in their search. Just stand by them, Mike. For
now, just be there for them as you are for me.

Your dear and trusting friend,
Mary

Nothing terribly revelatory there to my mind, nothing completely shocking. I'd experienced my father's silences and solitude myself, and had always accepted that they were rooted in a combination of professional failure and personal frustration. I had already learned that my mother and Ben Fries were close, although I was relieved to hear that she had not cheated physically on my dad. I knew already from Mike Slattery that my mother is what drew my father and Ben Fries together in their quest. The letter shed no more information on that mystery.

I was able to hear my mother's voice in the letter, the voice of a real, multivalent, conflicted woman, and that was reason enough to have read it. I expected to hear from one of the other River Rats, my cousin Andrew most likely, what exactly my mother's project was. To this point I had found nothing obvious in Heron's Nest and was in no condition to resume the search now.

What surprised me most about the letter was Mike Slattery's refusal to believe my mother's insistence that Napoleon's gold was real. What was holding him back? Did he know something that no one else did?

I asked him these questions when he stopped by Heron's Nest the day after I read the letter.

"I believe that if there actually were a chest of gold at the bottom of the river we'd know more about it," he said. "Why is the ship it came on and the location of that ship such a mystery?"

"I was hoping the River Rat Reporters would answer that question."

"One of them may yet offer an answer to it."

"That can't be your only reason not to believe."

"No, it's not the only reason. Don't you think it's strange that somebody hasn't found it already? Do you know how many people dive on the Saint Lawrence, especially since the zebra mussels came in the 1990s? Do you know how many treasure hunters there are out there looking for it, especially after Captain Pembroke started telling the story in the late seventies? Surely somebody would have come across it by now."

"Andrew mentioned other teams of divers," I said.

"None of the Undies has yet to find it, either. Believe me, they have been looking."

"It's a really big river ..."

". . . and it's clear as gin now that the zebra mussels are here. I can understand not being able to find it back then, when the water was more weedy and murky as mud, but not now, not since the early nineties, not with what those zebras have done."

I sighed and moved on to the topic I really wanted to know more about. "Not even my mother was able to convince you."

Mike Slattery shook his head.

"What was her project?"

"That's not my tale," he said.

"Who's tale is it then?" I was growing frustrated with the Reporters' elusiveness.

Slattery paused for a moment before answering, "Andrew's. Your mother's project is part of Andrew's story." He paused again and saw my frustration. "Look, Tom, I know you're getting fed up with receiving the story one bit at a time from one person at a time. We take these stories seriously. You need to let us do it our way."

"Why, Mike?"

"Because the stories are our memories. For most of us older guys, our stories are all we have left of better days gone by. Andrew's the exception, of course. He's young, just a bit older than you. For the rest of us, our stories are part of who we are. All we ask, Tom, is that you respect that."

I agreed that it was the least I could do.

MY MOTHER'S LETTER ALSO PROMPTED ME to embark on a project of my own. With my mobility impaired, yet with a high speed internet connection at the ready, I decided to sit in my recliner and do some research, the first I had done since leaving New York City three weeks before. My topic was a well-worn one to other historians but a new one to me: Napoleon Bonaparte himself, the ultimate cause of my father's quest, the man whose shadow darkened this river and several lives on it, thousands of miles from where and two hundred years from when he commanded the fates of millions. So while listening to my father's Beethoven records, which Martin Comstock had moved downstairs for me, I got to work.

Using my alumni borrowing privileges I collected several general biographies from the State University at Clinton Falls library, requested a few specialized monographs through the interlibrary loan service, and, via online databases, found a couple dozen good scholarly articles on Napoleon's conquests. In doing all this I was guessing that Napoleon's gold had come from somewhere that he had conquered. Italy was its source, perhaps, or Egypt, although I knew that most of the booty from that campaign, most famously the Rosetta Stone, had ended up in English hands due to Horatio Nelson's defeat of the French fleet at the Battle of Aboukir Bay. Or maybe the gold came from one of his later achievements against the Austrians or his not-quite-successful invasion of Spain. Even though the latter campaign would become his self-described "ulcer," there was still plenty of conquistador gold in Madrid to satisfy his appetite.

I made a reasonable assumption that the gold was indeed gold and not a metaphor for something else, a person, for example, like Baigent, Leigh and Lincoln's Holy Grail, or a description of Napoleon's prose in a theoretically lost or concealed manuscript. Overall I felt good about my work as I commenced it. By the time the Yankees and Diamondbacks started game one of the World Series I had received some of my books through Fed Ex and some of the articles via my inbox. I was ready to begin writing a summary of Napoleon's conquests.

I also consulted Mindy McDonnell, who was busy teaching in Buffalo, and with whom I had been more or less out of touch since coming North. We had exchanged a few emails, but neither of us was fond of having an extended conversation in that medium. Talking on the phone was a different story. We could do that for hours. In this call I updated her on the stories I had heard so far from the River Rat Reporters. I gave her my take on river life during the off-season. I described my accident, making sure to avoid melodrama and remain optimistic about my recovery. We talked for over an hour about these things. Then I read her my mother's letter, and shared my initial impressions of it.

"Nothing revelatory?" Mindy said. "Are you kidding?"

I remained silent and let Mindy continue.

"Tom, it's true your mother was living a double life, but she was living it well. She had one foot in the traditional world with her housewife and mother roles. She had the other foot in the modern world of choice and freedom. She said she was torn between two lovers, but she didn't utter one syllable of regret for the situation."

"She said she felt like a fool," I said, feeling at the same time that Mindy was doing a better job defending my mother than I was.

"Of course she felt like a fool! She had no choice. Society demanded that a woman who enjoys a deep and satisfying friendship with a man other than her husband *must* feel like a fool!"

"I thought you were a traditionalist."

"I am a traditionalist. But since when does tradition equate with gender slavery? Your mother was deservedly proud of the fact that she and your father made a vow and kept it. Well, we know at least she did, at least until 1978. Who made the rule that she had to stay barefoot and pregnant in the kitchen under that vow, serving up every need of you and your brother and silently obeying your father's every command?"

"My mom and dad had so much more before this all happened. Before 1976."

"You're looking back to the idyllic days of your childhood in that vacationland Camelot of yours," Mindy said. "You were a kid, for goodness sake. Your biggest concerns were probably where to swim, what Hot Wheels to play with and what flavor Kool-Aid to drink. You had no idea what was happening between them. Nor should you have. They had Heron's Nest. They had you and your brother. They'd been married for, what, a dozen years by the time she wrote that letter?" I affirmed her math. "That's what they had, and in the big picture that's pretty good. People change. Relationships change. Never should a relationship demand a complete monopoly on the other partner's love. Your parents were fortunate that they were able to change together, despite circumstances that might have caused them to grow apart."

"Why do you think she wanted my father and Ben to search together for Napoleon's gold?"

"It was more than money, I bet. Maybe she knew Napoleon's gold would never be found, but also that the continuing search for it would ensure, for her, the attentions of the two men she loved. Without the quest, the two men she loved would have been pulled away from her. That, for her, would have been disaster."

"I never thought of it like that," I said.

"Of course not. You're a man. Your job is to solve problems."

"I can be sensitive," I said.

"Of course you can. But I'm not talking about sensitivity. Some people, mostly men, see the world in terms of problems and solutions. Other people, mostly women, including your mother, see the world in terms of situations and circumstances. We make the best of what we have and don't always try to change things for the better by fixing something we mistakenly perceive is wrong. I give your father credit, by the way, because he never tried to impose an unnecessary solution on an imagined problem that would've inevitably torn his life apart. He stuck to what he could manage—his paper, his family, his search for Napoleon's gold."

"He never found it," I said. "He failed."

"See? Problems and solutions. Let me guess. You're working on a problem right now."

"I am, actually. I'm trying to figure out what Napoleon's gold actually was and is. I'm going straight back to the sources." To be honest, I did feel more comfortable now that we were talking about problems and solutions. However, I wasn't about to admit that to Mindy right now.

"Good. That's a good, manageable project. Any theories?"

"I think it literally is a sunken chest of gold. I've just started considering where Napoleon might have gotten it."

"You mean who he raped to get it?"

I coughed. "I suppose that's another way of putting it."

"I think you're on the right track, then. Maybe Napoleon himself was particularly fond of one of his chests of booty, kept it away from his raving rabid troops, and saved it to be taken into exile with him." Mindy chuckled. "The irony would be that the booty made it through while the rapist didn't."

"My mother loved Napoleon you know," I teased.

Mindy was on a roll and would not be denied. "No wonder. He was on the same knife's edge of being pulled towards both the past and present as she was. He had to figure out how to rule like an old regime tyrant, while at the same time fooling everyone else that he actually believed his own revolutionary propaganda. His conundrum was about how he would hold onto power rather than subvert it."

"Please don't hide your feelings about the man," I said.

"I won't."

"That's one of the more remarkable characteristics about him, you know. Even today he can elicit passionate opinions in people, opinions both favorable and unfavorable."

"Well, you know where I stand."

"Clearly."

"It sounds like you're on the right track. You want to e-mail me your findings?"

"I'd rather show them to you in person," I said. "I considered coming out to Buffalo to do some hands-on library work, but that won't be happening anytime soon with my broken foot."

"I almost forgot!" Mindy said. I could hear her hand slap the table. "I have a conference in Syracuse Monday and Tuesday the week after next. Will you be around before that?"

"Where would I go?" I asked. "Or more accurately, how would I get there?"

"Excellent! I'll come see you Friday evening, and I can stay until I have to go down to Syracuse Monday morning. Should I call a hotel?"

"You have your choice of guest rooms here. Heron's Nest will welcome you."

"Will I get to meet your new friends?"

"I can find out. On Saturday we can definitely go to Jimmy's and watch the Yanks."

"I have to warn you. I'm rooting for Arizona," she said. I could hear the teasing delight in her voice. "I'd be happy to watch the Yanks lose with you."

Part Two

Each year ... we have drawn a strange comfort from a timeless world compounded of earth, air, fire and water. Living close prisoner to the four classic elements, or living the close prisoner of a religion, helps anyone to be free to be himself. Twenty years ago we did not know this, but from the first moment we stood on the ancient stone beneath the wind shaped pines and looked down miles of glinting ice and water, we were sure that we were in the presence of a mystery.

John Keats
Of Time and an Island

Chapter Fourteen

I DID NOT HAVE TO WAIT LONG to watch the Yankees lose. They quickly got down two games to none against Arizona, soundly beaten both times, and it was obvious that they were flat, perhaps exhausted by the distractions of the terrorist attacks and aftermath that affected them like it did no other playoff team. But they had been down 2-0 against Oakland, too, and had come back to win that series.

I hoped the tide would turn when the teams played in New York, with Roger Clemens on the mound and with President Bush scheduled to deliver the ceremonial first pitch. Game three of the World Series was scheduled for Tuesday. I spent my time until then working hard on my research, wanting to kill time and conclude something before sharing my work with Mindy.

After a day and a half of work I arrived at the following hypothesis. Napoleon's gold was captured in either Italy (1796), Malta (1798), Egypt (1798-99), Austria (1805), Spain (1808) or Prussia (1810). Of these possibilities, Egypt was my best guess. The rationale behind the theory was simply the massive amount of gold available in Egypt and the fact that several French ships did get through to Marseille before the French lost the battle of Aboukir Bay and suffered under a British blockade.

Wherever it came from, I thought, the gold stayed in France during the invasion of Russia in 1812 and the Waterloo campaign of 1814—otherwise it would have been lost. During those last few weeks of his rule in 1815 it was probably in Paris, or perhaps at Malmaison, Josephine's chateau, where the now former emperor said a final goodbye to his mother as he wavered over the decision to flee to America or fight one more day.

At some point in late June or early July 1815 it was taken to the coast and loaded onto the mysterious corvette that sailed west in anticipation of its master. From there, the evidence sails out of the realm of supposition, through conjecture and into sheer guesswork. By late afternoon Tuesday I knew that no reading could help me pass that boundary. I could find no proof for what Ben Fries had told Mike Slattery and the others about Captain Terry and the chase to Brockville.

I also knew that what I had come up with in my frantic page-turning and note-taking amounted to nothing more than what I had known already, nothing more than a list of Napoleon's major conquests that, hopefully, even a first-year Western Civilization student could recite. Where was I, a trained and reasonably experienced historian, to turn? Was my sour mood just a factor of the Yankees losses and my anxiety over the upcoming games? Was I getting cabin fever? Were my feelings being dragged down again by current events? It was late Tuesday afternoon, and I had a highly accomplished historian scheduled to arrive at my door in a few days. I hoped Mindy would be able to help.

But by Tuesday evening I was to receive unexpected guidance from elsewhere, as the River Rat Reporters resumed their tales.

"May I come in?" Raphael Ostend shouted with the door open a crack, his voice rising above the strains of Beethoven's violin concerto, which I played thinking about my father after reading my mother's letter again.

"Yes, please," I said, setting Tulard's biography of Napoleon on my swivel table and turning the volume down with a remote.

"Are you in good spirits?" he asked as he entered the kitchen and took off his coat.

"I'm nervous about the Yanks," I said.

"You know, baseball is useful in times like these when other, far more important things are getting all our attention," Ostend said. "Diversions are necessary in difficult times. They can clear the mind rather effectively. May I sit?"

"Absolutely." I started to get up to neaten my piles of books, articles and notes on the couch and chairs, but Ostend waved me back to my recliner and moved a chair in from the kitchen.

"You're hard at work," he said.

"Investigating Napoleon's gold," I said.

"Trying to find out where it is?"

"Trying to find out *what* it is, and where it came from. I'm stuck in murky waters, though."

"Ah, yes. 'Waters shrouded by the uncharted mists of antiquity, where fact becomes legend, and legend becomes myth.'"

"Sounds like Carlyle," I said.

Raphael Ostend laughed quietly. "It was your father," he said to my surprise. "He could have been plagiarizing Carlyle, though, with a bit of Tolkien thrown in for good measure. What have you discovered?"

I recited to him my pedestrian research efforts, and since verbalizing them made their inadequacies even more evident I made up a lame excuse of not being able to access enough useful materials because of my limited mobility.

He responded with polite nods, then with a surprising fact. "You know, my family was in Vienna during the French occupation."

"They were?"

"In fact, my great-great-great grandparents knew Beethoven. They loved him, as both a person and a musician, despite his irascibility. They attended several of his premiers, including the *Eroica* and Fifth Symphonies, and this ..." Ostend waved his hand around the room to indicate the music, "the Violin Concerto, my personal favorite."

"You probably know the story of the *Eroica*, right?" I asked, excited about sharing something I had found in my research. "How Beethoven initially dedicated it to Napoleon, but scratched out the dedication when he heard the news that Napoleon had become emperor?"

"Of course I know it. My ancestors lived through that story. After Austerlitz they shared Beethoven's grief. They hated Bonaparte and his occupying army."

I thought for a moment. "So, in theory, Napoleon's gold could have belonged to your family at one time?"

"I don't see why not. But then again, Bonaparte robbed from so many people that it wouldn't much matter where his gold came from."

"Are there any documents? Journals? Letters?"

"Letters that describe a company of Alsatian thugs, braying out *La Marseillaise*, breaking down the gates of the Ostend Castle and stealing all the gold from the depths of the keep?" I nodded in anticipation. Raphael Ostend offered a slight smile. "No. There aren't."

"Oh, Mindy will love you," I said.

"Mindy?"

"Mindy McDonnell. A graduate school friend. She's coming to visit this weekend. You share a similar sense of teasing humor, and a jaundiced view of Napoleon."

Ostend picked up some of my notes on the Egyptian campaign and thumbed through them. He looked at one page for longer than a glance and then nodded. "Why are you taking this tack?"

"I'm tracing genealogy. I'm trying to establish my roots so I don't get blown over in the breeze, so I can get a firm, steady grip on what I know. The genealogy of Napoleon's gold."

"How much can you know?"

I sighed. "So far, I don't know much. That's the problem. I can't seem to find my way through those uncharted mists of legend."

" 'Uncharted mists of antiquity,' " he corrected, " 'where fact becomes legend and legend becomes myth.' " He paused. "Here's a question for you. If Napoleon's gold became legend and myth only when it came here and sank into our water, does it matter so much where it came from?"

"It might. Yes, to an historian, it does."

"Why?"

"I just told you. Genealogy."

"I can understand the genealogy reference because that is, in effect, what you're doing. Given your family's involvement, the reference may be even more appropriate than you realize. My question is, though, why does it matter to history? Isn't a chest of gold, no matter how valuable, just an object, or a collection of them? Isn't a chest of gold just a chest of gold?"

"It affected people's lives," I insisted. "It changed people. Ask Billy Masterson. Ask Jim Pembroke. I don't know, ask yourself."

Raphael Ostend nodded coolly. "Napoleon's gold did change people's lives, irrevocably so. It changed mine. But have you found any evidence that this chest of gold mattered one iota before it became part of our river bottom?" Ostend could read my frown. "There you have it. What Napoleon's gold was before it became myth is far less relevant than what it is as myth."

"I'm not going to relegate something this important to the status of mere myth."

"Why is it so important? Why did your father and Ben Fries want so badly to find it?"

"Because my mother wanted them to search for it."

"That just reduces the same question down one level. Why did your mother want to find it?"

"It would be worth a lot of money. Millions."

"Take it from someone who has enough money to know. It's not as valuable as it seems. I'm confident your mother knew that as well."

"There's the intrinsic historical value of it, then. If it can be found, examined, catalogued, it won't have to be relegated to the status of mere myth."

"First, do you think your mother cared about what a professional historian would do with this particular relic from the past?"

"I don't know yet."

"Second, why relegate it? Why not elevate it?"

"That's what I'm trying to do, elevate Napoleon's gold to the higher status of history."

Raphael Ostend shook his head. "In my opinion, you've got your categories backwards, Tom, your priorities in disarray."

"What do you mean?"

"Let me ask you another question, if I may. On what basis is the resurrection of Jesus the Christ history? What evidence is there that the carpenter's son, after being executed by the Romans, rose on the third day and appeared to Mary Magdalene, then to the twelve apostles, then to the four hundred others and then to Saul of Tarsus? How would you successfully argue against those who claim that Jesus the Christ's resurrection was a myth? If it were a myth, if it could be proven that the testimony of all those who allegedly saw the resurrected Jesus was mistaken, would the impact of the story on your life be lessened?"

"No."

"What basis do you have for that judgment? How would Jesus the Christ's resurrection matter if it was no longer, as you put it, an elevated fact of history?"

"Because Jesus' life would still have meaning. His teachings, his promise that the kingdom of God will arrive. His spiritual defiance of Roman power. The Gospels would still have meaning. Jesus' life and death would still have meaning." But I could feel the argument slipping away, and Raphael Ostend knew it.

"The Gospels? Be honest with me, Tom. Are you fool enough to think that those four disparate accounts written by four anonymous men can withstand even the most rudimentary tests of historical scrutiny?" He moved forward in his chair. "Assume the story is myth. Tell me why the resurrection of Jesus the Christ matters to you. Tell me, without using the word history."

"Because I believe the resurrection's message," I said, knowing full well the pit of historical uncertainty into which I had just cast myself. I nearly shouted the words, "Because I believe that through Christ God opened for me and for those I love, including my dead parents and dead brother, the way to eternal life."

We were both silent for several moments before Ostend spoke.

"Belief." He said the word slowly, and let it hang there for half a minute as he sat back in the chair and crossed his legs. "More human action has been motivated by belief than by any other stimulus. Belief, as a trigger for human action, some good, some bad, is to fact what a mountain is to a molehill. Facts may or may not be important. If one wants to truly understand human action, one must contend with belief."

"What do you believe?" I asked, my voice soft with humility after having been beaten in an argument, and soft with vulnerability after having revealed my deepest religious convictions.

"About the resurrection of Jesus the Christ?"

"Sure. For starters."

"I believe Jesus was a great man. A prophet and a healer. A teacher and a spiritual genius. I do not believe that Jesus died for my or for anyone else's sins. You might call me a Gnostic."

"Do you go to church?"

"I come over to Wellesley and attend Densmore on high holy days and for concerts. Also, I enjoy the vespers services over at Half Moon Bay. It is our culture, after all."

"Okay," I said hesitantly. "What do you believe about Napoleon's gold?"

Raphael Ostend stood and went over to the small liquor cabinet on the other side of the room. "May I?" he asked. I nodded. I waited quietly for him to sit back down. I watched him pour a glass of my father's scotch that had been sitting in the cabinet untouched for five years, and take a sip. Then he said, while looking into the glass, "When it comes to Napoleon's gold, I learned at an early age to believe everything my grandmother taught me."

Chapter Fifteen

RAPHAEL OSTEND, sipping the scotch and alternately sitting on the kitchen chair and pacing the floor, told his story.

"Let me begin by explaining my reactions to two films I watched countless times as a child. Both were about ancient Egyptian magic in the modern world. Both starred the great Boris Karloff, whom I once met, incidentally, here in the Thousand Islands, when I was a young man. One film was *The Mummy* and the other was *The Ghoul*. Do you know them?"

I thought I had seen *The Mummy*, but could not recall it nearly as well as I could the Scooby-Doo episode that featured a mummy searching for an ancient coin, or the recent film version with Brendan Fraser. I had never even heard of *The Ghoul*. I shook my head no.

"In *The Mummy*, Karloff plays an ancient Egyptian prince named Imhotep, who comes back to life when his tomb is raided by British archaeologists. Imhotep, posing as Ardath Bey, hypnotizes and seduces Helen Grosvenor, the reincarnation of his ancient Egyptian lover. The climax of the film comes when Helen's other love interest, Frank Whemple, attempts to save her from the ceremony of death and resurrection that Bey is about to perform upon her. Frank Whemple succeeds, but only because a statue of Isis strikes Bey down in anger at Bey's sacrilege. In *The Mummy*, the ancient magic is real, and it is the agent of the villain's undoing. It's through magic that justice triumphs over evil.

"*The Ghoul*, although seemingly similar in setting and

content, is actually very different in everything but form. In that film, Karloff plays Professor Henry Morlant, an Egyptologist who fully subscribes to the magical practices of the civilization he studies. Morlant is dying, and he has a jewel that will bring immortality to him upon the death of his earthly body. But when he dies the jewel is stolen. He comes back to find the thief, but not in the way we first think. As in *The Mummy*, there is a scene in the film's climax that involves the statue of an Egyptian divinity. This time, the god is Anubis, the god of embalming and entrance into the afterlife. This time, in complete contrast to *The Mummy*, the scene is devoid of magic and full of human agency. Magic in *The Ghoul* is trickery, is made a mockery of, and is used as a fraud to further the aims of criminals.

"These were my grandmother's films. Like all the copies in her collection they were 35-millimeter films, which we used to watch in a small theater either in my grandparents' Manhattan apartment or in our family home up here. Grandmother encouraged me to watch films just as much as she encouraged me to read. Books might give me knowledge, she said, but films will give me feeling. She was very keen on what I felt about these two films in particular.

"She asked me one day which film I liked better. My immediate reply was *The Mummy*. She asked me why. I explained to her that I found it more real than *The Ghoul*, although I couldn't explain why this was so.

"This was the situation for several years until one day— I must have been in my teens—it struck me. *The Mummy* was more real because it took its own material seriously. It accepted as a given, that Egyptian magic was valid and could affect the lives of the story's characters. It didn't try to rationalize or skeptically explain away magic as some human sleight of hand or, worse, ignorant superstition. It allowed the viewer to wrestle with the possibility that what was happening on screen was real."

"I got the same feeling while watching *The Amityville Horror* for the first time," I said.

"Yes, I suppose the comparison is legitimate. Remember, Tom, that *The Mummy* had few predecessors. Remember, too, that the scare of Tutankhamen's curse was fresh in the minds of many when both films premiered in the early 1930's. People all over the English speaking world were debating whether the curse was real or imaginary, whether Egyptian magic was real or imaginary."

"Why was your grandmother interested in your opinion?"

"It was a test," Ostend said. He stood, and, holding the glass of scotch, slowly paced back and forth in front of the chair. "She was testing me to find out if I would be receptive to her philosophical ideas. She called them that, philosophical ideas, although most people today would call them occult teachings or, worse, witchcraft."

"Don't tell me she believed she was Nefertiti reborn," I said.

"No, no, nothing pedestrian like that. Grandmother was a diviner, a seer. She could perceive things, read into people. She could learn lessons from nature that most people couldn't even begin to understand. Again, in the modern era, dominated by a limiting rationality, she was dismissed by some as a witch."

"You're one too?" The surprise, shock even, in my voice was evident, although I tried hard to hide it.

"No, not me. I experience déjà vu occasionally. Grandmother called them moments of clarity. But I don't possess one one-thousandth of the power she had. She was much more than this, mind you, but as a practitioner of astrology, geomancy, hydromancy, oneiromancy and scrying, among several other spiritual arts, she was an unsurpassed expert for many years.

"Grandmother was famous in some circles. During the summer season, men and women by the dozen came to visit her and hear her prophecies. Karloff was one of them. He wanted to discern whether he had anything left to contribute to the world of cinema. She told him he had one more great performance left in him. No doubt this turned out to be his voice work as the Grinch in the animated version of Dr. Seuss's tale, a classic performance by any standard.

"Grandmother would charge nothing for her insights, but she would conduct a long interview with every seeker to learn what his or her intentions were. If they sought her advice for their own personal profit or material gain she would not help them. If they sought her out for any other reason, to help solve a personal problem, heal a relationship, discern a way through a personal crisis or do good for others, she would stop at nothing to find the clearest route to certain knowledge."

"You believe that what she did actually worked?" I asked.

"I already told you that Grandmother called her knowledge philosophy. By this she meant exactly what the word means—the love of wisdom. But what is wisdom, Tom? Intellectual knowledge only? Facts arrived at by applying the scientific method of observation and conclusion? Grandmother rejected this limited, materialistic understanding in favor of a broader, truer definition of philosophy. To her, the love of wisdom was a deep appreciation of all knowledge, whether it was acquired through the logic of syllogisms or the repeated efforts of experimentation or the work of the mind, or, as in her case, the work of the soul. To Grandmother, this, the work of the soul, was, in the modern world, the lost component to a complete and true definition and practice of philosophy."

Raphael Ostend laughed quietly. "She used to say that philosophy, without the work of the soul, was like music on the page that was never played. It was there, it existed, but without the aural element it had little, if any, meaning. She also liked to cite Beethoven. Once he became deaf he could still hear with his soul, you know. That's why his music, coming straight from his soul, connects so readily with our souls."

"That also clarifies what you were saying earlier about elevating Napoleon's gold to the level of myth."

"Yes it does," Raphael Ostend said. "Grandmother insisted that the spiritual qualities of the world could be identified and interpreted just as thoroughly as the material qualities were, if one had the natural inclination towards the spiritual realm and took the time to learn the appropriate techniques."

"She was famous? Up here?"

"On the river, in Montreal, in New York, in Pittsburgh. She was famous to many men and women who longed for something more than what scientific materialism could provide. People from all stations of life came to see her. Wealthy capitalists. Explorers. Artists. River pilots. Reverends. Hollywood Actors. Military men. I was exposed to the great world beyond and all its possibilities by the people I met through Grandmother."

"Excuse me if this sounds rude, but your family is most famous for making hats."

"That's how we make money," Ostend said with a slight smile, "but neither making hats nor making money is or has been the most important pursuit in my family."

"What is?" I asked.

"Truth."

"That explains why you were a friend of my father's," I said.

"And of all the other River Rat Reporters," he added.

"What did your grandmother teach you about Napoleon's gold?" I asked. "With all your talk of spirituality, I'm beginning to think that the gold wasn't real gold after all. A holy grail type metaphor, maybe."

"It was no metaphor," Raphael Ostend said. "It was quite real, although I'd rather show you than tell you what

Grandmother knew about it. The second reason I visited you in person was to see how well you were doing, to see if you're in good enough health to attend."

"Attend what?"

He looked surprised that I did not already know. "The Ostend Ball, of course, held every year on the first Saturday of November at Valhalla. It was at the first one, held in 1886 to welcome home Captain Doctor Charles Obadiah Smithson from Egypt, that Grandmother initially became aware of Napoleon's gold. It's Smithson's tale and Grandmother's reaction to it that I want to share with you on Saturday. Can you come?"

We were silent for a moment as Raphael Ostend waited for my RSVP. I was doing some quick math in my head. "1886?" I asked. "How old was your grandmother?"

"Twenty-three. She married Grandfather in 1884."

"When were your parents born?"

"My father was much older than my mother. He was born in 1890."

"And you?"

"1925."

"You're seventy-six!?" Even with the white hair, he did not look a day over sixty.

"Seventy-six and a half. Longevity runs in my family, Tom. Grandmother lived almost through her hundred-and-second year. My father died at ninety-nine. Even those numbers are relative, of course." Ostend tipped the glass of my father's scotch. "Will you be able to come?"

"I guess so. I feel pretty good." I smiled. "Can I bring Mindy?"

"You'd better tell her the party is formal. Also tell her the party hasn't changed much, if at all, since the first one a hundred and fifteen years ago. I make it a point to inform new guests of such things so they're not overwhelmed when they arrive. Consistency is very important in my family. As for you, your father's tuxedo is probably still in his closet. If

I can take it with me today, I can have my seamstress alter the pant leg to accommodate your cast."

"Of course," I said, not knowing my father even had a tuxedo.

"Splendid. I'll drop it off for you at Jimmy's. It'll be waiting for you on Friday. I won't be there, of course, as I have too many preparations to complete, but your tuxedo will."

"Thank you," I said.

Raphael Ostend went upstairs and returned with my father's tuxedo, put on his coat, then rinsed out the glass he had used for scotch. Before leaving he said, "Your research is correct about several things, Tom. You're definitely on the right track."

THE CONVERSATION WITH RAPHAEL OSTEND sent my research in a different direction. Or, to be more precise, two directions that promised to converge on Saturday night at Valhalla, Ostend's island home. First, who was Doctor Charles Obadiah Smithson, the guest of honor at the initial Ostend Ball? Second, what could I discover about Lady Ostend, as Raphael's grandmother had preferred to call herself? I committed myself to answering these two questions as well as I could before Mindy arrived Friday evening and before we attended the affair on Saturday.

Captain Charles Obadiah Smithson, M.D. was a Canadian, appointed assistant surgeon to the Royal Military Academy in Kingston, Canada's West Point, in 1870. He served under Garnet Wolseley on the Red River expedition in what would become the province of Manitoba, a terribly difficult campaign of a thousand miles across rugged and dangerous territory. Under Wolseley's leadership and Smithson's medical care, the Canadians successfully suppressed the Métis rebellion there and repelled several American incursions from the south. Afterwards he organized the Canadian artillery corps. He served the Red Cross in the conflict between Russia and Turkey. He also visited Washington, D.C., to study what the American Army had learned about medical organization and practices during the Civil War, and applied what he learned to the Canadian military.

In 1884, Lord Garnet Wolseley was given command of the Nile Expedition, the purpose of which was to bolster the defenses of Khartoum, Sudan, a city under siege by Muslim Mahdists rebels. Wolseley had been so impressed by Smithson in Manitoba that he immediately called on the doctor to join the force of four hundred Canadian voyageurs he had recruited to help him navigate up the Nile River from Alexandria. The Canadians were chosen, as you might guess, because of the expertise they had acquired living and working on the Saint Lawrence and other Canadian rivers. It was the first overseas mission for any Canadian force under the British flag. Smithson served admirably in Egypt, as he had in Manitoba, although the Nile expedition was a failure overall and Khartoum was taken by the Mahdist rebels.

His adventurous life settled down after that. He returned to Canada in 1886 to serve as Chief Medical Officer at the Royal Military College in Kingston. It was his return to the Thousand Islands' first city that made him the guest of honor at the inaugural Ostend Ball in 1886.

Until his death in 1903, Smithson was also a prominent historian. Among the founders of the Kingston Historical Society, with a private collection of manuscripts and monographs that was the envy of many public institutions, Smithson authored several important articles on Canadian history, including two or three on the Napoleonic era.

So the connections certainly existed—his service in Egypt in 1884-85, almost ninety years after Napoleon was there; his historical investigations that must have made him familiar with the story of Napoleon's gold; his work at the Royal Military College which probably put him in contact with the French émigrés across the river in Cape Vincent. I would have to wait until Saturday night to find out if any of these connections were relevant.

I would also have to wait a few days to learn more about Lady Ostend, because information about her on the internet was scarce. She was mentioned in several new age articles as one of the most sought after diviners in the American Gilded Age. She was mentioned in several dispatches from the *New York Times* Thousand Islands correspondent as one of the most gracious hostesses on the river, especially after the Ostend Ball had been running a few years. The *Times*, however, missed the more important story, neglecting to mention Lady Ostend's spiritual work.

Most curiously, she was noted on the website of the Philosophical Research Society as an important benefactor to the Institute for Applied Philosophical Research at my alma mater, the State University of New York at Clinton Falls. This information also was absent from her *New York Times* obituary.

I discovered more about the Philosophical Research Society easily enough from the "About Us" page on their web site. The Society was founded by Manly P. Hall in 1934 in Los Angeles, California. It remains one of the most important libraries in the world for the study of spirituality, metaphysics, the occult sciences, and Freemasonry.

I had no success with the Institute for Applied Philosophical Research. I Googled it, and was directed to the home page, but all that contained was a banner and a log-in field. I tried my old SUNY username and password, still active thanks to alumni privileges, but was denied access, emphatically, with a screen that told me so in bright yellow Helvetica on a black background.

Might Mindy know more? I was impatient for her arrival on Friday evening, and even more impatient for our date to the Ostend Ball the following night. But I had the good fortune of being distracted by the Yankees' three tremendous victories back at the Stadium, especially by the most remarkable win in game four, when Derek Jeter hit the first November home run in baseball history to tie the series at two games apiece. After another memorable come-from-behind victory on Thursday, and with my father's Beethoven symphonies as my Friday soundtrack, I was nothing short of ebullient.

Chapter Sixteen

MY GOOD CHEER CONTINUED as I joined the other River Rat Reporters, minus Raphael Ostend, at Jimmy's on Friday evening, my transportation provided courtesy of Martin Comstock.

"Does your friend know where to meet us?" Comstock asked as he held the barroom door open for me and my crutches.

"She knows. She's been to Alex Bay several times with family. I gave her detailed directions just in case. Landmarks and all."

"Good man."

The Reporters were generous with their salutations, welcoming me back to the table, praising me for how well I was getting around with the crutches, coaching me on how to better perform some of life's other necessities, razzing me about Mindy's visit, echoing my excitement for the Yankees' comeback.

When I asked if I would hear a story that evening, Martin Comstock shook his head and explained we would be taking a night off from that, since I had other things to think about once Mindy arrived and since Raphael Ostend still "held the floor," and would continue to do so until his story was completed on Saturday night at Valhalla.

When I asked how we would deal with the scheduling conflict of game six on the same night, my cousin Andrew answered that he had already taken care of it by installing a satellite dish on the island and a high definition television in

Valhalla's smoking room, where we could retire two or three at a time—no more, per Raphael Ostend's instructions—to watch an inning or two of the game.

"Take it from someone who's failed in this department and has since learned his lesson," Jim Pembroke said. "Do not retire to watch any of the game without your date's permission. She takes priority."

"She's wearing a Diamondbacks colored gown," I said. "She might be in the smoking room as often as the rest of us, rooting for Arizona."

"Ouch," Mike Slattery said.

"We'll be tapin' the game, too," Billy Masterson added. "You can watch it later and fast forward through the commercials and pitchin' changes. You won't miss an inning."

"Thank you, gentlemen," I said, "for the advice and for the videotape."

We spent the next hour talking about baseball, the anthrax scare and how President Bush should continue to respond to the 9/11 attacks. I was surprised to hear a general skepticism and lack of enthusiasm for Operation Infinite Justice, or Operation Enduring Freedom or, in Mike Slattery's words, "whatever the hell they'll decide to call it next week." Mike then went into a long discourse on how Afghanistan had been a graveyard of empires for centuries, and would probably remain so for the Americans as well. I kept quiet as I was too busy watching the time, sipping alternately—and only sipping—from glasses of beer and water, glancing out the window at cars passing by Jimmy's and parallel parking on the street, and generally biding my time until Mindy arrived. I was also thankful that none of the Undies were there to spoil Mindy's appearance.

She arrived just a few minutes after seven. Martin Comstock greeted her with the same polite introductions he had extended to me. These were followed by polite inquiries into the ride across the Thruway and up I-81, and, finally, invitations to have, in Billy Masterson's words, "a beer or several."

As for my greeting, Mindy and I hugged as soon as she walked in the door, with my crutches awkwardly in the way but providing safety from a too obvious public display of affection. I watched her as the inquiries and introductions and invitations proceeded—we had not seen each other in almost a year—looked at her hair that she'd let grow past her shoulders and had highlighted with a hint of blonde, at the silk scarf that matched the burgundy lipstick she wore, at those grey eyes flecked with blue that had always attracted and sometimes mystified me. She caught me out of the corner of her eye, and while commenting on her thirst after the long drive gave me a smile and a wink before turning back to Mike Slattery and his question of what drink she preferred.

"Whatever's in the pitcher," Mindy said. Jim Pembroke had already gotten her a glass and had poured it full. "I love draft beer as long as they keep the taps clean," she added.

"Laurie, did you clean the pipes?" Pembroke asked. "Tom Flanagan has a special guest here tonight."

The bartender responded, "Twice as often as Comstock does over at Castello's."

"Great!" Mindy said, unbuttoning her coat.

All the Reporters' eyes were on her, and they gave loud sports fan groans when she revealed her Diamondbacks sweatshirt. They, along with several other bar patrons who were watching the arrival of an unfamiliar face, laughed and even clapped their hands when she handed me, with an exaggerated kiss on the cheek, the small National League Champion pennant she had been hiding in her coat sleeve. I felt myself blush with a combination of embarrassment and appreciation. It was, no doubt, exactly the response she had intended.

WITHIN FIFTEEN MINUTES WE WERE DISCUSSING more important

things than baseball again. Mike Slattery had started the shift in conversation by asking Mindy what kind of historian she was.

"The kind who studies the past," she said with a smile.

"Can you elaborate?" Mike asked.

"Seamus McNally, my mentor at Clinton Falls, used to say that history is everything that happened the day before yesterday. I agree with that. I study it all."

Billy Masterson nodded. "I like that. It's true. You need at least a day to let it all sink in."

"You have a Ph.D., right?" Mike Slattery continued. Mindy nodded. "What's your concentration?"

"My dissertation was on the intersection of the Women's Rights and Abolitionist movements in antebellum upstate New York. I teach a seminar on that once every couple of years, but I also teach the American history survey, both parts, the Gilded Age, twentieth-century American foreign policy, and a new course on contemporary American female culture. Since 9/11 I've also been team-teaching a seminar on America's image overseas."

"Damn," said Jim Pembroke. "You're busy."

Martin Comstock said, "Well, you probably need more than a day to get a grip on those 9/11 events."

"That is tough," Mindy said. "We're doing a lot of journaling. I want my students to be conscious of the fact that they are, right now, living through history."

Billy Masterson turned to address me. "Didn't you live through that shi ... I mean stuff, up close and personal?"

"I did," I said. "I was in Brooklyn, just across the river from the attack. It was horrible. I still have nightmares about being on the roof of my apartment building and watching the smoke. Sometimes I can still smell it, or at least the memory of it." I forced myself to smile.

"I'll tell you one thing. This war'll be the end of life as we know it up here," Billy said.

"Why's that?" Mindy asked.

"'Cuz they'll try to shut up the border tighter'n a clam shell," Billy replied. "They'll be stoppin' boats and scannin' retinas before you know it."

"They can't stop every boat," Mindy said. "Can they?"

"They're too undermanned for that," Andrew said. "Oh, they'll try some things. They'll put some new regs in place. They'll tighten up the crossing at the bridges. Maybe have the troops from Fort Drum on extra alert for border emergencies. They can't stop us from crossing on the water, though. Didn't work during Prohibition. Won't work now."

"Still," Jim Pembroke said, "things are changing. There's already talk among some river people of odd things happening here and there. Unmarked government freighters passing through in the night. Too many small craft still on the river, even though the season's over. Some say there's submarines patrolling off Cape Vincent. Andrew's Undee friends are getting restless. They want some Muslim blood."

"Undies?" Mindy asked.

"Undesirables," I said. "Andrew's name for a certain group of people on the river who never saw eye-to-eye with my father. From what I've seen I think Jim's right. The Undies are getting restless."

"Rumors born of high anxiety," Mike Slattery said. "As one of the greatest of men once put it, the only thing to fear is fear itself."

"Well, let's not put a damper on this occasion by discussing the uncertainties of the future," Martin Comstock said. "Think about what we've got. Mindy and Tom's reunion. The Ostend Ball. Let's talk about something else tonight."

Mindy nodded in agreement and complied. "Mike, did I answer your question?"

"Sort of. You told me what you teach, but I'm sure different historians approach each of those topics in different ways." Slattery paused and took a sip of beer. "Let me put it like this. As you probably know, Tom here is doing some research on Napoleon's gold. From watching him work it seems like he's taking an inductive approach, collecting evidence and laying it all out there, drawing conclusions carefully and only when enough evidence has been gathered to allow him to properly do so. Do you do that, or do you fill in the blanks imaginatively, based on your understanding of human nature? In other words, do you gather all the materials before you build, or do you build on top of what's already there, allowing room for creativity?"

"Damn, Slattery," my cousin Andrew said. "Where'd you come up with all that?"

"B.A. in philosophy," Mike Slattery said.

"B.A. in B.S. is more like it," Jim Pembroke commented.

"Besides," Slattery continued, "the second way, the deductive way, is how Charlie Flanagan did it."

"There's a place for each style," Mindy said. "It's more like a continuum than a hard and fast distinction. For example, Tom got as deep as he did into the Radisson family story by using the second technique. His father's way."

"I also learned it from you," I said.

"How would you approach the topic of Napoleon's gold?" Martin Comstock asked, addressing Mindy. "I assume Tom told you enough for you to form an opinion."

"First, from what Tom told me, it seems reasonable to conclude that there is a chest of gold somewhere on the river's floor. I probably would have gone about my research the same way Tom's father did, by looking, mapping things out, talking to people he knew, gathering evidence, making suppositions, keeping my eyes open for the lucky break. Most of all, I would have recognized that sometimes we historians have to settle in and prepare ourselves for the long haul. Sometimes answers don't come easily." Mindy took a sip of beer. "Is there a deadline for Tom's research?"

"Not really, as far as we're concerned," Martin Comstock said. He glanced at Jim Pembroke and then at Mike

Slattery, which told me there was more to his answer than he was letting on. "He's got two and a half more stories to hear, then he can do whatever he wants with the information."

"Mindy thinks I'm too much of a problem solver," I said.

"What's wrong with that?" Andrew asked.

"In your line of work, nothing," Mindy said diplomatically. "Things get lost in history, and we can't just go somewhere and order a new document or picture like you can go order sheetrock or a few two-by-sixes. Sometimes historians have to be satisfied with where we are and use our imaginations to invent."

"That makes sense," Andrew said.

"Tom told you our stories?" Jim Pembroke asked.

"He gave me summaries. Enough to make me curious, and definitely enough to whet my appetite for whatever's going to happen tomorrow evening."

"Oh, that'll surprise you," Billy Masterson said.

"By the way," Martin Comstock said. "I have a message from Raphael for the two of you. He's invited you to stay overnight. He said to make sure you bring a change of clothes."

I looked at Mindy and smiled. "Is it some sort of ritualistic thing?" I asked. "Something you guys do every year at the Ostend Ball?"

"It's a story," Mike Slattery said, "just like the rest of our stories. Each of us heard it, in one form or another, upon initially attending the Ostend Ball. That's the only time Raphael tells it, once a year at the most, on the first Saturday in November, and only when a new guest is there to hear it. This year that new guest is you. And you, too, Mindy."

"I suppose he has his reasons," Mindy said.

"Indeed he does," said Martin Comstock. "Indeed he does."

WE WERE BACK at Heron's Nest by nine. I gave Mindy a voice-guided tour of the place as I stood in the living room, supported by my crutches as she walked around, taking it all in and asking questions about my family and about my memories of specific rooms.

I told her my personal favorite memory, which was the time my father and uncle Jack spent an hour chasing a large bat around the house, both upstairs and down. My father eventually caught the bat in the screened porch with a fishing net, and released it outside. But the same one worked its way back into the house a half hour later. My uncle Jack got it that time, snapping it with a towel as if he were a high school athlete in the locker room. He took the stunned animal outside again, through the kitchen door, and returned through the screened porch wearing a black canvas tarp around his shoulders and face. He pulled the tarp down, revealing a pair of fake fangs that he had dipped in ketchup while he was out in the kitchen. Speaking in an excellent East European accent, he then proceeded to terrorize Andrew, Patrick and me until my brother laughed so hard that he wet his pants.

After the tour and a couple more stories, Mindy and I sat on the couch together, sipping glasses of a Finger Lakes riesling she had brought, listening to the Beethoven piano sonatas that played quietly in the background, and chatting about what else had been going on in our lives. I rested my leg on a large inflated yoga ball.

"I'm sorry I brought up 9/11," she said.

I waved her off. "That's okay. I'll have to learn to deal with it someday. I guess coming up here was one way to do it."

"A successful one from what I've seen so far. Can I tell you something selfish?" she asked.

"Of course."

"I wish I'd been the one to restore the connection with

you back in 1997. I wish I'd been the one to meet Ben Fries."

"You mean rather than Julianne Radisson?"

"Yes. I mean rather than Julianne."

"I'm sorry Mindy, I—"

"No, don't apologize. I know my feelings aren't rational, and I know you did what you did back then for very good reasons. It's just that, even five years down the road, I regret not having you all to myself."

"You're the only one here right now."

Mindy sat forward on the cushion and propped her arms on a pillow. "I'm grateful to be here now. And I find it an honor to meet the River Rat Reporters." She took my hand.

"But sadly," I said, "come Monday you'll be gone, back to Buffalo, four hours away. And how often do we see each other when we get back to our own separate lives?"

"I've been thinking about that since the day we talked on the phone for so long."

"Last week? When I read you my mother's letter?"

"No. Back in September. The day after the attacks." Mindy paused and sipped her wine. "Which leads me to another thing I'm selfish about. I wanted to see more of you after that. I was also angry that you didn't come see me. That you didn't escape west to Buffalo rather than north to the river."

"Well, I—"

"I won't let you apologize this time, either. I wanted to see more of you back in September. I still do. But after we talked for so long last week, and after finally seeing you here, I understood why you wouldn't want to leave now for anything. Which brings my next question. Are you going to stay here and become a River Rat yourself?"

"Apparently, becoming a genuine River Rat takes about forty years for someone not actually born here, even though I was born in the next county down. I am going to stay, at least for the time being. My plan is to live at Heron's Nest through next year's tourist season. In the meantime I'll work some with Andrew next spring and summer, reacquaint myself with the river, and look for different work to begin in a year or so. I'll keep the cottage, of course, and come back as much as I can."

"What work will you look for? Research? Teaching?"

I shrugged. "Perhaps."

Mindy smiled. "What?"

"What what?" I said.

"You're holding something back." She smiled and poked my forearm with her index finger. "You have a plan."

"Is it that obvious?"

"To me it is."

"Okay. What I really want to do is start my own business."

"Come on! What business?"

"You had to ask?"

"Yes, I did. Now you have to answer."

"I want to start a private investigator service. It's been my dream now for five years."

Mindy laughed. "What? Are you serious? Like on those old TV shows?"

I laughed too and shook my head. "No, not like Magnum or Banacek. Mine would be an historical investigation service. I expect I'd end up doing a lot of DAR genealogy work, title searches, stuff like that."

"Where would you work from?"

"Clinton Falls, most likely. It's more centrally located than up here, and the interstates would give me good access to the rest of upstate New York. In fact, Louie Fratello offered me some office space above The 357. Maybe I'll take him up on it."

"You'd certainly be good at it, given this adventure and with your Radisson family experience."

I took a sip of my wine and asked her a question. "Would you ever move back?"

"To Clinton Falls?"

"Yes."

Mindy paused and also took a sip of wine. "I hear whispers that Seamus McNally is done after next semester."

"Have you asked him about it?"

"I have. He would neither confirm nor deny. That, to my way of thinking, means yes."

"There you go."

"I'm up for tenure in a year, Tom. I'd be throwing it all away if I left."

"Are you kidding me? They'd welcome you with open arms at Clinton Falls. They'd give you tenure right away. They've been lost at sea without both Langley and Radisson. With McNally gone, the American history wing would be a shell of what it was only five years ago. Whittaker's probably close to retirement, too. You'd be the cornerstone of the rebuilding effort, Mindy. A franchise quarterback."

"I guess the timing *is* right," Mindy said slowly, mulling it over.

"In more ways than one," I said.

WE DID NOT SLEEP TOGETHER that night. After I kissed Mindy on the cheek she squeezed my hand lightly, then put her fingers around my chin and returned the kiss, this time on my lips. She gently rubbed the scars on my face and forehead with a feather touch. We hugged for a moment, then Mindy pulled away and smiled.

"I'm grateful and happy to be here, Tom," she said. "I mean that. I'm also *very* tired. If I don't get some good sleep I'll be a worthless lump of skin and bones tomorrow."

I said okay, then we hugged again, my nose against her hair as I drew in the scent of her. Mindy kissed me again, let go of my hand, and went upstairs to the room Patrick and I had shared as children.

THE NEXT DAY STARTED for me with the scent and sound of frying bacon as I awoke a little later than usual. I washed up, got dressed and found Mindy in the kitchen measuring coffee beans into the grinder.

"Good morning, Mr. Flanagan," she said with the exaggerated friendliness so common among bed and breakfast proprietors. "On the table this morning you'll find bacon, scrambled eggs, cantaloupe, coffee and fresh-squeezed orange juice. I hope you had an excellent night's sleep at the Heron's Nest."

"Don't you hate that awkward sharing of a breakfast table with people you don't know and don't particularly want to know?" I asked.

She laughed, then waited as she ground the coffee. "Does your foot hurt at all?"

"No. At worst it feels hemmed in, claustrophobic, like wearing a necktie."

"Or a girdle."

"I'd imagine, yes."

"Why don't you go check out the morning headlines and Yankee gossip, or whatever you do on Saturday morning, and I'll finish up here and give you a yell when the food's ready."

"Sounds good," I said.

"Say," Mindy said, picking up some tourist pamphlets she had been reading before starting breakfast. "Who's this William Johnston character they keep talking about?"

"The river's most famous scoundrel," I answered. "He was Canadian. He rebelled against the British, became what he called 'the Admiral of the Patriot Navy,' and recruited a few dozen of his countrymen and upstate New Yorkers to invade Canada. To pay for it all he tried to steal money from the *Sir Robert Peel* that ferried between Wellesley Island and the mainland, right where the bridge is now."

"Tried to steal money? Gold?"

"Some say it was. Others say it was a payroll."

"Was he caught red-handed?"

"Not exactly. He set the boat on fire and it sunk."

"He did? How many died?"

"None. Johnson and his mates got everyone off the boat before it sank."

"Oh, so he was a kind-hearted pirate," Mindy said. "Must be why they give him a leading role in this silly Alex Bay festival."

"Pirate Days," I said. "He and his men weren't that kind-hearted. They left all the passengers standing there on the shore."

"Where?"

"On Wellesley Island. We can go see it tomorrow. It's just off Peel Dock Road, my favorite road in the world because it goes under the bridge."

"Do you think Johnston knew about Napoleon's gold?"

I considered this for a moment and shook my head. "No, I don't. If he had, he would have publicized his search for it and we'd know. There wasn't much he could keep secret."

"What happened to him after the ferry incident?"

"He hid out in an island cave until the government caught him. He served some jail time, then the Americans hired him as a lighthouse keeper over on Rock Island, which is ..." I turned myself around and pointed with my crutch.

"Right over there," Mindy said, holding up one of the brochures. "Here at Heron's Nest, we'll soon offer a picnic lunch at the Rock Island State Park, the perfect complement to your island stay."

Smiling, I took a dish towel from the refrigerator door handle and tossed it at her.

"Go catch up on your Yankees," she said. "I'll bring you some coffee when it's ready."

"What are you up to today?" I asked.

"A boatload of grading," she said with a sigh. "It is

midterms, after all. I promise I'll finish it today, then we'll have tonight and all day tomorrow to ourselves."

Chapter Seventeen

"I ASSUME you've come prepared," Raphael Ostend said, "having already done some research on Captain Doctor Charles Obadiah Smithson." He directed the statement to me just before dinner, in the company of the other fifty-seven guests gathered around Valhalla's massive dining room table who were, thankfully, engaged in conversations of their own.

I say thankfully because it was not easy for me to respond, overwhelmed as I was by the evening's experiences so far.

First it was Mindy, who, at six o'clock, descended the stairs of Heron's Nest in her long black gown, feathered with subtle hints of green, blue and purple. Diamondback colors indeed, but still beautiful, especially on her. She had her hair up and wore a simple necklace of black pearls with equally simple earrings to match.

She said I looked good in my father's newly tailored tuxedo, the left leg bell-bottomed to fit over my cast. She was right, I must admit, but I looked nowhere near as good as she did.

"My goodness," I said when she stopped at the bottom of the stairs. "You'd fit right in with those red carpet starlets on Oscar night."

She smiled, raised her arms and did a spin. "Golden Globes, maybe. Oscars, no way."

We sat down at the kitchen table and had more Finger Lakes riesling, chatting about what we each expected to happen that night. We couldn't wait for it to begin.

The next overwhelming experience was our evening's transportation. Raphael Ostend's butler had called Saturday afternoon to tell me not to worry about how we would get over to Valhalla. I pressed him for more information, but he would give no further details. My curiosity at seeing nautical running lights approach the dock at six thirty thus turned to amazement as I realized the boat was the *Archangel* itself, piloted by Captain James Pembroke. He was accompanied by a very tall blonde woman in a sleek forest green dress. He introduced her as his "first ex-wife Margie." We boarded the boat with backpacks containing tomorrow's clothes, and set off expectantly.

The downriver journey along Wellesley Island and around Grenadier and into Canadian waters was leisurely paced and beautiful as we rode through the cool, starlit evening. Jim skippered, and Margie, Mindy and I enjoyed a bottle of Dom Pérignon, provided by Raphael Ostend, and some AM radio oldies. Mindy marveled at how peaceful the river was on a windless night.

I was even more overwhelmed by Valhalla itself. The castle was made of stone, quarried in the Thousand Islands, and was actually built on two adjacent islands, one wing on each. The wings, and therefore the islands, were connected by a bi-level stone walkway that accessed both the ground and upper floors. There were numerous gables and towers, and the whole structure was covered with red slate roofing.

I had seen it enough in the daytime on my various river travels by kayak, Lyman and tour boat. I thought I knew what to expect. But now, on Ostend Ball night, Valhalla was lit by hundreds of old fashioned naphtha lamps and torches that made the pink granite glow like fire itself.

The sight was spine-tingling and more than a little frightening. I was taking a swig of champagne from the bottle when I looked north past the Crossover Island Light and first saw it in the distance. Astonished, I pulled the bottle away before tipping it upright, spilling some of the expensive bubbly on my coat.

Margie wiped the champagne with the scarf she was wearing. "Impressive, huh?" she said, turning back to look at the castle. "I'll always remember my first time seeing it all lit up like that. What was it, Jimmy? 1984?"

"'81," Jim Pembroke said. "We split up in '84."

I nodded and handed Margie the bottle.

Captain Pembroke pulled the *Archangel* into the boathouse, where, with the half-empty bottle of champagne and our backpacks, we disembarked onto a torch-lit solid rock landing. We followed curving pink granite stairs up two flights to the main lobby, and then ascended a marble stairway to the second floor and its ballroom, dining room and smoking room. Sweating from the exertion, I asked why the hell Ostend hadn't built an elevator. Mindy replied, to the delight of Jim Pembroke and his ex-wife, that torches wouldn't work too well in elevators.

The oak paneling in the ballroom, the crystal chandelier as large as Heron's Nest's living room, the nineteen piece orchestra, the excellent champagne, the tuxedos, the women's gowns made of taffeta and silk and lace, the picture perfect fireplace in every room, the conversation and laughter and hors d'ouvres—all of it transported me, as if through time, to a world of such magnificence and beauty that I became dizzy from it all. Fifteen minutes after arriving, I hobbled over to the wall opposite the ballroom fireplace, sat down in one of the leather upholstered chairs set in a row for those who were not dancing, and listened to the strains of a Brahms tune. I marveled that I was there, at Valhalla, where my parents had been as well; my father in the same clothes that I now wore.

Mindy joined me after a time, and asked if this is really how things were, on a regular basis, back in 1886.

I nodded. "In season. The Ostends are odd, though, and always have been. One purpose of their ball is to weed

out those who only think about the river in the summer
from those who care about the place all year round. As you
can see, a lot of people took the effort to get here in early
November."

"It's spectacular, isn't it? It must have been even more
spectacular back then."

"A fool's paradise, some people call it."

"Why?"

"Things were like this here at Valhalla, at George Pullman's Castle Rest, Charles Emery's Calumet, Ed Noble's
Thousand Island Club, The Thousand Island House in Alex
Bay, The Frontenac Hotel on Round Island, The Columbian in TI Park. Summer was filled with high-end social
events where the rich and famous dressed to be seen, and
mingled and danced all night long. The river was full of
private yachts and steamboats shuttling people from one
party to another. Until the First World War the only competition as the premier vacation paradise for the elite was
Newport, Rhode Island."

"Wow."

"The *New York Times* even sent a seasonal correspondent up here to cover all the river's happenings. But it could
never last, hence the fool part."

"What happened to end it all?"

"The government requisitioned the yachts and steamboats for the war effort. The automobile eclipsed the train
as the elite's favorite mode of travel, which opened up Long
Island for their pleasure. Several of the great hotels—the
Frontenac, the Columbian—burnt down. The first generation of river gentry died off and their sons cast their eyes
elsewhere. After all this the Great Depression hit, and few
families besides the Ostends were able to maintain their
high standard of living. Even the Ostends cut back, closing
off one wing of Valhalla, dry docking the *Archangel* for a
time, and limiting their parties to the annual Ostend Ball."

"Sounds sad," Mindy said.

"The fool part or the end of paradise part?" I asked.

"Both."

"It is, in a way. Then again, you and I wouldn't be here if this place were still on the level of Newport."

"Very true," she said.

When the dinner bell rang, Mindy took my hand and led me to the table, where the guests were being seated for the meal.

RAPHAEL OSTEND HAD PLACED Mindy and me to his right, at the head of the huge oval dinner table. He had already offered a toast, pronouncing us the guests of honor. Mindy and I both raised our glasses of red wine and blushed as the River Rat Reporters, their wives and ex-wives and girl-friends, and other guests, including two state senators and former United States Ambassador to the Kingdom of Jordan, the Honorable Walter Maitland, applauded. Raphael Ostend offered grace using a traditional Anglican prayer sprinkled with thous and thines. When seated, the wait staff immediately began serving the first course—a chopped lettuce, apple and walnut salad, topped, of course, with Thousand Island dressing.

It was then, as people around the table began to start up their own conversations, that Ostend asked me if I'd done my homework on Captain Doctor Charles Obadiah Smithson.

"Uh, yes, I have. I found out a lot. I mean, I learned how impressive a man he was. The Red River campaign. The American attacks. Egypt. An historian, too. A good one."

Or something like that. All I remember of my first response was pausing to take a long draught of wine in the middle of it and having my glass topped off immediately by a waiter.

Mindy was paying no attention to us, concentrating in-

stead on a conversation with Phyllis Slattery that had something to do with knitting.

"I've told you Smithson was the guest of honor at the
first Ostend Ball some one hundred and fifteen years ago.
Now, tonight, you enjoy that same honor."

"Is there a plaque or something?" I asked, starting to get
comfortable.

Ostend shook his head no. "Records of guests, honored
or otherwise, are maintained in a journal I keep in my desk
drawer. As soon as tonight's festivities are over I will sip my
last glass of brandy and personally and proudly inscribe the
names Thomas Flanagan and Melinda McDonnell at the top
of the page dedicated to the 2001 event."

"So, yes, Charles Obadiah Smithson," I said. "Does
everyone else here know his story? The one involving your
grandmother? The one you're going to tell me?"

"They've all been told it," Ostend said. "Not all of
them, however, take it seriously. Your father did, of course,
as do most of the other River Rat Reporters. I hope, despite
your insistence that history be hidebound by rationalism,
that you'll take it seriously as well."

He leaned forward and said, "Tom, without making it
too obvious, look at the painting right behind me, above the
fireplace. Study it for a time. Observe it carefully, and tell
me what you see."

What I saw was a portrait of a magnificent, almost regal
woman in three-quarters profile. She was dressed in a black
gown with ruffles and a very large, very expensive looking
gold and pearl necklace. Her blonde hair was pulled back
into a bun, held together with pearl-headed pins, her ears
adorned with long gold and pearl ornaments that would
have been insulted to be called mere earrings. Her face was
exquisite—a high forehead, eyebrows with a slightly pointed
arch, blue eyes that sparkled like sapphire, long cheekbones,
a thin nose, a wide mouth that smiled but showed no teeth,
a chin that dropped into a slight point that echoed the arch

of her eyebrows. I took another sip of wine, and could have looked at her all night.

"My daughter and granddaughter look just like her," Raphael Ostend said. "Unfortunately they're not here." He leaned closer and whispered. "Or fortunately, perhaps, since if they were here you'd be unable to take your eyes off them either. Melinda may not mind you ogling over a painting of Grandmother, but she certainly would mind, and I would too, if it were my daughter and granddaughter you were casting your eyes upon with your mouth hanging open like a dog's."

That caught my attention, and I snapped my mouth shut with an audible click and turned back to meet Ostend's gaze. He was clearly amused.

"Sorry," I said. "I noticed the portrait earlier, but now that I've looked closely, you're right, I don't want to take my eyes off it."

"That's why I told you not to make it too obvious."

I was concerned. "Did I?"

"Hmmm." His smile grew.

I cleared my throat in embarrassment. "So that's Lady Ostend," I said.

"Yes."

"Is her beauty your story?"

"No. In fact, her outward beauty distracts one from the story. Look again, only this time try not to look at her. Look hard at the rest of the painting, observe it closely, and tell me what else you see."

It took me a minute of concentration to see it. Or see them, rather—the colors, hidden in shadow, that now appeared in each corner of the painting framing the woman, and seemed to emerge from the darkness and brighten as I continued to move my gaze from one to the other to the next.

"Who painted this?" I asked.

"The North Country's most famous native son,"

Raphael Ostend said with obvious pride. "It's a Remington."

That surprised me. "Frederic Remington painted this? It doesn't look like his stuff."

"It's very different from his usual style. No cowboys. No Indians. No horses. No broad landscapes. He painted it, however, right here at Valhalla, in 1892."

"The colors ..." I started to say, but my words trailed off as I looked again and saw them fade once more in the interplay of light and shadow.

"They come and go, don't they?" Ostend said. "Remington explained that the way the retina adjusts from the lightness of Grandmother's skin to the shadow of the background makes the colors seem alive, pulsing, as it were."

"He was right."

"It was a brilliant technique, brilliantly executed. He achieved his objective admirably."

"Why make them like that? What was his objective?"

"Remington was here when Captain Doctor Charles Obadiah Smithson told his story about Napoleon's gold. Remington witnessed Grandmother's reaction to it. Subsequent conversations and shared experiences with Grandmother convinced him that she was indeed someone special, someone who *knew* things that others didn't, someone worthy of a special technique."

"Smithson's story had something to do with these colors?" I asked.

The wait staff had cleared the salad plates and had brought the next course, a thick pumpkin soup spiced with nutmeg and pepper and garnished with croutons and herbs. I took a few spoonfuls as I waited for Ostend's reply.

"Yes. You've learned something about Smithson's life? I had a difficult time comprehending your answer earlier."

"I have," I said, without repeating the details. "He was an impressive man."

"Would you guess he was a reliable man? A man to be trusted?"

"Undoubtedly. He'd have to be to accomplish what he accomplished. You can't do what he did by lying and cheating. That stuff's for politicians." I glanced down the table to confirm that the state senators or the former ambassador weren't listening.

"Yes, Grandmother knew that too. She tested him nonetheless."

"The same test she gave you? To see if he was predisposed to receiving her philosophical ideas?"

"No. Simply to see if he was telling the truth." Ostend reached into his tuxedo pocket and produced an old photograph, which he placed on the table next to me as I finished the last spoonful of soup.

"What does this have to do with the colors Remington included in his painting of your grandmother?"

"Just look at the photograph. We'll return to the painting in a moment."

I examined it. The photo was of two men, both mustached, one in a military uniform, obviously British but with a Canadian flag insignia on his shoulder, complete with sword and scabbard. The other wore a simple Arabian robe and a matching turban. The military man, Captain Doctor Charles Obadiah Smithson no doubt, was substantially taller than the Arab, but both men exuded the same impressive power and confidence.

"Who's the man with Captain Smithson?" I asked as the server took my empty soup bowl and replaced it with a plate of bread and cheese.

"I'm glad you recognized Smithson," Raphael Ostend said. "The other man was an Egyptian guide who led the Canadian voyagers from Luxor to the second cataract on their way to Khartoum."

"Did he have a name?"

"He did."

I waited. "Well, what was it?"

Raphael Ostend didn't answer this question. Instead he looked down the table and caught Jim Pembroke's attention, then motioned for Pembroke to come over.

I took a sip of wine and waited again.

"This is where Raphael trots me out for dramatic effect," Jim Pembroke said as he approached the curve of the table between Ostend and me. "I've done this thirteen times so far since Margie and I first came here. Not since '96, though, with your cousin Andrew, so please excuse me if I seem rusty."

"Thanks for the commentary, Jim," Raphael Ostend said. "Would you please answer Tom's question?"

Pembroke stood at parade rest and smiled. "Shoot," he said.

I picked up the photograph. "Who's the man with Captain Smithson? The Egyptian guide who led the Canadian voyagers up to the second cataract?"

"The man with Captain Smithson, the Egyptian guide who led the Canadian voyagers up to the second cataract, was first known to me as the well-dressed Arab with the large ring on his finger. He was the man Charlie Flanagan met in Montreal, the man who told your father about Napoleon's gold. His name, at least as he gave it, was Naguib Malqari." Pembroke pointed to the picture. "See that? The ring is still there. Or was there, I should say."

I had a feeling this would be Jim Pembroke's answer, but I was still astonished when I heard it.

"This is Naguib Malqari?" I asked. "The same man from your story? In what? 1886?"

Raphael Ostend answered. "In 1885 actually, almost exactly a year before Captain Smithson told his story at the inaugural Ostend Ball and gave Grandmother this photograph. The photograph was taken by Lord Wolesley himself when the voyagers reached the second cataract. Malqari and Smithson had become good friends on their journey up the

Nile, exchanging notes on all sorts of interesting topics from riparian ecosystems to possible improvements to the Suez Canal to modern battlefield surgical techniques to the existence and meaning of a certain treasure taken from Egypt by Napoleon and carried first to France and subsequently to Canada."

I excitedly nudged Mindy at this news, causing her to spill a bit of wine on her plate of bread and cheese. "I knew it!" I said. "Of all the possibilities, I guessed first that it came from Egypt!"

"Settle down," Mindy scolded. "You're in polite company." She looked at Phyllis Slattery, smiled, and gestured towards me. "I can dress him up, but apparently cannot take him out."

"Would you like me to fill you in?" I asked more politely.

"I already have," Phyllis Slattery said. "We couldn't talk about sock monkeys all night, you know."

I showed the photograph to Mindy. "Malqari looks about fifty, maybe sixty, wouldn't you say?" Mindy nodded. "That means in 1976 he would have been between one hundred forty and one hundred fifty years old! I'm sorry Jim, Raphael, that can't be true."

"It gets stranger," Raphael Ostend said as Mindy took my hand beneath the table. "Captain Smithson told Grandmother that Malqari not only knew of Napoleon's gold, but, before Bonaparte left Egypt for France in August 1799, had helped load it onto the French ship *Egalité*. Malqari insisted on the veracity of this, proving it to Captain Smithson with written instructions, in Bonaparte's own hand, that 'the gift of gold and other various treasures should be loaded aboard the *Egalité* with urgency and taken with dispatch to Marseilles, where the cargo is to be kept under the strict and secret care of a Monsieur Champlain, who will be given further instructions upon my arrival in the Fatherland."

"Smithson believed all this?" I asked.

Ostend answered, "In addition to giving Grandmother the photograph, Captain Smithson also showed her the letter. The letter is now in the possession of the Kingston Historical Society, along with all of Captain Smithson's papers, which the Society received after his death. You can go see it if you like. There's no question it's from Bonaparte's own hand."

"Malqari could have gotten it anywhere. From a pawn shop in Cairo, for example. Or from his grandfather. Right, Mindy?"

"He could have," Mindy said. "He also could have gotten it directly from Napoleon."

"That would make Malqari over two hundred years old when Jim encountered him on the CANCO-2000 and my father met him in Montreal!"

"That's correct," Raphael Ostend said. "Of course, neither Jim nor your father knew that at the time. Your father found out only after attending his first Ostend Ball in 1978. By then he'd also learned that Malqari was dead."

"No wonder he was frightened by Malqari when he met him in Montreal."

"I found out in 1981," Jim Pembroke said, "which, as I told you on the way here, was my first Ostend Ball." Pembroke glanced at his watch. "If my part is done, Raph, and if you don't mind, I'd like to retire to the smoking room for a moment between courses. It should be at least the fourth or fifth inning by now."

To be honest, I hadn't remembered about the game. Nor was it a top priority at this moment.

Raphael Ostend thanked Jim Pembroke and said to me, "Now back to Grandmother's portrait and those colors. On the night of the first Ostend Ball, with Frederic Remington as a guest, Captain Smithson also told of Naguib Malqari's claim that Napoleon's gold had certain 'guardians' in this river to protect it. Grandmother knew exactly what he meant when she heard this, because she had, in fact, already encountered these guardians. She tested the veracity of Captain Smithson's story, and found his honesty irreproachable. Naguib Malqari, it seems, had indeed helped load Napoleon's gold onto the *Egalité* in Egypt and, moreover, knew that the gold had ended up in our Saint Lawrence in the care of these strange guardians."

Instead of speaking I took a drink of wine and returned my gaze to Lady Ostend's portrait.

Without turning around, Ostend continued, "Now, beginning in the top left corner and moving clockwise, tell me what colors you see."

"Red with some hints of orange. Royal blue. Grayish-brown—that one's the hardest to capture. And finally green. No wait, blue, a deeper blue than on top, with accents of green and of robin egg blue. Incredible. That one's pulsing more than the others."

"Very good. Now what if I told you that each color represented one of the four classical elements of the universe?"

"Okay," I said, without a clue as to what the connection was between the colors, Napoleon's gold and Naguib Malqari. "That makes them, again going clockwise from the top left, fire, air, earth and water."

"Correct. But the colors don't actually represent the elements themselves. Rather, the colors represent the spiritual component of each element, what you might have heard called, collectively, the elementals."

"You mean ..."

Mindy let go of my hand and pointed, as if counting off. "Salamanders, fairies, gnomes and mermaids," she said.

"Salamanders, sylphs, gnomes and undines," Raphael Ostend said. "Let's all use the technical terms, please, rather than the corrupted ones from childhood stories."

"The elementals?" I said, somewhat confused.

"Yes. Deep knowledge of the elementals and their power goes back several thousands of years. The Mesopotamians, Egyptians, Chinese, Greeks, Romans and most other civilizations knew the truth of the elementals' existence. The great scientist and philosopher Paracelsus was the first Westerner to accurately explain what each elemental was. In the five hundred years since his time, many more great men and women knew and know the same truth. Did you learn, Tom, that Bonaparte even knew one?"

"He did?"

"Yes, a salamander, or perhaps a gnome. Le Petit Homme Rouge, the French called him. He first appeared to Bonaparte during the Egyptian expedition, in fact, and explained that he had advised French leaders for centuries, albeit with mixed results—their fault rather than his, of course. The creature agreed to a ten-year pact to advise Bonaparte and guide him to victory. He sealed his promise with a prediction that the Egyptian campaign would fail because of a naval defeat, but that Bonaparte himself and the French people would achieve unprecedented victories on land nevertheless.

"The Red Man led Bonaparte back to France and to the consulship. He prompted him to invade Austria. He warned him not to invade Russia. But as was often the case with Bonaparte, the advice of his advisors, even this one, fell on deaf ears. Of course, not many people take the relationship between the Emperor and the Little Red Man seriously today, but it was well known and widely accepted back then."

"I know Napoleon believed in all kinds of spiritual insights and prophecies," I said, calling to mind some information I had come across in my recent research. "But why would Frederic Remington represent the elementals in a portrait of your grandmother?"

"Because knowing them and learning from them was one of Grandmother's greatest gifts. She, like Bonaparte, had listened carefully all her life to what they had to teach her. Her divination, her deep investigations into the spiritual world, everything she did best came back to what she learned from the elementals. Furthermore, she knew when she heard Captain Smithson's story that the 'guardians' were none other than a group of elementals— specifically, in this case, a group of undines."

I was astonished. "Mermai—sorry—undines? Here? In the Saint Lawrence?"

"Of course. It's an ancient river, Tom, secluded from civilization for millennia until Americans and Canadians started settling on and around it in large numbers in the 1870's. The river was theirs for much longer than it's been ours. In Grandmother's time, the river was full of them."

"Lady Ostend knew them? Learned from them?"

"On the night of the initial Ostend Ball she took Captain Smithson, Grandfather and Frederic Remington down to the landing where you disembarked from the *Archangel* earlier this evening. She summoned several undines, who, in due time, approached from their hiding places and affirmed that Napoleon's gold was indeed in the river."

I could not believe what I was hearing, and Raphael Ostend knew this. He also knew that trying to explain or rationalize anything to me at this point would be fruitless. He continued his story much as he had to every other first-time guest at the Ostend Ball at Valhalla. I tried to keep this fact in mind as I listened.

"There's more to this story than Malqari's longevity or his connection to Napoleon's gold. The undines also thought they *knew* Malqari. According to Grandmother, they could feel his presence on this river, both before and after he visited here."

"How?" I asked.

"Grandmother had two theories. First, that somehow and without consent, perhaps by force, Malqari had drawn power from them, or from another elemental or set of elementals. She admitted that exactly how this was done was well beyond her understanding. Elementals guard their secrets jealously, and would not have given up any of their knowledge or, especially, their powers to anyone they mistrusted without a fight or, as with Le Petit Homme Rouge and Bonaparte, and much more rarely, by strict agreement."

"How would the undines know *that*?"

"Grandmother said that all elementals have a unique ability to communicate over long distances. 'Community without propinquity,' she called it rather ostentatiously. Perhaps the undines from whom Malqari took his power passed the information to the undines here."

"What was her second theory?"

"Grandmother's second theory was that the undines knew that Malqari's longevity, his very being perhaps, was irrevocably bound together with Napoleon's gold. As long as the gold remained hidden, Malqari remained alive. Someone finding the gold, on the other hand, or, perhaps, someone extracting it from the river, would mean his demise."

Now my head was spinning. I could not help wondering if Malqari was the man who had caused my father to crash into a dock and wreck the family Lyman, killing him and my mother and brother. Impossible, I thought again, as Malqari would have been more than two hundred fifty years old by that time, and dead for almost twenty years to boot. But if there was anything I should have learned from the Ostend Ball that night, it was that the presumably impossible was not so certainly that. I made a mental note to check my father's map and note cards for the initials "N.M."

"You said Malqari visited the river. Did your grandmother ever meet him?" I asked.

"She did. It was the year after the inaugural Ostend Ball. The *New York Times* even wrote a story about his visit. 'An esteemed personage from Mohammedan lands journeyed to the Thousand Islands region of the Saint Lawrence River last week,' it said. 'One Nagub Malkree spent three whole days touring the river, inquiring into its unique properties. Mr. Malkree would not say exactly what those properties were.' As usual, then as now, the *Times* was both inaccurate and incomplete in its reporting."

"Did Lady Ostend know why he was here?"

"She had no doubt that he wanted to find and capture an undine."

"Was he successful?"

"We do not know."

"Did Malqari really die in Beirut, as my father heard from one of his contacts in Montreal?"

Ostend looked me square in the eye. "That question is best discussed in private."

As I was running the calculations of Malqari's presumed age through my mind again, Mindy asked one of the several other questions that was racing through my brain. "The undines spoke to Lady Ostend? In English?"

Ostend smiled and looked aside for a moment, then returned his gaze to Mindy. "That is difficult to explain. They communicate subsonically, if you will, not in English or in any other human language. Not in the languages of dolphins or whales, either, as those mammals have been studied recently by marine biologists. But Grandmother could understand them. Hear them in her soul, as she once told me." Ostend chuckled. "Nor, by the way, did they speak in that high-pitched, glass-shattering squeal that Darryl Hannah's mermaid used in *Splash*."

"I didn't want to embarrass myself by mentioning that," I said.

"We've all thought of it, hon," Phyllis Slattery said. "That movie and a few others and a few books are all most of us have to go on. Try to forget about what pop culture has taught you. Try to forget everything you already might know about mermaids. In this case, you'll be better off."

"Phyllis, do you believe?" I asked. In the back of my mind, I was also thinking about what Billy Masterson had told me about how he communicated with fish in the same silent manner.

"Unlike my hard-headed husband, yes, I do. I believe in the undines and I believe in Napoleon's gold."

Mindy continued her questions. "What do they look like? Are they really *there*? I mean, are they physically present? If an undine swam up next to the *Archangel* right now could we go down and *see* it?"

"Yes and no. You would see them as you see them in Remington's painting, with the difference being that they would be three dimensional, of course, and each in its own element rather than on a two dimensional black background shrouded by charcoal shading. The undines would be an almost transparent presence, a shimmering of delicate substance in the water. There, but not there. Visible, but just barely, and only to the well-trained eye, or rather, the well-trained soul."

"Do they look like fish?" Mindy asked. "Or do they look half-human like in all the children's tales?"

"They have the attributes of fish in the sense that water is to them like air is to us, a transparent substance through which they move with ease just as we move with ease through the atmosphere. They also admire humans, despite our carelessness towards them and their world. Paracelsus wrote that over the millennia they have learned to take on human attributes. The half-human image, however, is a complete fiction."

"As I already mentioned," Phyllis Slattery said, "you'll be better off if you forget about all that kid's stuff."

Ostend took a sip of wine and held up a finger. "Also, they hate boats, especially power boats, which disturb and pollute their water, and stay away from them as much as possible."

"Tough to do up here," Mindy said.

"For a few months, yes. For most of the year the river is theirs, as it has been for centuries. They're probably starting to emerge from their hiding places right about this time of year."

"The river's still filled with them?" I asked.

"Yes. One just needs to know where to look, and, as I've already explained, how to look."

"Where would one look?" I asked. "Have you seen one?"

"I have not," Raphael Ostend said with clear regret. "I was with Grandmother once when an undine saved our lives." He smiled and shook his head. "I was a young boy at the time. It was an extraordinary experience that I'll never forget." He paused, and I wondered if he was going to tell us the story or keep it private. He took a sip of water and, to our satisfaction, continued.

"It happened in the autumn of 1934. We were in the *Archangel*, which we'd bought from an upstate New York glover just the year before. My parents, Grandmother and I actually lived on the *Archangel* for much of that summer, before we dry-docked it for the remainder of the financial crisis. We were on the boat one evening in July, having just finished checking on Valhalla. We were heading upriver towards Gananoque when a thunderstorm developed off Lake Ontario. We turned around with the intention of finding shelter back here until the storm passed.

"As we approached the Lost Channel Grandmother let out a shriek that nearly stopped my heart and caused my father to stop the boat as quickly as he could. We all came to her. Grandmother smiled and explained that she screamed so loudly and so suddenly because a sharp pain had filled her head in the area just behind her eyes, but had just as suddenly subsided. We heard the crack of thunder as the storm drew closer. Grandmother advised my father to get back to Valhalla as fast as the *Archangel* could take us.

"Then something strange happened. As soon as we started to move, Grandmother screamed again in pain. My father stopped the boat. The pain subsided. This time, however, she suggested we should drop anchor and get below decks to wait out the storm where we were, rather than try to reach Valhalla. We all agreed. When the storm began to sub-side an hour later we moved on.

"My mother was the first to smell the smoke, and Grandmother was the first to place a direction to it. As we approached the Lost Channel, and as Georgina Island came into view, we saw what was causing the smoke—a copse of pine trees high on a cliff that had been struck by lightning. The trees were now burning and bubbling as their sap cooked in the flames. A few of the trees had fallen into the water below. The branches not yet submerged were still burning and a heavy steam rose from the water next to them. My father thought for a moment, then looked at Grandmother with an ashen expression on his face. He carefully drove the boat around the fallen trees.

"Several years later Grandmother told me what had really happened. She had not only been struck with a deep and unnerving pain, she had also received a voiceless com-mand, 'Stop! Stop or you will die!' " Ostend paused and took another drink, of wine this time.

"It was the first time in a long while that an undine had communicated with her. The undine told her to stop. Her shrieks of pain twice caused my father to stop the boat. Grandmother was certain that had we kept going we would have been struck by that lightning or, worse, been hit by one of the falling, burning trees that had been struck."

"Wow," Mindy said.

"Was that the only time something like that happened?" I asked.

"Yes, the only time. On all the other occasions, the un-dines communicated only when asked a question, or ap-peared near the surface when Grandmother was alone."

"Do you know anyone other than Lady Ostend who's seen one?" Mindy asked.

"Yes. Several others who sit or once sat at this table have seen an undine."

I looked around. Phyllis Slattery shook her head no. But

as if on cue, and like Jim Pembroke playing his part, Billy Masterson stopped talking with his date, Laurie, from Jimmy's Tavern, and nodded and tipped his wine glass my way. Then Andrew Hibbard, three seats down from Mindy, leaned back in his chair, cleared his throat, and silently mouthed, "Me too." Finally, from farther down and across the table, former Ambassador Walter Maitland nodded to me and smiled.

No one else responded, and then it struck me why Raphael Ostend had chosen his verb tenses so carefully.

"My parents once sat at this table," I said. Ostend raised an eyebrow. I looked at Mindy and then back at our host. "And they saw an undine," I added.

"They did indeed," Raphael Ostend said. "Both your mother and father did see an undine. Several of them, in fact. But that story will have to wait for another time, and another teller."

"Andrew's tale," I said. I looked at Mindy again. She smiled, and I became silent.

The questions shouting in my mind were quieted for a moment by the satisfying return of my parents into the tapestry woven before me.

Chapter Eighteen

THAT WAS NOT THE LAST of Raphael Ostend's surprises, although he kindly waited until after dinner, dessert and the resumption of dancing to disclose the others.

The dinner alone would have made the rest of the evening extraordinary. After the bread and cheese came several other traditional Thousand Island courses, all made with local food, including baked filet of river bass with roasted tomatoes, leg of lamb with caper sauce, and roast duck with stuffing. Billy Masterson himself had caught the river bass. Mindy's duck still had a few pieces of shot in it, which she found endearingly wholesome. The vegetables were salt potatoes, onions, peas, string beans and beets, all of them grown in Valhalla's garden, which Ostend tended himself on a nearby island. For dessert, we had a choice of crème broulee or blueberry pie with homemade vanilla ice cream. Mindy chose the former, I selected the pie, and we shared our plates enjoying both offerings, a perfect conclusion, we agreed, to one of the best meals of our lives.

I sipped a glass of thirty-five-year-old Madeira as the orchestra, playing big band, jazz and some reworked rock and roll to facilitate the dancing, resumed. I apologized to Mindy that I wouldn't be able to join her on the floor.

"Don't worry about that," she said with a wave of her hand and a teasing smile. "My dance card is full as it is."

"Really? Full? With whom?"

"All the River Rat Reporters, State Senator Fucillo, Ambassador Maitland, our host if I can find him, and, let's see ... oh, yes, Margie if they play *YMCA*. But I doubt that'll happen at this party."

I laughed. "No, I don't think so." My smile faded. "What am I supposed to do while you dance the night away?"

"Mingle. Or go back to the leather chairs and just sit there and wait for people to come to you." She smiled and then spoke in a whisper. "Or you can go watch the Diamondbacks march on to game seven."

"You mean watch the Yankees win the World Series?" I countered. I'd forgotten about the game again, but now that Mindy mentioned it, I did indeed want to see an inning or two of what was bound to be, in my own mind at least, an historic victory for New York.

"Perhaps, if they can come back from fifteen runs down."

I stood up, and my cast made a thud against the table leg. "What?"

Mindy took my hand and smiled. I could swear I actually saw her bat her eyelashes. "Sorry to break the news, darling, but it's true. Unless your Yankees can score sixteen runs before the Diamondbacks get twelve outs, we'll be watching baseball tomorrow night, safely ensconced at Heron's Nest."

Jim Pembroke stood behind me now. "It's true, Tom. Andrew and I watched the D'backs knock the cover off the ball in the bottom of the third, right after I answered your question about Captain Smithson's Egyptian friend. And the Big Unit's shutting the Yankees down. The situation's bleak. It looks like it'll be up to the Rocket tomorrow night."

"I might as well drink up," I said, and drained the little glass of wine that no doubt cost as much as a night's worth of beer at Jimmy's.

I STILL WANTED TO WATCH some of the game, as much to get

some sense of normalcy back into my life as to see if what Mindy and Jim had said was true. I was also having a hard time watching Mindy dance—swaying, spinning, laughing—as I just sat there against the wall, thinking about Naguib Malqari and the undines. As she hit the dance floor for the second time with Ambassador Maitland to a jazzed up Beatles medley, I excused myself from a conversation with Laurie and made my way down the torch-lit hallway and around the corner to the smoking room.

The television set provided the only light in the room. I saw from the box score that the Yankees had scored two runs, but knew that a comeback was futile, since it was the top of the seventh inning with two outs and no one on. I watched the camera pan the crowd. Since the volume was muted I saw, but did not hear, the ecstatic cheers of the Diamondback faithful as they celebrated their impending victory. This wasn't quite the normalcy I was looking for.

I was about to turn around and leave when my attention was drawn away from the television by two voices coming from a dark corner of the room, about twenty feet away. I could not tell who the men were, but I correctly assumed that one of them was Raphael Ostend. I cleared my throat and tapped my crutch on the door as if knocking.

"Ah, Tom," Ostend said. "My condolences on the Yankees' impending loss. No doubt they'll rebound and triumph tomorrow. Shut the door please, would you?"

I hesitated because the hallway torches were the only source of light I had besides the television. When I heard the other man speak, however, I obeyed Ostend's request with a push of my crutch.

"I sure as hell thought Pettitte would come through tonight," the other man said. "I thought he'd come back strong after giving up that big homer in game two. Those Diamondbacks are pesky, though. I'm not sure Clemens'll be able to contain them much more effectively tomorrow night."

It took a moment for the voice to register in my memory, but when it did I was as shocked as I had been by any of the evening's revelations. I had not heard it in almost five years, but it had lost none of its upstate New York edge. Hearing it now caused me to swoon sideways a bit. I was glad to have my crutches.

"Ben?" I said, my voice shaky. "Ben Fries?"

Raphael Ostend turned on a desk lamp, and I now saw the two men seated, Ostend in a leather swivel chair and Ben Fries on the desk itself. He looked exactly the same as he had on the day I had last seen him, bidding farewell from the front porch of his cottage just a few doors down from Heron's Nest. He was tall, about six four, and with his long grey hair and beard he resembled a thinner and more sinewy Mike Slattery. His eyes held the same power that I remembered from the time Julianne Radisson and I had visited him five years before. Now, they were, if anything, even more intense.

I hobbled over to him, and he pulled around a chair for me. I offered him my hand, but instead he looked down at it, back up into my eyes, and nearly picked me off the ground in a magnificent bear hug to which I feebly reciprocated with weak arms.

Here was the man I'd hoped to encounter in my travels north but whom I had least expected to see. Here was the man my mother had loved as much, albeit differently, as she had loved my father. Here was the man whose own life was as inextricably bound up in Napoleon's gold as my father's had been and as mine was becoming. I felt, to use one of my mother's favorite expressions, utterly flabbergasted. I did not know what to think, much less say. I sat down and kept quiet.

Raphael Ostend spoke first. "This ... reunion was supposed to happen later, Tom, with at least one of the other River Rat Reporters or with Melinda by your side to give you comfort and strength."

"The others are busy," I replied curtly. "And I don't need Mindy."

The two men exchanged a long look, then Ostend invited Ben Fries to answer the question that was foremost in my mind, why he was here, at Valhalla, on the night of the Ostend Ball.

"Five years ago, Tom, on the night before your father died, he told me something I could not believe was true." Ben Fries turned to face Raphael Ostend. "You've told Tom Lady Ostend's story?"

"Yes," Ostend said. "All of it."

Ben nodded and returned his attention to me. "You understand about Naguib Malqari and his extraordinary lifespan?"

"I do," I said.

"Very well. On the night before your father died, he told me he'd just found out that Malqari was still alive."

"How?" I asked. "I thought Malqari died in Lebanon sometime in the late seventies."

"We all did. But your father talked with him face to face in 1996, as he had in Montreal twenty years before. The meeting was arranged in an attempt to bring the two men to a common purpose. They met at night, on the dock of George Boldt's yacht house on Wellesley Island, just across from Boldt Castle. Your father was astonished, as you can well imagine. Apparently, he was again frightened by Malqari's intentions, as he had been in Montreal in 1976. He decided to change his mind and join your mother and me in protecting the gold rather than hunting for it."

I paused for a moment and felt the anger build up inside my gut. "He told *you* this?" I asked. "He told *you*, when he knew full well that you were the one driving the wedge between him and my mother? Twenty years of knowing you were in love with his wife and he told *you?*"

Ben Fries fell silent for moment. With his eyes cast down and his arms folded, he said, "Charlie expressed the same misgivings, of course. But he and I both knew that our lives were following parallel paths in more ways than one. He and I both knew that we had to work together if we had any hope of stopping Malqari from taking the gold."

Raphael Ostend was watching me carefully, gauging my reaction. When I looked his way he caught my eye and held it. My breathing began to slow down and deepen. The pulse in my temple stopped hammering.

"What happened at this meeting?" I asked. "What exactly did my father and Malqari talk about?"

"We don't know exactly what they discussed," Ostend answered, speaking slowly and holding my gaze. "We were supposed to find out the next evening, on Labor Day, at an emergency meeting of the River Rat Reporters called by your father. As you know, your parents and brother didn't live to see Labor Day evening."

"That's why I'm here," Ben Fries said, "because from the day your parents died I've been tracking Malqari across half the globe, trying to catch him and ask him what he discussed with your father that night, ask him why your father suddenly changed his mind and decided to protect Napoleon's gold rather than hunt for it, and to discern why your father was so afraid of the man, except for the obvious reason of his supernatural longevity, of course."

"You've been tracking Malqari?" I asked.

"Raphael bought me a boat, a good one, and he and the other Reporters have generously subsidized my work for almost five years now, since I left the river after my January 1997 encounter with you and the Radisson girl.

"I've traveled to Paris, London, Berlin, Cairo and Islamabad. I've followed Naguib Malqari across half the globe. I've gotten beaten up twice, stabbed once, shot at once and threatened more times that I can remember." Ben leaned forward towards me. "Just last week, Tom, I followed Malqari for an hour through Montreal's Old City before he finally eluded me. That was the first time I've found him in North America in five years. His presence in Montreal leaves me with no doubt that he is here or is on his way back here, back upriver, back to the Thousand Islands."

I took a moment to consider the information Ben Fries had just imparted. Raphael Ostend handed me a glass of brandy. I sat back, took a sip, and followed that with a deep breath. I sipped the drink again, looked at Ostend, looked back at Ben, and finished the brandy in one swallow.

"I think I do need Mindy," I said.

Chapter Nineteen

RAPHAEL OSTEND FULFILLED MY REQUEST quickly and efficiently by placing a call via an intercom on his desk. In what seemed to me only a minute later Mindy knocked, opened the door and said, with her newfound sports fan exuberance, "See! I told you the D-backs had kicked their ..." Her voice trailed off as she saw the three of us at Ostend's desk, and her expression became concerned both with the look on my face and with recognition of the identity of the third man in the room.

"My God," she said, a phrase she usually avoided. "You must be ... you can't be ... Professor Hartman? Benjamin Fries?"

"And you must be, can't be, Melinda McDonnell." Ben said this with a smile, trying with some success to lighten the mood.

Without the same hesitation that had silenced me, Mindy unabashedly asked another question, "Did you love Tom's mother as much as she loved you?"

Ben blushed a bit as he turned towards me, then regrouped and looked Mindy square in the eye. "I did love Mary Flanagan, deeply and truly. It was my good fortune to know her and love her, my better fortune to be loved by her. I felt neither jealousy towards Tom's father, though, nor the urge to compete with him for Mary's affections. Charlie and I both loved Mary Flanagan. I'd like to think that the combination of our loves completed her as a human being."

Mindy considered this for a moment, then nodded and smiled. "You pass the test," she said. She stepped forward and offered her hand. "Ben Fries, it's a pleasure and an honor to finally meet you."

Ben smiled, too, and shook her hand with a respect that was admittedly well earned.

Raphael Ostend filled Mindy in on the discussion thus far. She listened with the same gravity that had characterized the conversation before she entered the room, nodding her head slowly as she heard and weighed each point. She also looked puzzled at the way I looked, or rather refused to look, at her.

"Should all this concern me?" I asked when Ostend had finished summarizing things for Mindy.

Ostend answered. "We have no doubt that Malqari is looking for you."

"Looking for me? Why would he want to find me? I have no more knowledge of Napoleon's gold than I did before I got here. Well, beyond what the Reporters have told me so far in their stories." I paused. "Why are you wasting my time telling me your stories?"

"Our stories are hardly a waste of time," Ostend said with a hint of anger himself. "The day your father died he asked the Reporters to tell him our stories. He wanted to hear our stories because he suspected they held the key to what he was looking for."

He breathed deeply and continued in his usual, calmer tone. "Tom, back when we met for the first time at Jimmy's, Andrew and I both assured you that the River Rat Reporters were not trying to manipulate you," he said. "I reassure you of that right now. Gold that glows underwater, the 'French evil' that Hassan the wheelman feared, the rivalry between Ben and your father for your mother's affections and their first quest for the gold, the undines and Malqari's connection to them: all these and more are pieces of a puzzle that we've been trying to fit together for five years without knowing how the puzzle is supposed to look when it's finished."

"I don't know what it's supposed to look like either!" I said, sitting forward in my chair, my voice getting louder and higher in pitch as I spoke. "When I first met Martin Comstock at Castello's and again that first night at Jimmy's you guys treated me like I was some kind of savior or something, here to heal you, to restore your lost paradise. I can't do that." I was shouting now. "I don't have it in me to do that!"

"Why did you come here, then?" Ben Fries asked quietly.

"I didn't know what I was looking for, beyond some vague sort of personal healing. But after a month here I know what it is. Turns out it's the same damned thing I was looking for when I left five years ago. I want to find out how and why my parents and brother died and I want to do something about it. I want to find this drunk speedboater and, and …" I couldn't continue, couldn't even identify in my own mind what I would do when I found the man.

Raphael Ostend moved around his desk and placed a hand on my shoulder. "I think we can help you find what you're looking for, Tom. Come, follow me."

OSTEND LED US DOWN THE HALLWAY in the opposite direction of the ballroom, turned a corner and entered a second library. He had taken a torch from the hallway wall and now held it just inside the door so we could all make our way inside the room. He directed our attention to a large bookshelf in the corner, where he removed a few books, reached to the back of the shelf, and turned a mechanism that made a loud click. The bookshelf moved away from the wall. Ostend reached behind it and swung it open. Ben, Mindy and I silently followed him into the hidden passageway and Ben closed the door behind him.

Descending the slight incline of the passageway with my

crutches was easy enough. It was turning that was difficult because the torchlight did not reach all the way to the floor. We were moving at a fast pace. I could not stop and bumped into Ostend when he halted suddenly at another hidden door. Mindy wondered aloud why I wouldn't give her one crutch to hold and take her hand. I did not bother to answer.

"Before now, I've shown what you're about to see to no one," Raphael Ostend said. "The Reporters will understand why, when I deign to show them. Ben, you'll understand why when you see it. As for you, Tom, I hope you'll forgive my secretiveness. We all agreed and hoped that secrecy was for the best."

Ostend opened the door and led us into a cold, damp room that seemed immense behind its shadows and beyond its echo. When he lit the torches that hung two on each wall, I saw that the room was only about twenty by forty feet. On one end was a set of sturdy wooden doors. In the middle of the room was an old, burned out wooden boat, about twenty feet long, its paneling removed from one side.

I dropped one crutch to the ground and moved to the wall using my other one for support. I grabbed a torch in my free hand and moved as quickly as I could around the boat, my shoe, the crutch, and their echoes making an odd, horse-clomp sound on the stone floor.

I stopped when I got to the back of the boat. I lowered the torch to cast more light on the writing shellacked with stain a shade lighter than that which covered the boat's siding. It said *"No Name,"* my father's homage to Ulysses and a personal jibe to all those boat owners who named their vessels pretentiously, as he said, as if the wooden or fiberglass constructs in which they sat were members of the family. Even something as well built as a Lyman Islander, he said, was still just a thing.

I LOOKED UP AND SAW that Raphael Ostend had moved beside me.

"Why do you have my father's boat at Valhalla?" I asked, angry and puzzled in equal measure.

"I paid some men to raise it," Raphael Ostend said. "They did it on September 11, 1996, the night of the funeral mass, after you stopped looking for the drunk speedboater."

"Why?" I asked.

"Because I hoped to show it to you one day," he said.

I repeated my question.

"Right now, in order to answer all your questions, there are three things you need to know. The first is this."

Ostend moved over to the Lyman's open panel and moved the torch closer to it. I followed him, got down on a knee and tried to see what he was showing me. Mindy stood behind me, looking over my shoulder.

"See that?" he asked, using a pen for a pointer. "See that fuel line? See the lengthwise cut right there, about three inches before the section that was melted in the fire? The fuel line's been tampered with, Tom. It's been cut." He looked at me, his face glowing eerily in the torchlight. "Tom, your father's boat was sabotaged."

"By whom?" I croaked.

Ostend seemingly ignored the question and stood up. He handed the torch to Ben, who was standing next to him now, wide-eyed at the burnt hulk before him.

"This note that was found in your mother's pocket when she was pulled out of the water is the second piece of information you need to know. Here. Read it."

He handed me a torn slip of paper that he'd taken from his tuxedo coat pocket. The words written on it were in my father's distinctive handwriting. It was difficult to read because of the disintegration brought on by the water and by time. The note read,

Thank ... my dear, for yester ... versation and
thank ... for rec ... g my ... veness. I promise you:
I'll do ... thing I ... ful ... l our shared task. Malqari
may ... live, bu ... he ... 't stop us. Nor can
Ma ... me ... my ... pose. It may only be a matter ... time before he ... gold is. He may
already ... what the ... I will do everything in
my ... to prevent ... taking it.

"Malqari," I said, looking at Raphael Ostend and Ben
Fries and raising the torch so I could see their expressions.
Mindy took the letter from my hand and read it herself. I
spoke carefully. "Malqari told my father that he knew where
the gold was and that he was going to take it. When my
father found out, he committed himself to protecting it, to
keeping it safe in our river, where it belongs." I lowered the
torch and moved it back and forth along the Lyman's hull.
"When my father refused to help Malqari get the gold,
Malqari sabotaged his boat, or paid someone else to do it."

Ostend nodded and said nothing.

Mindy handed me the letter. I folded it in half and put it
in my inside coat pocket. I recalled the week I had spent on
the river looking for the man who'd allegedly killed my parents and brother, the week which would connect my personal grief to the national grief of the 9/11 attacks. I now
knew those were wasted days in more ways than one.

"Malqari did it by sabotaging my father's boat," I said.
"Which means the third piece of information is that there
never was a drunk speedboater."

"It was a cover up," Mindy said. "You and the rest of
the Reporters invented it."

"Yes," Ostend said, "and Tom, for wasting your time
on your pursuit, I and the other Reporters are deeply and
truly sorry."

"Why did you do it?" Mindy asked.

"The drunk speedboater was code language," Ben Fries

explained. "We decided upon it back in '76 or '77, before your father heard that Malqari was dead. We agreed back then that if any of us were injured or killed doing anything involving Napoleon's gold, and especially if we were any closer to finding it, we would use coded language. An injury would be caused by a reckless speedboater. A death by a drunk speedboater. They're common enough here on the river for the explanation to be plausible in just about any circumstance."

"My father was in on this?"

"He came up with the idea," Ben said. "True, he wanted to find the gold back then and remove it from the river. In that we were divided. But he also wanted to ensure that no one else got it, especially Malqari. Thus, the coded language. The need for it seemingly faded when we heard that Malqari was dead. Frankly, I'm astonished your father remembered it when he discovered that Malqari was still alive."

"What if someone was out on the river alone?" I asked.

"We didn't go out alone," Raphael Ostend said. "We always went in pairs, and we always ..." he paused to glance at Ben Fries, "except for one occasion, that is, we always let one of the other Reporters know where we were going."

"The exception was the time you paid Billy Masterson to dive." I said. "You never told anyone where you went."

"That's true," Ben said, "and I'm still not sure whether my secretiveness was a mistake."

"What do we do now?" I asked nervously. "Run? Hide? Confront Malqari together? Try to bait him into revealing whatever it is he's up to? What do we do?"

Ostend answered. "In our opinion, we should do nothing beyond being more vigilant and cautious. I talked to Andrew at dinner earlier, and he's agreed to set up a surveillance camera on a buoy offshore from Heron's Nest. He and Billy have also agreed to stay with you for a while."

"Do you think I need protection?" I asked.

"Better safe than sorry," Ben Fries said. "Malqari might

believe that you've learned all there is to know about Napoleon's gold since moving in to Heron's Nest. If that's the case, he might try to convince you, too, to help him, just as he tried to convince your father five years ago. If you refuse, it's likely that he'll try to harm you as well."

"I think I'd like to go home," I said.

Mindy looked at me with a puzzled expression. "We're not staying?"

"I'm going home," I said. "You can join me, or you can stay here with Ambassador Maitland all night. It's your call."

"All we did was dance," she said.

"For now," I snapped.

Raphael Ostend stepped between us. "It's probably for the best that you leave sooner rather than later anyway, for reasons that Ben will explain in the company of the other Reporters. Do me one favor, though, both of you. Please keep the whereabouts of your father's boat a secret. I would find myself facing substantial difficulties with the American authorities if they found out the boat was here."

Ostend took a cell phone from his pocket and instructed his butler to gather together the Reporters and take them to the *Archangel.* He moved over to the large oak doors, and unlocked and opened one of the them. I then saw that the storage room we were in was adjacent to the landing where the *Archangel* was docked. I turned around to face my father's burned out Lyman one more time. Then I walked through the door and prepared to board the boat that would take me home.

Chapter Twenty

ONCE THE OTHER RIVER RAT REPORTERS had joined us around the *Archangel*, Raphael Ostend asked Billy Masterson and my cousin Andrew to accompany Mindy and me back to Heron's Nest. He also asked Jim Pembroke to take us there, after dropping off Ben Fries at his boat, which was anchored just off the western tip of Tar Island.

Ostend moved to the edge of the landing and placed a hand on the gunwale. "Gentlemen," he said. "I just shared with Tom and Mindy the two pieces of information that point towards Naguib Malqari as the killer of his parents and brother—his father's note and the true meaning of the words 'drunk speedboater.' Now Ben has some information to share with all of you, which I have no doubt you will find most unpleasant."

Ben cleared his throat as he stepped among us. "Just yesterday I discovered that one of Raphael's distinguished guests this evening has, for several years now, been Naguib Malqari's associate in pursuit of Napoleon's gold. He's been his informant on the river. He's also been recruiting several local men to help them find Napoleon's gold."

"Who is it?" I asked, wondering if it was, and hoping it wasn't, one of the Reporters.

"Former Ambassador Maitland," Ben Fries said. He looked at Mindy, whose jaw dropped in shock and perhaps shame, and then he looked directly at me.

My heart sank, even with the relief of knowing it wasn't

one of the Reporters, even with the jealous satisfaction I felt at seeing Mindy pricked by the news.

Ben Fries smiled, his eyes still on me. "Maitland was in that clique of New York politicians your father sought out to support Preserve the Islands, Tom. He was also an old friend of Harold Radisson's and a college classmate of Hillary Clinton's. Your father admired and respected him."

"If memory serves," Mike Slattery said, "you didn't trust him one bit."

"True. That was a major point of contention between Charlie and me in the early years. I'm sad to say I was right."

"I danced with him three times," Mindy admitted. The others turned to face her, looks of reproach on a few of their faces and confusion on a couple of others. I heard a hint of residual pride in her voice, however, and looked away and scowled. "He asked me all kinds of questions," she continued, "and I answered them. Where I live, what I do, the conference I'm supposed to attend on Monday. I even told him what perfume I was wearing."

I turned to face her. "You told him what?" I asked, feeling my pulse quicken. "You never even shared that with me."

"Oh shit," Billy Masterson said.

"Did you talk about Tom?" Raphael Ostend asked with some urgency.

"No, not beyond confirming that he's here as my date."

"You shared your perfume with him," I said.

"Did you talk about Napoleon's gold?" Ostend asked, trying to ignore my jealousy.

"He said, and I quote, 'it's an interesting proposition, this gold.' "

"The undines?"

"He said he's seen one as well."

Billy Masterson exchanged a look of concern with Raphael Ostend.

"Where?"

"I asked, but he wouldn't tell me. He did offer to show me, though, if I came up here next summer."

"Did you accept?" I asked, almost in a shout.

"Yes, Tom," Mindy said. "I accepted." She spoke the next words very slowly, *"for both of us."*

"Did he mention the *Archangel?*" Ostend asked quickly.

"He didn't seem very interested that I'd come over to Valhalla on it. Why would he be?"

"The *Archangel's* our ace in the hole against Malqari," Ben Fries said. "If Maitland didn't talk about it then he either knows about it already or didn't know enough to ask. Either way, we're left with as little knowledge, and thus with as little certainty, as we had before." Ben sighed.

"Maitland left the party," Mike Slattery said. We all turned to look at him. "Phyllis and Margie saw him say goodnight to Senator Fucillo, then saw him practically run down the stairs to the other boathouse."

"That can't be good," Billy Masterson said.

"Perhaps not," Ostend said. "How long ago was this, Mike?"

"Just a few minutes ago, as your butler was gathering us to come down here."

"So it hasn't been very long," Martin Comstock said, looking at Mike Slattery and then at Raphael Ostend.

"If the two of you would like to try and follow him, you can be my guest," Ostend said.

"Well, he might lead us right to Malqari," Comstock said.

Mike Slattery started for the stairs. "We'll take my boat, Martin. Jim, I'll have Phyllis drop Margie off at her place."

"Thanks," Jim Pembroke said. "She's not cut out for adventures like this."

"Trust us, Tom," Martin Comstock whispered as he walked by me on his way up the stairs.

"Kingston docks on Tuesday?" Mike Slattery asked as he was halfway up the stairs.

"Yes," Raphael Ostend said, "just as we planned."

WHILE MINDY, BEN AND BILLY were preparing to board the *Archangel,* and while Andrew was engaged in a heated discussion with Raphael Ostend about something, I stood on deck with Jim Pembroke, who was checking the gauges and instruments one final time before we embarked. "You're the only living Reporter to have seen Naguib Malqari," I said.

"That's right."

"Do you think he's two hundred fifty years old?"

Pembroke checked a few more gauges, opened and closed a small fuse box below the dashboard, then sat down in the pilot's chair. "What are the other possibilities? That his distant ancestor looked exactly like him and wore the same ring? That the picture was doctored? The first is too much of a coincidence. Lady Ostend ruled out the second. I think I'll trust her judgment. Why, what do you think?"

"The doppelganger ancestor theory is reasonable to me," I said. "If he knew his ancestor had loaded Napoleon's gold onto a French ship in Egypt, then he'd have even more motive to keep searching for it."

"The ring's the most interesting aspect," Pembroke said.

"Yes, I meant to ask you about that, too. In the picture, it looked to me like an ouroboros, a 'tail-devourer,' a serpent eternally eating itself and being recreated. Do you remember anything like that from the CANCO-2000?"

Pembroke paused and then nodded. "It was that. Your father called it the deathless snake. He was convinced that Malqari himself was deathless, like that snake. Like Lady Ostend said. He thought he was wrong about that after hearing Malqari was dead, but it just goes to show ya', Tom, that sometimes we can never be sure what's the truth and what isn't."

"The ring could be a family heirloom," I said, not want-

ing to believe the most outrageous theory. I added, feeling
the butterflies in my stomach, "Jim, do you think Malqari
had anything to do with my parents' and brother's deaths?"
Mindful of Raphael Ostend's instructions, I was careful not
to mention the sabotaged boat behind the closed and now
locked oak doors.

Pembroke paused again, but this time shook his head.
"Honestly, Tom, I'm not sure I believe that."

"Why?"

"I can't see the motive," he said. "If Malqari was after
the gold, or after the undines, what good would killing your
father do?"

I had several more questions I wanted to ask, but as I
was about to respond, Jim stood up and nodded towards
the landing. "There are the others, Tom. We should be off.
Who knows, maybe, in three days, you'll be able to ask your
questions to the well-dressed Arab himself."

MINDY AND I SAT on different padded benches in the
Archangel's aft cabin, not saying a word. I watched her crying
while I seethed over the flirting she'd enjoyed with Ambassador Maitland, the ally of the man who'd killed my parents
and brother.

We remained silent and separate for an agonizing half
hour or so, until suddenly we heard Billy Masterson yell
Mindy's name, and then "Get out here! Quick!"

We glanced at each other, then Mindy ran and I
crutched out the cabin door into the cool November air. I
expected to see another *aurora borealis* light show. By time I
got outside Billy had already taken Mindy by the arms, dancing to an old Van Morrison tune.

Billy said, "The party shouldn't end just because the
band's not here!" He spun Mindy around with a speed that
almost made her trip. "Hell, Mindy," he added, "I've made
several mistakes in my life worse than you dancin' with
Maitland. I'm still doin' fine, ain't I?"

Mindy began laughing through her tears as she danced and the others were smiling. I couldn't help cracking a smile myself.

Andrew then joined Van Morrison in song, singing about singing on a caravan. He reminded me of Mike Slattery's story wherein Andrew's mother and mine shared songs as part of their lives. Andrew, unlike me, had inherited his mother's musical talent. Ben and I clapped in time, and after a couple verses joined in on the dance.

After more dancing and clapping we all joined in on the final refrain. We shouted the "La la's" as loudly as Van Morrison's backup singers did on the recording, a bit too loud for Jim Pembroke's comfort, albeit in harmony. He turned off the radio and told us to shut the hell up because there's no goddamn way we'd be mistaken for a flock of geese.

We settled down as we moved out into open water. Pembroke turned off the running lights, slowed the *Archangel* to a crawl, and directed our attention to the sky. We saw the Big Dipper, of course, the Milky Way, Orion, Cassiopeia and several other constellations that we named and pointed out to each other. We stood there for a few minutes and silently watched the sky, seeing a meteor or two and several airplanes alight under the stars. Billy Masterson kept humming the Van Morrison tune, until Jim Pembroke switched the running lights back on, hit the throttle, and brought us back to the reality of our journey.

A FEW MOMENTS LATER Mindy sat down across from me, next to Andrew, and laid a hand on his. She said, "Andrew? Don't you have a story to tell?"

I did not want her help, and tried to indicate this with a stare and shake of my head. She ignored me.

"Never thought I'd have to tell it in front of so many people," he said. "I thought it would be just me and Tom out on the lawn of Hibbard Island, with a few beers each and a bag of chips."

"Better get on with it," Jim Pembroke said. "You know as well as the rest of us that this is the one he most needs to hear."

"Does your story involve my mother?" I asked.

Andrew nodded and scrunched up his bottom lip. "Your mother and my father," he said. "It's our family saga." For the first time that evening I noticed that he had shaved off his goatee.

"Our family saga? How come I don't already know it?"

Andrew paused, and in a second his face grew red. He took off his glasses—I had never seen him wear them before—and said, with his voice growing louder and higher pitched than usual, "You don't know the story, Tom, because you left. Once you got your first summer job down in Clinton Falls you came back to the river, what, once a year, tops? You left, cuz. You were always much more of a city boy than a river rat." He sighed and motioned with up-turned hands towards me. "Now you're here. The prodigal son has returned. Now I'll do my duty and tell you what you should already know."

"He's not a prodigal son," Mindy said, also with anger. "He's a son restored from exile. Prodigal means ..."

"I know damn well what prodigal means!" Andrew said. "Don't you think I've sat through sermons about it at Densmore? Just because I'm Methodist and not Catholic doesn't mean I don't know anything about the Bible. And you know what, Mindy? He is prodigal."

"He is not."

"Who put him through college? Uncle Charlie and Aunt Mary. Who left him Heron's Nest? Uncle Charlie and Aunt Mary. Is he using those years of college? Has he done anything with Heron's Nest in the past five years before deciding he wanted it back and just showing up to claim it?

Without even a phone call? My dad was right. I should have changed the goddamn locks."

"Whoa," Billy Masterson said, holding out his hands towards Andrew. "Down boy."

I shook my head. "No, Billy, it's okay. My absence from the river and from Heron's Nest has bothered me all these years, too. For moving away so suddenly and completely, I do deserves Andrew's criticism."

"What you don't deserve is the underlying envy," Mindy said. Andrew turned and shot her a look. I shot her a look. She ignored us both. "Don't try to deny it, Andrew. I can see it in your eyes every time someone mentions Heron's Nest. I can hear it in your voice when you say the words. You want it, and you're jealous as hell that Tom has it and you don't."

My mouth fell agape, as did Billy's and Jim's. But Ben Fries, sitting in the bucket chair next to Captain Pembroke, which he had swiveled in our direction, just smiled slightly and nodded his head. Andrew disengaged his gaze from Mindy and lowered his eyes. He shook his head and laughed, and mumbled something about a goddamn Diamondbacks fan. He looked back up at me, his expression mellowed from the confrontation.

"She's right, Tom," he said. "I'm jealous as hell and I always have been, ever since we were kids. I always knew Heron's Nest would stay in your side of the family, even if it meant it would sit vacant for five years. I always knew it. But I never accepted it."

"You've got a beautiful island, Andrew," I said, "with plate glass windows and a hot tub."

"That I do have," he said. "I also have the pride of having helped my dad build it and improve it. But it's only a rock in the water, cuz. Without a family or a history it's only a building with a basin full of inefficiently overheated water and a few more sexy perks." He laughed. "Just like Napoleon's gold is only a chest of gold without what Heron's

Nest brings to it. Actually, that's one thing Ostend has been right about all these years."

"What do you mean by that?" Mindy asked. "What's Heron's Nest got to do with the gold?"

"What I mean is that Tom's been looking in the wrong place for answers, and at the wrong person."

"What?" I said, echoing Mindy.

"You're looking for answers in your father's study, thinking that you'll get them there and from him." Andrew started getting angry again. "He didn't *have* any answers, Tom. He didn't know shit. From the day he started looking to the day he died your father had no answers. Hell, I bet he didn't even know the right questions."

"My mother ... ?"

"Yes, who was also my aunt, please don't forget."

"She knew the answers to Napoleon's gold?" I looked at Ben, who, with his eyes and a nod, redirected my attention to Andrew.

Andrew laughed loudly, drawing a rebuke from Jim Pembroke to quiet down. "She knew, all right. She knew all the answers. More importantly, she knew that you don't start building with the crow's nest. You start building with the foundation. And get this. She never told your father a damned thing about it until the day they died."

Chapter Twenty One

ANDREW'S STORY, the story of our family tree, is best shared beginning with my mother and uncle and proceeding backwards from there to the earliest years of river settlement, when most of the islands were still owned by the various First Nation tribes.

The first fact Andrew explained was why my mother and not her older sibling Jack had inherited Heron's Nest. The reason why was simple. Learning it provided me with the understanding that Andrew's jealousy was in part born of his frustration at having choices that should have been his, made for him instead.

Our grandfather, George Hibbard, was an island contractor in the glory days of vacation real estate development. He never added it all up himself, but legend has it that George Hibbard Construction had built over two hundred homes of all shapes and sizes on the river. These ranged from the smallest two or three room cottages for extended families to share on a weekly basis to large summer mansions for executives from General Electric in Schenectady, Endicott-Johnson in Binghamton or Eastman Kodak in Rochester. He had trained his son, Jack, to follow in his footsteps. When his eldest child reached the age of eighteen, George offered him the choice of inheriting either Heron's Nest or the family business. Jack chose the latter, and, adapting to changing times, became a master in the art of home renovation and historical restoration.

When Jack moved south permanently in 1992, he

passed the business on to his son Andrew. Just as George Hibbard had groomed his son to run the family business, so, too, did Andrew's father. Thus, without a choice in the matter, Andrew ended up the third generation owner and operator of George Hibbard Construction, Inc. By default, I ended up the owner of Heron's Nest.

The question hanging from the next branch down on the family tree surprised me, both for its content and for its unexpected connection to the larger story of Napoleon's gold. Why was my mother the lone Roman Catholic in a family of more or less faithful and committed Methodists? Why did she become Roman Catholic, marry a Roman Catholic, and raise Patrick and me as the same?

Perhaps a little more background is necessary here, especially in this day and age when a family's religious affiliation matters far less than it used to. The Hibbards are not only of Methodist descent, they are the closest thing possible to Methodist royalty. Far down the family tree is the Reverend William Hibbard, one of the most widely traveled and influential circuit-riding preachers in the first generation of American Methodism. Billy Hibbard was a spiritual wonder, a prophet whose dreams were filled with divine interpretations of events in his own life and accurate predictions of events to come in others' lives. He was a fiery preacher whose stories, condemnations and calls for repentance could bring an audience of a thousand to tears and a witness to miracles who saw a dead woman returned to life. Andrew insisted that Billy Hibbard's spiritual gifts ran in our bloodline, even though he claimed he had never experienced them and even though I knew I hadn't either. Then again, Andrew and my mother both had seen an undine.

Back to the family tree. Billy Hibbard was also a "croaker," a first generation American Methodist who, in the 1820's and 30's, bemoaned the luxury-seeking new generation of Methodists, striving to be part of the new American establishment rather than striving towards spiritual perfection. Rejecting power and wealth as the corruptions of the Devil, Hibbard was a populist, raging in his sermons against the wealthy, comfortable, spiritually empty Congregational churches of New England served by the over-educated graduates of Harvard Divinity school and other establishment seminaries.

This anti-establishment populism remained strong in the family blood. None of the Hibbards had gone to an Ivy League school. Most, like my grandfather George, had struck out on their own in small, family-owned businesses after graduating from high school or, at best, community college. My mother, of course, had married Charlie Flanagan, the high priest of populism, as one of his newspaper colleagues called him, who spent his entire career exposing the frauds and follies of the powers that be. But my mother was also the most well-educated family member before me, earning an M.A. in English Education from the SUNY College at Geneseo and using it to pursue a career in high school teaching before resigning to raise her sons.

Back to the religious connection. Reverend Billy and all the Hibbard family line up to my mother were as hard-core Methodist as Methodists could be, opposing slavery, advocating temperance, eschewing profanity, and singing their way to spiritual perfection. Methodism is how the Hibbards ended up with Heron's Nest.

Many people who live in and visit the Thousand Islands don't know that Thousand Islands Park, the community where Heron's Nest is located, was founded in 1875 as the Methodist "Thousand Islands Camp Meeting Ground," modest in its architecture, emphasizing the needs of the many rather than the rights of the individual. It still functions this way, and in clear and dramatic fashion. When I inherited Heron's Nest, what I actually received were shares in the Thousand Islands Park Corporation rather than a private title to the property. Any changes I might wish to make to the building or grounds must be approved by the shareholders. If I sell the cottage, the buyer must be approved by the other share-owning residents. I am as responsible as any of my neighbors for the upkeep of the whole community. While this arrangement has become more common these days in urban and vacation condominium living, it was unique back in the 1870's and, for an entire village community, remains so today.

People forget the village's Methodist heritage because most of the remaining buildings in TI Park come from the same culture of wealth and upward mobility that gave Billy Hibbard such fits when it first appeared in the 1820's and 30's. The village is dominated by beautiful, ornate cottages in the Victorian, Queen Anne and Craftsman styles. Few of them have less than three colors of paint on their siding and trim work. Most of them sport gables, turrets, gazebos or at least screened in sleeping porches decorated with arabesque fascia frames. The historic jewel of TI Park, the Columbian Hotel, may have burned to the ground in the early twentieth century, but its memory lives on in the many cottages that echo its grandeur. The whole community is now on the National Register of Historic Places.

Heron's Nest, however, while historically important in more ways than one, is not one of the grand gingerbread houses that make TI Park so picturesque. It is a simple bungalow, built by the hands of Thomas Hibbard, Reverend Billy's grandson, with a dormer and crow's nest added by my contractor grandfather George Hibbard. According to Andrew, it has been painted white with green trim since the time it was built. The black and white photographs on the living room wall testify to that fact as well as two-tone pictures can.

The Hibbards were old school Methodists. My uncle Jack and aunt Nancy and cousin Andrew are still Methodist, at least on paper. I've heard them called "Creasters" in reference to the two holidays they do regularly attend church. My mother was a Roman Catholic who went to mass every

Sunday and on most holy days of obligation. This fact is explained by the marriage match between my grandfather George Hibbard, who bequeathed Heron's Nest to my mother and the family business to Jack, and my Roman Catholic grandmother Marie Louise Dindeblanc, who hailed from a family as staunchly Catholic as the Hibbards were staunchly Methodist.

How did the match happen? The question may seem less than relevant today when men and women cross all kinds of religious lines to marry. How was their marriage connected to Napoleon's gold? From what Andrew told me, it seems the one question cannot be answered without also answering the other.

The Dindeblancs, from southern France via Montreal, were first drawn to the upper river and then to Thousand Islands Park for the area's diversity and tolerance. TI Park started as a Methodist camp but, along with attracting the establishment, it quickly became a spiritual haven for non-Methodists as well. Frederick Douglass stayed there. Susan B. Anthony visited. The most famous and influential vacation resident of the Park was the Swami Vivekananda, founder of the international Hindu Ramakrishna Order, whose mission, I discovered later on the group's website, is to promote the divinity of the soul, the universality of religion, and the unity of the Godhead.

Swami Vivekananda stayed in TI Park for two months in the summer of 1895 before returning from a long series of travels in the United States to his native India. While here he conducted spiritual seminars for regular Park residents and for visitors who came exclusively to be instructed by him. He was beloved by the river people, and he reciprocated that love. When Vivekananda left TI Park after his summer stay, he blessed the river and its islands and called them good. He said later that the time he'd spent in the Thousand Islands were the happiest days of his life.

The Hibbards, who had become good friends with

Vivekananda, were tickled to hear that he had declined chairs in Eastern Philosophy at both Harvard and Columbia and chose instead to return to India.

Vivekananda and his stay in TI Park marked a positive change for the Hibbard family from Reverend Billy's time, at least from my early twenty-first-century point of view. Less critical, less dogmatic, less closed-minded, the stewards of Thousand Island Park around the turn of the twentieth century welcomed new and innovative ways of thinking just as much as they celebrated their Methodist roots. They listened to Vivekananda and took him seriously. They accepted him openly when he told them, "I do not come to convert you to a new belief. I want you to keep your own belief; I want to make the Methodist a better Methodist; the Presbyterian a better Presbyterian; the Unitarian a better Unitarian. I want to teach you to live the truth, to reveal the light within your own soul." Whereas Billy Hibbard would have scowled and shouted out words of condemnation against that philosophy, the Hibbards, living a century later, accepted Vivekananda's teachings and opened wide their hearts to his message that revealed the light within.

Thanks in large part to Vivekananda, TI Park became a progressive, open-minded community of tolerant and curious people who enjoyed life on the river and let other people enjoy it too; in whatever way they saw fit. Thus, when the Dindeblanc family arrived in 1903 and began telling their story, the Methodists of Thousand Island Park, including and especially the Hibbards, were predisposed to listen to their claim that the sacred nature of their shared river was more meaningful than even Swami Vivekananda had known.

Questions arise here. Did Swami Vivekananda know about Napoleon's gold? About the undines? It seems hard to believe that he didn't, as tuned in as he was to the spiritual nature of creation and as appreciative as he was of the river's spiritual dimensions. Hearing his part in the story, having already heard Lady Ostend's, I started to understand that the late 1800s were important years in the developing appreciation of the Thousand Islands region in more ways than one. Unfortunately, if Vivekenada did know something about the gold and its guardians, he wrote nothing about them.

According to Andrew, the match between George Hibbard and Marie Louise Dindeblanc was made before the Hibbards heard the story of Napoleon's gold. Marie Louise didn't mention it during the courtship phase, which proceeded traditionally first with chaperones, then without them. When George Hibbard asked the elder Dindeblancs for their daughter's hand, and again when he rowed Marie Louise to Bluff Island, dropped to a knee and proposed to her, he knew nothing about Napoleon's gold. This fact of chronology relieved me because—with Reverend Billy's populist blood in my veins, after all—I didn't want to suspect that the Hibbards, too, had sold out to the establishment and were merely seeking wealth through new family connections.

The Dindeblancs, you see, insisted that Napoleon's gold was theirs. It was their family ancestor, they claimed, who had conveyed the gold aboard the *Egalité* from Brest to the Saint Lawrence in 1815. It was their ancestor to whom the gold was entrusted by Napoleon himself, to be kept secret until the exiled emperor arrived in the New World. It was their ancestor who had saved the gold from the wreckage of the *Egalité* and had safely hidden it elsewhere on the river.

And where was it hidden? Apparently, my grandmother Marie Louise was prepared to tell my grandfather George exactly where it was hidden during their first night as wife and husband. But George had already found it on his own, and he told her the location first, which she then confirmed as correct. Andrew told me the same on the *Archangel* as we headed upriver from the Ostend Group. Napoleon's gold was located in an island cave, about twenty five hundred feet offshore of Wellesley Island, due south of Heron's Nest.

I LOOKED AT BEN FRIES after Andrew finished telling the story. "Did you know this at the picnic back in 1976?" I asked. "The one where you told my parents about the gold?" I was thinking back to Ben's comment, made to my father and relayed to me by Mike Slattery, that Napoleon's gold might be located right offshore from Heron's Nest, exactly where, it turns out, my maternal grandparents insisted it was indeed located.

"No," Ben Fries said. "I was just guessing. Blindly throwing a dart at the board. Sometimes, you know, you hit a bull's-eye. It turned out to be a mistimed shot, but it was a bull's-eye nonetheless."

"Your mother didn't know the specifics either in 1976," Andrew said. "She learned the full story only after Grandma Marie died in 1978 and left your mother an unorganized mess of documents, notes and pictures. What your mother did with them is in a safe deposit box in the Citizens Bank of Clayton. She called it her project."

Andrew reached into his pocket, took out his keychain, removed a small gold key and held it up. He looked it over as if it were Napoleon's gold itself. "I'm supposed to give you this," he continued. "I was supposed to give it to you five years ago when your parents died."

"Why didn't you?" Mindy asked for me. She knew me better than anyone back then, and was thinking, no doubt, about how different each of our lives would have been had Andrew followed through on what he was supposed to do.

"I already explained that," Andrew said. "You were gone, Tom. You decided to remain in Clinton Falls. What good would the knowledge do you there, what good would it do us on the river, with you not even here?"

"Have you seen these papers?" I asked, becoming suspicious.

"No, I haven't. I promised not to look at them. I keep my promises."

"Who'd you promise?" I asked.

"Your mother. She gave me the key when my parents moved to Florida. She gave it to me in trust, for you. I warned her that I wouldn't give it to you unless you came back." Andrew laughed. "She shrugged and said she couldn't do much about that now." Andrew handed me the key, which I placed in my inside tuxedo jacket pocket. Mindy breathed a sigh of relief.

I thanked him, then asked, "Was what you said before the truth? About my father not knowing?"

Andrew looked at Ben Fries, who answered for him. "Charlie learned about the French corvette at the June 1976 cookout, about the 'French evil' when the CANCO-2000 ran aground a few weeks later, and about the gold specifically when he visited Naguib Malqari in Montreal in November of that same year. He'd already heard the rumors of gold in the river, everyone had, but up to that point he lacked an historical anchor to tie it to.

"Your mother finished her research project on the gold and her family history, the project that's inside that safe deposit box, in 1990. She told your father parts of the story, including what Andrew just told you, but not the entire story. That new bit of information, plus the clearing up of the water by the zebra mussels, led your father to resume his search."

"Why'd he have the markings and note cards on the map if he and mom both knew it was offshore from Heron's Nest?"

"Because he didn't know that for sure," Andrew said. "The gold had been sighted in more than one place, Tom. That's the strangest thing of all. Billy Masterson, Hassan the wheelman, several of your father's diving friends, both your father and mother themselves, even some of the Undies."

Andrew shook his head. "All of them swore that they saw the gold, but in a completely different place on the river."

"What do you mean? It wasn't where Grandma Louise and Grandpa George both said it was?"

"They thought so," Andrew said. "Your mother thought so. This didn't make any sense to your father, who'd been down there and saw nothing even remotely connected to Napoleon's gold. He started to keep track. The markings on his map and the note cards record where and when the gold was seen and who saw it."

"There was more than one chest?" Mindy asked. Her eyes widened as she considered another answer. "Or the gold itself *moved*? That can't be."

"Can you come up with another explanation?" Andrew asked.

A disturbing thought came to my mind, and I looked at Billy Masterson. "Andrew said you told my father you saw the gold, Billy. You told me you didn't tell him until much later. Did you see the gold more than once? Did you see it more times than that one when you were with Ben? The one you told me about?"

Billy held up his hands. "I saw somethin' those other times, Tom, and, yes, they were in other places, but those other times were nothin' like the time I told you about. I swear, that was a once-in-a-lifetime experience. That was the real gold."

I looked at Ben. "You never told Billy where this once-in-a-lifetime experience took place. You didn't tell my father which of Billy's dives was the different one, the really important one." I paused as another thought crossed my mind. "You did tell my mother, though, didn't you? She knew. She knew that you used Billy and kept what you knew secret."

Ben slowly nodded. "Hear me now, Tom. Listen carefully. Your mother and I had committed ourselves to protecting the gold. Until the very end, your father had committed himself to finding it and taking it. We tried over and over again to change his mind, but he wouldn't change it, especially after he lost his newspaper. There was no stopping him after that, especially when he got his motivation back and resumed his search in the early 1990's."

"Well, where is it, then?"

Ben shook his head. "I can't tell you just now. Wait, please, until we meet in Kingston in three days."

"You still know where it is," I said. Ben nodded. "And that day you took Billy out? It's still there, isn't it?" Ben nodded again.

"Why didn't you tell me?" Billy said, taking rightful ownership of the conversation. "You know I've been lookin' for it all these years. Why didn't you effin' tell me?"

"I promised Mary I would tell no one. I wanted you …"

Billy stood up and sprung across the boat towards Ben. Andrew caught him just as he was about to deliver the punch. Andrew held Billy's cocked right arm at the elbow, keeping the fist a good two feet from Ben's face.

Ben didn't flinch, didn't even move. He spoke carefully. "I'm sorry, Billy. It had to be that way. I had to confirm that what Mary had told me about Napoleon's gold was true. I needed you to confirm it for me."

"I never told you!" Billy shouted, his breathing heavy as he exerted himself against Andrew's restraint. "When I came up, I never even told you what I saw!"

"You didn't have to tell me!" Ben said, finally standing, but for emphasis rather than to protect himself. "You didn't have to tell me because I could see it in your face when you came up out of the water. Remember what Swami Vivekananda once said about the light within our souls? It was like you were a different person when you came out of the water that day. It was like a light inside your soul had been turned on. I knew only the gold could do that."

I moved around to the port side of the boat and could see Billy's face, his eyes wet, his mouth curled, his skin flushed red with emotion.

"Eff you, Mister Freeeeeze," he said, with more grief than anger. "You could have saved me twenty-three years of pain by tellin' me one simple fact."

"It's the pain that made you who you are, Billy," Ben said gently. "It's the pain that's made you a good man."

Just then Jim Pembroke interrupted to inform us that we were nearing Tar Island and thus Ben's boat. Relieved that the conflict between Ben and Billy was over and at the same time regretting that Ben was leaving us, I looked to the port and saw the lights of Rockport flickering in the distance.

"Billy," Ben said, pulling his backpack over his shoulders and then offering his hand. "I am truly, truly sorry. I hope you can find it in yourself to forgive me."

Billy Masterson took Ben's hand and wordlessly shook it, his mouth closed tight in a scowl and his eyes no longer able to hold back the tears.

Chapter Twenty Two

WE SAID OUR GOODBYES QUICKLY and reconfirmed our rendez-vous at the public docks in Kingston on Tuesday morning. As Ben stepped from the *Archangel* to his Sea Craft, that old sense of uncertainty suddenly returned and I had no idea whether I would ever see him again. Part of me didn't want to see him again. I was angry at his betrayal of Billy and his withholding of information from my father.

Mindy sensed this, moved next to me and tried to take my hand. I pulled away. Behind me I heard Billy Masterson mutter, "Fare thee well, you old son of a bitch." I was too absorbed in my own sense of renewed anxiety to turn around and respond.

Jim Pembroke turned the boat starboard and hit the throttle. As we passed the western end of Deer Island and approached the channel I heard Andrew whisper "Holy shit," and then say it again louder. Mindy turned and gasped, then moved her hands to her mouth and shrieked.

I rotated on my crutches to see what was bothering them, and gasped myself when I saw, moving upriver, a massive ocean freighter, under the Canadian flag, its hundreds of running lights reflecting into the water off its silver steel hull, its seven searchlights scanning the water until they fixed on us. The ship's bridge seemed to touch the sky, its deck was busy with activity as some men ran and pointed towards the *Archangel,* and others shouted instructions in several languages that I could not understand. All of this illumination and activity was happening beneath the smokestack, which was decorated with a white on black picture of the tail devourer, the deathless snake, Naguib Malqari's ouroboros.

"I'll be damned," Jim Pembroke said. As a former river pilot he was clearly fascinated by what he saw. He slowed the *Archangel*, then started offering measurements of length, beam and draft, ballast figures, I.M.O. numbers, probable engine sizes. None of it meant anything to the rest of us, besides Andrew. "How the hell'd that thing get through the locks?" Pembroke asked. How the hell'd it get past customs?"

"What do you mean?" I asked.

"The Seaway's maximum length is 766 feet," Jim said, "but doesn't it look bigger than that?"

"It's hard to tell," I said, also fascinated. "I don't think I've ever seen anything *that* big."

"Save the discussion for later," Andrew said. "We've got to get out of here now."

"Where?" Mindy asked, her trembling hand again reaching for mine.

Jim Pembroke, shaking off his fascination, took action. He steered the *Archangel* hard port and then back around, away from the shipping channel and towards the maze of islands near the Canadian span of the international bridge. "That ship won't be able to follow us where we're going," he said.

"Those will," Billy Masterson said, pointing south and then east towards at least a dozen small watercraft approaching us from all directions. We saw small skiffs and two person jet skis and Zodiac rafts fitted with outboard motors. At least one man on each craft was armed. In the air, we saw three small helicopters that were normally used for crop dusting.

"We're effin' screwed," Billy added, "by a shit swarm of Sea-Doos."

"Not yet," Andrew said as he looked back at the watercraft closing in on us. "Jim, get us out of here. Go into the islands, away from that damned ship. Make this thing fly!"

Andrew reached under the starboard bench and produced two shotguns. To my relief he gave one to Billy and not to me. He told Billy to aim at the helicopters first, then at the Sea Doos.

"Just what I thought," Andrew said as he raised the gun and sighted. "Several of 'em are Undies."

We were moving into a group of tightly clustered islands now, Jim Pembroke turning the wheel this way and that in order to avoid hidden shoals and, worse, exposed cliffs. Some of the boaters didn't turn as fast as they should have, and either ran aground or screeched the hulls of their crafts into the cliffs.

Andrew instructed Mindy and me to get down below deck immediately. We had a hard time doing so with the *Archangel* zig-zagging so fast.

While making my way aft I peeked overboard at the point where Jim Pembroke opened the throttle full bore. I swore I saw the *Archangel* rising out above the water.

From below deck, through the windows, Mindy and I saw what was happening around us, at least directly to port and starboard. We saw the smaller craft catch up to us and heard Andrew and Billy fire the shotguns. A couple of the boats capsized as they swerved to avoid Andrew and Billy's shots. One of the jet skis was hit and fell into the water, its driver and passenger bailing out just in time. We also saw the number of our enemy growing as we moved out into open water and more craft joined the chase. There were, no doubt, even more of them behind and in front of us, outside our field of vision. Most worrisome, we heard and felt the increasing barrage of shots hitting the *Archangel* from every direction. Mindy moved away from the window.

After about five minutes the gunfire from above deck stopped. Andrew ran down the stairs, shut and locked the door behind him, and started opening drawers below the sink and stove. He pulled out a roll of duct tape and a large Ziploc freezer bag. He looked at me then at Mindy, his eyes flashing with anxiety. "Billy's been shot," he said.

"You're fixing him with that?" Mindy exclaimed.

Andrew smiled. "No," he said. "Tom, come over here. Give me back that key."

"No, Andrew. It was meant for me. You can't change things now."

"I don't want to change things!" Andrew said.

He looked behind him as we heard voices nearby shouting in the same languages that we'd heard from the deck of Naguib Malqari's ship. Mindy confirmed that some of the talking was in French, but the voices were too muffled for her to translate.

Andrew raised his hands, holding the duct tape around two fingers. "I'm trying to help you, for Christ's sake. Get over here now and give me the damn key."

When I did so Andrew reached down and quickly unbuckled my belt and unclasped the fly of my pants. He pulled the pants down. He forcefully pressed the safe deposit box key onto my inner thigh just below the hem of my underwear, and securely fastened it with the duct tape.

"Pull your pants up," he instructed. "No one gets that key, you understand? No one!"

I nodded.

Andrew reached down and undid the boot from my left foot. He took it off and replaced it with the freezer bag, which he also secured with duct tape.

"What are you doing?" Mindy asked.

Andrew ignored her, put the boot on his left foot, and got my crutches. "Can you swim with one good foot?" he asked.

"Well enough, I think."

"Good, because that's your only option."

Andrew gave me a slick black turtleneck, reached under the dining table and produced an air tank and mask. "Take this. Billy says it's got plenty of oxygen. And change into that diving top. They'll see you a mile away in a white shirt."

I followed his instructions, giving the tuxedo jacket to Mindy, who put it over her shoulders.

The voices sounded closer. One came from above us, arguing with Jim Pembroke in broken English.

Andrew looked up. "Hurry, dammit. We're running out of time." He went back under the table, pulled back the carpet and unlatched a hidden door, which slid open to reveal a cargo compartment down into the hull. "The *Archangel* was a smuggling boat before the Ostends bought it and rebuilt it," he explained. He grabbed me by the collar and pushed me through the hatch. "Now go, Tom. Crawl aft. You'll find another door just above and to the left of the engine compartment that'll let you out. Hurry. If we're lucky Pembroke'll hit the throttle in thirty seconds. If we're not lucky the boat's already theirs. Swim away from here and protect yourself. Don't worry about us."

"What are we going to do, Andrew?" Mindy asked.

"I'm Tom now," Andrew said, leaning on the crutches. "You understand that, Mindy? I'm Tom Flanagan now."

She looked at me, back at Andrew, then took in a deep breath. "Yes, I understand," she said. "But why?"

Andrew pointed down at me. "Hopefully, it'll buy him some time."

Mindy knelt down as I lowered myself into the hull. "Be careful, Tom," she said as she reached down and touched my cheek with her palm. "I need you to make it through this. I love you."

"Go!" Andrew shouted. "I'll do my best to protect her!"

Just as I made it safely into the hull, Andrew quietly but quickly slid the door shut. I crawled aft, as instructed, and despite the darkness was still able to find the hatch to the outside. I noticed a strange metallic sound as I crawled along—strange for a wooden boat, I thought—but, given the circumstances, didn't make much of it at that moment. I placed the breathing mask over my nose and mouth and slid my arms into the straps holding the tank. As I slipped out of the *Archangel* and closed the secret hatch I could hear the voices getting louder, all of them, thankfully, coming from the bow. The majority of the voices were French. They were definitely aboard and had probably taken possession of the boat.

I fell into the water and swam down. I knew from the pressure I felt from behind and above me that Jim Pembroke or someone had hit the engines and moved the boat forward. I felt another wave of pressure, looked over my shoulder and saw the wake. The water churned, then cleared. The *Archangel* was gone. The only question I had was who, exactly, was at the helm.

Part Three

I do not know much about gods;
but I think that the river
Is a strong brown god—
sullen, untamed and intractable,
Patient to some degree,
at first recognized as a frontier;
Useful, untrustworthy, as a conveyor of commerce;
Then only a problem
confronting the builder of bridges.
The problem once solved,
the brown god is almost forgotten
By the dwellers in cities—ever, however, implacable.
Keeping his seasons and rages, destroyer, reminder
Of what men choose to forget.
Unhonored, unpropitiated
By worshippers of the machine,
but waiting, watching and waiting.

T.S Eliot
The Dry Salvages

Chapter Twenty Three

AT FIRST, I THOUGHT THEY WERE UNDINES in their mythical half human form. At first, and for a long time thereafter, I thought they were mermaids. The trio of women seemed to hover above me as I lay supine on a shelf or table. They were pressing something wet onto my head, which didn't make sense because my other working senses told me that I was still underwater. My vision was clouded, my hearing muted, I tasted and smelled river water and seaweed. I thought these undines must have some liquid more viscous than water that they used the same way we humans used a cold compress.

They had also removed my cast. I was due to have it taken off in two weeks, but now it was gone, and my lower left leg, which they had placed in a cylindrical tub filled with liquid, was numb to any sensation from whatever the substance was.

I must have said something to this effect, because they answered me, in English, "Your foot is fine. The bones are healed. The contents of the cylinder in which your foot is contained will give it strength."

They answered me. It seemed that all three of them spoke at once, as if in three-part harmony.

"Where am I?" I asked.

"You're safe," they said. "You're in our care."

"What happened to the others? What happened to Mindy?"

"We don't know. But you're safe."

"What happened to me?"

"We found you washed up on our shore. The current must have carried you. Don't tell us now where you came from. Don't speak at all. Now you must be silent. Now you must heal."

I was not under water after all, but on an island. Which one? Who were they?

"We're the Sisters of Mercy," they answered. "This is Magdalena Island. Our island. You're safe here, Tom Flanagan. You're in Canada." They reached down and stroked my brow. "You must rest. Rest will help you regain your strength."

Next, in what I knew was three-part harmony, they sang to me a song I remembered from my past. I couldn't make out the Latin lyrics, but I knew the tune, a song to the Virgin Mary. I knew I had heard it before, sung by my mother at Saint Cyril's. I remembered all this, and immediately fell into a peaceful sleep.

"LOOKS TO ME LIKE ANOTHER SITUATION of bewilderment and pain," a voice said as I awoke.

I knew who this voice belonged to, even before I opened my eyes. When I opened them and my vision cleared, I first saw the clerical collar around his neck and then his features—grey hair cut short, full red lips curled into a smile, frameless glasses. A sagging face more tired than it had been five years ago when he had buried my family.

"Bishop?" I asked. "How did you find me?"

The bishop stepped aside to reveal the three women who had treated me. "The Sisters called me when they finally got you to fall asleep yesterday morning. They knew you were an American. When they described you, Thomas, I had no doubt it was you."

"Yesterday morning?" I asked. "What day is it?"

"Tuesday, November 6, 2001," he said.

"What time?"

"Two o'clock in the afternoon."

I sat up too quickly and felt an instant ache in my temples. The Sisters of Mercy immediately gathered around my bed. Six arms gently eased me back down.

"I need to go," I said. "I need to go now. I was supposed to meet someone in Kingston this morning. It's very, very important."

"You'll see Benjamin Fries soon enough," the bishop said. "Before that we need to get you to Clayton. First to the bank, so you can retrieve whatever it is inside that safe deposit box, and then to sanctuary at Saint Mary's, where you'll have time to peruse and, hopefully, understand it."

"How did you know?" I reached down to my groin and felt for the key.

The bishop produced it from a pocket and placed it on my chest.

"How did you get that?"

Before the bishop could answer I saw behind him, and behind the Sisters of Mercy, Billy Masterson, with a bandage around his head and his arm in a sling.

"Welcome back, pilgrim," he said, cocking the finger of his slinged hand in an imitation of shooting me. "Let's let these fine ladies pray over you one last time before we board the bishop's boat and get the hell out of Dodge."

ON THE BISHOP'S BOAT, on our way across the river to Clayton, I remembered what happened to me and learned what happened to Billy Masterson.

I swam. As best I could with my weak and not yet healed foot duct-taped inside a Ziploc freezer bag, I swam. I must have gone almost due north, towards the Canadian mainland, before I surfaced and took in my surroundings. I could see nothing except for water and the stars in the darkness above. Determined to get somewhere, I swam some more.

It was at this point that things got hazy. I recall swimming again under the water, feeling light-headed, worrying that the oxygen was running out. I surfaced again with the intention of removing the mask and tank. I tried to turn downriver a bit to be carried by the current and save my strength. But I blacked out, and became aware again after the Sisters of Mercy found me, carried me inside, and tended me for more than a day.

I was confused about several details. The Sisters of Mercy said I had washed up on their shore. Magdalena Island was in the Admiralty Group, upriver rather than downriver. The current could not have carried me to Magdalena Island. How, then, did I get there?

"You were lucky they found you," Billy Masterson said.

"Luck had nothing to do with it, William," the bishop said. "Thomas was guided to the Sisters by God, who knew exactly what to do with this pilgrim, as you so aptly described him. Or rather, He knew that the Sisters knew exactly what to do with him."

"What exactly did they do?" I asked.

"First, and most significantly, they pulled you out of the river. That's what saved your life. The water's getting cold, Thomas. You shouldn't have been in it. Although your Methodist cousin had few, if any, other options, he put you in great danger by sending you off to swim without the proper gear. You lost consciousness because you were approaching the point of hypothermia."

I was about to mention the diving shirt in Andrew's defense. Only then did I realized that the Sisters had outfitted me in a pair of cotton khakis, a blue button down shirt and a new pair of leather shoes.

"Second," the bishop continued, "the Sisters prayed over you, prayed for hours that you would be able to let go of things that are beyond your control."

"What things?" I asked.

"The fate of the river. The destiny of Napoleon's gold.

The survival of the creatures that guard it. Even, still, the well-being of your family." The bishop looked my way.

"How did they know?" I asked. "Did I tell them all that in my sleep?"

"You told them nothing," he said with a smile. "The Sisters read your soul. That's what they do."

I looked at Billy Masterson and then back at the bishop. "What did they see?" I asked.

"They saw a young man struggling with guilt, a young man chasing a chimera in the hopes that he'll find answers to the unanswerable questions of his past. They saw you trying to heal yourself of a self-imposed wound, trying to absolve yourself of the sinful guilt you bear for your parents' and brother's death."

I was speechless at this. Billy Masterson shook his head and said, "Damn, I thought I had issues."

The bishop continued. "Third, Thomas, they healed you. They healed your physical injury, of course, but they also healed your soul."

I considered this for a moment. "Why don't I feel healed?"

"You wouldn't yet, just as after undergoing open heart surgery you'd still experience severe discomfort for some time. You're healed, but you still need time to recover."

I felt strangely disoriented just then, as if there was something missing from what we were talking about, something more than the mystery of how I got to Magdalena Island and what happened when I got there. We were approaching Clayton, though, and I wanted to hear Billy's tale, so I promised the bishop I would pray over it. I then asked Billy to tell his story.

"I got picked out of the river, too," he said, thumbing his free hand towards the bishop. "He was on his way to rescue you from the mercy of the Sisters when he came upon me sittin' on a shoal." Billy narrowed his eyes and smiled slightly as he looked at the bishop, who was concentrating on his piloting. "Perfect timing," he added. A thought had entered his mind. I made a mental note to ask him about it later.

"Andrew said you were shot," I said.

"I was. Took a nice chunk of skin off, too." He rubbed his shoulder. "Nothing a little river water couldn't clean, though."

"Who took the *Archangel*? Did the Undesirables get it? Did Andrew and Jim fend them off?"

"None of the above," Billy said. "Soon after Andrew bailed out of the firefight and went below deck with you and Mindy, Malqari himself came aboard."

"Malqari!" I shouted, fearing the worst.

"That's when the shootin' stopped," Billy explained. "You might have noticed that. That's also when I high-tailed it out of there, shot shoulder and all."

"You abandoned them? What about Mindy?"

"I was told to leave them," Billy said. "One of Malqari's men held his gun to my heart, and Malqari himself ordered me to abandon ship. 'He will not miss this time,' the ageless son of a bitch told me. But then he said—listen to this—'I have Flanagan and Pembroke. They're the ones I need. The girl can come with them.' "

"Andrew's trick worked!" I said. Billy nodded. I frowned. "Where'd he take them?"

"I don't know," Billy said, "but he made a big mistake lettin' me go and thinkin' that I can't find the *Archangel*. Wherever the eff he took it."

THE BISHOP DOCKED at the Clayton waterfront, then drove us the block and a half to the bank. After I retrieved the contents of the safe deposit box, a plain letter-sized manila envelope, he continued inland to Saint Mary's Roman Catholic Church and placed us in the protective care of Father Dominic Ianelli.

"I must leave you here," the bishop said when we were

safely ensconced in a basement reading room. "I have an emergency meeting in Clinton Falls that I cannot miss."

"Thank you, bishop, for everything," I said.

"One final thing," he said as he held open the door on his way out. "One final piece of advice that pertains to my meeting. Difficult times are coming to the Church. A storm is on the horizon, a terrible one. When the storm hits remember that the Mother Church is a human institution, susceptible to failure and sin and the arrogance of pride, as is any other human institution. Remember also, Thomas and William, that God is not fallible, God does not sin, God is omnipotent and gave up that power only when He humbled Himself through His son on the cross." The bishop paused and looked down at the floor, then returned his gaze to Billy and me. "I tell you about this storm in confidence. Remember those truths about your church and about God when the storm hits. Remember them, and your faith will survive the deluge." The bishop closed the door and was gone. Neither of us, at that time, had any idea what he meant.

"You sure we can find them?" I asked Billy Masterson when the bishop had left.

"One way or another," he said. He pulled out his pack of cigarettes, saw that he had none, and tossed the empty container in the garbage. "Mindy told me somethin' when we were dancin'," he added.

"What?"

"Basically, that she's crazy 'bout you."

I sighed. "Why'd she spend so much time dancing with Maitland and paying no attention to me?"

"He's an attractive guy," Billy said. "Rich, handsome, charmin'. Don't forget, she danced with me, too."

"Yeah, I know," I said.

"Jealousy sucks," Billy said.

I opened the manila folder and pulled out the document.

"You need me to stick around while you read that?" Billy asked, pointing down to the table.

"No," I said.

"Good. I need smokes and some food."

"Go ahead. But Billy, do you already know what's in here?"

"All I know is what your mother told your father, then what your father told us. That's what, third-hand knowledge? I bet I don't know half of it. You want somethin' to eat?"

"No thanks," I said. But I felt that odd sense of incompleteness again, the same sense I'd felt on the bishop's boat as we approached Clayton, but this time, I thought I remembered what was missing.

"Billy," I asked, "who won game seven?"

"Oh shit," Billy Masterson said under his breath. "I was hopin' you had amnesia and forgot about that."

"The Yankees lost?"

"Worse than that."

"Worse? How?"

"Rivera blew the save in the ninth. Threw the ball away, plugged a batter, allowed two hits. It was as ugly as they come. I could barely watch it myself."

"Wait, you saw it? I thought you said you were on a shoal Sunday night?"

"And most of Monday."

"So …"

"The Sisters had it on tape," Billy said. "I never would've guessed they were baseball fans." He looked away. "I asked them to heal you of that, too."

I thought about it for a moment and smiled. "I think it worked, Billy. At least the Yanks gave us all we needed in those game four and five comebacks. And I'm really glad for Mindy." Still wanting to be angry, I also wanted those last words back right after I said them.

"We'll find her," Billy said with conviction.

Chapter Twenty Four

My mother's project consisted of twenty-four typed, double-spaced pages. "November 27, 1989," was typed on the top right corner of the first page. I knew this was the day my mother had completed the project she had mentioned to Mike Slattery in her 1978 letter, the project that I now held in my hands.

The document also completed Andrew's tale of our family history. He had covered the Hibbard branch of it well enough for a man of action, not words, as he described himself. Now I could read, in my mother's own writing, the story of the Dindeblanc side back to its earliest days on the river. I went to the door, locked it, then sat down at the large oak table to read what my mother had written.

I could begin with the most clichéd of all biographical openings—"Marjorie LaPlace was born on October 4, 1769, to a poor peasant family on the outskirts of Paris—blah, blah, blah, blah, blah." Starting thus would do justice to neither her nor her story. Her, because the substance of her life didn't actually begin until just before her twentieth birthday, for reasons I should get to by the next paragraph. Her story, because everything that happened in her life, and her country's history, was devoid of justice before 1789.

I reread Dickens this past summer. Charlie chided me for it—"You haven't memorized that

yet?"—but I got as much from *A Tale of Two Cities*
as I have every time I've read it, perhaps more now
that Marjorie's story is finally coming together for
me. This time, it was the arrogance of the French aristocracy that came through most clearly. The Evré-
monde clan, even beloved Charles, believed he knew
what was best for everyone, even if most everyone
didn't agree. True, the book has some continuity er-
rors and chronological difficulties. Ben faults it for
that. The arrogance of the aristocracy rings true to
me historically, even though the recent spate of
American and British bicentennial studies (but not
the Canadian ones) highlight instead an "enlightened" and "reforming" elite that was on its way,
little by little, to creating a new and better France, if
only the people hadn't gotten in the way. Only when
the dam broke and the people became active in public affairs did the "enlightened" aristocratic vision
fade into darkness. One high and mighty Harvard
scholar demeaned the people's activism as the
"politics of turpitude." But that view of history is an
elitist one that privileges the elites. It is, in other
words, a load of manure. The truth is, as *Tale* clearly
shows, that the pre-1789 French aristocracy was
convinced it knew how to do things better than anyone else.

Manure and its uses, in fact, provides a good example. Rather than learning about farming the way
French peasants knew about it, by getting their
hands dirty in the soil and in the manure that fertil-
ized it, French aristocrats tried to reform agriculture
by amassing statistics and citing scientific formulas.
They called themselves physiocrats, which was an
appropriate label in more than one sense. They were
arrogant, and mistaken in their arrogance, in matters

much more important than manure. They'd begin dying for it in 1789.

Back to Marjorie's story—I see I've already fallen two paragraphs behind. She and her mother were at the Bastille when it fell on July 14. Even better, they returned to Paris on October 3 and were in the 7,000 strong vanguard of revolutionary women who, the next day, on Marjorie's birthday, marched to the palace at Versailles and demanded justice and bread from their king, queen and elected representatives. Almost ten times that number made the return trip to Paris on October 6. Later in life, Marjorie would recall these October Days with the same swell of tears and pride that I've seen from black women in Mississippi and Alabama as they remembered and relived the Freedom Marches. They were all good people, caught up in the great events of their age.

Things quieted down for a few years as Marjorie returned to the rhythms of a young woman's daily life. It wasn't to be, however, for a second storm broke. Once again not turpitude, as the Harvard (or was it Princeton?) professor wrote from his ivory tower, not the senseless violence of a mob, but justified vengeance was the convective force beneath these acts of turbulence. This time it was the Second Revolution of 1792. The storming of the Tuileries Palace. The defeat of the Swiss Guard and capture of King Louis and Queen Marie Antoinette. The September Massacres, ill-labeled by another enemy of the revolution who no doubt wore his academic regalia like an *ancien régime* reenactment costume.

Only this time Marjorie's life changed even more, for her vibrant patriotism caught the eye of a soldier, Gerard Dindeblanc, who had traded his patrimonial occupation of raising and butchering Bourbon Reds for the more patriotic work of unveiling and butchering Bourbon sympathizers. He was marching into Paris on July 30, 1792, with his company from Marseilles. They were singing a war song recently composed by Rouget de Lisle, a song that would become the French national anthem. Marjorie's telling of the meeting, written some years afterwards in her incomplete attempt at a memoir, described it in suspiciously clichéd terms. They looked, they talked, they professed devotion, they kissed, they married.

After that they hardly saw each other for almost six years, a separation that probably accounts for the aforementioned clichés. By that point their son, Jean Baptiste Dindeblanc, was dressing up for play as the young Corsican general who was the hero of his (never met) father and the bane of his (widowed?— she had received no letters) mother. Napoleon Bonaparte would define Dindeblanc family lives for generations, much in the same way he would define the lives of tens of thousands of other French families over the next seventeen years of his ascendancy and beyond.

Gerard returned home after six years of war in Belgium, the Vendee, Austria and Italy, but only long enough to introduce himself to the boy, pledge his eternal devotion to his wife, and insist that he'd been "true" to her all these years. "Loyauté" was the word he used. It had a nice revolutionary ring to it.

He was home in May 1798, but left Marseilles for nearby Toulon after a brief stay. This time he returned to serve his fatherland and his commanding general from Corsica with his wife in tow, not by his invitation but at her insistence. Jean Baptiste, the boy, was placed in the care of a Dindeblanc aunt and uncle on the family farm outside Marseille.

In Marjorie's tale, the events that came before May 19, 1798, even the great days of revolution, were nothing but prelude. The true adventure of her life, the events that would define it, began the day Gerard smuggled her aboard the *Egalité* in the great harbor of Toulon, a city returned to the Republic five years before by the courage and cunning of Bonaparte himself. There were many whispered rumors of the fleet's destination among the soldiers and the wives that surreptitiously accompanied them. That the destination was Egypt became certain, courtesy of a proclamation issued by Napoleon, and only after a month on the water. Sea sickness was rampant, mice and rats were in the grain, meat rotted in the heat of the ships' holds, and the women who snuck aboard those ships were forced to hide in those same holds from the men who had left their wives at home.

Marjorie had little trouble dealing with the last challenge. When approached by an officer and offered money in exchange for amorous favors, or when threatened if she didn't provide the favors willingly, she instead sat the officer down and regaled him with stories of those early days in Paris. Without these uprisings, she insisted, Napoleon would be just another Corsican officer of low rank, ambitious for glory but without the means to achieve it, stuck at the rank of lieutenant or, if he got lucky, captain. Valmy, Toulon, Italy, Egypt. She insisted that none of these great conquests would have happened or be happening without those early risings of people in the streets. She concluded with the assurance that she had already provided enough favors for French men, because without her and her sister Parisians, they would not be having this encounter in the first place, en route to what promised to be the most glorious of all French conquests. Most suitors left her company intimidated by "La Citoyenne," as she quickly became known, and regretting having asked for or demanded favors from her.

In time, Napoleon himself learned that Marjorie Dindeblanc was aboard one of his ships. He wanted to hear her tales firsthand. He ordered Gerard to appear before him. Gerard, of course, feared the worst —abandonment on a Mediterranean island, painful lashes on the deck of the flagship *L' Orient*, execution at sea and an undignified burial. What he received instead was a mild rebuke for allowing his wife to sneak aboard and an invitation to join General Bonaparte, his staff, and a few of the savant scientists who were also on the expedition for dinner that night in Napoleon's lavish dining quarters.

"It seems you bring some unique experiences to this expedition, my intrepid lady," General Bonaparte said as the company sipped a fine Bordeaux after an exceptional dinner.

"I have learned to approach life with the courage necessary to challenge tyranny," Marjorie responded to the delight of the table.

"Do you consider me a tyrant?" Bonaparte wanted to know, perhaps thinking back to his own behavior a few years before when he had opened fire on a crowd of 25,000 protestors outside the National Convention in Paris.

"Not yet," she answered, "but only not yet."

That threw the general into a fit of laughter. When he calmed down he complimented Lieutenant Dindeblanc on his choice of mate, absolved him of allowing his wife to sneak aboard the *Egalité*, and promised him that he would someday have the opportunity to serve his commander well.

Marjorie sat with a frown. The general met her eye, having expected she'd be satisfied with the pardon he'd granted her husband. When questioned, she said, imprudently, "I chose to marry my husband, General Bonaparte. I chose to board the *Egalité*. I am a free woman of the French Republic. I needn't ask permission to do anything, from my husband or from you."

This gave the general pause. He thought through his reply carefully and asked her why, then, she chose to join the expedition.

"My husband and I made a vow to proceed through life together," she said. "I am proud that he serves the Republic well. I wish to provide the same service, regardless of who is in command."

This brought the evening to a satisfactory conclusion. Napoleon rose and thanked his dinner companions for reminding him of the truth of revolutionary principles, so often lost in the complicated necessities of the moment. He wished the Dindeblancs well, and reiterated that they, together, would someday have the opportunity to serve him well. He emphasized the pronouns as he repeated his promise, both the one he changed to the plural and the one that remained singular.

Once the *Egalité* reached Egypt, Gerard Dindeblanc was too involved in the demanding everyday challenges of the expedition to ponder Napoleon's promise of opportunity. The challenges included a difficult disembarkation in Alexandria, a grueling march through the heat of the desert to Cairo, the unsettling phenomenon of mirages, which even the most brilliant of Napoleon's savant scientists didn't understand, the victory over Murad Bey at the Battle of the Pyramids, in which Gerard played a heroic role, the fear and reality of anti-French insurrections in Cairo, and, finally, ophthalmia, which left his eyes and the eyes of thousands of his fellow soldiers swollen, stinging and oozing a thick, yellow pus.

Marjorie Dindeblanc had fewer duties, and thus waited more impatiently for her opportunity to arrive, thinking about it often. This is not to say that she did or saw nothing in these early weeks of the expedition. In fact, her actions in response to danger were decisive, her observations acute and revealing.

She was among the last to disembark at Alexandria. She was horrified by an incident on her way to Cairo, in which a distraught Egyptian woman and her child were given food and water by the French, only to be killed by the jealous fury of a man Marjorie took to be the woman's husband. She rallied the soldiers' courage as the water of the Nile seemed to "overflow its very banks" and then recede into illusion as the army drew closer. She joined the other officers' wives and non-combatants on the Nile river flotilla to Cairo, growing close to several of Napoleon's savants, especially the artist Dominique-Vivant Denon. She tended the wounded at the Battle of the Pyramids, although their number, just over 100, paled in comparison to the numbers she had tended in Paris in previous Revolutionary and Napoleonic battles. She comforted them, she tells us, by inventing stories of how the impressive Giza Pyramids in the distance were built and what they represented. Finally, she negotiated with some success the cultural gulf between the French occupiers of Egypt and the native population by adopting a few forms of Egyptian dress and by inviting the Egyptians to tolerate the strange new customs of the Frenchmen in their midst.

Finally, in early November 1798, Napoleon

presented his opportunity. The order came in Bonaparte's own hand:

> You shall accompany the group of scientists,
> led by Dominique-Vivant Denon, headed up-
> river on the Nile. With them, you shall, for the
> glory of the Republic, investigate and catalogue
> the ancient wonders that you will find there.
> Through you, the greatest civilization of modern
> times shall encounter the greatest civilization of
> ancient times. Lieutenant Dindeblanc, it is my
> order that you guard Professor Denon from the
> Bedouins and other dangers that lurk in the
> desert or lay submerged in the river. You will
> protect him until you join the main body of the
> southern army led by General Desaix. Citoyenne
> Dindeblanc, it is my order (or request, if you
> prefer) that you assist the Professor in all his en-
> deavors.

Denon, who had already climbed the Pyramids
and measured the Sphinx, sailed south with his company on an Egyptian flat-bottomed boat. Marjorie,
his friend, recorded everything she saw. There were
villages on the shore that were dirtier and more in-
hospitable than Cairo, their populations infected by
numerous diseases, including ophthalmia. There
were well irrigated fields and orchards that grew
everything from wheat to oranges to dates in an
abundance that astonished her. There were ibises
and ducks on shore, hippos and large, strange fish in
the water. Marjorie at first thought the ophthalmia
was affecting her sight when she saw what looked to
be a giant brown monster, twenty feet long, sidle its
way off shore and into the water. She discovered

later that other soldiers and scientists had the same doubts upon their first crocodile sighting as well.

And she saw the ancient ruins, the true object of Denon's quest, and was left breathless by their size and majesty. Thebes, Dendara, Karnak and the others are common destinations today to those who can afford them, and are learned about easily enough in books by those who cannot. In those days, few outside Egypt, and perhaps no one in Europe, knew the full scope and measure of the temples, tombs and treasures therein that the French found on their journey up the Nile. Marjorie Dindeblanc was even more unique. She was one of only a handful of European women to lay eyes on this part of the world until the new tourist industry began selling Egypt as a destination in the 1870's.

Marjorie Dindeblanc was overawed by the temples and tombs, especially by the great zodiac of Dendara, which, she insisted to Denon, must have been the work of a people great and free. Apparently, she did not share the realization of several other French witnesses that only a highly centralized, rigidly hierarchical society could build on such a grand scale. This was a peculiar blindness on her part, as her beloved Paris had virtually nothing in the way of monumental architecture from the revolutionary years to compete with what had been built under the French kings. Even the greatest of all revolutionary icons, the Arc de Triomphe, would be completed by governments that relied much more on centralized authority than the original revolutionary one had.

Marjorie was so awestruck by what she saw on her voyage up the Nile that she kept a keen eye out for some way she could help Napoleon, whom she now adored for sending her on this journey. She wanted to find some gift, devise some gesture, that would repay him for what he had done. She found it in the most exotic of all encounters the French army would face in their time in Upper Egypt.

She was in Girga, just downriver from Dendara, with a detachment of soldiers. Their orders from General Desaix were to procure food and supplies for the long and grueling chase of Murad Bey and his Mameluke army upriver past Thebes, past Aswan and the first cataract, perhaps into the completely unknown (to Europeans) kingdoms of Nubia. Marjorie was impressed at the quantity of goods available in the small city, and at how cheap these were, despite the upward pressure of demand applied by the arrival of so many new mouths to feed. She bought ducks, chickens and pigeons, beans, oranges and dates, leather for boot repair and cotton cloth to replace the heavy, stifling wool worn by the French.

On New Year's Eve (just another day according to the French revolutionary calendar), as she and the troops were about to return to the main army with their stocks, she was astonished to see entering the city a caravan of two thousand camels making its annual trek from Darfur to Cairo. The caravan was led by a "happy, intelligent, lively, charming" Nubian prince who immediately took as much a liking to the French as they did to him. They feasted together. Marjorie Dindeblanc and the French listened to the Prince's tales of Mecca and India and the strange city of Timbuktu, where gold was so plentiful that it was less valuable than cotton. They discussed the ancient origins of Egypt, the Nubian sharing with them the (now) famous creation story of Isis, Osiris, Seth and Horus. The Prince insisted that these gods

were real, and had once ruled Egypt and Nubia in a
golden age of prosperity and wisdom.

They spoke of the Nile, the mighty river, the
Life-Giver to all of northeast Africa—to all humanity, the prince claimed, since the river's spiritual
power had imbued the earliest of human civilizations with the spiritual underpinnings necessary to
create great things. From this central place, and
from those earliest times, the life-force of the Nile
had spread far and wide throughout the world.

The French wanted to know what makes the
Nile different from the Seine. The prince answered
them simply. He hadn't even heard of the Seine and,
he surmised, before coming to Africa, the French
had most certainly heard of the Nile. The French
persisted. What was so special about this river? Why
was the Nile so essential to the well being of humanity? What made it different from other rivers?

The Nubian prince offered them a demonstra-
tion. He called forward a certain camel, outfitted
with the finest leather halters and silk brocades, decorated with gold loops hanging from its ears, nose
and tail, and guarded by three large, well-armed soldiers. He led the camel to the river. He produced
from its gear a polished wood container, about the
size of a modern shoebox. He explained to the fifteen French soldiers and one French citoyenne
gathered around him that the contents of this box
originated in Nubia, and could now be found in
rivers throughout the world. He took a handful of
the substance, a fine powdered gold that glistened in
the sun as some of it sifted through his fingers and
back into the container. He poured half a handful
into the river. It made the water foam as it hit the
surface, then its glitter turned to glow as it dissolved
into the water.

A moment later the water itself seemed to undulate, flow back in on itself in a manner that amazed Marjorie Dindeblanc and the French soldiers who watched the scene with her. She would write to Napoleon that

> . . . the water seemed to come *alive*! It took on shape, although the shape was hard to discern since it was constantly moving. Actually it took on shapes, separate entities that clearly interacted with each other in their movements and seemed to communicate with each other as well.
>
> What is this magic powder that the Nubian prince has shown us? He explained that it was simply powdered gold, drawn from a vein at the true source of the Nile river, the place where all life once began.
>
> And the water-shapes? My dear General, the Nubian prince assured us that the shapes are real. They are, in fact, water beings, actual creatures, living entities that weren't created by the powdered gold but were, rather, called forth or summoned by it. Awakened by it, perhaps, is the best way to describe the effect. This gold, this fantastic powder taken from the source of the Nile and thus the source of all life, is received by the water beings as a gift. It tames them, the Nubian prince told us, prepares them to fulfill any request that the giver might ask.

In other words, Marjorie Dindeblanc and the soldiers with her that day witnessed the Nubian prince call forth a group of Nile river undines. She suspected, and no doubt Napoleon himself decided when he received her letter, that the general must have as much of this powder as he could get his

hands on. Bonaparte knew, although Marjorie probably did not go this far, that he must find the source
of this powder and possess it.

TO MY REGRET, MY READING WAS INTERRUPTED at this point by
Billy Masterson's return. I opened the locked door for him
when he knocked, and he sat down in an upholstered chair
in a corner of the room.

"Learn a lot yet?" he asked.

"I have. You want to hear it all?"

"Tell me. I'll let you know if you're on the right track,"
Billy said.

"My ancestors, Gerard and Marjorie Dindeblanc, were
part of Napoleon's Egyptian expedition," I said.

"Check."

" 'Citoyenne' Marjorie made quite an impression on
Bonaparte."

"Check."

"She and her husband traveled up the Nile with General
Desaix, having been ordered by Napoleon himself to protect the artist Dominique Vivant-Denon, whose task it was
to draw the ancient wonders there."

"Check."

"While in Girga, Marjorie and several French soldiers,
not including her husband apparently, met a Nubian prince
who showed them the incredible powers of a powdered
gold substance that seemed to summon from the water of
the Nile a group of living beings."

"Check."

"What Marjorie saw were undines."

"Check."

"Some quantity of the same powdered gold came into
Napoleon's possession and made its way to the Thousand
Islands in 1815."

"Check."

I looked down at my mother's document and flipped

through a few pages. "My mom's story breaks off with Marjorie seeing the undines in the Nile, and resumes with the *Egalité* leaving Brest for America. That's a gap of sixteen years."

"Check."

"Gerard wasn't there. Marjorie sailed with her son, Jean Baptiste, the one she left with family in France when she and Gerard went to Egypt."

"Check."

"Can you help me out with something more than 'check'?"

"Check," Billy Masterson said, cracking a smile. "Accordin' to your father, your mother knew several other things about the Dindeblancs. Gerard died of plague durin' the French siege of Acre, which explains why Marjorie ended up here alone with her kid. Also, those two were the only ones to survive the wreck." He motioned towards my mother's project. "That's in there. Do you want to hear it from me or do you want to read it in your mother's words?"

"I'll let her tell the story," I said. "No offense."

"None taken." Billy Masterson said. "Besides, I should find an ash tray."

As he was about to leave the room I asked him one more question. "Billy, why did you say Napoleon's gold was water from the river of heaven when you already knew from my mother via my father that it came from the source of the Nile?"

He looked at me and said, "How do you think it ended up at the source of the Nile? Where do you think it came from? You don't think it grew there do you, Tom?"

"I guess not," I said. "Can I ask you one more question?"

"Fire away."

"Can you tell me about the time you saw an undine? Was it like what my ancestor described seeing in the Nile?"

He nodded. "A lot like she said. Remember I mentioned to you about swimmin' with a sturgeon?"

"The six footer."

"Yeah. It was a powerful beast, that fish. I was about ten feet away from it, and if it turned towards me it would've crushed me like a bug. I felt the same way with the undine, except it was invisible, like Wonder Woman's airplane, only underwater. If that thing'd turned towards me it would've obliterated me like a bug hittin' one of those blue zappers. There's no question about it in my mind."

"It wouldn't have done that, right? It was friendly?"

Billy Masterson considered this for a moment. "It was beyond friendly, I think. Beyond mean, too. It was beyond most things we think and feel. On a completely different level." With that he left the room and closed the door.

Alone again, I read the final five pages of my mother's story.

Marjorie Dindeblanc, like many of her compatriots, was thrilled with the Emperor's return from his Elban exile in 1815. Many modern observers, especially those American historians from Harvard and Princeton and their British counterparts from even more elitist institutions, wonder how this was possible. How could a nation ravaged by over twenty years of almost constant warfare welcome back with such glee the man who was single-handedly responsible for most of those years of war? The answer, as I see it, comes in two parts.

First, and most obviously, France had won most of those wars. Except for the naval battles of Aboukir Bay and Trafalgar, and except for the Spanish draw and the Russian disaster, the people's army of France, whether revolutionary in nature or under the command of Bonaparte, defeated the abominable, and heretofore indomitable, royal armies of

Europe. We Americans of French descent remember this better than others. We live in a land from which the tyranny of kings was first dispelled. The blood flowing through our veins was spilled in great quantities to lay that tyranny to waste forever. Who says history lacks meaning?

History provides another reason for the French people's devotion to their Emperor. Napoleon Bonaparte, although not quite a god, was certainly more than just a man. The best way to describe him is as a force of nature, a being whose will dominated an era and whose accomplishments and failures defined several generations' worth of people's lives.

Napoleon was irresistible, a quality matched by few in history. Alexander, Jesus, Muhammad and Gandhi are the ones that immediately come to mind by way of comparison. It wasn't just Napoleon's conquests. It wasn't just his ability to lead people and convince them to follow him into danger. It wasn't just his incredible knack of leading them *through* that danger to victory. It was, rather, that like the other men listed above, Napoleon personally and completely embodied an idea, a principle, a way of thinking that was so new and so fresh that the idea not only gave him purpose but also used him as a means to achieve its own end of becoming the defining idea of the age. With Alexander the idea was power. With Jesus it was love. With Muhammad it was submission. With Gandhi it was non-violence. With Napoleon that idea, that principle, was revolution.

He was born as part of the revolutionary generation. He became a man during the opening years of revolution. His first real opportunity came in the context of the revolutionary struggle against tyranny. His armies spread revolutionary ideas and institutions throughout Europe. He tamed the revolution like no other man was able to do, transformed it into a creature of his own devising, reflecting his own personality. He took the principles of revolutionary power as far as they could go before they imploded on the frozen hell of Moscow and beyond. In the spring of 1815 he resurrected the revolutionary idea, if only as a ghost of what it once was and if only for a hundred days. And with the help of Marjorie Dindeblenc, "La Citoyenne," who also had been at the center of the great revolution since the beginning, he tried to bring to bear upon the revolution's enemies the sublime and ancient power of nature itself.

He found her in Marseilles. He asked her for one more favor. He told her that a man named Champlain—of course she knew him—had been keeping a treasure of his that had come from Egypt, a treasure about which she had first told him and which he had subsequently acquired from the Nubian prince. She was surprised to hear that a quantity of the powdered gold had made it to France. She did not know how much of it Napoleon had acquired from the Nubian prince, although she did know that Napoleon had not succeeded in finding the gold's source. He asked her to take the gold to Brest, to board the *Egalité*, the ship that had carried her to Egypt in the first place, and wait there for his orders.

The gold was essential for victory, he said. The gold, if properly used, could bring him what he had not yet been able to achieve—victory over the English on water, the element of the undines. He would raise an army, the largest army yet deployed in his war against tyranny. His army would be victorious, he promised, would achieve another crushing victory on land that had become a hallmark of Napoleon's success. Victory won on land, he would use the gold to call forth the creatures of the sea, the water beings that Marjorie herself had seen in the Nile. The undines would serve him in achieving a second victory that would bring peace to France for ages to come.

What could Marjorie Dindeblanc say? She packed a trunk for herself and her son, visited Monsieur Champlain and procured the gold. She and Jean Baptiste rode a carriage from one corner of France to the other to await her Emperor's orders.

She waited in Brest until she received the news of Waterloo early in the morning of June 19, 1815. She was devastated that Napoleon had failed. She boarded the *Egalité* and waited some more. Two days later she received word from Napoleon's brother Joseph that the ship would disembark immediately for America, with Napoleon to follow, if all went according to plan, as soon as possible. Her hope was renewed. The *Egalité's* crew was sparse, composed of Captain Marceau, a few hand-picked sailors, and the Dindeblancs, mother and son. The gold was hidden in the hold beneath a pile of crates which, said the labels, contained clothing.

The crossing was uneventful once the ship eluded the British blockade and reached the Saint Lawrence. There was no resistance at Louisburg. Jean Baptiste suggested that the British there already knew what had happened at Waterloo and were still celebrating their victory. If true, it was the exiles' good fortune. The *Egalité* passed Montreal on August 4, at which point the captain realized that they were being followed now by the British aboard the *Goodspeed*. They pushed the corvette hard, Jean Baptiste and even Marjorie herself taking the helm so they could keep their distance and perhaps even pull farther ahead of their pursuers.

Catastrophe struck suddenly. It was nighttime. The crew did all they could to avert disaster, but to no avail. The captain followed his charts as best he could, but they were outdated, soon to be replaced by the precisely surveyed and expertly drawn work of William Fitzwilliam Owen in 1816, another victory, this time a cartographic one, for the British. The leadsman took proper soundings with his headline and communicated the depths to the captain, but channels rose to shoals and fell back again too quickly and too unpredictably for him to keep up. Add to that the strong and erratic current and the danger of being caught, and the result, while not inevitable, was at least predictable.

Marjorie was not sure what shoal they hit, or where the ship went down. Soon after they hit ground a familiar (to us) wind rose from the west and with it a severe storm. Marjorie and Jean Baptiste went belowdecks to try to save the gold as soon as the vessel started to lurch starboard. They were fortunate in making this choice. Most of the others who died did so while on deck, some after being struck by rigging or broken pieces of mast, others from being thrown into the water by the sideways lilt of the ship and drowning. The Dindeblancs remained belowdecks in an air pocket long enough for the boat to sink. They were able to float up and out of a deck hatch while buoyed by the chest of powdered gold.

But the danger did not end there. Several years later, from memory, Marjorie described what happened next:

The chest began taking in water. Also, we

could see, illuminated as the sky was by flashes of lightning, a small trail of powder seeping out of the bottom of the chest. Jean Baptiste, that ever-faithful boy, took my hand and prayed for our coming demise.

The chest sunk lower, and we could no longer maintain a hold on it above water. We were both too tired to swim. We could only try to keep ourselves afloat. I thought, but did not say, that Jean Baptiste's attentions could best be applied to treading water rather than praying. That was an unfair thought, because neither of us could hold out for much longer. Jean Baptiste began to complain of a sharp pain in his upper leg. I felt around the area and touched an open wound. I could also feel the warmth of his blood flowing out into the cold river water.

Following this, something extraordinary happened. As in Girga, so here, the powder from the chest began to glow, the water began to strangely undulate, and since we were in it rather than on dry land watching it, we could feel the gathering water beings around us.

The water beings gathered first around Jean Baptiste's leg. He gasped, then in a brief moment his breathing returned to normal and his face took on a relaxed, almost tranquil appearance. I returned my hand to his leg, and felt my fingers being guided to the spot that had been wounded and bleeding, but was now closed, now healed.

At that moment we became suddenly and unexpectedly buoyant. We rose—were lifted, it seemed—out of the water enough to breathe and were moved towards the dry rock of the shoal upon which the *Egalité* had foundered.

Since that day, I have swum in the strong current of this river. I know how it feels to be carried forward by the water. This, however, was
different. It was as if the water was distributing
itself across our bodies, taking on our weight,
and raising us, lifting us, to a place where we
could reach forward and pull ourselves up out of
danger.

Jean Baptiste later said it was the hand of
God. I knew it was something much different.

There is little of the tale left to tell. Municipal
and church records show that Marjorie (to her chagrin, no doubt) and Jean Baptiste (to his delight) were
taken in, clothed and fed by the Montreal branch of
the Roman Catholic Angelic Sisters of Saint Paul.
After several years they established themselves in
the Côte-des-Neiges neighborhood of the city,
where they enjoyed some degree of prosperity in the
shipping trade. Jean Baptise married in 1827. Marjorie died in 1851. In 1863, Gerard and Nanette
Dindeblanc, Jean Baptiste's son and daughter-in-
law, moved to Cape Vincent, where several cousins
had settled after the first Bourbon restoration. Gerard, who had first heard the story of Napoleon's
gold and its arrival in the Thousand Islands from his
grandmother, passed down the story to his children,
and they to theirs. Finally, Marie Louise Dindeblanc,
who would later marry George Hibbard, began to
trace its historical meaning while she was still a
child. Her voluminous but unorganized collection of
notes formed the basis for my essay.

Genealogy alone doesn't tell the tale. If the undines hadn't saved their lives, Marjorie and Jean
Baptiste Dindeblanc would have surely died in the
wreck of the *Egalité*. If it weren't for the undines, my

branch of the Dindeblanc family would not have set roots along the Saint Lawrence, and neither I, nor my sons Thomas and Patrick, would be here today. I suspected as much beginning over a decade ago. I've *sensed* my obligation to *something* in this river ever since I was a little girl, looking down into the water and feeling the magic contained therein.

It's no exaggeration to say that I have the undines of the river to thank for my very existence. I will do whatever I can to protect the water beings and the gold they love, the gold my family brought to this place.

Chapter Twenty Five

AND THAT'S WHERE MY MOTHER'S PROJECT ENDED. No doubt she ended it there because she had answered all her own questions and had completed it to her own satisfaction. As much as I wished it were otherwise, the fact was that she wrote her project for no one but herself, to work through the perplexing questions and difficult problems surrounding her family and her family's relationship to the river she loved.

I thought back and tried to recall any clues she might have dropped that the undines were that important to her, or even existed for that matter. If there were any hints they were oblique ones, comments about her deep appreciation for the river and her hope that Patrick and I would stay connected to it in our lives, her promise that Heron's Nest would always be there for us as a refuge from the harsh realities of the world. I tried to recall if she had told us any bedtime stories about the gold or the undines, but all I remember were other stories taken from published sources like *Winnie the Pooh, Jack and the Beanstalk,* and *The Hobbit* when I was older. She did enjoy reading *The Little Mermaid* to me, but millions of other parents have read it to their children with not a clue that undines actually existed. By the time I started pulling away from the river to pursue my own life, I'd lost interest in anyone else's stories and was intent on creating some of my own. Andrew was right. I didn't know about these deeper themes because I wasn't around to learn about them.

I had become an historian. My father was proud of this

choice. I can recall him telling me so directly one evening that I did join him and mom on the river. My mother, on the other hand, warned me about the inherent dangers of studying history. It might stifle my imagination and it might cause me to favor certain techniques borrowed from other disciplines over my own intuition, which she insisted was true and accurate. Worse yet, history might lead me to a false certainty that I had found some eternal truth, which was, to her, the most elusive certainty that existed, and was best approached through emotional and spiritual channels rather than intellectual ones. My mother mistrusted the pursuit of objectivity. To her, any truth that could be arrived at via historical investigation was fleeting at best. I imagined her worrying that history and its overwhelming evidence would cause me to view Napoleon as a monster rather than as a hero of the revolutionary age. She would have been right.

She held back her knowledge of the family from me, and perhaps from Patrick as well. Maybe she hoped I would encounter this knowledge myself after she was gone. Having now read her project, I could appreciate her worry. Would I dismiss her family history as foolishness? Would I set it aside as an insufficient replacement for an objective truth that was lost, to use my father's words, in "the uncharted mists of antiquity, where fact becomes legend, and legend becomes myth?" Systematic analysis and interpretation were useless to me now. Having read my mother's story, all I could do was accept it as a real and vital part of who she was. And thus, a real and vital part of who I am.

So much for my analysis of the past. After a few moments of such reflection, I redirected my thoughts to what to do in the present. When I wasn't reading my mother's family history I was thinking more and more of Mindy, kicking myself for having been so angry at her during the final hour or so before our separation.

I glanced again at what Marjorie Dindeblanc had written about how she and her son had survived the wreck of the *Egalité*. I leaped up in sudden shock as a question was answered in my mind. How had I been carried upriver to Magdalena Island? By the undines. The water beings had saved me just as they had saved my ancestors.

I was about to go find Billy when I heard footsteps approaching down the hallway. I went quickly to the door and started talking loudly before I answered it.

"I'm done reading, Billy," I said. "Let's go find a map. From what my mother wrote we might be able to figure out where you …"

I looked up and saw Billy Masterson, as expected, but with a sheepish look of defeat on his face. An instant later I saw the reason for his embarrassment. Behind Billy, and seemingly moving him down the hallway by force, was a tall man with a large head and perfectly styled short grey hair. I recognized him immediately. He had about him the same aura of privilege and confidence that I had seen at the Ostend Ball, even though he was wearing khakis and a pullover shirt now instead of a tuxedo.

"Ambassador Maitland?" I said, confused by his presence.

"I'm sorry, Tom," Billy said. "I went out to the corner store for a pop. He found me a block away." Billy turned his head to face Maitland and scowled. "This is a church, for Christ sake, put the damn gun away. Besides, we're in the basement. Where the hell we gonna go without you knowin' it?"

Maitland smiled calmly and did as requested, then shoved Billy into the room and locked the door.

"You work for Naguib Malqari," I said. "You told him I was at Valhalla. What else did you tell him? What does he want from me? Where's Mindy and the others?"

"I work for no one," Maitland said calmly. "But yes, I did tell Malqari you were there. He and I were partners once. For a long time, our interests converged." He shook his head. "Presently, due to certain circumstances, our interests do not converge. Our partnership has ended."

"How 'bout the bishop?" Billy said. "You workin' for him?"

"We have … certain arrangements," Maitland said.

"Was reading Mary Flanagan's story one of 'em?" Billy asked, to my surprise.

Maitland looked at me and smiled, not at all sheepishly.

"What're you talking about, Billy?" I asked.

"Remember when we were in the bishop's boat?" Billy Masterson asked. "When I told you the bishop picked me up, too?" I nodded, recalling that I'd made a mental note to ask Billy about what had crossed his mind at that moment, causing him to smile. "Well, the bishop did pick me up, but only the second time he passed by. I didn't realize it the first time because my wound was feelin' better and I was startin' to enjoy myself on that shoal, bein' all alone with the river and all. But when he did pick me up, I knew I'd seen him come downriver and back up a couple hours before. His non-answer to your question of how he knew about the document made me even more suspicious."

"Would you care to explain your theory in further detail?" Ambassador Maitland said, leaning against the door with crossed legs.

"Sure would," Billy said. "The bishop got the call from the Sisters that Tom was convalescin' on their island. He went out there to make sure it was really him. He came to Clayton with the safe deposit box key, got Mary Flanagan's document, made a copy of it, returned the original to the bank, gave the copy to you, and returned to the Sisters, pickin' me up along the way. He gave the key back to Tom, tellin' him that the Sisters found it when they undressed him. The whole operation would've taken an hour and a half, two hours tops. My only question is why you weren't here waitin' for us the first time."

"Congratulations, Mr. Masterson," the Ambassador said. "I certainly underestimated your intelligence."

"Among other things," Billy muttered.

Maitland, however, was too proud of having succeeded in his plots and plans to pay Billy any heed. He continued, "I did not meet you here earlier for two reasons. First, I wanted to give Tom the opportunity to read his mother's tale. He deserved at least that much after all these years of waiting. Second, I was reading the Dindeblanc family story myself." He shook his head and laughed through his breath. "It is a fascinating tale, which provides ample supporting evidence for what I already knew."

"What is that?" I asked.

Maitland looked at his watch, which to me looked even more expensive than Raphael Ostend's. "We have to go now," he said. "If Mister Masterson promises to pilot us to our destination without any shenanigans, I promise in return I'll tell you what I know once we're aboard."

"Aboard what?" I asked, thinking of Naguib Malqari's behemoth that we'd encountered earlier. Ambassador Maitland, who had produced the gun again and was motioning Billy and me out the door, did not answer. Billy looked at me and smiled. I followed, and Maitland closed the door behind me.

As we were walking to the docks, Ambassador Maitland did answer my next question of where exactly we were going. "We're going downriver," he said as we walked downhill towards the village docks. "We're going to stop your friends from doing something very, very misguided."

As we approached the docks, I got the answer to my earlier question of what boat we were boarding. I had to blink to make sure that what I saw was real and not an illusion—the *Archangel*, moored perpendicular to three slips, dwarfing the few other boats there at this time of year.

Billy reached back and poked me in the ribs. "Told you I'd find her," he said. "Better yet, now I get to pilot her!"

"You said Malqari took her," I said, confused. "What about Mindy, Andrew and Jim?"

"Malqari did take the yacht," Maitland said, "and then he gave her to me. Don't worry about your friends. They're fine."

"Wait a minute, you said back at the church you and Malqari were at cross-purposes."

Maitland nodded. "We wanted to find the same thing, which we've now successfully done. Now that we've found it, we want to do two very different things with it. Naguib, however, may not yet know that."

" 'It' refers to Napoleon's gold," I said.

"The only thing worth looking for," Maitland said as he loosed the aft mooring and jumped onto the boat.

"My mother's tale helped you with that," I suggested.

"Her tale confirmed what the gold was, what it could do. Her tale may have offered an answer to where the *Egalité* went down and where the chest of Napoleon's gold was lost. However, that's not exactly what Naguib and I have been looking for all these years. There's another answer, another location, that is far more significant."

Billy Masterson helped me aboard, then grabbed the second rope and jumped on deck himself. Billy started the engine. Maitland and I sat in two of the leather passenger seats.

Maitland turned towards me, and made a steeple of his hands in front of his face before speaking. "We know where the gold is," he said coolly. "Now that we've found it, Naguib and I have very different ideas about what should be done with it." He placed his hands on his lap. "Naguib would rather see the gold remain in the river, inert, useless, slowly dissolving into the cold water until, in time, it is inextricable and as useless as saturated paper."

Like my mother, Ben and, eventually, my father, I

thought. Given what I thought I knew about Malqari, this claim confused me even more. "And you?" I asked.

"I want to raise the gold from its obscurity, use it the same way Napoleon Bonaparte used it to achieve his greatest successes after he first discovered it in Egypt."

"He didn't discover it," I said. "Marjorie Dindeblanc did. My ancestor did."

The Ambassador dismissed my comment with a slight wave of his hand. "Be that as it may, it was Napoleon who discovered the power of the gold, discovered what exactly it was capable of."

"What do you mean?" I asked. "He had the gold loaded aboard a ship and sent to France. Seventeen years later he had it loaded aboard the same ship and sent to America. He never once used it."

"That's where you're mistaken, Mr. Flanagan. Your mother, despite the impressive thoroughness of her project, could have never discovered the missing chapter of the gold's story. Your father and the other so-called River Rat Reporters could've never known it."

"Why not?"

"Because this chapter of the story was hidden for years, locked in a secret library deep within a Galilean monastery belonging to Syriac Catholics. I found it during my time of service in that part of the world. Would you like to hear it?"

"Tell me," I said.

Maitland nodded. "Have you heard of Mount Tabor?" he asked.

"It's biblical right? I remember three scriptural mountains. Sinai, Horeb and Tabor."

"Yes, Mount Tabor overlooks Nazareth, Cana and several other villages mentioned in the life stories of Jesus. It's less than ten miles from the Jordan River and Lake Galilee. Do you recall from Sunday school what happened there?"

"The transfiguration?" I guessed, referring to Jesus' spiritual encounter with God while Peter, John and James slept nearby. Maitland shook his head. "The Sermon on the Mount?"

"Tabor is where Jesus encountered Satan," Maitland said. "Do you know the story?"

I nodded. "Jesus fasted for forty days, then was tempted by Satan to do three things: turn rock into bread to feed his hunger, assume power over all the kingdoms of the earth, and rule as high priest over the holy city of Jerusalem. Jesus parried off the Devil on all three temptations. Satan fled, as the Gospel says, 'until a more opportune time.' "

"Very good."

"I hope so. My mother was my Sunday School teacher."

Maitland laughed. "Do you know what happened to Napoleon on Mount Tabor?"

"I didn't even know Napoleon visited Mount Tabor."

"He did, during the eastern portion of his Egyptian campaign against the Mamelukes. He fought a great battle there, destroying a massive Turkish/Mamaluke army with his usual brilliant battlefield strategy and execution. After the victory he looked down from Mount Tabor and recalled what had happened to Jesus there." Maitland paused. I glanced at Billy Masterson, but he was paying no attention, it seemed, clearly enjoying himself during his first and only opportunity at piloting the *Archangel*.

"What's this particular victory have to do with the gold?" I asked.

"Have you ever heard of Napoleon's friend, Le Petit Homme Rouge?" Maitland asked, perhaps knowing full well that I had heard the story of the influential gnome just a few days before at the Ostend Ball. I simply nodded. "Well, Bonaparte didn't, or couldn't, resist the same temptation. He made a deal with the Little Red Man the day after his triumphant victory, a deal that would lead him to even greater triumphs—Marengo, Austerlitz, Jena, Friedland, Wagram—but a deal that would also cost him dearly in years to come and, ultimately, precipitate his downfall."

"Wait," I said. "Are you saying that this imaginary man, a figment of Napoleon's imagination, was the same being that tempted Jesus in the gospels?"

"I'm not just saying it," Maitland insisted, "I know it. I spent half my lifetime there, Mr. Flanagan, under the pretext of diplomacy, trying to parse out the truth to what began as a mere whisper of legend in my ear. Thanks to those Syriac monks, I know for certain that Napoleon's Le Petit Homme Rouge was the same supernatural being that Jesus encountered almost two thousand years before, on that very same summit. Believe me, the pursuit of this knowledge cost me dearly." Maitland paused. "You might also consider your words more carefully before you dismiss the Little Red Man as a figment of Napoleon's imagination. Recall, Tom, that your mother, father and cousin, as well as our pilot, all claim to have witnessed a similar elemental creature in these very waters upon which we now move."

He was right, of course, and could have also mentioned Marjorie Dindeblanc, Lady Ostend, and who knows how many other witnesses of the undines, including me. I returned to the main point of his story. "Napoleon could not do what Jesus did," I said. "Napoleon couldn't resist the temptation."

"Nor did he want to," Maitland answered. "Napoleon *wanted* that power, *craved* it. He actively sought it. In Egypt, Napoleon was able to procure several chests of powdered gold from the same Nubian prince that your ancestor met in Girga. On Mount Tabor, he was fortunate to encounter the one being who could grant him that power."

I nodded. "He exchanged his powdered gold for the promise of unlimited power. The gnome, like the undines, considered the gold a great gift." Somehow, despite my best rational judgment, it all made sense to me.

"Exactly," Maitland affirmed. "Do you also see the mistake he made?"

I thought for just a moment, recalling my conversation

with Raphael Ostend a few nights before. "Napoleon exchanged the chest of powdered gold with a gnome," I said, "whose only realm of existence is land. Napoleon achieved victories only on land, one after another, until his failure to defeat the British navy and secure the sea caused Spain, and then Russia, to successfully resist him."

"Yes," Maitland said. "His downfall began with his failure to successfully challenge the British navy and British mercantile power. First came resistance in Spain, supplied with British goods and weapons by sea via Portugal, then came the resistance of the Russian Czar, whose courage was bolstered by British propaganda and the promise of British help via the North Sea. Then, of course, came Waterloo." Maitland laughed. "A land battle to be sure, but do you see the obvious irony of the name?"

"What did my mother's project reveal?" I asked rhetorically, once again taking up Maitland's train of thought. "Napoleon realized the extent of his mistake too late in the game. It was only while mustering his forces for Waterloo that he decided to use more of the powdered gold from Nubia, perhaps his last chest of it, to attract and ally himself with the undines, the water beings. He believed that with their help he could defeat the British at sea. By then it was too little, too late."

Maitland nodded. "By then Le Petit Homme Rouge had abandoned Napoleon, leaving him, for the first time in over a decade, to his own devices."

"Do you have any of this gold?" I asked him directly.

Maitland reached into his pocket and withdrew a small silk pouch. "Only this," he said. "There's enough of it here, however, in this river, to bring victory and supremacy to our nation for generations to come. I'm one of the few who know this, Tom, and long years of study have taught me how to transform the power of the gold into the power we need to defeat our enemies once and for all."

"How?" I asked. "By offering it as a gift to the undines? Then what?"

"Then the undines are on our side. Then they willingly provide us with a gift, the greatest gift that humanity can receive."

"Long life? Like Malqari?"

"The real question, Tom, is how that long life comes about."

I searched my memory for some clue that I had already received from the River Rat Reporters or read in my mother's project. Then, in another moment of clarity, I remembered again my experiences with the Sisters of Mercy.

"The cylinder," I said. "They used it to heal. It contained an undine."

Maitland looked confused by this, but then he said, thinking along a parallel track with the one I was on, "Yes, the undines healed Jean Baptiste Dindeblanc. They wrapped themselves around his leg and closed his wound, which was most likely fatal. I suppose you could call them a cylinder."

"They heal," I said, careful now not to reveal my own experience, "which means our soldiers would be pretty much invincible. All you'd need is an undine in a tank back at base camp."

"Dozens of them," Maitland said. "Hundreds. Feed them some powdered gold, and the work of recuperation begins. Our enemies would never be able to keep pace. We'd swamp them with sheer numbers of invincible men."

I considered those enemies, as I had several times before that moment, thinking back to the 9/11 attacks and the immediate aftermath of them. The Al-Qaeda terrorists, of course, were obvious enemies and had to be dealt with severely and mercilessly. But how many other people would fall innocently into that compartment labeled "enemy?" How many other people would fall victim to our nation's wrath? Many of them, no doubt, were men and women who were probably not much different than we were here on the river, torn between two worlds, confused at the rapidity of the changes around us, wanting nothing more than to be left alone to live life and enjoy the brief time we have to do so.

I also thought about the river itself, this place of serene and powerful beauty, this place of healing. Our river was filled with the golden water of heaven, as Billy Masterson saw it, or filled with the grace of God's sublime creative love, as others saw it, or filled with simple fresh air and clean water and freedom, as most of us lived our lives upon it. However we described the spiritual power of this river, we agreed that the power is timeless, beyond the reach of human frailty and foolishness.

And I had just learned, like few others had before me, that the power of the river was, at least in part, perhaps in large part, a gift of the undines. As Marjorie Dindeblanc had tried to describe, the water beings were summoned, called forth, awakened, *given life*, by the powdered gold that they loved. What if, from here, from our river, this healing goodness of creation could be brought to all humanity, and not just to those serving the violent ends of an angry nation? If I had ever wavered in my thinking before, at that moment I did not. The gold must stay here, in the river that received it so long ago. The gold, if used at all, must be used for good.

"Do you see this, Tom?" Billy Masterson suddenly asked me, as I could feel him throttling down the *Archangel*. We were just past Alex Bay and the Summerland Group, and were about to turn north and head into Canadian water near Grenadier Island. I swiveled my chair around and saw in the channel Naguib Malqari's massive freighter. There were dozens of smaller craft too, as there had been at our earlier encounter, and they were, as before, mustering around the *Archangel* itself. This time I noticed an obvious difference. They were not preparing to attack Ostend's boat but to join the *Archangel* in attacking the ship that towered before us.

Chapter Twenty Six

WITH A SERIES OF HAND SIGNALS Ambassador Maitland issued orders to the men on the smaller boats to move forward and surround Malqari's freighter, which I now called, for its notable lack of an official name, the *Ouroboros*. I saw one fishing boat, a larger vessel than the others, move aft towards the starboard side of the freighter and rendezvous with a smaller tug that was anchored there. Meanwhile, the other craft were zigging and zagging around the *Ouroboros*, holding their fire.

"They're a diversion," Billy Masterson whispered as Maitland continued with his hand signals. "Keep your eye on that trawler and tug. They're the ones about to do something." He strained to see onto the *Ouroboros'* deck. "Damn, I wonder if they're seeing all this."

"Who?" I asked.

"Malqari, for sure. Pembroke and Hibbard and your girlfriend, too, if my guess is right."

"Look," I said, and pointed.

We both saw the plan unfold. The fishing boat moved astern the tug. Men aboard it took hold of a thick steel cable and secured it to a winch at the fishing boat's aft. The tug raised anchor. Together the two boats moved some distance apart and lowered the cable into the water. Billy and I both understood what was happening. They were trying to disable the freighter's aft propellers by snagging them in the cable. It was a dangerous operation because, if the engines were activated, the force of the propellers could easily pull both boats down. But the diversion at the fore of the *Ouroboros* seemed enough to give the men time to complete the maneuver.

Billy moved closer and whispered. "If you can disarm Maitland, we can move the *Archangel* around to the stern of that freighter. I know there's a welding torch down in the cabin here because I stowed it before we set off from Valhalla. If you get me back there I think I can get down to that cable and cut it."

"There's no air tank," I said. "Remember? Andrew gave it to me when we were attacked the first time."

Billy looked over his shoulder and saw Maitland still turned the other way, still giving signals. He shook his head. "Doesn't matter. I can hold my breath long enough to get the job done."

"What about your shoulder? Where you were shot?"

Billy waved me off. "No worse than being snagged by a decent-sized muskie lure."

"What about those cables? That's some powerful steel they're made of."

"Nothing your basic torch can't handle."

"Are you sure Maitland's the guy we want to stop? Are you sure we want to help Malqari?"

"Maitland wants to take the gold away from our river, Tom. The bishop helped him get your mother's project. That's bullshit. That's enough proof for me."

"Okay, so how do I get the gun from him?" I asked. "And what do we do about them?" I motioned towards the Sea Doos and other boats.

Billy smiled, bent his knees and slowly opened the leather-cushioned beer cooler to his left. Looking one more time at Maitland, he motioned for me to reach into the cooler. I did, and was surprised to feel not the cold tin of a can but rather the cold steel barrel of a rifle. I looked up at Billy, surprised.

"The magazine's new," he whispered.

I slowly pulled the gun out, then pointed it at Walter Maitland, sliding the bolt and clicking off the safety as I did so.

"Jig's up, Ambassador," Billy said.

Maitland stopped giving hand signals and turned around to face us.

The Ambassador was confused. "How did you get that?" he asked. "I searched the whole boat."

"Forgot to check the beer coolers," Billy said. "If you want to make it work on this river, you've got to pay attention to the beer coolers."

Maitland dropped the handgun and lowered his arms to his sides. "I'm no good at intimidation anyway," he said.

"We figured that out back at the church," Billy said.

"Call them off," I said, waving the rifle back and forth to indicate the other boats out on the river.

"There's no need for that," Maitland said. "We've already accomplished the first part of what we set out to do. Malqari's freighter is disabled."

"What's the second part? What're you doing next?" Billy asked.

"*We* are going aboard said freighter," Maitland said. "Together *we'll* sit down with Mr. Malqari and the rest of your friends and talk. I'll convince you with words if I can. If not ... well, I have other means of persuasion available."

"What if we don't want ..." I started to say, but then stopped when I heard several clicks of rifles and shotguns and who knows what else being loaded behind us. I turned around to see eight men on jet skis, a few of them Undesirables I recognized, who had coasted to a stop next to the *Archangel*. They all had weapons resting on the boat's gunwale, pointed at us.

"I thought you said you're no good at intimidation?" I asked as I clicked on the safety and lowered the rifle.

"I'm not," said Maitland, smiling, "but I make damn sure to hire men who are."

Billy raised his hands and spat into the water. "Effin' Sea-Doos," he said.

WE MOORED THE *ARCHANGEL* against the vastly larger *Ouroboros*, then climbed a pilot's ladder up to the deck. I was astonished at how bright everything was; not new but polished to a near-reflective sheen. From the deck we followed Maitland through a doorway, down several flights of stairs and down a long hallway with a low ceiling. He stopped and opened a door to the right. We walked through the door and into a large, cedar-paneled state room with a large oak table in the middle and bookshelves on two walls.

"Tom!"

I heard Mindy's voice the instant I stepped through the door. She rose from her chair and ran to me. We hugged for a long moment, before she pulled away and expressed how surprised she was to see me; how no one knew if I was okay; how they didn't even know where to begin looking for me.

"I'm so sorry you missed your conference, Mindy ..." was all I could say in reply.

"I'm just glad you're okay," she said. "I meant what I said when you were leaving the *Archangel*, Tom." Then she whispered, "I love you." She moved her arms to my side and looked at me and then behind me when she felt no crutches. "Your leg," she said, looking down. "It's ... better?"

"All fixed up," I said, "courtesy of the Sisters of Mercy. Courtesy also of ... but we'll talk about that later."

She removed my tuxedo jacket. "Here. You look better in this than I do."

"And you, Billy!" Mindy said, reaching out and placing a hand on his injured shoulder.

"I'm all fixed up courtesy of the eau de Saint Laurent," Billy Masterson said.

I looked over Mindy's shoulder and saw the remaining

River Rat Reporters seated around the table, along with the man I immediately recognized as Naguib Malqari. Another Arab was seated between him and Jim Pembroke. I guessed this was Hassan the wheelman, finally back on the river to face the man whose reputation he'd destroyed. Ben Fries was there, too. He had a small cassette recorder on the table in front of him.

"Maitland," Raphael Ostend said with derision when the ambassador walked through the door. "It was bad enough when I found out you'd been secretly sharing information with a presumed enemy. It was worse when I discovered my presumption about Malqari was wrong, and that you'd been double-crossing all of us as part of your own nefarious game."

Maitland gave a quick laugh. "Please, Raphael. Nefarious? You've got to stop watching so many of those 1930's movies." He quickly became serious again. "I assure you that what I do is for the good of us all, including Naguib and Hassan, although they might not yet understand it."

"None of us understands it," Jim Pembroke said, "which is why we agreed to attend this damn meeting in the first place."

"Captain Pembroke, you didn't have a choice," Maitland said.

I just stood there with Mindy's hand in mine, becoming more and more confused by the conversation and its meaning. Naguib Malqari sensed this, walked over towards me and Billy Masterson and motioned for us to sit at the table.

"My apologies are especially for you, Tom Flanagan," Malqari said. "There were certain ... communication difficulties over the years that allowed misperceptions to arise as to my intentions. Some of these difficulties caused your cousin to employ unnecessary measures which put you in danger. Others placed Mister Masterson in harm's way. I can assure you, however, that I meant no harm to come to either of you, or unnecessary anxiety to come to Miss Mc-

Donnell." Malqari bowed slightly and lifted his arms, palms upturned.

"He really didn't mean any harm, Tom," Mindy said to reassure me. "Everyone from Lady Ostend to Jim Pembroke to your father misunderstood his intentions."

"Maitland told us," I said. I looked at Malqari. "You want to save the gold, not manipulate it. Protect the undines, not take them and use them for conquest."

Malqari nodded slowly. "I am the recipient of a great gift from these beings," he said. "I would never consider harming them, or taking from them the gold they love."

I sat down next to Mindy. "Is this true?" I asked, looking at Mike Slattery for an answer.

Slattery just nodded. I wondered if he'd converted into a Napoleon's gold believer, or at least was on his way to becoming one.

"I still don't trust him," Andrew said. When I looked at my cousin I saw for the first time how uncannily we resembled each other when he shaved his goatee and put on glasses. I smiled at the recognition.

Naguib Malqari saw my smile and guessed its meaning. "It wasn't until you walked in the door and I saw Mindy's reaction that I knew for sure it was you, Tom," he said. He turned towards Andrew and bowed again as he had to me a moment before. "I congratulate you, Mister Hibbard, on your talent for disguise and for your loyalty to protecting your family. I truly appreciate such things."

This seemed to disarm Andrew a bit, who started to say something, a thank you perhaps, or maybe another point of suspicion against Malqari, but then stopped.

Ambassador Maitland sat in the remaining chair at the table, while Billy Masterson remained standing near the door.

"I assume we are through with reintroductions and clarifications?" Maitland said. He looked around the table.

"Good. Tell the others, Naguib, why you are really here. Then I will tell you all what you should be doing."

Malqari bowed curtly towards Maitland, with his hands crossed this time instead of upraised. Then he spoke. "All of you know or have experienced something of the phenomenon known among the people of this river as Napoleon's gold. The name is appropriate for you who live here, because your first introduction to the gold was through a chest of it brought to this river in Napoleon Bonaparte's name, intended for his use upon his anticipated arrival at the place called Cape Vincent.

"Alas, this particular hope of Napoleon's friends and family was never realized. Defeated at Waterloo, captured by the British, exiled on the remote island of Saint Helena, and guarded there by British soldiers, Napoleon never arrived in this place. His gold is here, though, faithfully delivered in service by his friend Marjorie Dindeblanc, whom Bonaparte first met en route to Egypt.

"It was there, in Egypt, on the Nile River, that Marjorie Dindeblanc first saw the incredible properties of the gold and experienced the power that it possessed over the water beings you call undines. It was there that Marjorie Dindeblanc first told Napoleon Bonaparte about these properties and powers. It was close by there, in Galilee, that Napoleon himself first saw and experienced them, in the company of La Petite Homme Rouge. I know all this because I was there in my younger years, one of the few in Cairo who shared the enthusiasm of the French for the particular kind of enlightenment they brought with them."

Malqari gave a nod towards Raphael Ostend. "Here, on this river, my friends Lady Ostend and Captain Doctor Charles Obadiah Smithson were among the first non-indigenous people to make the connection between the properties of the gold and, first, the presence, and then, the powers of the water beings. They made these connections, of course, in relation to the chest of gold sent by Napoleon, although they did not know where that gold was.

"When I first heard whispers of such things I knew that the gold brought here by Marjorie Dindeblanc was an insufficient quantity to have any lasting effect on the elementals. I knew there must be more of the same golden powder somewhere, here in this river. I knew, in fact, that to attract and sustain such a large concentration of undines as Lady Ostend insisted were here, this Saint Lawrence River must contain a source releasing at least as much, if not more, of the golden powder as the Nile River contained when I was in Egypt as a young man. This is what I learned when I visited the Saint Lawrence River for the first time in 1887."

Naguib Malqari looked down at the table. None of us made any more noise than we had to.

Malqari continued. "I began surveying the Saint Lawrence River, when I could manage to do so, in search of the source of the gold. Events intervened and upset my plans, however, as they did for so many people caught up in them. World wars, national revolutions, economic crises, and regional conflicts among my people all necessitated my attention. Travel to Canada was difficult. I did manage to come to the river, briefly, only twice, in 1935 and again in 1959.

"The latter date is significant. By then, as you all know, the river had been irreversibly transformed by the dredging of its bottom and the damming of its waters, albeit transformed in more ways than most people understand. Since the middle of the twentieth century the undine presence in this river has increased, you see, not slightly but rather dramatically. I quickly developed a theory of why this had happened, a theory related to the presence of the gold. I needed more time and more opportunity for observation before I could test my theory's validity."

"Your theory is?" Mindy asked. The rest of us except Maitland looked at her.

"The increased undine presence in the river could have only one explanation—the existence in the river of more powdered gold after the creation of the Seaway than before the creation of the Seaway." Malqari nodded curtly towards Mindy and continued.

"I finally had my chance to thoroughly survey the river in 1976, only to have my work complicated by the terrible accident of the CANCO-2000. That tragedy was the result of a confluence of factors.

"My friend Hassan had been down this river before. His spiritual astuteness is keen. He knew there were water be-ings in this river, just as he knew that the same were in the Nile of his native land. Unfortunately, Hassan is a Coptic Christian. He was taught from an early age to be suspicious of the lesser spiritual beings, just as his ancestors had been suspicious of the jinn that appear in so many tales from our lands. He was misinformed by his spiritual leaders to under-stand the elementals as 'demons,' enemies of the divine, rather than as creations of the divine hand and partners in the sustaining of that creation. Hassan became frightened when I suggested we must find the undines and follow them to the place where they rested. He overreacted to Captain Pembroke's insistence that the boat carry on despite the presence of what Hassan called 'the French evil.' Most im-portantly, he is, Captain Pembroke, deeply sorry for the pain he has caused you these past twenty-five years."

Thus prompted, Hassan stood, then bowed as Malqari had earlier, only lower, and said twice what sounded to me like "Na-asif."

Jim Pembroke understood the gesture as an apology and rose and took Hassan's hands in his. "Don't sweat it," Pem-broke said, looking him straight in the eye. "You can take the wheel of my boat anytime you like."

I was struck by the magnanimity of each man's gesture, and smiled at Mindy, who smiled back and squeezed my hand.

Both men sat, and Malqari nodded slowly. He resumed his story.

"My survey ended incomplete because of the CANCO-2000 tragedy. Soon thereafter, I was again distracted by events in my homeland. I believed my quest had failed. I believed I would never discover the secrets of this river. I came close to death once, but had the good fortune to be found, and then nursed and healed by the same men who would, several years later, explain to Ambassador Maitland the effect the powdered gold has on the elementals. To my continued astonishment, these men who healed me were my enemies. I continue to meditate upon the beauty of their commitment as true followers of Jesus.

"I did not expect certain men and women of this river to begin independent searches for the gold so soon after I was forced to abandon mine." Malqari nodded towards me. "Charlie Flanagan made me aware of this when he visited me in Montreal in November of 1976. He was obviously committed to finding the chest of Napoleon's gold, although he had no concept of what it actually was or what it actually meant. I was most astonished for this news on that occasion because I did not know when I would be able to return. Perhaps my astonishment was interpreted as a threat by Mr. Flanagan. Yet in my heart, I was reassured that the search for Napoleon's gold was in good hands." Malqari paused and shook his head. "I am sorry, Tom Flanagan, deeply sorry, that I never had the opportunity to see your father again after that initial meeting in November 1976."

As Malqari began his apology I bowed my head slightly, thinking that he might be apologizing for his involvement in my parents' and brother's deaths. Somehow, I was prepared to forgive him for that, a feeling that surprised me. But when I heard the implied claim that he was nowhere near the river at my parents' and brother's deaths, contrary to what Ben Fries had told me at the Ostend Ball, my head shot up and my eyes found Ben. He was equally astonished.

Malqari saw this, but continued his tale nevertheless. "Others became interested in the special properties of this river as well." He nodded towards Ben Fries. "The organization known as Preserve the Islands, begun under the leadership of Benjamin Fries, has worked in the undines' best interests, albeit mostly unknowingly, by protecting the river from all that would harm it, beginning with the fight against year-round shipping on the Seaway. I am forever grateful for their blessed work.

"Mary Flanagan …" Malqari nodded towards me again, "concentrated her energies on the extraordinary tales of her ancestors that confirmed to several of us in this room, including my friend Ambassador Maitland, that the gold in this river did indeed have the same set of powers that we thought it did.

"I knew all of this indirectly. I also knew that Charlie Flanagan, Captain James Pembroke and others did not trust me. Nor did I try to explain my intentions and earn their trust. Perhaps this was a mistake. Perhaps I should have made more careful attempts at communication. To explain myself, it was in my interests, as I perceived them, to reveal my intentions only when my observations were completed.

"I made my next visit to this river twenty years later, in October 1996, with the intention of completing my observations. Unfortunately, this visit came after Charlie, Mary and Patrick Flanagan had met their ends. Again, Tom, I am truly sorry that I could not be here for them."

I remained silent and let Malqari continue.

"The delay caused by the deaths of Charlie Flanagan, who was closer than anyone to discovering the true source of the gold, and Mary Flanagan, who already understood its true nature, did serve to provide time for me to acquire more of what I needed to make an exhaustive search for where the source of the gold could be." He extended his arms and moved them from side to side. "Now, five years after that loss to us all, and with another set of events intervening to threaten the accomplishment of my goal, I have everything I need aboard this boat. Just these past weeks I have recommenced my search."

"You swear you're not here to steal it?" Andrew said, his voice lacking the suspicion he'd had before.

"I swear," Malqari insisted. "I am here to study it. I am here to discover how the gold of this river attracts these elemental beings, how it awakens their healing powers, and how the ability of other rivers to do the same can be restored." Malqari looked around the room. "The undines of the Nile are disappearing, my friends. Those of the Jordan are all but gone. The Tigris and Euphrates, the Oxus, the Ganges and the Yangtze are all becoming empty of the spiritual power that made them such powerful magnets for the first civilizations. I have not yet studied the rivers of Europe or other parts of the Americas, but I suspect the situations in those streams are similar. Here, however, the river is quite alive, and I want to know why and how it is happening."

"Find anything yet?" Jim Pembroke asked.

Malqari shook his head. "Nothing. Nothing yet. But I suspect the answer lies downriver, where we are headed ..."

"*Were* headed," interrupted Ambassador Maitland. "Your ship is stuck. My ship is already there, Naguib, doing what should have been done years ago."

"Taking the gold," Mindy said. "But, tell us, why?"

"He wants to use it for the war in Afghanistan," I said. "He thinks he can do with it what Napoleon tried and failed to do. He thinks he can successfully channel the power of the gold to convince the elementals to do his bidding and lead the United States to victory."

"He's full of pipe dreams," Mike Slattery said. "Leaders have tried to harness spiritual power for their own belligerent causes for millennia. It never works quite the way they plan."

Maitland held up a hand. "Ah, but this war is different,

Mayor Slattery. This war is one of good versus evil, a cru-
sade as the president so wisely said back in October."

"Bullshit," Jim Pembroke said. "This war's no different
from any other war. You think the people of Afghanistan or
Lebanon or Somalia see America as the force of good while
American bombs are raining down on their homes, killing
their kids? The only difference now is that America's been
attacked. As much as I feel for those people in those towers
and their families, I feel sorry for the Afghans and Lebanese
and Somalis, too. As far as I'm concerned, you're finally getting a taste of the world's own medicine."

"Might I remind you," Maitland said, "that the Canadians, too, are part of the coalition of the willing? If we
don't stop terrorism, then terrorism will strike your shores
as well."

"Might I remind you ..." Pembroke said with a pointed
finger, then backed away. "Shit, Malqari, let's get this boat
the hell out of here and start doing what you brought us
here to do. Come on, Hassan, let's get to the bridge."

"I think you'll find your ship quite immobilized at this
juncture, Captain Pembroke. No one can get those cables
untangled from the propellers."

"You were right about the ca ..." I started to say to
Billy Masterson, only to turn and realize that he was no
longer in the room. Not knowing how long he'd been gone,
but knowing exactly what he was planning to do and how
dangerous that plan was, I let go of Mindy's hand, leapt up
from the table and ran out the open door.

Chapter Twenty Seven

I RAN AS FAST AS I COULD with my left foot still weak and with little memory of where we actually were. A couple of wrong turns took me down near the engine room, but at least that indicated I was heading in the right direction. I ran up a final set of stairs and fell against a door that I hoped would lead me out to the deck. When I opened it and saw sunshine I resumed running, determined to stop Billy from jumping overboard to try to release the ship from the cable that had immobilized it.

"Billy!" I yelled. "Billy, are you up here?"

When I reached the aft railing and looked down I knew right away that I was too late. There was no shooting, no yelling, only several boats and a couple Sea-Doos gathered in a loose circle, facing the body that floated face down at its center. The men in the boats with weapons were holding their guns loose by their sides. Whatever threat there had been, if any, had passed.

Two men approached Billy's body, tied a vest around him and pulled him to a boat with a low gunwale. One of the men on a Sea-Doo looked up, saw me, and tried to explain what had happened. I couldn't understand his French.

"He climbed aboard the wooden boat. A moment later, he jumped feet first off the deck into the water," Naguib Malqari said behind me, translating. "We could not know the object he was holding until we saw the flame underwater and saw the steel cable snap. We did not fire, according to the Ambassador's instructions. Soon the broken cable hit him and the torch was extinguished. His body sunk, then floated ... no, was ... was raised out of the water. After this the cable came to the surface as well, and then sunk. All this lasted only a minute. When he came up, we saw no breathing."

At this, the man in the Sea-Doo turned to face the boat where two other men performed mouth-to-mouth and then CPR on Billy Masterson's body. They looked at him, then up to the deck of the *Ouroboros*, where Mindy, Ambassador Maitland, Hassan and the other River Rat Reporters had gathered behind me and Naguib Malqari. Both men below simultaneously shook their heads and frowned.

"No," I shouted, looking back and catching the shock on Mindy's face and the disbelief on the face of each of the Reporters. Hassan had his head bowed and was praying. Ambassador Maitland's expression told me nothing. Perhaps he was thinking about what to do now that his plan of disabling Malqari's ship had been foiled.

"No," I cried again, turning back down to the water. I saw what Mindy was already pointing out—a faint golden glow rippling at the water's surface where Billy's body had been "raised," in the words of the French sailor. I saw it, and I quickly jumped onto the deck railing with my right foot, threw my left foot over it and fell into the water, aiming for the golden glow.

I would later compare the sensation to landing on one of those Moonwalk bouncy houses I used to love as a kid, then slowly submerging into the water before I was indeed raised by something more powerful than an ordinary swell. Having jumped into the river from plenty of tall island cliffs while growing up, several of them the height of the deck of the *Ouroboros*, it felt nothing at all like I had expected.

At that moment my attention was focused on trying to reach the boat that Billy Masterson's body was in. When I got there the two men who had tried to revive Billy helped me aboard. I dropped to a knee and took Billy in my arms. There was, as I had already been told, no breath at all.

I started crying, the tears mixing with the river water that was falling down my brow, and I continued to cry even though I saw that Billy's face showed the most contented smile I had ever seen on another human being, alive or dead. I assumed, and still believe to this day, that Billy had seen his golden glow, dropped from the river of heaven, one more time before he died. I held him in my arms and rocked back and forth for what seemed to me like a very long time.

"GET HIM UP HERE!" I eventually heard Ambassador Maitland say, in a tone that indicated he had had to repeat the directions several times already.

The men rowed the boat over to a second pilot's ladder, about a hundred feet from where the *Archangel* was moored. Andrew waited there for us, standing on the bottom rung. One of the men and I picked Billy up and handed him to my cousin, who slung him over one shoulder and climbed back up the ladder using only one arm to navigate the rungs. When he reached the top he gently pushed Billy onto the deck, then climbed up himself, none the worse for wear.

I followed Andrew up the ladder and onto the deck, where Mike Slattery grabbed me and threw me down onto the cold metal.

"Why'd you go and do that?" he yelled, still holding my shoulders.

"He's dead, Mike ..." I managed.

"I know damn well he's dead. The river does that, Tom." I tried to look away, but he grabbed my head and turned it back to face him, then returned his grip to my shoulders. He did speak in a softer voice, however. "You need to learn this. When the river says you go, you go. When the river says you stay, you stay. There's no way to fight it. There's no way to change it. Billy appreciated that. Billy accepted that."

"It's just that …" I tried to tell him that the undines were supposed to heal.

"Save your words!" Slattery said while giving my shoulders a harder push against the metal deck. "Pay attention to what's happening here and to what your part in it is. And shut up. This isn't the time for words."

He lifted me off the metal, turned me around and walked me over to where Billy lay.

The River Rat Reporters and Mindy joined us, while Naguib Malqari, Hassan and Ambassador Maitland remained back a few steps. We stood around Billy's body for what must have been five minutes, each of us silent and engaged in our own private prayers, thoughts or memories.

It was Andrew Hibbard who broke the silence. He hummed the tune, barely audibly, then sang Van Morrison's *Into the Mystic*. He only made it to the end of the first verse, purposefully perhaps, or because he could not go on. Crying, he slipped back into our shared silence.

After a few more minutes Ambassador Maitland said quietly, "Gentlemen, I never meant for this to happen. No one was supposed to get hurt. All I want is for you to understand how important my work is for all of us—"

"Billy's dead," Ben Fries interrupted. He looked at Ambassador Maitland. "We won't let him die in vain. We won't let you take what he loved and appreciated far more than any of the rest of us and corrupt it into something destructive. We won't let you take the soul of our river and use it for any other purpose than for the support of life."

"I second that," Mike Slattery said. He slowly moved back and behind Ambassador Maitland. Andrew did the same from the opposite direction. Moving quickly, the two men secured Maitland, Andrew holding him in a tight half nelson, and walked him to an open doorway that led below-decks.

"You can't stop me," Maitland croaked, barely able to breathe. "What this river contains is needed for the defense and security of our homeland. I will obtain the authority to claim it by eminent domain if I have to." He was about to say something else, but Mike Slattery stopped his words with a punch to the face.

Andrew closed the door with his foot and Mike locked it. Raphael Ostend, taking a rope from a storage bin, tied Maitland up to the diagonal metal hand bar on the door. Andrew and Mike let him go with a push into the door, which produced a loud thud.

"Well, we've got things to do," Martin Comstock said, wiping a final tear from his eye. "We can mourn later and for as long as we have to. Right now we've got things to do."

"I suggest we understand exactly what it is we're about to do before we proceed," Ben Fries said. "Please, friends, join me back in the stateroom. It won't take long. I've got something you all need to hear." He then looked at Naguib Malqari. "I think I'm about to save you a lot of time."

WHEN WE HAD TAKEN OUR SEATS around the table, Ben Fries put an index finger on the play button of the cassette recorder he had before him. "I recorded this conversation a few days ago," he said. "The meeting I had with this man was the reason why I needed a few days alone before our planned rendezvous in Kingston. The rendezvous didn't work out as planned, but I did get the interview. One voice you'll hear is mine. The other speaker is a man named Edwin Nighthouse. He's an Algonquin and a lawyer, and he lives on Princess Street in Kingston, though he spends much of his year in Ottawa. I found him at home at Kingston. He ... well, I'll let our conversation speak for itself. Please, friends, listen carefully. Nighthouse is about to tell us exactly what Billy died for."

Edwin Nighthouse: Not at all.

Ben Fries: Thank you. I know how awkward these things can be.

EN: As I was saying, the work on the Seaway helped pay my way through college.

BF: Queens College, you said?

EN: Yes. I studied history there, then received a full scholarship to Toronto University's law school. I passed the bar in 1966. I returned to Kingston and have been a practicing attorney ever since; here and in Ottawa.

BF: Mostly indigenous rights cases, correct?

EN: And international law. The two go hand-in-hand since our national borders are not necessarily your national borders.

BF: Of course.

EN: My business should pick up quite a bit now that America's been hit and will no doubt turn itself into a fortress. (Sighs) I wish I weren't so old and tired. I could work sixty hours a week on those cases, especially for the unfortunate Saint Regis people.

BF: Back to the Seaway, were there many other First Nation workers besides you?

EN: Not many dredgers. Most worked on the lock and dam projects in Massena. There were a few who'd come upriver now and then. They'd work for a couple of weeks to get the job done on time or to get us back on schedule, then head back east.

BF: You got behind schedule often?

EN: Oh, yeah. Dredging this river was the most difficult aspect of the entire Seaway project. Not the most complicated—that award goes to the actual dam construction. But dredging was definitely the most difficult component.

BF: Why?

EN: Ever look closely at the river floor? Ever notice how it's made up of one of two things, either rock or mud? Well, that rock is glacial till, left over from the retreat of the ice sheets tens of thousands of years ago. Some of it's pebble size, some of it's boulder size. Most of it's in between. What it all has in common is that it's incredibly hard, very difficult to break through and scoop up, even with the strongest of shovels. Much of it had to be blasted before it could be scooped up to begin with.

The other stuff, the mud, well that's clay, and it turns to soup when it's dug out and stays wet. When it's cold, that clay freezes like a giant popsicle right in the back of the dump trucks. Either way, clay or till, the job was much more time-consuming than anyone thought it would be. Broken equipment, frozen equipment, hell, just getting the stuff up out of the water took a lot of time and a tremendous amount of horsepower.

BF: You did it. You dredged not only the canals

around the power dams but also the channels themselves.

EN: We sure as hell did. Shallow bottoms, shoals, even entire parts of islands were taken out to make room for the damn cargo ships.

BF: You don't sound too proud of what you did.

EN: I am in a way, because at the time it was the greatest construction show on earth, as we used to say. It quickly became less relevant, however. Today, it's almost obsolete. Did you know that only four percent of the world's ships can even fit through the Seaway? Four percent!

BF: Why not dredge more? The equipment must have improved since the late fifties.

EN: Sure the equipment's there to do it, but expanding the Seaway, like the American Corps of Engineers wants to do, would destroy the river. Sure, the work I did helped change it beyond recognition. Anything beyond that and our river would be destroyed. If that happens, I'll blame no one but myself. Although I don't think it'll happen in our lifetimes.

BF: But the money you earned did put you through college and law school. You're helping a lot of First Nation people with your work. Admit it, you probably wouldn't have been able to earn enough doing any other line of work, at least not in those days.

EN: Back then, no. You're right. It's two sides of the same coin.

"All right," Ben Fries said as he stopped the tape. "Now let me fast forward. Nighthouse and I talked about a few of his cases, but most of that isn't really relevant here. What is relevant is his answer to my question of why the Saint Lawrence River is so special. The question arose in relation to a recent lawsuit involving a large fish kill caused by another round of dredging in Canadian territory about fifty miles downriver from Massena. Nighthouse and his clients lost the case and were denied any financial reward, but only because the judge ruled that they failed to prove conclusively that the kill was caused by the dredging incident and not by one of several other assaults on the river that happened around the same time, including a chemical spill, a sewage leak and even an earthquake. The judge made it quite clear that the First Nations were legitimate victims of environmental damage, whatever the cause. Nighthouse spoke of how important this legal point will be in future litigation. Here's what he said."

EN: ... and for the first time a Canadian judge allowed evidence that relates to the spiritual beliefs of our people. She overruled the defense's objections that talk of water-beings was based on unsubstantiated myth rather than observed reality. She accepted the idea, insisted upon by us for centuries, that the natural world is filled with unseen, non-material beings that are nevertheless disturbed or even destroyed by modern industry's use of their habitat as a dumping ground.

BF: Or in this case, a dredging ground.

EN: Yes. It all comes down to the same thing, you see, because the point of the dredging is to make the

Seaway easier to navigate for the toxin-carrying ships that modern industry needs to survive.

BF: And grain and corn.

EN: Of course, grain and corn downriver, toxins upriver, on the return trip.

BF: These spiritual beings. They're here, in the Saint Lawrence?

EN: Of course. They are here and they always have been. My people call them *nibiinaabewag* or *niibin-aabekwewag*, "watermen" and "waterwomen." Your people most often call them mermen or mermaids. They are not half-human as so often portrayed in your children's books and Hollywood films. A *nibi-inaabe* is actually almost invisible to the human eye when in its water habitat, which it rarely leaves.

BF: And you've seen, or perhaps encountered them?

EN: Of course. Up and down the Saint Lawrence.

BF: I've heard rumors of them in our river. I've also heard stories that they're attracted to, or perhaps fed by, a unique golden powder …

EN: Of course. All great rivers have the power that emanates from the gold, although modern industry and its concomitant pollution has reduced the amount of gold in many of the world's rivers. My people have known this, too, for many, many years. Incidentally, we're not the only ones to know of and identify this substance. The Egyptians called it the tears of Horus that fed the Nile. The Hebrews called it manna. (Laughs.) Did you know that Western scientists actually claim that manna is insect shit? You'll never hear a more revealing misreading of a spiritual truth than that one.

BF: The gold is here in the river. Where exactly?

EN: Everywhere.

BF: Where does it come from?

EN: (Laughs.) I can tell you that, too, because I was at least indirectly responsible for dramatically increasing the amount of it in our river.

BF: How?

EN: That takes us back again to the Seaway construction days. I was working up near Brockville. We removed tons of glacial till from the area around Three Sisters Islands. The work was very difficult, as I explained earlier. Downriver, at Massena, they had these monster shovels they called the "gentleman" and "junior," brought in from coal-mining country in West Virginia because the shovels they started with weren't doing the job. Upriver, where I was, we still had the shovels we started with. So we blasted with dynamite first to loosen and break things up. Then we could scoop it out. Not easily, mind you, but at least we could get it done.

One day, towards the end of the job, I was working the backhoe when I saw a glow over the side of the barge. I want to be specific here. I saw a glow, not a glitter. I saw an expanding area of light coming from below the water, not a reflection of the sun upon it.

At first I thought it was a piece or two of dynamite that hadn't exploded but had been ignited. But the glow remained, and increased in intensity as I continued to dig.

BF: The glow was the golden powder.

EN: Yes, it was. But the strangest thing was that it started to move, to spread upriver, against the current. Was it alive? Was it being carried by the watermen? I didn't know and I still don't know the answer. What I do know is that the dredging I did during those last days of the project uncovered a source of the golden powder, perhaps the largest source in the Saint Lawrence. It's the largest source I know of anyway, and I've been looking for others since that day.

"That's what's relevant to us," Ben Fries said. "Over the years Nighthouse has found other sources of the gold, including some that correspond with Charlie Flanagan's findings, as recorded on his map and notes. Your father couldn't understand why it was that Napoleon's Gold seemed to move from one location to another. He couldn't understand because he was mistaken. He was asking the wrong questions, as Andrew said a few days ago on the *Archangel*. He didn't know that the gold was coming up and out from below the water, from fissures in the bedrock of the rive floor.

"There are five of these sources. One is between Carleton and Wolfe Islands, where there was also dredging during the Seaway project. Another is at the west end of the American narrows offshore from Heron's Nest, where George and Marie Hibbard believed and where I guessed that Napoleon's gold went down. A third is at Stonycrest Island, which was literally blasted in half to make the channel wide enough for two ships to pass. Another is just offshore of the Darlingside Palisades, where the First Nations left their most impressive petroglyphs. The final source is on the eastern end of the Admiralty Group, in the deeper waters off Forsyth Island, where many people believed the *Egalité* actually went down."

"Stonycrest Island," I said. "Wasn't that where Hassan said the French evil was? Right next to Cherry Island?"

Naguib Malqari translated, and Hassan nodded his head and mumbled something in Arabic.

"That's water under the proverbial bridge," Jim Pembroke said. "It is a relief to know Hassan was right about the gold and undines being there."

"Where's Maitland's boat headed?" I asked.

"Our guess is the Brockville Narrows," Raphael Ostend said, "near Three Sisters Island, where Edwin Nighthouse's own dredging opened up the largest source of the gold. We also think Maitland's ship and his men are already there, perhaps extracting the gold as we speak."

"Extracting it? How would they extract it?" Mindy asked.

"A drill, vacuum hoses and filters," Naguib Malqari said. "Although I have not yet identified his refining process."

"How do you know his men are there and not at one of the other locations?" Mindy asked.

"Because we've had people out recently checking all the other areas," Ben Fries said. He smiled and let out a soft laugh. "I doubt Maitland realizes his men are in Canadian waters."

"That would cause him a heap of trouble," Mike Slattery said. "Still, I think it's best we follow through on our plan."

"What is your plan?" I asked.

"We figured this part out before you got here," Jim Pembroke said. He looked at his watch. "We'd better get our rears in gear if we're gonna get it done in time."

"Get what done?" I asked.

"We're gonna scuttle Maitland's ship," Pembroke said.

Chapter Twenty Eight

WE FOLLOWED JIM PEMBROKE and Hassan out of the room and onto the deck, where Billy's body had been wrapped in a canvas tarp and weighed down with chains. I continued behind the two men as they began climbing down the pilot's ladder to the *Archangel*, but was stopped when Raphael Ostend placed a hand on my shoulder.

"They're doing this alone, Tom," he said. "Our job is to watch, and then to share with others the truth of what we know."

"They're using the *Archangel* and not the *Ouroboros* to scuttle Maitland's freighter?" I asked, incredulously. "How?"

"I modified more than the engine," Ostend replied. "Underneath the wood veneer, the *Archangel's* hull is ribbed with titanium-reinforced steel. I'm surprised you didn't notice when you were climbing around my secret chambers."

"I did notice something metallic," I said, "although I didn't have much of an opportunity to investigate." I paused for a brief moment to consider what Ostend had just told me. "Why'd you modify it like that?"

"We knew the *Archangel* might be needed in one of several possible ways. We considered all options and took nothing for granted. It was expensive, but if it helps to protect the undines and save our river it will be worth every penny."

By this time, Mindy and the other River Rat Reporters were by Ostend's side. Also, several of the men who had been working for Ambassador Maitland, including a few of the Undesirables I recognized from Jimmy's, had boarded the *Ouroboros* and were now talking to Naguib Malqari. We turned to listen to their discussion.

"Some of you are men of this river," Malqari said in English. "Others of you are from far, far away. Wherever you call home, I assure you that I will make it possible for you to return there as very rich men." Malqari sighed and shook his head. "I know that I, as an Arab, may be mistrusted by some of you. I assure you that I despise the men who destroyed the towers as much as you do. Barbarism has no place in my philosophy." Malqari held up his hands. "My friends, I hold no ill will towards you for aiding Ambassador Maitland in his pursuits. I, too, was mistaken into thinking that his purposes were benevolent. I admit my ignorance, and I ask nothing more from you than the same. Now, I ask you to work for me. If you do, I will not forget the services you provide."

Malqari turned around and stepped away. The men he had been talking to said a few words amongst themselves, nodded enthusiastically and called him back. One man, the one who had told me about what Billy Masterson had done, offered a hand for Malqari to shake.

"Good allies to have, those," Martin Comstock said.

Quickly, Naguib Malqari motioned for several of the men to join Jim Pembroke and Hassan on the *Archangel.* Other groups of men took their stations on the *Ouroboros.* Within a minute, I could feel the propellers engage. We began moving downriver.

MINDY AND I HAD MADE OUR WAY to a bench when Martin Comstock walked over our way. We separated and Martin sat between us.

"Well," he said. "I guess you already know the theme of my story."

"I'm guessing it's about how my parents and brother

died," I said, "which would explain the question marks on my dad's list."

"Yes," he said, "back then I didn't have a story. I wish I still didn't."

"Do you have to tell it now?" Mindy asked. "Look at him, Martin. He's exhausted."

"It's okay," I said. "I'd rather hear it now, before anything happens, than have to wait until later."

Comstock sighed and placed his hands on his knees. "In truth, my story's the most straightforward of them all. No mysterious glows. No strange, ageless men. No grandiose speeches. No highbrow galas. No exotic adventures in foreign lands. My story is a simple one, Tom, perhaps the simplest kind of story a person can tell on this river, and I've been waiting a long, long time to tell it."

"What's it about?" I asked.

"Well, it's about forgiveness, more than anything," he said. "The one thing in the world we all want, and the one thing above all others that's hardest to give."

Mindy and I stayed silent and waited for Martin to continue.

"My story begins at Il Castello's, on the Saturday evening of Labor Day weekend. A bunch of us were hanging out in the lounge after a long, beautiful day on the water. Your parents were there, along with the Slatterys and Jim Pembroke and his new wife. Your father seemed more light-hearted than usual.

"I especially remember *Bridge over Troubled Water* coming on the radio and your father asking your mother to dance. Now the song itself might not sound too light-hearted, but both your parents had the biggest smiles on their faces as they moved around the room. It was impossible for me not to notice. The Slattery's noticed it too. We hadn't seen your parents dance like that in ages, not even at the Ostend Ball.

"And what a song! After the oil spill of '76 that song meant more to us than any other, especially to your parents;

more so, of course, to your mother. To her, the bridge over troubled water was an actual steel construction. Your father was adding another layer of meaning by laying himself down to help your mother proceed to the other side, just as the song says. Damn, Tom, even now, five years later, I couldn't think of a better song for them to dance their last dance to." Martin Comstock smiled at the thought, then sighed and wiped away a tear.

"Anyway," he said, "I was getting ready to open up the next day when your father came to see me. He sat at the bar and drank Sprite, which was my first indication that something strange was happening. He told me that he and your mother had had a long talk before coming out the previous night, talked all morning and all day, as a matter of fact, trying to sort things before the sun set on another day of disagreement."

"What were they trying to sort out?" I asked.

"Well, the surface issue was the accumulation of rifts going back twenty years, to the summer of 1976, when your mother fell in love with Benjamin Fries and he with her. Mary and Ben had agreed to agree, contrary to your father's wishes, that protecting the gold rather than extracting it was the proper course of action.

"The underlying issue was exactly that, whether the gold should be left in the river and protected, which your mother wanted, or taken from the river and used responsibly for the common good, which your father wanted. True, he didn't have the technology to actually extract it back then, nor the financial means to arrive at that technology, but he did have Ambassador Walter Maitland's ear, and Maitland was very, very interested in hearing how your father's search for the gold was progressing. That was the issue that really tore your parents apart, Tom. That was the issue they finally came around to discussing at about two or three in the afternoon. It must have been terrifying for them to start down that road, more exhausting for them to continue. It had been a stumbling block between them for twenty years of their life together, after all. That's a long, long time. In the end they made the journey, and I'll be damned if they didn't make it to a destination, too." Comstock paused, smiled and shook his head.

"What do you mean they made it to a destination?" Mindy asked.

"Well, Charlie Flanagan sat there in front of me that Sunday afternoon, sipping his Sprite, and had a smile on his face bigger than any smile I'd seen on him in years, even larger than the one he had had the night before. You know what he said? He said he'd finally come around to seeing your mother's point of view. He said he was hereafter committing himself to protecting the gold."

"Why?" Mindy asked. "Why the change of heart?"

"I'll get to that," he answered.

"I never knew about this conversation," I said. "The last time I talked with them was a week before Labor Day, a week before they died." Then I asked, "Did Patrick know?"

"According to what your father said, the three of them had Sunday brunch together that morning at the Rondette and talked the whole issue through. Your parents told Pat about the gold and the undines for the first time. Apparently, that was also when your dad made an open plea for forgiveness to your mother. He asked your mother for forgiveness, right there, on his knees, before all the other diners in the little round restaurant that morning."

"Patrick must have gotten a kick out of that," I said, recalling my brother's mocking responses towards all things sentimental.

"Yeah," Comstock said. "The upshot of the conversation was that your father asked for forgiveness, received it, and then came 'round to seeing your mother and Ben's point of view about the gold. As a matter of fact, that's why he was in Il Castello's that Sunday afternoon, to ask me if I would gather up the River Rat Reporters 'for a monumental meeting,' as your father put it, a meeting that would include Mary, to discuss and decide upon a proposed course of action concocted by he and your mother during their long conversation the day before."

"Is this also when he asked to hear your stories?"

"Yes, it was. He was supposed to begin recording them the next day, at our monumental meeting."

"You haven't mentioned Malqari yet," Mindy said. "Did Tom's father tell you he was alive? Did he tell you about the conversation they had together?"

"He did not," Comstock said. "I knew nothing about Malqari until Ben Fries told us after your parents had died. My guess is that the meeting with Malqari is part of the answer to your earlier question, Mindy, of why Charlie changed his mind." Comstock paused. "Odd, though, don't you think, that Malqari said the last time he saw Charlie was in 1976?"

"I was surprised to hear that, too," I said. "Obviously Ben was as well."

"Well, maybe that was part of what your father was going to tell us at our meeting." Comstock shrugged. "We were supposed to meet and discuss their proposal on Monday, Labor Day, at a special session at Jimmy's, scheduled for seven o'clock. Of course, we never found out what their proposal was. The others never told Charlie their stories. As a matter of fact, the Reporters never discussed Napoleon's gold again until you showed up, Tom, five long years later."

"Really?" Mindy asked. "You never discussed it at all? With Billy Masterson longing for his golden glow? With Jim Pembroke telling the story to tourists on the *Thousand Islands Queen*? With Raphael Ostend regaling new guests with tales of undines and ageless men? You never even mentioned it?"

"Well, after the accident Billy retreated into his shell and didn't say a word about his glow. Pembroke went through the motions of telling a truncated version of the story on his tour boat, but emphasized the clichéd tale of George and Louis Boldt instead. Until this year, Ostend hadn't told his story since November 1996, when he told it to Andrew simply to keep someone from the family in the loop. It was at that year's Ostend Ball, in fact, in 1996, that we formally decided to give Napoleon's gold a hiatus."

"I bet Andrew didn't appreciate that too much, having been recently initiated a Reporter," I said.

"No, he didn't. His frustration kept him quiet all these years, too."

I laughed all of the sudden, no doubt as my brother would have, thinking back to the image of my father on his knees declaring forgiveness to my mother. "A public act of forgiveness," I said out loud.

"That was his act of forgiveness," Comstock said. "Your mother apparently had a plan, too, which she meant to share on Labor Day, their last day, as it turned out, and was also meant to show how the healing of a relationship worked best when it was a two-way street."

"What did she plan?" I asked.

"It was a secret. Your father didn't know."

"My guess would be that she was going to show your father the gold," Mindy said. She held up a finger. "The question is whether it was the gold from the *Egalité* or the powdered gold coming up out of the river."

"You think she knew where it was?" I asked. "She didn't indicate that in her project."

"I don't know if she did," Martin said, "and I honestly don't know what her intentions were."

"You know what happened," Mindy said.

Comstock nodded. "They took out the Lyman, which they didn't use that much now that they also had Jack Hibbard's Chris-Craft. It was obviously a special occasion. Their idea was to go around to one of their favorite picnic spots in the Canadian park islands and enjoy the afternoon.

Eat, drink, swim. Reconnect before Patrick was to go off for his final year of college." Comstock paused. "By the way, I know for a fact that once they set Patrick on his way, your father was going to call you and apologize."

"For what?" I asked.

"For clamming up so often when he got angry. For not playing ball as much as you wanted him to. For spending that extra hour at his Olivetti rather than with you, Patrick and your mom down on the lawn. With the prospect of Patrick going, I think both he and your mom wanted you here more often. Your father hinted that they were even going to tell you about Napoleon's gold, like they told Patrick at brunch on Sunday morning." Comstock paused again and shook his head.

"Martin, you told me when we first met that my father was again very close to finding the gold. At the Brockville Narrows, right? Right where we're headed?"

"I believe so. I think your parents' intention was to reveal to the rest of us where this source was, then to convince us to swear to protect it. Hell, they might've even wanted to create an organization similar to Preserve the Islands. Protect the Gold, maybe."

"Or Save the Source," Mindy said.

"That would've been nice," Comstock agreed.

"He told you all this that Sunday?" I asked.

"He hinted at some of it. Told me the rest outright." Comstock sighed. "I don't know, but when I saw him that Sunday it seemed like he knew something was about to happen, about to change. I don't know, maybe it was just me."

"Do you think he knew he was going to die?" I asked. "Mike Slattery told me earlier, with Billy gone, that all of you realize that the river'll take you sooner or later. Do you think my father believed that?"

Martin Comstock nodded. "You know how Jim Pembroke put it? He says that every rock out there has one of our names on it."

"It wasn't the river that took him," Mindy said, shaking her head vigorously. "It wasn't a shoal either. Nor was it a drunk speedboater. Ostend already told us all that."

Martin Comstock looked quickly away and then back to me. I knew he found something uncomfortable with what Mindy had said.

"Tom, trust me on this one. If there's anything difficult about my story, this is it."

"What?"

"I was there, Tom," he said carefully. "I was with them that day. I saw and heard everything that happened."

I STOOD UP, moved over to the railing and looked out at the river. The island cliffs we passed were like a cubist painting in the mid afternoon sun and shadow. Captain Pembroke, Hassan and several of the *Ouroboros* sailors were in front of us on the *Archangel*. We were getting close to the Brockville Narrows.

"I want to remind you of something first," Martin Comstock said, "before I tell you my story. As a bartender, a significant part of my job is to remember. I remember what people order. I remember what people tell me. I remember what they want me to remember and what they want me to forget. You have to know, Tom, and you too, Mindy, that you should have no doubt whatsoever that I remember what happened that day. Do you understand?"

"Yes," I said. Mindy nodded and swallowed hard.

"Well, here's what happened," Comstock said, licking his lips. "Your father crashed into a dock because he was distracted. He was distracted because, just a moment before, your brother Patrick jumped out of the boat and into the water."

"He did?" I asked. "Why?"

"Well, to be with the undines."

"How do you know that?" Mindy asked.

Comstock stood and began pacing in front of the bench

where Mindy still sat. "As I said before, I was there. I was also out with Billy Masterson and the Slatterys on their boat that day; independent of your parents and brother. We were headed upriver from the bridge and saw the Lyman, and went over to say hello. We were about fifty feet away when I saw Patrick jump into the water. Then I saw your father clip the dock on the starboard side of the Lyman, sending your mother hurtling sideways into the river. I thought he must have ruptured a gas line too, because the Lyman caught fire right after that happened."

I glanced at Mindy and she nodded slightly. I recalled, as she did, Raphael Ostend's request to keep our knowledge of my father's sabotaged boat to ourselves. I was also silently confirming that the Lyman caught fire *after* the boat had hit the dock.

Comstock continued. "Billy Masterson dove into the water, going after your mother. He got her up, but just like it happened with him earlier today it was too late. I got your father out of the Lyman just before it really flamed up. Unfortunately, it was too late for him, too, but he was able to talk, and told me several things."

"What?" I asked impatiently, closer now than I'd ever been to finding exactly what I was looking for.

"First, he said 'drunk speedboater.' As I understand it, Raphael already explained that the words were coded language."

"He did," I said.

"Well, Billy, Mike and I knew right away what he meant; that we were to say nothing of why Charlie was on the water that day. Instead, to divert attention from Napoleon's gold, we were to testify that he was run down by a drunk speedboater. What we didn't know, and what made the situation very complicated for us, was whether someone else— Naguib Malqari, Ambassador Maitland, one or several of the Undesirables, another person who had it in for your father—had been involved in the crash. Believe you me, that uncertainty set us on eggshells for years, especially after we saw the note that was in your mother's pocket."

I remembered the note, which I had placed in my tuxedo jacket pocket, which I had given to Mindy on the *Archangel* and which she had returned to me on the *Ouroboros*. I took it out and read it again.

> Thank ... my dear, for yester ... versation and thank ... for rec ... g my ... veness. I promise you: I'll do ... thing I ... ful ... l our shared task. Malqari may ... live, bu ... he ... 't stop us. Nor can Ma ... me ... my ... pose. It may only be a mat-ter ... time before he ... gold is. He may already ... what the ... I will do everything in my ... to prevent ... taking it.

I moved beside Martin Comstock and pointed at the partial name in the fourth sentence.

"*Maitland* knows the gold's here," I said. "He's the one my father should have been looking, or watching out, for. Not Malqari. Maitland. My father realized he'd been double-crossed," I said.

"He apparently knew Maitland was dangerous," Comstock said.

"Why?"

"Well, drunk speedboater, for one. The code was meant to shield us from trouble." Comstock breathed deeply be-fore continuing. "Also, Tom, because your father asked me not to tell you the truth of what had just happened. Only if you returned to the river, which he trusted you someday would, could we, the Reporters, involve you in what we knew of Napoleon's gold. He made us promise that we wouldn't reach out to you while you were living your life elsewhere, but would open up and tell you our stories when you arrived. As I mentioned at Il Castello's when we first met, we waited five long years for that."

I went back to looking out at the river. "Let me get this straight," I said. "I thought it was a drunk speedboater because my father wanted me to think it was a drunk speedboater?"

"Yes, exactly. He wanted everyone to think it was a drunk speedboater rather than something having to do with the gold. He wanted you, especially, to think it was a drunk speedboater."

"It was convincing," I said. "I remember thinking as I went up and down the river for a week that on some days a third of the speedboaters up here are at least buzzed."

"True enough," Comstock said. "I want you to remember, though, that your father also okayed the discussion of Napoleon's gold when you came back to the river. He wanted you to know. He wanted you to be part of it. It just had to be by your choice. It had to be something you wanted to get involved in. He was big on that, you know, the freedom of choice."

"You said Tom's father told you several things," Mindy said, watching Comstock as he paced. "Were those two it?"

"No, they weren't," Martin Comstock said.

I waited. "What else?" I finally asked.

"Well, the third thing your father told me was to let Patrick be."

I turned from the railing to face him. "To let Patrick be?"

"Yes. Once Billy got up with your mother, he dove back in to look for Patrick. Your father told me no, to get Billy back up here, to not search for Patrick, to let him be."

"Why?" I asked.

Martin Comstock stopped pacing and moved next to me at the railing. "Well, that was my question exactly. Your father answered that it was time for him to go off on his own now, to do what he had to do."

"His senior year of college?" I asked, perplexed. I remembered what Comstock had told me earlier, and looked over at him. "Not the undines," I said.

"Your brother jumped into the water," Comstock said. "That's the last anyone saw of him. We certainly didn't see him from our boat, even though we were only fifty feet away. Naturally, Billy and I both thought he'd drowned. Your father seemed to have a different idea." He saw my reaction of non-comprehension. "You didn't know this about Pat? You didn't know that his body was never recovered?"

"No one ever told me," I said, paying careful attention to my words. "The bishop said nothing about Patrick's body. All he said was that there'd be closed caskets. I remember that like it was yesterday."

"Well, the bishop was the one who was supposed to tell you," Comstock said. "He told us he'd rather break the news, since it was such a delicate subject and all. Huh. I wonder what happened."

"Okay," Mindy said, trying in her usual way to make some sense of it all. "You're saying Patrick's body was never recovered. Was there a search?"

"Yes, the police and Coast Guard both sent divers down. That was before you came up from Clinton Falls, Tom. It must have been the morning after the crash. Then, a week later, after you'd stopped running up and down the river, Raphael Ostend hired a private group of divers to search some more. Nothing. Not a trace."

I thought of Ostend's secret again, and shared another look with Mindy. "Why haven't I heard about any of this? Why didn't someone tell me at the funeral?" I asked.

"I'm sorry, Tom, but I already told you. Your father instructed us to tell you the details only when you indicated you were ready. I can't guess at the bishop's motives."

We stood in silence for a moment. Then, forcing myself to speak the words I was thinking despite the lump in my throat, I asked, "Martin, do you think Patrick could still be alive?"

"Well, perhaps," Martin Comstock said coolly, most likely having thought this through several times himself over the past five years. "I don't know for sure, and I don't think any of the other Reporters do either. The best I can come up with is that your father's invocation of the drunk speed-boater was meant to protect both of his sons."

I turned back towards the railing in shocked silence and again looked out at the river. I saw the city of Brockville rising proudly up its hill on the mainland. I saw patches of cumulous clouds that might soon threaten a storm. Farther east, I saw a ship, stopped and facing upriver, which must have been Maitland's.

Hiding my face from both Mindy and Martin Comstock, I lowered my gaze overboard and, for the second time that day, cried.

Chapter Twenty Nine

I STOOD THERE, looking out and down at the wake of the *Ouroboros* as we sped over the river's surface.

After a while Mindy came to join me. She stood beside me in silence for just a short moment, then placed her hand upon mine.

"You'd better come forward," she said. "We're getting close."

"Where's Martin?"

"He's at the bow with the others. His story is over, Tom. We'd better go join them."

I walked with her towards the bow of the boat, where the other River Rat Reporters and Naguib Malqari had already gathered. I caught a peripheral glimpse of Maitland, and several important details suddenly came together in my mind. I jogged away from Mindy and took hold of Maitland's chin. As I lifted it up he opened his eyes a crack and tried with little success to focus them on me.

"You manipulated my father, then killed him," I said. "First, you staged the meeting at the Boldt Yacht house on the night before Labor Day, the night before he died. Malqari said he didn't see my father again after their only meeting in 1976. It was someone you hired to convince my father that Malqari was alive and was going to extract the gold out of the river. You didn't know that my father had changed his mind just that day, that he and my mother and Ben Fries were now in agreement that the gold should be protected rather than harvested."

Maitland tried to mumble something. "Shut your damn mouth," I said, gripping his jaw tighter. "At some point my father had a conversation with you." I reached into my coat pocket and took out the note that had been found in my mother's pocket. I put it in my palm and slapped him across the face. "He realized you were the one he should've been after. He realized you were the one that posed the greatest threat to the gold, to the undines and to the river itself."

Now I put the note back into my pocket and, using my free hand, lifted Maitland higher off the deck by the shirt collar. I could hear his difficulty breathing, but I didn't care. "You sabotaged his boat, you son of a bitch. You knew that only my father could garner the necessary support to stop you."

Twice I cranked up my grip on Maitland's collar and chin. He raised his eyes to meet mine, and for the first time in the man I saw fear. I also saw, looking deeper, my own soul's undoing if I took advantage of that fear to hurt him any more. I still couldn't forgive my parents' killer, just as I hadn't been able to on the day the bishop convinced me to lay my parents to rest. At least I had the choice now to do no further harm.

Without saying another word I released my grip on Maitland's chin and collar. He slumped back down with a groan.

Martin Comstock patted me on the shoulder as I passed by him and took my place to view what was about to happen. For the next several minutes I watched and listened like a spectator, feeling that my part in the story had ended as quickly and decisively as my mother's and father's had.

"YOU SURE HE KNOWS what he's doing?" Ben Fries asked Raphael Ostend.

"Jim knows what he's doing," Ostend said. "By narrowly averting so many collisions over the years, he's learned exactly how to commence one."

"What exactly will happen to the *Archangel* if and when this collision commences?" Mike Slattery asked.

"We'll see," was Ostend's reply, spoken with expectant sadness. "We'll just have to wait and see."

Turning to my right, I saw several of Malqari's sailors with wetsuits, air tanks and coils of rope. Andrew, surprisingly, was among them. They were gathered around three inflatable Zodiacs, which they were preparing to drop into the water when we got close enough to Maitland's freighter. A rescue crew, I guessed, in case Jim did not know exactly what he was doing or, perhaps, even if he did.

Raphael Ostend drew our attention to the *Archangel*. We looked and saw Hassan at the wheel and Jim Pembroke standing next to him, pointing out sites on nearby islands and on the river. Pembroke looked back to the *Ouroboros* and signaled with a thumb's up.

The *Archangel* started taking on speed. I now saw for sure what I thought I had noticed before when we were fleeing from the *Ouroboros*. The boat actually lifted out of the water as it accelerated at an incredible rate towards Maitland's freighter.

Ben Fries, who, along with Naguib Malqari, had a pair of binoculars, mentioned that the sailors on Maitland's freighter definitely knew the *Archangel* was coming. Soon enough, the rest of us could see them pointing and scurrying about the deck. We could hear the freighter sounding its horn in the traditional five blast warning of oncoming danger.

No signal could stop this danger from approaching, however. Hassan kept the throttle at full bore, Jim Pembroke kept pointing out minor adjustments to their course, and the sailors who had boarded the *Archangel* from the *Ourorboros* stood resolute and firm, some of them with guns and others with tools that I could not identify; others, with similar equipment, held at the ready by the men. Andrew stood to my right, behind me.

Strangely, Maitland's freighter, the *Avenger*, identified by the black letters on the bow, turned to the port and started to move across the river in a southerly direction. Just as Naguib Malqari had surmised, there were large opaque hoses coming out of the water, connected with machinery on the deck. From there, another set of smaller hoses led to what were no doubt holding tanks in the hull. Somehow, Maitland had figured out a process for extraction and, perhaps, refining of the powdered gold as well.

It seemed clearer than ever to me that for good reason the crew was in disarray. As the *Avenger* pulled away trying desperately to gain speed, the hoses, still connected to their underwater attachments, began to tear at the water line. Water frothed up above the surface. I could see small streams of gold pouring back into the river.

Hassan turned the *Archangel* slightly to port, presumably to line up the boat to strike the large freighter ahead. Without warning, without a single blast of a horn or the merest flicker of the running lights, the *Archangel* picked up even more speed.

We were about two hundred yards away and could see everything that was happening.

Raphael Ostend couldn't believe what we saw happen next.

"Hassan's turning!" Ostend shouted. "He's not following through!"

"Dammit!" Mike Slattery said, slamming his fist down on the railing. "I knew Pembroke shouldn't have trusted him." He then turned away to look at Naguib Malqari.

Indeed, instead of striking the *Avenger*, the *Archangel* blew past it, then disappeared behind it for a moment, then reappeared on the port side, coming upriver, bouncing over the freighter's wake.

"There they are again," Ben Fries said.

"What the hell's he doing?" Martin Comstock asked. "Doesn't look to me like he's retreating."

The *Archangel* turned again, completing a full circle around the large freighter. It slowed, turned hard port, and lined up again, facing the *Avenger* bow to bow.

Meanwhile, the freighter had also resumed moving straight upriver after making its long and awkward turn.

"I'll be damned," Slattery said. "Naguib, my apologies for making that hasty comment about your Egyptian."

"What is your meaning?" Malqari asked.

"Have one of your men get us a chart, would you please?"

Malqari spoke Arabic to a sailor standing beside him. The man ran fast down the length of the ship to the bridge and returned a moment later with an official NOAA nautical chart that showed the river from Morristown, New York, to Butternut Bay, Ontario, and contained the Brockville Narrows.

Mike Slattery tapped the laminated paper with his index finger and laughed. "I will be damned," he repeated.

"Why?" Raphael Ostend asked.

"Because, Raph, he's not only going to scuttle Maitland's freighter, he's going to save your precious boat as well. Look here."

With his finger Slattery indicated on the map what was about to happen, or, more accurately, where it was about to happen. There was a shoal in the dangerous narrows that the *Avenger* was now heading straight towards.

"Hassan and Pembroke are playing with this guy!" Slattery said. He tapped the chart again. "Look, they've maneuvered the freighter so it's got nowhere to go but into that shoal!"

Just as Mike predicted, a minute or two later there was a loud scraping sound, then a bellow that sounded like an amplified out of tune double bass. The *Avenger* lifted out of the water, but, unlike the *Archangel* earlier, was propelled by the force of the collision rather than by the energy of acceleration.

The *Ouroboros* sailors and Andrew moved into action, securing their scuba gear, hoisting and then lowering the inflatable Zodiac rafts overboard to commence the search for anyone who might survive the collision and the *Avenger's* inevitable sinking. As they approached the scene, we could see people already in the water, some of them with air tanks and rope; others needing the help that was coming their way.

The *Avenger* began listing to the starboard. The *Archangel* moved closer, dangerously close, I thought. I could see several sailors from the smaller boat jump into the water, swim over to the freighter, and scale the side of the boat up to the deck.

"What are they doing?" Mindy asked.

"The *Avenger* has to be moved," Martin Comstock said. "If not it could get hung up on the shoal and not sink for hours, or at all. What they have to do is make it to the bridge and pull the boat forward a bit. It'll slide right off and sink."

We heard a few shots of gunfire. After a minute or two of silence we heard the engines of the *Avenger* engage the propeller. With the sound of the steel hull tearing against the shoal, the freighter moved forward, then bounced into the water up to its ballast line. Finally, it began to sink.

As the *Archangel* passed across the freighter's bow and returned to the *Ouroboros*, Jim Pembroke hit the horn in three short bursts and one long one. Those of us on deck let out a loud cheer. Ben Fries slapped Naguib Malqari on the shoulder. Malqari paused, but then slapped him back. Mike Slattery initiated a hug among the three of them. I picked up Mindy, twirled her around, and we hugged and kissed.

I SOON LEARNED that just as my father and the River Rat Reporters had concocted a "drunk speedboater" story to deflect attention away from the true nature of any Napoleon's gold-related casualty that might someday happen, so too did

Naguib Malqari have a plan for deflecting any suspicion that might be directed towards him and the *Ouroboros*.

The rescuers spent a hurried fifteen minutes searching for and bringing back anyone they could find. There were twelve sailors from Ambassador Maitland's *Avenger* and six from the *Ouroboros* who had transferred to the *Archangel*. All of them were physically okay, except for a sailor on our side who had been shot in the leg. The twelve men from Maitland's freighter were given the same speech about working with him that Malqari had given earlier. All of them took him up on the offer.

After taking care of the people in the water, a smaller team, led by Andrew, disconnected and removed the hoses that had been used to draw the gold out of the water. We didn't see any more of the substance from our vantage point on the *Ouroboros*, but Andrew told me when he got back on board that the tanks were empty. I asked him about the fuel in the freighter's tank, and he assured me that the tank was intact; that the Canadian authorities would have the fuel cleanly and safely pumped out in a matter of days.

Walter Maitland's journey went in the opposite direction than that of his men, off a boat rather than onto one. Mike Slattery outfitted the still unconscious Ambassador with a life vest and, inviting me to help, unceremoniously dropped him into the river. We later learned that when Maitland was found he was immediately arrested and put under the custody of the Royal Canadian Mounted Police for attempted theft of public property, to be specific, a large pile of two hundred year old logs, worth tens of thousands of dollars, that sat at the river bottom near Brockville. I also learned that Naguib Malqari had thoroughly framed Maitland for the crime when he'd found out, months before, that Maitland had been attempting to double-cross him.

"Who exactly," Mike Slattery said with a smile when he heard that part of the story, "was zooming whom?"

Back on the *Ouroboros* itself, with Maitland's ship on its

way down to join the two hundred year old logs, Naguib Malqari sent messages to the Canadian Coast Guard and to the Lebanese Embassy that a terrible accident had occurred, presumably due to the inexperience of the unlicensed pilot aboard the *Avenger*. He stated that he and several other witnesses could, at the Coast Guard's earliest convenience, corroborate the navigational failure that caused the tragedy to occur.

Raphael Ostend coached us on the scripts that Naguib Malqari had provided, and both men assured us that all would turn out well if we followed the scripts exactly. They were right, although it took a couple months and several awkward visits with investigators to work itself out.

Jim Pembroke, who climbed back aboard the *Ouroboros* that day with Hassan to a hero's welcome, was later shielded from having to appear before investigators for a second time because Raphael Ostend testified that Pembroke was working on an especially difficult repair job in the Valhalla boathouse at the time of the accident. According to the testimony, Ostend himself had been piloting the *Archangel*, taking it on one final trip past the great city of Brockville before the *Archangel* was handed over to the Antique Boat Museum in Clayton. Pembroke's first ex-wife Margie gave witness for the alibi. Ostend declared that he had borrowed Pembroke's captain's hat to make the *Archangel's* last run feel more official.

A couple of days after the investigation was closed, Captain James Davis Pembroke sealed the story by presenting Laurie at Jimmy's with a gilded captain's hat on a wooden plaque, the engraved text of which read "This is Lord Ostend's headwear, worn when he showed no fear, aboard the *Archangel* he did ride, with NO OTHER CAPTAIN by his side, and fortunately for us he'd learned how to steer."

Epilogue

IT WAS A COLD, CLEAR FIRST DAY of winter when we laid Billy Masterson to rest in the water he loved. The river was glazed over near the shore that day but hadn't yet frozen. We followed Billy's instructions, given to Jim Pembroke several years before, exactly as he had written them.

The five remaining River Rat Reporters were with me that day. Mindy was, too, having returned to the river from Buffalo after finishing the semester. The seven of us drove to the top of the American span of the Thousand Islands bridge and stopped our three vehicles to unload Billy's wrapped body from the back of my pickup. At the exact moment of the winter solstice, at 2:22 in the afternoon, a Canadian bagpiper played *Amazing Grace* as we lifted the body over one railing and onto the pedestrian walkway, one hundred fifty feet above the Saint Lawrence.

When the bagpiper finished, I recited the passages from Revelation that Billy and I had talked about back on Snell's island in the Summerland Group, "'Then the angel showed me the river of the water of life, as clear as crystal, flowing from the throne of God ... down the middle of the great street of the city. And there will be no more death or mourning or crying or pain, for the old order of things has passed away.'"

"Amen," the others said in response.

"A-effin'-men," I corrected.

I stepped back from Billy's body and stood next to

Mindy as we all quietly laughed. Martin Comstock and Jim Pembroke picked him up and balanced him on the railing.

"Well, any of you have last words to share?" Comstock asked.

"You were a good man, Billy," Mike Slattery said.

"The best damn fisherman on the river," Raphael Ostend added.

"A great dancer," Mindy said through her tears.

"I'll miss you, buddy," were Jim Pembroke's words.

"Ere the bonnie boat was won," Andrew Hibbard said.

"Well, then, good night and good luck, my friend," Comstock said.

After another moment of silence, Comstock nodded to Jim Pembroke. The two of them pushed Billy over the railing, and he fell, feet first, all the way down to the water, which he hit with hardly a splash.

"This might not be the proper time to ask," Andrew said hesitantly, "but did you weigh his bottom half down?"

"No," Comstock answered. "We did not. I suspected that that's the way they wanted him to go."

I was watching the water. Given the low angle of the ecliptic on winter's first day, it was difficult to tell whether the brightness of the water was a glimmer of reflection from the sun or a glow that came from the beings of the deep, receiving from Billy Masterson his final and most significant gift.

BEN FRIES WAS NOT THERE, of course. After the *Avenger* went down he remained on the *Ouroboros* with Naguib Malqari, and returned with him to Montreal. He and I hadn't said much in those last few moments before the rest of us climbed down the pilot's ladder to the *Archangel*. I didn't mention what Martin Comstock had told me about Patrick, still trying to sort it through in my own mind and knowing there wasn't time to receive any significant answers from him at that moment. Ben said nothing about what he was feeling as the stream of events that had begun twenty-five years earlier came to its conclusion. I wasn't upset by our parting because Raphael Ostend and Ben himself had assured me that Ben and I would remain in touch at least once a year at the annual Ostend Ball.

AFTER BURYING BILLY AT SEA, and after saying goodbye to Mindy as she departed south to spend Christmas with her parents in Binghamton, I drove down to Clinton Falls, to the Roman Catholic Diocesan office, where the bishop was offering confession on an extended schedule as the Advent season came to a close.

"How have you sinned, my child?" the bishop asked through the thick, dark red curtain.

"I trusted a man I shouldn't have trusted," I said. "He led me astray."

The bishop cleared his throat. "Was this a matter of pride?"

"For me or for you?" I asked.

"My son, I do not understa ..."

"By giving Ambassador Maitland my mother's history project you betrayed my trust as well as hers," I interrupted.

"Maybe you and I should discuss this in private," the bishop said quietly.

"This confessional is as private as it gets, bishop. It's just you and me and God now."

The bishop sighed. "Ambassador Maitland's intentions were well-founded."

"He double-crossed and tried to murder my father," I said. "But I'm here to talk about you."

"This affair is much larger than you can imagine," the bishop said.

"By giving him my mother's project, you also directly contributed to Billy Masterson's death."

"William was a troubled soul," the bishop replied.

At this I pulled the curtain of the booth open, leapt out

of the box, and tore the curtain to the bishop's booth off its rod.

"Billy was a good and honest man," I shouted. "Infinitely better a man than you'll ever be."

I was shocked by the bishop's haggard appearance. He seemed to have lost half his hair, his eyelids were droopy, and he had very little color to his face. He reached towards me with a shaking hand, but still mustered some authority in his voice.

"This is a sacrilege," he said, standing up. "I've always been suspect of your lack of respect for authority, Thomas. Now I know my suspicions were warranted indeed."

"I am suspect of authority," I said. "It's one of the most admirable traits I inherited from my parents. In fact, I wonder if my brother shares that trait."

The bishop caught the verb tense. He looked down at the faded maroon carpet. "Shared, Thomas. Shared. Your brother Patrick is dead."

"Tell me, bishop, what will I find if I go up there right now and excavate his grave? His body? Someone else's perhaps? Or did you at least stop your desecration at leaving the casket empty rather than placing a substitute corpse where you said my brother would be?"

The bishop turned more pale at this comment, which seemed impossible given the shade of his skin already.

I continued before he could reply. "Don't worry. For Patrick's sake I'll keep quiet. No one but I, and the few close friends I've already told, will know what a lying snake you are. From the looks of you, you've got enough on your plate as it is."

With those words I turned away, walked down the long aisle of the Cathedral and out the door. I didn't care whether the three elderly men and women waiting behind me for confession had heard any or all of what I had said.

I was thinking, "I'll keep quiet, bishop, at least until I find my brother."

I STAYED AT HERON'S NEST that whole winter, reading books and reflecting upon what had happened and what I should do next. Most of all, I could not help but marvel at how the river changed on a daily basis as the ice ebbed and flowed and cracked and groaned, as alive as it was in its liquid state. I joined the River Rat Reporters on most Fridays, our conversations more subdued now without Billy. Together we relived our autumn adventure, each of us embellishing our own parts in it. When I asked if anyone had seen the golden glow since that day the *Avenger* went down, they all just shook their heads and sipped their beer. Perhaps they were waiting for spring.

After visiting her parents for Christmas, Mindy returned north for the long New Year's weekend. She had applied for and had accepted the offer of a tenure-track teaching position in Clinton Falls. It was hard for the Reporters to tell which one of us was more delighted with this turn of events.

We made love through much of the afternoon on New Year's Eve, then went to Il Castello's for dinner and wine before enjoying the spectacular fireworks display over Boldt Castle. The air was cold and the show was long, but we enjoyed every moment of it, cheering and clapping as the finale gained momentum.

When the sight of the last burst had faded and the countdown to the new year had ended, I removed my gloves, then removed hers and took her hands in mine.

With the waning full moon shining above us, I looked her in the eyes and asked her to be my wife.

"That was done traditionally," she replied slowly and with a smile.

I waited for an answer, watching her eyes while brushing the hair off one reddened cheek, tucking it back under her knitted hat.

"Well, will you?" I finally asked, trying not to sound impatient.

"Sorry," she said, keeping my gaze. "I just wanted to be here for a while, just you, me and that question of yours. Just the three of us, just for a while."

"There's room for your answer, too," I said pathetically.

Mindy laughed. A tear came down her other cheek where her hair still curled out from underneath her hat. "Why didn't you ask me five years ago?" she asked.

"I'm younger than that now," I joked, borrowing words from a Bob Dylan song.

"Yes, in a sense, we both are." She laughed again, then became serious. "Yes, in fact, I will be your wife," she said, "but only if we can be married in Ostend's castle instead of that one." She let go of my hand and pointed in the direction of George Boldt's tragic gift of love to his bride, Louise. "That one's got way too much baggage," she said.

We laughed together. As I placed my hands on either side of Mindy's face, she placed hers on mine, and we kissed once and then held each other for a very long time as the last of the New Year's revelers passed by.

Then a warm breeze from somewhere beyond the frozen river blew and embraced us as tightly and as lovingly as we embraced each other.

Fin

The love of glory is like the bridge that Satan built across Chaos to pass from Hell to Paradise: glory links the past with the future across a bottomless abyss. Nothing to my son, except my name!

Napoleon Bonaparte*
April 1821

*From the valediction in his will, and thus his last public words, as quoted by Steven Englund in *Napoleon: A Political Life* (2004).

Afterword

NONE OF THE RIVER RAT REPORTERS are real people. Nor are they based on any of the river people I knew while writing this book. Any similarities to year round residents or summer vacationers are entirely unintentional. If needed, an apology is herewith offered.

Albert Hartman/Ben Fries is the one exception. He is based on a real person, Abbie Hoffman, who went by the name Barry Freed during the time he spent in Fineview on Wellesley Island. I did not know Hoffman/Freed in the years my family vacationed in Westminster Park. But the stories my older brothers told me about seeing him outside his cottage mowing the lawn on their trips across the island for potable water, or of running into him on their bar-hopping adventures into Alex Bay, filled me with the hope that I, too, might catch a glimpse or exchange a word or two with the great outlaw. The possibility of such an encounter fed my imagination for years, even after Hoffman turned himself in and served his time; even after Abbie died in 1989.

It fed my imagination because Abbie Hoffman/Barry Freed, however flawed, was also a great man for the same reasons that made the fictional Albert Hartman/Ben Fries a great man—the founding of an organization that still serves to protect one of the most magnificent natural treasures in the world, our beloved Saint Lawrence River and the Thousand Islands that lie upon it like jewels.

I took it as a given that if I wrote anything in life I would someday write something about the river and the people who love it. I would write not just for my own satisfaction, but also as a gift to them and to our river. As usual, when love appears, love for the river is a complicated emotion, able to germinate and grow in people as diverse as an outlaw, a river pilot, a fisherman, a wealthy industrialist, a newspaper reporter, a contractor, a national defense hawk and even a two hundred-year-old (at least!) man. If there is one thing that the existence of Save the River has taught us, it's that even when divided by class, race, gender, nationality, politics or religion, we can come together and agree to protect something so intrinsic to who we are as human beings.

Some real people deserve real thanks for being there along the way. To my parents (again) for taking me to the Thousand Islands as a child. To Carol Brown for use of the cottage. To Kristin and Bradon for opening up their lives to what the river might offer them. To Susan Smith for allowing me to see more of the river than I ever dreamed existed. Her web magazine, *Thousand Islands Life*, is essential reading for anyone who loves, or wants to know more about, the region. To my friends at the Antique Boat Museum for the boat rides and for keeping the Lyman, and all the other nautical treasures, in such good shape. To Larry and Ellen Hickey for introducing me to the French Festival. To Shelley Higgins and the Cape Vincent Chamber of Commerce for keeping the story of Napoleon alive in the Thousand Islands. To Warren Roberts of the University at Albany for injecting France and Napoleon into my historical imagination. And to Napoleon Bonaparte himself, or rather to his brother Joseph, for concocting the getaway plan that formed the kernel of the *Napoleon's Gold* story.

Napoleon Bonaparte, of course, was a real person—but what kind of a person? Having studied him for twenty years, I don't yet know whether I love him or hate him. What I do know is that neither I nor anyone else can be indifferent to his legacy. This is as true in the Thousand Islands as it is anywhere else in the world outside France. Reminders that Napoleon mattered are everywhere, and not only on the streets of Cape Vincent during the second weekend in July. Look around. You'll see them.

Is the golden powder, Napoleon's gold, real? Do the creatures that live in symbiosis with that powder really exist? I don't know for sure. As a child and still as an adult I have often stared deeply into the waters of the Upper Saint Lawrence, wondering and hoping. Sometimes, like Tom Flanagan in the boathouse of Valhalla, I saw nothing but water. Other times, still seeing nothing with my eyes, I certainly *felt* something in my soul. It was something powerful, something beautiful, something that exists beyond the five senses that we human beings rely on for most of what we perceive.

I know this much—whatever it is that I see with my soul on these occasions is definitely a worthy and welcome resident of our sublime Saint Lawrence. When you gaze soul to soul into our river, I hope you know this too.

Annotated Bibliography

The following is a list of books and websites that were useful in writing
Napoleon's Gold, *and, for the books, some comments on how each
one relates to the story.*

Books:

Anonymous. *Densmore Church: Wellesley Island NY.* Wellesley
    Island, NY: Densmore Church, Inc., 2004.
    This booklet celebrates the 100th anniversary of the
    beautiful stone church on Wellesley Island.

Anonymous. *A Story by a Water Sprite: the Fairy Land of Amer-
    ica.* Alexandria Bay, NY: Combined 1000 Island Boat
    Tours, Inc., undated.
    I remember reading this pamphlet when I was kid, stay-
    ing at the Brown cottage in Westminster Park on
    Wellesley Island. Did it plant the seed of the undine
    story? Perhaps it did.

Burleigh, Nina. *Mirage: Napoleon's Scientists and the Unveiling of
    Egypt.* New York, NY: Harper Collins, 2007.
    Tells the tale of the *savants*, the scientists who accom-
    panied Napoleon on the 1798 Egyptian expedition.
    Dominique-Vivant Denon, Marjorie Dindeblanc's
    friend in this story, is one of Burleigh's main characters.

Coristine, Ian. *The 1000 Islands*. Ontario, Canada: 1000 Islands Photo Art, 2002.
Now hard to find, Ian Coristine's first book of photography still dazzles.

—————————. *The Very Best of Ian Coristine's 1000 Islands*. Ontario, Canada: 1000 Islands Photo Art, 2009.
This one dazzles more: a new photo printing process makes, in the author's words, "each page a cover." Both books contain the best map of the 1000 Islands region I've ever seen.

Couch, Skip and Dennis McCarthy. *Shipwrecks of the Thousand Islands*. Clayton, NY: Blue Lodge Systems, Inc., 2010.
I don't dive myself—have never much enjoyed being in water above my head, in fact—but this book takes me down below the surface with its excellent descriptions and clear photography. The historical sketches of the dives are impeccable.

Englund, Stephen. *Napoleon: A Political Life*. Cambridge, MA: Harvard University Press, 2004.
My favorite among the many, many biographies of Napoleon. Englund captures the Romantic nature of Napoleon's personality better than anyone. Englund's understanding of how Napoleon's shadow is still cast over so much of our world was also an inspiration to me as I wrote this book.

Ennis, Rex. *Toujours Jeune, Always Young: Thousand Islands, Emery and the New Frontenac Hotel*. Rogersville, TN: Abendroth and Root Publishing, 2010.
The Gilded Age comes alive in Ennis' fine local history. It's not just the research that comes through while reading these pages, it's also the feeling that Ennis is an au-

thor who has walked these island pathways, paddled through these waters and breathed this air.

Grocott, Terence. *Shipwrecks of the Revolutionary and Napoleonic Eras.* London, England: Chatham Publishing, 1997.
Taken from the original reports as found in English newspapers, this compilation was invaluable in providing an understanding of how the wreck of the *Egalité* might have happened. Grocott's introductory essay on how shipwrecks happened two hundred years ago is fascinating reading. There's even a Captain "Pulliblank" in there, who was apparently quite the hero aboard the HMS Pigmy on December 15, 1793!

Hall, Manly P. *The Secret Teachings of All Ages, Reader's Edition: An Encyclopedic Outline of Masonic, Hermetic, Qabbalistic, and Rosicrucian Philosophy.* (1928) New York, NY: Jeremy P. Tarcher/Penguin, 2003.
The subtitle is sort of misleading because the book discusses much more than those themes. Everything Lady Ostend believed and practiced is here. Each chapter opens a window into a new way of thinking, and sent me off to the library or, less reliably, the internet for more information.

Keats, John. *Of Time and an Island.* Syracuse, NY: Syracuse University Press, 1987.
One of the most beautiful books I've ever read. It's not just about Keats' time on Pine Island, it's also about a disappearing way of life, a slower way of life that's gentler on both the earth and the soul. Thankfully, it's a way of life that my family and I have come to hold dear.

Le Lievre, Roger. *Know Your Ships, 2010: Guide to Boats and Boatwatching Great Lakes & Saint Lawrence Seaway.* Sault Ste. Marie, MI: Marine Publishing Co., 2010.

A great way to learn about the vessels that navigate through the 1000 Islands is to read Le Lievre's annual guide. The book also helps put the ships we see into the larger perspective of international commerce.

Lunman, Kim, ed. *Island Life: 1000 Islands ... 1000 Stories.* Brockville, ON: Thousand Island Ink, 2010 and 2011.
Filled with great pictures and great stories. Hopefully this periodical will become a permanent part of river literature.

Malo, Paul. *Boldt Castle: In Search of the Lost Story.* Fulton, NY: The Laurentian Press, 2001.
Although some people took issue with the way "Mr. Thousand Islands" fictionalized certain aspects of George and Louise Boldt's lives, there's no question that a wealth of verifiable information can be found in the first book of Malo's trilogy. What Malo also captures is the romantic allure of Boldt castle. This book is a must-read for anyone who values the Boldt legacy.

—————. *Fool's Paradise: Remembering the Thousand Islands.* Fulton, NY: The Laurentian Press, 2003.
Here, Malo introduces us to Julia Bignham McLean Hass, who took him, and thus takes us, on a trip back in time to the river's gilded age. Malo's own pictures, taken as a boy, adds depth to what, in the end, is an unforgettable journey.

—————. *A Floating World: More People, Places and Pastimes of the Thousand Islands.* Fulton, NY: The Laurentian Press, 2004.
My personal favorite of Malo's trilogy. This book is more idiosyncratic than the other two, and Malo's pictures are even better. I couldn't have written the Ostend Ball scenes without Malo's historical guidance.

Mondore, Patty. *Proclaim His Praise in the Islands*. Baltimore, MD: Publish America, 2003.

As a pastor, I turn to Mondore's spiritual reflections for insight into the ways God works in creation. What makes her book even more beautiful is the way it's so tied to this particular place, a sacred place for her and for me. Too bad Billy Masterson never had a chance to read this book!

Parham, Claire Puccia. *Saint Lawrence Seaway and Power Project: An Oral History of the Greatest Construction Show on Earth*. Syracuse, NY: Syracuse University Press, 2009.

The recorded conversation between Ben Fries and Edward Nighthouse was inspired by Parham's excellent history. Always fascinated by the seaway, I'm grateful for having been told its story in such a humane and respectful way.

Strathern, Paul. *Napoleon in Egypt*. New York, NY: bantam Books, 2007.

This has become one of my favorite history books. The descriptions of the Battle of the Nile and of Desaix's pursuit of Murad Bey are thrilling. All aspects of the French invasion are handled brilliantly.

Thompson, Shawn. *A River Rat's Guide to the Thousand Islands*. Erin, ON, Canada: The Boston Mills Press, 1996.

This is the book that reintroduced me to the river after several years away. All the stories I remembered from my childhood are here. If there's one book that's essential reading for a brief trip through the 1000 Islands, this is the one.

——————. *Soul of the River: Life in the Thousand Islands*. Burnstown, ON, Canada: General Store Publishing House, 1997.

In this book, the stories of real people and how their personalities were shaped by the river gave me the initial inspiration to write this book. After several readings, I feel like I know the characters that Thompson describes so well.

Websites:

Thousand Islands Life: *www.thousandislandslife.com*

Ian Coristine's 1000 Islands: *www.1000islandsphotoart.com*

1000 Islands Images: *www.1000islandimages.com*

Save the River: *www.savetheriver.org*

Antique Boat Museum: *www.abm.org*

The Ship Watcher: *www.theshipwatcher.blogspot.com*

Paddling the Thousand Islands: *www.paddle1000.com*

Napoleon's Gold Playlist

Music was an essential element in the lives of the Flanagan and Hibbard families and their friends. Here are some of their songs as found in the story, songs that sound especially good on a bright, summer day. I hope you enjoy these songs as much as Charlie, Mary, Nancy, Tom, Andrew and the others did.

1. *Before The Deluge*, Jackson Browne
2. *Jesus Savior Pilot Me*, Hopper/Gould
3. *Symphony #7 in A—Allegretto*, Beethoven
4. *Authority Song*, John Mellencamp
5. *Bohemian Rhapsody*, Queen
6. *I Write the Songs*, Barry Manilow
7. *Waterloo*, ABBA
8. *After the Gold Rush*, Neil Young
9. *You Don't Bring Me Flowers*, Neil Diamond with Barbra Streisand
10. *Torn Between Two Lovers*, Mary Macgregor
11. *Concerto for Violin And Orchestra in D Major—Larghetto*, Ludwig van Beethoven
12. *Caravan*, Van Morrison
13. *Sisters of Mercy*, Leonard Cohen
14. *Blessed Be Thou Heavenly Queen*, Anonymous
15. *Into the Mystic*, Van Morrison
16. *Bridge Over Troubled Water*, Simon & Garfunkel
17. *My Back Pages*, The Byrds

Further Resources

Please visit the *Napoleon's Gold* page at
www.SquareCirclePress.com to download
Book Club Discussion Notes and find links
to the songs on the Playlist.

Also available from
Square Circle Press

**Cornflower's Ghost:
An Historical Mystery**
by
Thomas Pullyblank

Cornflower's Ghost is a vastly entertaining novel, replete with mysterious deaths, romantic intrigues, political deceits and historical schemes covering more than 200 years. Implicated in these antics are professors and graduate students at a modern university, 1960s radicals, leaders of the American Revolution, 18th century politicians, and the specter of an Iroquois ghost. Thomas Pullyblank weaves this tale with a keen eye for detail and a storyteller's gift. But there's more than just a good story here: at the center of *Cornflower's Ghost* is history itself, and how we use the past to define ourselves and give meaning to our current struggles. Amid all the intrigue and suspense, Pullyblank's characters are fighting to claim the past and to understand it, since only history can reveal the answers to the secrets at the heart of *Cornflower's Ghost*. It's a novel that pulls you in and keeps you thinking long after you've turned the last page.

—*Brian Carso, Ph. D., Assistant Professor of History, Misericordia University*

To view our full catalog, visit www.SquareCirclePress.com

CPSIA information can be obtained at www.ICGtesting.com
Printed in the USA
269959BV00001B/2/P